Beat the Drum for Justice

Beat the Drum for Justice

A HISTORICAL NOVEL BY
CHRISTOPHER C. CROSS

Denizen Publishing
Centennial, Colorado

Denizen Publishing
Centennial, Colorado
https://beatthedrumforjustice.com
Paperback ISBN: 979-8-9911258-0-2
Hardcover ISBN: 979-8-9911258-1-9
Ebook ISBN: 979-8-9911258-2-6
Library of Congress Control Number: 2024914344

Disclaimer:
This is a work of historical fiction. While the author has made every effort to accurately depict historical events and figures, some liberties have been taken with the timeline and dialogue for narrative purposes. Any resemblance to actual persons, living or dead, is purely coincidental, except where explicitly stated.

The characters in this book who are not identified as historical figures are fictional. Any similarities to real individuals are unintentional.

The author acknowledges the sensitivity of certain language used in this book, including racial slurs. These terms are employed solely to reflect the historical context and the attitudes prevalent at the time. They are not intended to offend or condone such language in the present day.

For any errors or omissions, the author welcomes feedback and can be contacted at beatthedrumforjustice.com or beatthedrumforjustice@gmail.com.

Editing by Mark Chimsky and Amy Chamberlain
Book design by Journey Bound Publishing

Front cover image of snare drum: Originally posted to Flickr by Minnesota Historical Society at https://www.flickr.com/photos/7409083@N03/5712800301. Retrieved from: https://en.m.wikipedia.org/wiki/File:Snare_drum_made_in_Winona,_Minnesota.jpg. License: https://creativecommons.org/licenses/by-sa/4.0/deed.en. Coloring adjusted slightly.

Printed in the United States of America
First Edition

In memory of my father,
the consummate storyteller

and my mother,
the quintessential listener

and
to my wife, Nancy:
I could not have done this without you.

Contents

Part III Supreme Shame

Author's Note

I tried to make this story as historically accurate as possible. Any misinterpretations, mistakes, or lack of understanding about the history portrayed are solely mine.

Most of the depicted events involving actual historical figures, such as John Brown, Abraham Lincoln, Frederick Douglass, and Albion Tourgée, indeed happened (see Appendix A for a list of historical figures appearing in the story). As often as possible, words, phrases, and sentences uttered by historical figures in this book are reproduced directly from that person's speeches and writings as quoted in the sources cited in the online bibliography, with some paraphrasing at times.

There are a few intentional modifications of the timing of actual events to fit the story (e.g., Lincoln's "bad week" in Cincinnati occurred after John Brown left for Kansas, not before, and Walt Whitman's poem "Beat! Beat! Drums!" was written in September 1861, not April 1861 as implied). The only historical person I moved from one time period to another is Edna "Aunty Jack" Jackson: she was not an Underground Railroad conductor as depicted; rather, born into enslavement and freed by the Thirteenth Amendment, she was the longstanding housemother for the Mu Chapter of Sigma Chi at Denison University until 1934. Similarly, although William Parham was an actual person, as far as I know he was not involved in the *Plessy v. Ferguson* case. As much as I could, I intended the actual people involved and the dates and chronology of historical events to be accurate.

I often use characters' first names, but when historical figures' names overlap (John Parker, John Rankin, John Brown, several Williams, etc.), I have chosen to use last names rather than to change their first names, by which I mean no greater respect or distinction from the other actual characters. All nonhistorical characters are purely fictional amalgamations and caricatures from events in the author's personal and family history. The reader should not construe them as depicting any actual person.

I tried to be historically consistent in spelling. For instance, the Jefferson County, Virginia, historian Doug Perks informed me that "Charlestown" was the correct spelling for Charlestown, Virginia,[1] in 1859 (and the way John Brown spelled it), but "Charles Town" was also used at the time and in history books. Jeff Garringer, president of the Fayette County, Ohio, Historical Society, said to use "Washington C. H.," although its official name was just Washington. Likewise, the official government account of John Brown's raid spelled "Harper's Ferry" with the apostrophe, although many scholars prefer the name without it. Other places also had alternate spellings (e.g., Greensboro and Greensborough). When confronted with a spelling dilemma,

---

1 Now, West Virginia, which did not become a state until 1863.

I simply had to choose.[2] Also, some of the letters in the Civil War chapters are direct excerpts from actual letters, and thus the language of the time might seem odd to modern readers.

To be clear, I am a white man attempting to tell an American story set in the 1800s that centers on racism. I do not mean for the dialect I attribute to African American characters and others in the book to be offensive. For dialog, I developed a "vocabulary" by examining how others in museums, pamphlets, books, and other writings, including many by Black authors (e.g., James and J. Rosamond Johnson's *The Books of American Negro Spirituals*, especially pages 43 to 46; the poetry of Paul Laurence Dunbar; and *James* by Percival Everett), depict the dialect of this story's time and place. Through their speech, I intended to add character to the people depicted and, in some cases, demonstrate the progress of their educational development, without implying they have lost their Black voice. In all, my intention in this book is to show the horrific historical treatment of people of color, not add to the existing insensitive and discriminatory attitudes. I am deeply apologetic if I have failed at this.

I also apologize to those I might offend by including the "N-word" and other offensive terms. I have used them only where I felt it helped convey the racist views and prejudices of

---

2 An interesting historical spelling error occurred in the *Dred Scott v. Sandford* case. Scott was owned by a man named "Sanford," but a clerk's error at the Supreme Court spelled the case name "Sandford."

both Northerners and Southerners. My use of the words "Negro" and "colored" is an artifact of the time when "African American" was not in use ("African" and "Africamerican" were, however). "Black(s)" was also used during this period, although probably not as commonly as today. Likewise, although I would prefer to use "Native American," that term was not used in the 1800s, so I reverted to "Indian." I use the term "white supremacy," or some variation of it, because I've found references to it during the late 1800s. Finally, I chose to capitalize "Black" but not "white" in the current editorial style.

If you believe there is an error in this book, please contact me at beatthedrumforjustice@gmail.com.

Part 1
Shameful History

ONE

"CANADA, WHERE COLORED MEN IS FREE"

October 16–18, 1853

Wh-tsh. "G'YUP, girls!" Gabrial Adams cracked the horse whip again. *Wh-tsh.* "For the love of God, Nellie, YUP! Maggie, YUP!" *Wh-tsh.*

Gunpowder exploded behind him. He spun his head to look over his shoulder. Another shot boomed. Gabe had never used the whip or reins so violently, but at fourteen, no one had shot at him, either. *Wh-tsh.* "G-yup! YUP!" He came to the last turn before reaching his family's farm. *Oh no. Too fast*, he thought. The wagon careened onto two wheels and almost flipped. Gabe turned the horses slightly, regained control, and the wagon landed on its four wheels with a *whomp.*

The full moon illuminated Gabe's father, who had rushed out of the house at the first sound of gunfire, riding his large roan that stood ready for such an emergency. He galloped past Gabe, sweeping his arm backward in a "hurry" motion as if that would increase Gabe's speed. *Stall them, Pops*, Gabe thought.

The pounding hooves of the slave catchers' horses signaled the gap was closing. "G-YUP, girls! YUP!" *Wh-tsh.*

The four-man posse, riding full speed with unholstered guns gleaming, slid to a stop when they saw Atticus—known to his kids as "Pops" but to all others as Reverend Atticus—blocking the road with a rifle across his chest.

"What's all the shooting? Why are you chasing my boy, Richard?" Atticus demanded, recognizing Richard Mitchell, a well-known bounty hunter.

"Me and my partner been trackin' some runaway slaves, and some folks in Ripley thinks they might be in that there wagon," answered Mitchell, a weather-beaten man wearing a slouch hat low on his forehead, so that just his beady eyes, thin lips, and stubbled cheeks showed. Flicking his eyes and his head toward the men to his side, the grizzled leader said, "I ran into these two who seen the wagon and didn't like the way your boy was actin'. We was firin' warnin' shots to get him to stop. I aim to rid him of his load. They's wu'th a lot of money."

Atticus winced, hating that he had to deal with the likes of these devilish men, but kept his composure. "My son was in Ripley picking up supplies, not Negroes."

"We got every right to check. It's 'gainst the law to harbor fug'tives."

"I know the law. Holster those guns," Atticus calmly stated, "and come see for yourself." He turned and led them toward his farm at a pace meant to infuriate the impatient bounty hunters.

Meanwhile, Gabe turned through the gate next to the barn where his mother was waiting. He jumped from the wagon and, despite his hands shaking as if afflicted with palsy, tethered the horses to a post as she hurried to get the precious cargo out of the false bottom of the wagon. A girl who looked a bit younger than Gabe got out first. The girl's eyes darted as if afraid of what she might see. A boy, maybe ten or eleven, climbed out and grabbed the girl's hand. A woman clutching a baby came out of the wagon, followed by another woman whose knees were shaking so hard she had to grab the wagon wheel to keep from falling.

"Hurry," Gabe's mother, Ailene, pleaded in a whisper, her heart racing. Holding a lantern, she rushed the group into the barn.

She pulled a bale of hay back from near the corner of the barn, uncovering a trapdoor. Lifting the door, she lowered her lantern, illuminating a ladder descending into a large, dirt root cellar. "Get in the cellar," she said gently but firmly. "Be as quiet as possible. Set the latch on the trapdoor, and don't unlatch it until you hear someone say 'menare.'" The code word, meaning "to lead someone on a journey," was used by conductors on the Underground Railroad. "Don't light the candle yet."

Before Ailene closed the trapdoor, the group had enough time to glance at their new surroundings and see food, water, blankets, and a large chamber pot in the cellar.

Ailene heard the latch scrape closed. She threw the bale over the trapdoor, spread straw around the area, and hurried back to the house, straightening and smoothing the print dress she had sewn years before.

The cellar was pitch black, cool, and musty. "I's more skeered now than when we was on our own," one woman whispered to the other. "How's we knows we can trus' dem? Dey's white."

"We's got to," said the other—although she was having the same thoughts. "We's got no choice."

"I's hungry," the little boy whined.

"Hush, chile," she said as she began feeling for food, passing the provisions to the others. Still gripping each other's hands, the two children bit off chunks of jerky. The equally tense women swallowed their first sustenance in days. The baby began fussing for nourishment and then found his mother's breast. In silence, they wrapped themselves in the warmth of the woolen blankets and hopeful prayer.

Gabe unhitched Nellie and Maggie, calming them with his touch and whispers. He looked younger than his age. Although thinner and shorter than most of his friends, Gabe made up for his small stature with determination and grit. He had a ruddy complexion marred with teenage acne and a head full of reddish hair that was always mussed. The group of hopeful souls looking for freedom wasn't the first load he had transported, but it was the first time he had encountered bounty hunters. *Phew, I got them here. But is Pops okay?* Gabe wondered, still breathing hard. He heard hoofbeats approaching. *I must not have been careful when I left Ripley. Pops won't be happy with me.* Gabe led Nellie into her stall as Atticus escorted the four men into the barn.

"Take a look around. No one here," Atticus declared.

Mitchell turned to Gabe. "Why was you runnin' so hard from us if you ain't got nothin' to hide?"

Gabe looked down and said, "I can't say in front of Pops."

"Yes, you can, Son," Atticus urged. "I sent you to Ripley to pick up supplies. Why were you running from these men?"

"I stole some watermelons from ol' man Sommers's field, and I thought these men were his hands," answered Gabe.

Feigning anger, Atticus scolded, "We'll deal with you later—take care of the horses, then get in the house." Atticus knew it was risky to send Gabe to make the run alone. Word had come from Reverend John Rankin in Ripley, Ohio, that some "freight" needed moving. Atticus's well-known abolitionist views made him a target of slave catchers, and it was dangerous for him to transport fugitives. Gabe's two older brothers were away from home, and Atticus felt confident Gabe was capable. Gabe had made the nine-mile trip before without any trouble and was less likely to attract attention or, if caught, to suffer any severe consequences.

The men looked around the barn and saw nothing in the wagon except smashed watermelons and farming supplies in disarray.

"You ready to leave?" Atticus asked, but it was more of a command.

Mitchell's partner, his sallow, pockmarked face twisted as if in pain, said, "We's knows you is runnin' darkies, and we's watchin' you. Catchin' fug'tives turn a nice profit."

"Watch all you want." Atticus gave them an icy glare. "You'll make no money off me, and don't be messin' with my children.

We have nothing further to discuss. I kindly ask you to be movin' along." He made a slight movement with the rifle to remind the men they were not welcome on his property.

Gabe finished tending to Nellie and Maggie and went into the house. Atticus rode the farm's perimeter and ensured the men left the area.

Two days earlier, the group of six runaways—three adults, two youngsters, and a baby—had reached the Ohio River. The Jordan, the man had called it.

"Y'all hide here whiles I go look for da signal 'crosst the river," a tall, broad-shouldered man of about thirty told the others.

"Oh, Geo'ge, be careful," urged one of the women about the same age and dressed in a muddy, torn, homespun dress.

"I will, Rose," George replied. "You and Hattie keep ebry-one hid."

Sometime later, the bark of a gun startled the group, awakening those who had let sleep overtake them.

As dawn broke, George had not returned.

"We's got to stay hidden 'til Geo'ge come back," said the children's light-skinned mother, Rose, plump after years of working in the kitchen.

"What happen if he don' come?" asked the slim little girl with darker skin than her mother.

"I don' know, Jasmine. I jes don' know."

The sun crept across the sky and over the horizon—still no George.

"We gots to find de light 'crosst the river. We can't stay here," George's sister, Hattie, urged. Wiry-thin, having worked in the field all her life, Hattie was darker and taller than Rose and wore a plain brown dress and a matching piece of cloth wrapped around her short, curly hair. She straightened to her full height and, with resolve, said, "'Member what Geo'ge say: 'If we get separated, keep goin'. Don' look back.'"

Hattie led the group as they picked their way downriver—the way George had gone. They came to a strip of land jutting into the water. High atop the hill across the river, a pole extended upward with a lantern perched at its top.

"Dat's da sign we was tol' 'bout," Hattie said.

"Wha' we do now?" asked the other child, a young, husky boy.

"Well, Levi, we lights a candle and wave it in de air three times, wait a minute, and do it again," answered his mother, relying only on faith as she repeated the information passed along from others planning to escape.

Rose hid everyone in the thick brush, waved a candle as instructed, and then joined the others in hiding. Shortly, they heard several horses approaching. The runaways clung to each other as the horses stopped so close the group could smell their warm, peat-like odor. Thankfully, the baby slept.

"This here place gotta be near where we saw the light," one man said to the other.

Just as Rose moved to greet her rescuers, she heard one of the men chuckle, "I wonder how much we'll fetch for catchin' a couple a nigras?"

She slunk further back into the bushes, put her fingers to her lips, and gently covered the baby's mouth with her dress in case the little one stirred. They all held their breath as the men used the barrels of their rifles to poke at the bushes. Finding nothing, the men drifted off to continue their search.

Not much time passed before the hidden group heard something scraping against the rocks.

"Hello," came a man's soft voice. "Where are you? I'm here to take you to safety." He held his light close to the ground near where the other men had been standing.

Silence.

"I'm here to help," he said, a bit louder. "I'm a friend. Please come out."

From their hiding place, Rose peeked out. To her great surprise, illuminated by the lantern was a Black man wearing a long coat and a floppy black hat.

"It's all right. I'm your friend," he repeated with a gentle, reassuring voice.

Rose crept out of the bushes.

"Are there more?" the man asked.

"Yes'ir. Three plus a baby."

Hattie, holding the baby, came out shaking. Jasmine and Levi followed.

"Oh my," he said, taking off his hat and wiping his brow. "I'm not sure y'all will fit in the boat. But we have to leave, quick."

"My man is missing. We can't leave without Geo'ge," Rose pleaded, her eyes trying to pierce the darkness.

"We can't wait. I've got to get you across the river."

Rose hesitated but then joined the others in the small rowboat. The man shoved off and pulled on the oars.

"Mama, I is skeered we'll sink," Jasmine whispered.

"Jus' sit still as stones," Rose replied, trying to take the fear out of her voice.

"Just as sure as my name's John Parker, I'll get you across," the man said. The boat was halfway there when two men on shore started yelling at the group in the boat. Parker pulled harder and faster. "It will take a while for the men to cross the river downstream and back to where we'll land," he told the passengers.

When the boat hit land, Parker hurried them ashore into the woods, where they began climbing a steep hill.

"Hurry, Mama, hurry!" urged Levi.

"I'z doin' de best I can," Rose said, holding his hand, the baby cradled in her other arm.

"You can make it," her son said just before he fell on the slippery wooden steps dug into the muddy embankment.

Parker, Jasmine, and Hattie were having the same difficulty. "C'mon, Auntie. We're almost to the top," Jasmine said, helping Hattie to her feet.

The fleeing group continued to claw their way up the hill, where an older white man and his teenage son were waiting to meet them.

"Thanks for getting them here," Reverend Rankin said to Parker. His eyes darted to the frightened escapees. With urgency in his voice, he said, "We need to get you inside."

An hour after Gabe and the escapees arrived at the farm, Atticus, Ailene, Gabe, and his twelve-year-old sister, Caroline, returned to the barn and moved the hay bale covering the trapdoor. "Menare," Atticus said in a firm voice. A few seconds later, they heard a scratch as the latch slid back. Atticus opened the door and held a lamp at the opening. Four faces seared with fear stared back at him, and a baby slept soundly in his mother's arms. "We can't move you tonight," Atticus told them. "You are safe here and can come out."

The escaping slaves climbed out of the cellar. They all stood motionless, the two children partially hiding behind the women.

"Come, sit down and eat," Atticus said, pointing to the fried chicken, sweet potatoes, and corn on the cob Ailene and Caroline were holding.

Jasmine and Levi looked at their mother, not knowing what to do. No white person had ever served them food. Rose nodded in encouragement, and the children reached for the food.

Caroline stared at Jasmine, who was about her age but taller, with black, tightly curled hair bunched into pigtails. Trying to make her more comfortable, she said, "My name's Caroline. What's your name?"

"Jasmine," the girl replied softly, her eyes avoiding Caroline's gaze.

"That's a pretty name," Ailene added. "And who's this handsome young man?"

"Dis is my li'l brother, Levi."

"And how about you?" Ailene asked, turning her head and using her eyes to point to the woman holding the baby.

"I's Rose. I's Jasmine an' Levi's mother, and dis is my baby, Benjamin." Looking toward the other woman, Rose said, "Dis here is Hattie, my husband's sister."

"I'm Ailene. This is my husband, Atticus, and our son, Gabe."

"Nice to meet all of you," Atticus said. "Where are you from, Hattie?"

"We's from Massa Murphy's place in Kintuck, near Lexin'ton."

"How long have you been gone?" Ailene asked, looking at Rose.

"We left 'bout five or six days ago," Rose said. "We hid during de day and went as far as we could at night. We follow de Drinking Gourd like we wuz told. We is so thankful to you, but we is so worried 'bout my husband, Geo'ge. He went to get help at the river, we heard a shot, and he never came back."

Gabe noticed the worry lines on his mother's sun-worn face deepening.

"I'm sorry," Ailene said. "You've been through a lot."

As they ate, Rose told the Adamses about getting to the river and about Parker's and Reverend Rankin's help before Gabe picked them up.

Gabe took the story from there. "After we left the Rankins, two of those men who ended up chasing us stopped me and asked what I was doing out so late. I told them I had gone into Ripley for supplies, but a bad wheel had held me up. They came closer to the wagon, asking questions. I pretended to cry and told them I was scared to be out alone at night and just wanted to get home. I guess they believed me, because they rode off toward Ripley. I was almost home when I heard horses galloping behind me, and then they started shooting." He turned toward the fugitives. "I hope you're not hurt. That was a pretty rough ride."

"We bruised, but we free," answered Rose, wiping a tear from her cheek and rubbing her hip. "Glory be, we free."

"Not yet," Atticus said, cleaning his glasses with a rumpled handkerchief he pulled from his overalls. He sighed, and his shoulders drooped. "Ohio may be a free state, but you have a long way to go before you are safe and truly free. Many people in Ohio don't like what we do, and bounty hunters are everywhere. There's big money in catching runaways. We'll get you moving as soon as we can."

Everyone was quiet. Just the sound of crickets punctuated the cool autumn night. "That's enough for tonight," Ailene said softly, her hand pressed over her heart. "There are mats and blankets in the cellar. You can light the candles now. Go on back down and get some sleep."

As the Adamses walked away, they paused, then realized the women were softly singing a poem to the tune of "Oh! Susanna." They listened:

I's on my way to Canada,
Dat cold an' dreary land,
De dire effects of slavery,
I can no longer stand,
My soul is vexed within me so,
Ta think dat I'm a slave,
I's now resolved to strike da blow,
For freedom or the grave.

I've now embarked for yonder shore,
Where man's a man by law,
Da vessel soon will bear me o'er,
To shake the Lion's paw.
I no more dread de Auctioneer,
Nor fear the massa's frowns,
I no more tremble when I hear,
Da baying Negro-hounds.

Farewell, ole massa,
Dat's enough for me,
I's going straight to Canada,
Where colored men is free.

TWO

"LET MY PEOPLE GO!"

October 19, 1853

Atticus was up early, as was his usual routine. He dressed quietly, went to the kitchen, rekindled the fire, and began making a pot of coffee. Rubbing her eyes, Ailene followed and started making breakfast, calling for the children to get up.

After finishing his coffee, Atticus went outside into the cool fall morning to check on the latest arrivals. He checked around the barn to ensure no predators were lurking. He slowly opened the barn's large entrance door, letting the morning light flood the interior. He closed his eyes and breathed in the fresh smell of recently cut and stored hay merged with the pungent odor of manure and urine. The gentle whinnies from his horses comforted him.

Atticus was of medium height and sinewy, with a Romanesque nose and a strong chin. He never complained about his arthritic thumbs or his painful toes caused by wearing ill-fitting hand-me-down shoes from his brother, Nathaniel, during his youth. Atticus's deceased father, Caleb, was a prim Presbyterian minister with a small church on the west side of Cincinnati and was active in the nascent abolitionist movement, a cause which Atticus passionately joined. Atticus's mother, Sarah, also deceased, was the definition of a schoolmarm, sang in the church choir, ran the church school, and raised the two boys. After finishing his studies at the Lane Theological Seminary in Cincinnati, Atticus preached at the Georgetown Presbyterian Church, managed their farm, and worked part-time at Jesse Grant's tannery to help make ends meet.

The task at hand forced Atticus out of his reverie. He walked to the corner of the barn and pulled back the hay bale. "Menare," he announced. Hearing the latch slide back, Atticus pulled the door up, exposing four faces covered with grime from a week on the run.

As each cautiously climbed the ladder, heads poked above the floor one by one, and then they scanned their surroundings in wonderment.

"We jes can't believe we is here," said Rose, who seemed to be more talkative than the others. "All my life, I dream of bein' free. Now, me and my chillen will be."

Atticus went outside to the well, partially filled Ailene's wash tub with water from the hand pump, and carried it back into the barn. "Here, you can wash up. The outhouse is right behind the barn." He handed Rose a shawl and said, "Put this over your head when you go there. We'll be back soon with breakfast."

A short time later, Atticus, Ailene, Gabe, and Caroline walked into the barn carrying trays of warm biscuits smothered in sausage gravy and a pitcher of milk that Gabe had just squirted from their Jersey cow's udder.

"Food neber taste so good," Hattie said softly. "Dis here is 'freedom food.'"

"Mother and I made it just for you," Caroline beamed.

"We're going to move you as soon as it's safe," Atticus told them. "First, Gabe and I are going to look for George."

"Oh my. You do dat for us'ns?" Rose asked in disbelief.

Jasmine looked up at Gabe and said, "Please fin' him. I jes know you will."

"We'll do all we can," Gabe said, rubbing his toe in the dirt.

"While they're gone," Ailene told the group, "we'll get you all bathed and into clean clothes. Get that Southern dirt off of you."

"Dat mean you, too, Levi," Rose said with a smile.

Rose gave Atticus a description of George while Gabe saddled his horse, Major, and his father's roan, Maverick. They stuffed the saddlebags with food and took off at a trot toward Ripley, where they would cross the Ohio River into Kentucky.

"We'll stop at Reverend Rankin's," Atticus told Gabe. "John may have heard something about George."

Reverend Rankin was well known in the area, more for his abolitionist activities than his preaching. A ransom was on Rankin's head due to his reputation as a conductor on the Underground Railroad, but he considered it a badge of honor. Rankin's and Atticus's supporters called them "Freedom's Heroes," but their detractors used more unseemly names.

"Good morning, Atticus, Gabriel," Rankin greeted them from his porch with his usual gentle, kind demeanor. Rankin's house, located at the crest of Liberty Hill overlooking the Ohio River and the town of Ripley, was the first stop toward freedom for many people escaping enslavement. The Rankins lit a lantern atop a thirty-foot pole every night as a beacon. One of Rankin's nine sons kept watch, looking for a light waving across the river. Continuing the escapees' trip north was always challenging, as slave catchers hid in the woods nearby and patrolled the roads going north from Ripley, searching for valuable prey. "I didn't expect to see you so soon, Gabe. Is everybody all right?"

"Good morning to you, and it's good to see you," Atticus replied, smoothing his close-cropped brown hair, which was graying at the temples. "Yes, everyone's safe, but it was a close call. Those damned patrollers are getting bolder and more dangerous. And now we must worry about our greedy sheriff trying to collect his share of the bounty. The group Gabe moved last night," Atticus continued, "had a man who got separated from them at the river. Have you heard anything about him? We're going to try and find him."

"Parker told me the same thing, but I haven't heard anything else," Rankin replied, his clean-shaven face displaying a firmly set jaw. "He found the women and children across the river at 'The Point.' It might be best to start there and make your way to Maysville." He looked at his pocket watch. "The ferry doesn't leave for over thirty minutes. Come on in for some coffee. Jean just pulled some biscuits from the oven. The boys are all out hunting. They'll be sorry they missed you."

"I'll miss seeing the boys, but we wouldn't miss Jean's biscuits, would we, Gabe?" Atticus said, smiling.

"No, sir!" Gabe said, excited because it appeared his father would include him at the table.

They went inside the red brick, one-story house with a high peaked roof. Gabe always wondered how Reverend and Mrs. Rankin and their thirteen children managed in such a small space. He drew in a deep breath, enjoying the smell of just-baked bread.

They took seats at the kitchen table. Jean offered Gabe some hot cocoa.

Being with the adults, Gabe answered, "No thanks. I'd like some coffee, too."

Atticus smiled and winked at Jean, a plain woman with hollow cheeks, sunken eyes, and hair pulled back into a tight bun.

Gabe carefully studied the two men to see how much sugar and cream to put into his first cup of coffee before taking a sip. *Yeow, that's hot! Yuck! How can they drink this? Maybe if I put in a little more cream and sugar.*

Picking up a book from the kitchen table and handing it to Atticus, Rankin asked, "Have you seen Harriet's book?"

"Sure did," replied Atticus, examining the cover of *Uncle Tom's Cabin: Or, Life among the Lowly* by Harriet Beecher Stowe. "She was kind enough to send me a copy." Rankin also had attended Lane Theological Seminary and occasionally taught there. He and Atticus were close friends with Lyman Beecher, the seminary president, and his family, including his daughter Harriet. The escaping slave "Eliza" in *Uncle Tom's Cabin* came directly from Rankin's story about a runaway he had harbored in the 1830s, who escaped by crossing the Ohio River in winter, jumping from ice floe to ice floe while holding a baby in her arms.

"We read the weekly installments published in the *National Era* last year," Gabe interjected, forgetting he was to be seen and not heard.

Noticing that Atticus was about to reprimand Gabe for his impudence, Rankin quickly stated, "Her note with the book said about 300,000 copies have already been sold! Let's pray it affects public opinion about the 'Peculiar Institution.'"

"Amen." Atticus took a sip of coffee. "Anything new with the election?" he inquired, knowing Rankin was intently following the presidential race, with the election several weeks away.

Rankin's face turned hard. "That fool Pierce is going to win. Our Free-Soil man, Hale, can't get enough traction in the North, and no one in the South will vote for him."

"Pierce is nothing but a doughface," Atticus added, wrinkling up the corners of his mouth as if he just bit into a persimmon. "He'll give the South everything it wants."

The ferry whistle interrupted the men's conversation, which blew sooner than Gabe would have liked. "We best be moving," Atticus said, rising from his seat. The two guests thanked Mrs. Rankin for the coffee and biscuits, and she gave them several to take with them.

They all walked outside and took a minute to admire the spectacular view from Rankin's house. The day was clear, and they could see upstream and downstream for miles. The trees on the rolling hills and bluffs on either side of the river were changing to breathtaking colors. No painting could capture the vibrant reds and greens and subtle pastels. Their beauty, however, only disguised the disgusting dealings that lay beneath.

"The river is such an enigma," Rankin mused, as if delivering a sermon to an invisible congregation. His deep, penetrating eyes gazed over the Ohio River into Kentucky. "That thin ribbon of water separates this nation between enslaved and free. It carries the produce of the North and the immorality of the South. Someday, our efforts will flow like that mighty river and flush away the yoke of oppression, and purge our nation from the abominations of slavery—a never-failing fountain of the deepest source of human misery."

Atticus thought for a moment, then added, "The future of our country depends on the extermination of this evil, a concept that must be obvious to every enlightened mind."

"Amen, my friend. Amen."

They bid goodbye. Gabe and Atticus rode down the hill to the ferry and walked their horses onto its wooden planks. They assisted the ferrymen in pulling the rope to move the ferry across the river.

After landing on the Kentucky side, they rode for The Point, a short distance upstream from the ferry landing. The two rode in silence, scanning the scrub brush and listening for any sounds. After going a short distance, Gabe saw two men off their horses, searching the ground.

"Don't say anything," warned Atticus. "Let me do the talking—but, in case they ask you, we're from Cincinnati looking for fugitives."

A filthy, unshaven man looked up, pulled out his gun, and pointed it directly at Atticus's chest.

"Whoa there, fella," Atticus said to the man as he reined in his horse. "Is that any way to greet a man and his boy?"

"Don't need no darkie lovers interferin' wid our bizness," snarled the man with the gun, who, considering his greasy hair, filthy face, and gravelly voice, apparently preferred whiskey over a bath.

"Then we're after the same thing," Atticus said casually. "Me and my son are looking for some runaways. I'd be obliged if you put that gun down."

"Who you workin' for?" the man asked skeptically, still pointing his revolver at Atticus.

"Man by the name of Furman hired us to hunt down some Sambos who ran away from the Murphys," Atticus lied, figuring the worst-case scenario was that these men were after the same prey.

"Why do you have your boy with you?" the other man asked, glaring at Gabe under a wide-brimmed hat that accentuated a large scar from his eye to the corner of his mouth. "This is a man's work."

"He can smell a coon a mile away and can track one who walks on air," Atticus said, inwardly shuddering at his choice of words.

"Smell anything, boy?" the man with the gun snickered.

"Not yet," Gabe said, in a voice as deep down as he could reach, his boots shaking in the stirrups.

"Well, you might as well keep sniffin'," the leader grumbled as he holstered the pistol. "Ain't nobody here. We're lookin' for runaways from the Harlans in Kintuck, but we lost their trail upriver a piece. There's some blood down the way," he said, gesturing with his thumb, "but nothin' else. How's 'bout we split the bounty if either of us find what the other is lookin' fer?"

"Agreed," Atticus replied. "Gentlemen," *and I use that term loosely*, he thought, "it's time we get movin' on," and spurred Maverick.

Gabe felt sweat running down his sides as he tipped his cap to the men and turned Major to follow his father.

About a hundred yards away, they found the pool of blood the man had mentioned and what appeared to be the signs of a struggle. Gabe dismounted and picked off a large, torn piece of rough homespun cloth stuck on a briar.

"That's slave cloth," Atticus said. "I won't call it what Southerners do."

Gabe and his father followed a trail of red blotches toward the wagon road that paralleled the river and made their way toward Maysville. They frequently stopped, calling out softly for George and listening intently for any sign of a rustle in the scrub.

Hearing a noise, Atticus whispered, "George? Is that you? We're here to help. We are friends. Rose, Hattie, and the children are safe." The bush moved slightly. "George? Come on out. You are safe with us."

Out of the undergrowth stepped a young man, his eyes bulging, with every muscle tensed.

"I ain't Geo'ge, but we needs help. I is Bernard and dis here is Estella." An even younger woman, obviously pregnant and trembling uncontrollably, stepped out of the bushes.

"Where are you from?" inquired Atticus, his soft eyes and voice reducing some of the fear on both runaways' faces.

"We is from Massa Harlan's," the young man said.

Gabe and Atticus shared a knowing glance. "Men are hunting for you down the way," Atticus told them. "We must attend to some important business right now, but we'll send somebody for you as soon as possible. Stay hidden here. Don't come out until you hear somebody call your name and say, 'It looks like it might rain.'" Atticus and Gabe gave the young couple the food from their saddlebags, including Mrs. Rankin's biscuits, water, and the wool blanket Gabe had tied behind his saddle.

"Go' bless you," Estella said softly, her lowered eyes trickling tears that dripped off her chin.

Atticus gave her a smile of reassurance. "God bless you, too. Stay quiet and stay hidden. We'll send a friend. We promise."

Gabe wanted to say something but had no idea what it should be, so he parroted, "God bless you."

The fugitives returned to the brush, and Atticus and Gabe rode toward Maysville. When it appeared to Gabe that his father was picking up the pace and not as earnestly looking and listening, he asked, "Pops, how did slavery start?"

"Slavery has been around as long as mankind. The slave trade flourished in Europe and Asia long before Christopher Columbus discovered the islands in the Caribbean. But, if you are talking about Negro slavery in the New World, it began shortly after Columbus's discovery."

"Wow, that was a long time ago."

"By the early 1500s, Spanish and Portuguese traders were kidnapping or buying Africans and bringing them to South America and what was then called Hispaniola to work in fields and mines. Some early explorers of America paid for their explorations by capturing Natives and selling them as slaves in Hispaniola and Mexico."

"When did African slaves first come to America?"

"In the early 1600s. Many Black and white workers came as indentured servants, providing labor for a few years in exchange for the costs of bringing them here. Some Indians in America were enslaved, but not on a large scale. As the need for laborers increased, more Africans were brought over. Enslavement became an economical way for landowners to increase their wealth and power."

"I don't understand why slavery is based on being a Negro."

"It wasn't always. People enslaved those they conquered or captured. Sad to say, but Negro slavery because of the color of a person's skin started in America. I think that some impoverished whites began treating Blacks as lesser humans to feel better about themselves. Whites didn't like competing for jobs with Blacks. Laws were passed, called Black Codes, which made the white race legally superior to the Blacks."

"Black Codes?"

"Laws allowing Negroes to be bought and sold like animals, and saying a child born to a slave remains enslaved and is the property of the mother's owner. They made it a crime to teach slaves to read or write, or to travel without a pass. And many more laws like that."

"How did states become free or slave?

"Well, Son," Atticus began, "enslaved people lived in all states for a long time. But slave labor was in more demand in the agricultural South than in the North. Gradually, some Northern states began abolishing slavery, and all Southern states passed laws allowing it. The Continental Congress passed the Northwest Ordinance, which excluded slavery in any state formed in the Northwest Territory. In 1820, Missouri's desire to join the Union as a slave state caused a heated debate. Congress worked out what was called 'The Missouri Compromise.'"

"What did that do?"

"It allowed Missouri to join as a slave state and created Maine as a free state. More importantly, it established the dividing line between free and slave states along the southern border of Missouri, running west across the remaining Louisiana Territory."

"Is that how it is now?"

"No," said Atticus. "After the Mexican War, territory was added all the way to the Pacific Ocean, and Congress had to figure out what to do about slavery there."

"What did they do?"

"They reached another compromise, called the Compromise of 1850. California, much of it below the slave line, joined as a free state, but settlers in the New Mexico Territory, below the line, and the Utah Territory, above the slave line, could decide whether to be free or slave. That's called popular sovereignty. As part of the compromise, Congress also strengthened the Fugitive Slave Law, which some call the Bloodhound Law."

"What's that?"

"To get the South to ratify the Constitution, the Founding Fathers wrote into the Constitution that an escaping slave, if caught, had to be returned to the slave's owner. When that provision wasn't being enforced, Congress passed the first Fugitive Slave Act, but Northerners ignored it, too."

"I'll bet that made Southerners mad."

"Yes, it did. So, as part of the 1850 Compromise, the new Fugitive Slave Law imposed severe penalties for people harboring or assisting escapees. Slave catchers bring any Negro they capture—free or slave—to the constable and obtain a reward. The constable also gets paid for turning the alleged slave over to the person claiming to be the owner."

"Then why do we help them escape if it's illegal and so dangerous?"

"Because I believe every human deserves to be free. You know what the Declaration of Independence and the Golden Rule say: we should treat everyone, not just white men, as equals and the same as we want to be treated. I agree with Reverend Rankin that disobedience to the Act is obedience to God."

"What happened last night showed me how dangerous helping fugitives is," Gabe said. "Until then, I thought it was sort of a game."

"It's no game. It's serious business. This slavery thing is going to divide this country one way or the other. Some even think it could lead to a conflict where we are fighting against each other."

"Why is the South so concerned, since half the country is free and the other half slave?" Gabe asked.

"Because more states will be formed out of the territories north of the slave line than below it. People in the slave states think the North is doing all it can to abolish slavery, as Great Britain did, and end the foundation of their economy. They need to keep the number of slave and free states equal to keep the balance of power."

"It's all very confusing."

"And very complex," Atticus added as they reached Maysville. The pair went straight to the house of Atticus's abolitionist friend Jonathan Bierbower.

"Good morning, Jonathan," Atticus said, extending his hand. "This is my youngest son, Gabriel."

"Hello, Atticus. Hello, Gabriel," Bierbower replied, shaking with a hand made strong by his work building fine carriages. "What brings you to Maysville?"

"Gabe picked up a load of fugitives last night from Reverend Rankin. They told us that a man they were with went missing. They heard a gunshot and fear he was killed or captured. We saw some blood and signs of a scuffle but nothing else. Did you hear about any captures?"

"I heard that bounty hunters brought several fugitives in. I saw a poster they were being sold today at the courthouse up in Old Washington," Bierbower said, stroking his firm chin. "I don't know anything more than that."

"We better get up there, but there is one thing," Atticus said, telling Bierbower about Bernard and Estella, their hiding spot, and the secret phrase.

Bierbower nodded. "I'll take care of them."

They said their goodbyes, and Atticus and Gabe headed up the hill to Old Washington, which was about three miles away. As they rode, Atticus told Gabe, "The courthouse in Washington is where Harriet Stowe witnessed the slave auction she wrote about in her book." He paused a moment, choosing his words carefully. "Son, you are about to see something that will make you *very* angry. You must keep your composure."

Gabe had rarely heard his father sound so serious. His heart began beating hard and fast, and his leg muscles were taut, pressing into Major's flanks.

As they approached the two-story limestone courthouse, blood-curdling screams filled Gabe's ears. He saw a Black woman stripped naked from the waist up, her wrists and ankles in chains that were attached to a bolt embedded in the platform. Gabe immediately saw the reasons for her anguish, and her words became clear: "DON' take my babies!" she cried, trying to rip the manacles from her wrists. "No, no, no, NO! Buy me, too! Don' take my chillen aways from me. Please, JESUS!" she screamed.

Gabe blanched in horror. He wanted to shut his eyes to close out the scene, but he couldn't for reasons he didn't fully understand.

To the left, a man tugged on a chain attached to two slave collars that were around the necks of two young Black boys, probably about six or seven, who appeared to Gabe to be twins. The man pulled the boys toward their new owner as they struggled to return to their mother. Angry that his tall felt hat fell into the dirt during the tussle, the auction assistant yanked on the fetters, causing the boys to fall to the dusty ground and scream in pain.

"C'mon, you filthy little pickaninnies," he growled, dragging them away from the wailing woman, who was still pleading with God, Jesus, and everyone within earshot. One boy appeared injured and had stopped resisting. The other, giving up his hope of returning to his mother, assisted his brother.

The mother's screeches turned to deep, grieving sobs.

Stunned, Gabe felt the blood drain from his cheeks.

The auctioneer returned his attention to the half-naked woman and continued the bidding. "We're at nine hundred. Who'll give me a thousand?"

"I'll buy the Nigra for one thousand dollars," yelled a well-dressed man wearing a swallow-tailed coat, a vest, and a silk top hat. "I need a strong, fertile woman for my breeding house."

Gabe felt sick. He turned to his father for some sign of hope but saw the look of steel in Atticus's eyes, his clenched jaw and knuckles white from squeezing the reins.

The woman's sobs continued as another man pulled her back to the slave pen in the opposite direction from her children. The slave-handler dragged a man to the platform, chained like a wild animal. He was howling, "I'm a free man. I'm not a slave. I was kidnapped. Help me, somebody. I'm from Cincinnati. I work at Josiah Iliff's tannery. My . . . ," but the handler cut his words short, smashing him across the shins with a wooden board and dropping him to his knees.

"Shut up!" the slaver yelled. "You're a no-good liar."

The man began to protest again, and the handler swung the board, which looked like a sawed-off rowboat oar with holes in the blade to give it more force, and hit the Black man's back, knocking him to his elbows. Gabe winced as if he could feel the blow.

"Oh, please help me," the man pleaded to those watching. Another blow, bursting the skin on his back and exposing dark red muscle, silenced him. He fell forward on his face.

Gabe laid forward, burying his head in Major's mane to find comfort in its warmth.

The man was sold, grabbed under his armpits, and, pleading for mercy, dragged back to the holding cage.

While struggling to make sense of the madness he was witnessing, Gabe saw another man being yanked toward the sale platform by a slave collar. Steel tines stuck out a foot from the ring around his neck, and fetters shackled his ankles and wrists. He was a large, well-built man with tattered pants and a bloody shirt barely hanging on his body. He had what appeared to be a nasty flesh wound on his shoulder and cuts and abrasions on his chest, face, and arms. Gabe pulled the homespun piece he had taken off the bush from his pocket. It matched the man's shirt, just as the prisoner matched Rose's description of her missing husband. There was no doubt it was George.

Reaching the same conclusion, Atticus looked at Gabe and said sternly, "Stay where you are." Moving toward the stairs where the slave-handler was leading George, Atticus told the handler that, before he bid, he needed a closer look at George's shoulder.

"Sure, why not? It's a free country," the oppressor said, the irony of his words totally lost on him.

Atticus approached the prisoner's side and pretended to look at the shoulder wound. Avoiding the long tines, he leaned into the man's ear and whispered, "Rose, Hattie, and the children are safe. I'm Atticus Adams from Georgetown, Ohio. Come find me when you can."

Atticus's words were cut off by the slave jockey jerking on the chain attached to George's neck collar and demanding, "Let's go. It's your turn." The handler turned to Atticus and said, "He'll heal. Animals clean their own wounds."

The handler pulled George onto the platform. His wrist and neck chains rattled, and the ankle irons scraped across the wooden platform. Gabe got a better look at George's eyes—intense yet seemingly looking far away. *Was that a smile?* He saw George give an ever-so-slight nod to Atticus.

The auctioneer announced, "This here darkie is a runaway, and his family got away. He'll run again. He needs to be taken far down the river. He's worth over fifteen hundred dollars. Bidding'll start at five hundred." The bidding quickly reached nine hundred and fifty dollars, then narrowed to two bidders.

"A thousand," yelled one sporting a prominent potbelly, leathery skin, and a week's stubble on his double chin.

"Thousan' fifty," the other countered, raising his arm. His emaciated body, crooked nose, and long fingers made ugly look good.

"Eleven hundred."

"'Leven-fifty," the loathsome man said, running his fingers through his grimy hair.

Gabe felt as helpless as a babe just out of the womb. He wanted to break George free of his chains.

The low bidder didn't raise the price. "Once . . . twice . . . SOLD to Butcher Dan," barked the auctioneer with a bit of a smirk.

Gabe watched the crowd enjoying the despicable scene. Over the jeering and laughter, Gabe heard the women in the pen begin to sing, trying to comfort and give strength to the mother who had just lost her sons:

When Israel wuz in Egypt's land
Let my people go.
Oppress' so hard they could not stand
Let my people go.
Go down, Moses
Way down in Egypt's land.
Tell ol' Pharaoh
Let my people go!

THREE

"SOMEHOW, SOMEDAY, SOME WAY"

October 19–20, 1853

Atticus returned to his son and whispered, "Let's get out of here."

Gabe pulled Major's reins, glancing over his shoulder for another look at George. He wished he hadn't. The slave jockey yanked George off the raised platform, causing him to trip and fall down the steps. He then kicked George in the ribs and yelled something Gabe didn't understand. Clenching his jaw and choking the reins, Gabe spurred Major and caught up to his father.

As they started down the hill toward Maysville, Gabe asked his father questions rapidly like a two-year-old: "Why didn't we buy him? Can we rescue him? Where will they take him?"

"Son," Atticus said softly, "I couldn't buy him if I wanted to. I don't have a thousand dollars. No, we can't rescue him. People get killed trying to rescue slaves. As for George, we'll do what we can to find out who bought him and where they're taking him. At least we know he's alive."

"I almost threw up watching."

"So did I. What they did to that woman is the vilest part of slavery. Any culture that separates families and justifies its actions by claiming Negroes don't have feelings is an evil one."

"How are we ever going to find George?" Gabe asked.

"I don't know." Atticus pulled out his crumpled handkerchief, blew his nose, and wiped his eyes.

They rode silently for a few minutes, then Gabe broke the silence. "Pops, when they wrote the Constitution, why didn't they get rid of slavery?

"Son, the Southern states would not have ratified it unless it had the provisions that enabled enslavement to continue."

"What kind of provisions?" Gabe asked.

"The Constitution allowed for the importation of slaves until 1808, required the return of fugitive slaves, and counted slaves as three-fifths of a person for determining the population for the House of Representatives."

"I don't get that," Gabe said. "How can someone be three-fifths of a person?"

"That's a good question. The country intended to tax the slaves as property. The South demanded that, if they were going to be taxed on slaves, slaves should also count toward representation in Congress. The Founders compromised by counting slaves as three-fifths of a person for both purposes. One Southerner with five slaves has the same power as four Northerners. The more slaves in a state, the more representatives the state has."

"That doesn't sound fair," Gabe said.

"It isn't. The Founders hoped that slavery would eventually die out. But if it didn't, they knew they were deferring the problems to a later date," Atticus sighed. "Later, I'm afraid, has arrived."

"Pops, why do you hate slavery?"

"Son, slavery is wrong. Your grandfather instilled in me the belief that all people are God's creatures and each deserves basic human rights. I am doing what I can to give them freedom."

The downbeat travelers arrived at the Bierbower house. Atticus related the events and asked, "Who is Butcher Dan?"

Bierbower looked at his shoes and shook his head. "He works for a company that takes slaves to New Orleans and sells them to owners of sugar cane plantations or salt mines. It's the nastiest, hottest, most dangerous work for an enslaved person."

"Is there any way to find out where George ends up?"

"Maybe," Bierbower said. "They keep pretty good records of sales. I have some contacts. I'll see what I can dig up. By the way, I've already sent a couple of my hands to help the runaways you came across. They should be across the river by now."

"Thanks," Atticus said with a sigh. "That's the only good thing I've heard today."

Atticus and Gabe said their goodbyes. They crossed the river on the Maysville ferry and rode toward Ripley along the north bank. It was hot and humid for a fall day, and the horses and their riders wilted in the low afternoon sun that burned their eyes. The road had dried out, and each time a hoof hit the ground, it raised a cloud of dust and a swarm of grasshoppers.

"Do you think slavery will ever end?"

"Not unless something drastic happens. The Southern economy depends on slaves to maintain a comfortable lifestyle and culture. The North is as much at fault as the South, reaping huge profits by trading for sugar, coffee, rice, tobacco, and cotton produced in the slave states. Your Aunt Rebecca's family in Cincinnati got wealthy by turning Southern cotton into cloth. At this point, slavery is a large part of the nation's fabric."

"Is that why Northerners don't fight harder for Negroes' freedom?" Gabe asked, feeling like the day's heat had become even more oppressive.

"Correct. There are just as many prejudiced and greedy people in the North as in the South. Most Northerners, including many abolitionists, don't see Negroes as equals, and claim Negroes lower a community's moral standards and bring disorder. It will take more than a political compromise to resolve this dilemma."

Emotion overwhelmed Gabe as he wrestled with these new insights and his visions of the distraught mother losing her children and the slave jockey kicking George in the ribs. Gabe came to an absolute resolve: *Somehow, someday, some way, I will do my part to end this horrible plague.*

Dusk gave way to night, and the day's heat finally surrendered. A bright moon lit the way back to Georgetown. Mosquitos and the sound of chirping crickets filled the cooler air. The two pushed hard and arrived at their homestead, hungry as bears coming out of hibernation.

Hot venison stew with potatoes, onions, and carrots from their garden filled a pot hanging over the fire. Freshly baked bread and a tub of the day's churned butter was on the table. Gabe couldn't breathe deeply enough to take in all the aromas.

Atticus gave Ailene a long, loving hug and kiss. "I cannot tell you how much I needed to see you. What a day."

"I love you," Ailene said, returning his kiss. "I'm so glad you're home. Our visitors are eager to hear from you."

"We'll go see them and take care of the horses after we get washed up and eat."

Caroline joined them at the table. Atticus gave the blessing. Before the "n" of "amen" had left his father's lips, Gabe was digging his spoon into the bowl set before him.

Between bites, Atticus related the day's events.

Tears ran down Ailene's cheeks as she heard about George's circumstances and, most likely, his future. "I don't know how we'll tell our guests."

Gabe came up for air when he had finished his second helping of stew, half a loaf of bread, and about a quart of milk. "Good dinner, Mommy!" Gabe thought it was silly to keep saying the words he had said as a toddler, but his mother thought it was cute, so he still said it after every meal.

Ailene looked adoringly at him. *He's still my little boy, but he's the spitting image of his father,* she thought. Despite her demanding life on a farm and raising four children, Ailene, with crystal green eyes and an engaging smile, appeared younger than her thirty-seven years. She had below-the-shoulder auburn hair that was always a bit disheveled, and tonight, as usual, it had a streak of white from the flour left behind when she had pushed it out of her face. An inner warmth drew others to her like moths to a flame.

Ailene was born to poor farmers near Washington, Pennsylvania. When she was young, her family moved down the Ohio River onto a small farm outside of Cincinnati. She met Atticus at his father's church. Atticus, two years older than Ailene, was quite smitten by her and tried, at first unsuccessfully, to impress her. She still laughed at the memory of watching Atticus suffer in silence, tears streaming down his face as if nothing was happening, after Nathaniel had urged him to eat a handful of hot pepper seeds to show off his masculinity. Eventually, they had a lovely courtship, and a year later, Atticus asked her father for her hand and his blessing. Ailene was with child for much of the next six years, with Michael, now eighteen, Raphael, almost seventeen, Gabe, and Caroline.

After dinner, the four made their way to the barn.

Atticus closed his eyes, took a deep breath, and exhaled slowly. "Menare."

The latch scraped. Gabe opened the trapdoor, welcoming the small group into the lantern-lit barn.

Ailene held Rose's and Hattie's hands as Atticus told them and the children about finding George. He spared them the ugly details but explained how he managed to whisper a few words of comfort to George.

"You should have seen his smile," Gabe said, looking at Jasmine, trying to give her and the others hope. "He looked relieved that all of you are safe."

"But we could not stop him from being sold," Atticus said.

Rose pulled the hem of her dress up to her face to muffle the sobs she could not choke back.

The two children sat in stunned silence, worried sick about their father's fate.

Hattie squeezed her eyes shut. Her thin, weather-beaten face twisted in agony.

"I don't know what else to say," Atticus said, his voice barely audible. "We'll let you be. We better call it a night. It will be time for you to head north tomorrow."

Returning to the house, Gabe climbed the ladder to the loft he shared with Michael and Raphael when they were home. As he washed his face in the water basin, he thought about Jasmine and her family. *I've gotten them this far, and after what I just saw, I want to make sure they are safe. I want to take them to the next stop. I wonder if Pops will let me.* He fell into bed and was asleep before his head hit the pillow.

Morning dawned. Gabe wasn't certain how to raise the subject of helping take the group farther north with his parents. As he descended the ladder, moving slowly toward the kitchen following the scent of a hot breakfast, he overheard a conversation between Atticus and Ailene.

"It's too dangerous," his mother said tensely.

"He's up for it. He proved that yesterday," Atticus countered. Then, seeing Gabe, both stopped talking and focused on eating. The room's only sound was the scraping of knives and forks.

Gabe's favorite breakfast was on the table: eggs smothered in leftover stew with a piece of warm flatbread. Not sure what to say, he began devouring the food like he did dinner the night before.

"I understand you might like coffee with your breakfast," his mother teased, trying to ease the tension.

"No, thank you. Just milk," Gabe replied, turning a dark shade of pink.

"Son, we've got a problem," Atticus said. "We've got to get the folks moving, and with the harvest, we don't know who can come get them. We're unsure how long Raphael would take to get here from Lane Seminary. I cannot risk getting caught, as it would threaten our existence. I'd surely go to jail, get fined, or worse." He hesitated, glancing at Ailene. "We're thinking you can take them."

"You want me to take them to the next stop?" Gabe's stomach somersaulted, surprised his parents were suggesting what he had hoped for.

"Maybe even farther than that," answered Atticus, glancing at Ailene's worried face. "If I can get Nathaniel to let Marcus go with you, we will have you two take them to Oberlin, and then Michael can help the rest of the way."

"You want me to take them the whole way?" Gabe said, his voice going up an octave.

"Only if Marcus can go," Atticus said. Marcus, almost seventeen, was the youngest of Uncle Nathaniel and Aunt Rebecca's three children. "If he can't, you'll take them to Hillsboro, and it will be up to others to get the group to Canada."

Good God. Not Marcus. I'd rather take the risk alone. Gabe despised his spoiled cousins, especially Marcus, partly out of jealousy but mostly because they looked down their noses at others who were not as privileged. They lacked nothing, and lorded that fact over others in a manner that Gabe couldn't abide. Marcus's brothers had bullied Marcus, and he took great pleasure in dishing out the same treatment to others, especially Gabe, the little brother he didn't have. Adding further insult, that morning as every morning, Gabe was wearing hand-me-downs from Marcus. Gabe was often frustrated and angry that Atticus didn't notice his nephew's ill behavior and let the belittling continue. *Maybe he won't be able to go.*

"I don't want him to go *at all*, even with Marcus," Ailene snapped as she abruptly got up, snatched two plates off the table, and headed toward the open kitchen just a few feet away.

"Honey, we've got to move them," Atticus said, then turned toward Gabe. "Here's what I'm thinking. You are the best wagon teamster around, and I believe you can get the group up north. You could go from station to station during the day until you get to Oberlin. Two young boys traveling in daylight won't attract much attention."

"But what happens if we get caught?"

"That would be horrible for the passengers, but you'd both probably get a good hickory switch whipping and told to go home," Atticus said. "Bounty hunters want the fugitives, not a couple of boys, although they might still come after me."

"I say no," Ailene said, all the while knowing she couldn't stop the inevitable once Atticus had made up his mind.

Gabe couldn't believe what he was hearing. The trip to Oberlin would take six or seven days. It would not be easy, with fugitives in the wagon and putting up with Marcus. His stomach continued to churn. "Aw, Mother. I can do it!" Gabe announced, although reality was already replacing bravado.

"I see no other choice. I'll be off to Nathaniel's," Atticus said, leaving Ailene fuming at the sink. Nathaniel, Rebecca, and their boys lived in Georgetown, the county seat of Brown County. Nathaniel was a lawyer, and Rebecca's family was among the wealthiest in Cincinnati. Rebecca's father was also a lawyer and a former United States senator. "Get everything ready," Atticus said.

Ailene looked at Gabe in resignation. Forcing a thin smile, she said, "Let's do as your father said."

They went to the barn, where their guests sat huddled together on hay bales, eating a breakfast of eggs, thick slabs of pork belly, and fresh bread. In the corner, Caroline was rocking the cooing and smiling baby. Caroline loved helping her mother care for others, especially babies.

"Enjoying your breakfast?" Ailene asked as she greeted them, trying to sound cheerful.

"Yes, Miss Ailene," they all said in unison.

"Hello, and good morning," Gabe began. Jasmine looked up at him with big, dark eyes. Gabe was taken aback, then embarrassed that he found her so pretty. Although he had flirted with girls his age, Gabe wasn't sure how to act with an escaping slave. He stammered a bit but tried to sound grown-up when he told them, "I'm going to be taking you up the line today. We need you to prepare for the trip. It won't be very comfortable. You'll have to stay in the box in the wagon all day."

"Yes, Massa Gabe," Jasmine said, looking at Gabe as though no one else could take her to safety.

"Please don't call me that," Gabe pleaded. "I'm your friend. Call me Gabe."

"Yes, Mass . . . yes, Gabe," Levi said, as grown-up as he could. With his father missing, he was the man of the family.

Ailene put blankets and padding in the false bottom of the wagon, noting what a tight squeeze it would be for the passengers.

Gabe readied the horses. He had been driving Nellie and Maggie since he was eight. They responded to him like no other driver. For years, Atticus and Ailene had bragged to friends and family what a great teamster Gabe was, and he took immense pride in it. However, he was having trouble with the reins and hitches this morning, something he could normally do in the pitch dark. Gabe's fingers were not cooperating, and he fumbled with the tack. *I can do this*, although his body was sending a different message. As he struggled to get the hitch right, he heard the sound of horses. *Damn, that can only mean one thing. Marcus is coming.*

Barging into the barn ahead of Atticus, Marcus snidely greeted Gabe. "Ready to go on an adventure with your better-lookin' cousin? Hey, nice shirt."

Atticus and Ailene laughed, but Gabe turned back to the horses.

"I'm not sure I'd call it an adventure," Gabe said, yanking the reins harder than he needed to. "It'll be dangerous."

"I'm here to protect you," Marcus crowed lightheartedly, waving his rifle above his head. "I'll ride shotgun."

"I need you to start as soon as possible to get to Hillsboro before dark," Atticus told Gabe, giving him directions to the first stop at the Hibbens' house. "Someone at each stop will give you names and directions for the next stop until you get to Oberlin."

Ailene went to the house to finish packing enough food for the first day of travel. On the top and to the sides of the secret compartment, Atticus put hay for the horses and a few supplies Michael had requested. Gabe managed to finish hitching the horses while Marcus tied his horse to the rear of the wagon.

Still cuddling the baby, Caroline led the runaways to the outhouse. As they started back to the barn, Rose and Hattie were singing softly, readying themselves for the next step toward freedom:

> Swing low, sweet chariot
> Comin' for to carry me home.
> Swing low, sweet chariot
> Comin' for to carry me home.
>
> I looked over Jordan and wha' did I see
> Comin' for to carry me home?
> A band of angels comin' after me
> Comin' for to carry me home.

When everything was in order, the fugitives approached Ailene and Atticus.

"Miss Ailene, you is a Godly woman. We don' knows how to thank you," said Rose. "We can't never repay you."

"No need," replied Ailene. "We just want you to get to Canada safely."

Atticus gave Rose a slip of paper with his name and their farm's location.

"We's can' read this," Rose mumbled.

"Just keep it," Atticus said gently. "You'll learn to read, or someone can read it for you. Contact us when you get settled. I will do what I can to locate George, and I need to know where you are. If something happens," he warned, regretting he had to give such an instruction, "you must eat the paper. We can't have us or our location disclosed."

Rose nodded her head in understanding. It dawned on her and the others that real freedom was still far away, and this freedom could end in a moment.

Everyone loaded into the wagon except the baby. Caroline didn't want to give him up and sniffled as Ailene gently took Benjamin from her and handed him to his mother.

Gabe jumped into the lead seat on the right, and Marcus, not looking quite so cocky as before, hopped onto the seat next to him. As Gabe bent down for a tender hug from his mother, Ailene wrapped a large, knitted scarf around his neck as if it were a shield for his safety.

Gabe snapped the reins on the horses's rumps. "Hie, Nellie. Hie, Maggie," he commanded with as low and grown-up a voice as he could muster, and the wagon jerked forward.

"Be safe, be careful!" Atticus called after them, his voice cracking, matching the uneasy feeling in his heart.

Ailene held her hand to her mouth, tears in her eyes.

Caroline waved to the hidden cargo as the wagon disappeared down the lane.

FOUR

NOTHING BUT SILENCE

October 20–21, 1853

Thanks to a mostly flat road, the apprehensive cousins and the quiet passengers arrived in Hillsboro before sunset. "There's the house," Gabe said, remembering the Hibbens' home from a previous delivery he had made with Raphael several years before. He was relieved they had made it, because clouds were building, a storm was brewing, and the temperature was dropping.

"Hello, Mrs. Hibben," Gabe said as the large wooden door opened.

"Hello," responded Margaret Hibben, a middle-aged woman with an ear-to-ear smile and a prominent double chin that hung like a rooster's wattle. "Are you Gabriel or Raphael?" she asked. "I'm sorry, I don't remember."

"I'm Gabe, and this is my cousin, Marcus."

"Glad to meet you, Marcus. And it's nice to see you again, Gabriel," said Samuel Hibben as he joined his wife at the door. Dark eyebrows on his thin face accentuated white, curly hair. Gabe stifled a chuckle because seeing Mr. and Mrs. Hibben reminded him of a nursery rhyme his mother recited: *Jack Spratt could eat no fat, his wife could eat no lean.*

"Your father's telegram didn't say who was coming. It just said to expect four volumes of *The Irresistible Conflict*."

"That telegraph thing is amazing," Mrs. Hibben added, shaking her head. "I wish someone would explain how words get sent on a wire."

"Bring the wagon into the carriage house, and let's get your people inside," Mr. Hibben directed.

Gabe did as he was told and helped the passengers out of the box, each one stretching and taking deep breaths of fresh air. Rose comforted an increasingly fussy Benjamin as Mrs. Hibben escorted them into the house.

Mrs. Hibben settled the pilgrims in a cubbyhole behind a movable bookcase and provided them with water, bread, cheese, and beans. She placed the same meager meal in front of Gabe and Marcus, then sat down with them but did not set anything for herself or her husband. Gabe guessed the reason the Hibbens were not eating had more to do with lack of food than having already eaten.

"How are your mother and father?" Mrs. Hibben asked with a charming lilt. "We haven't seen them in quite some time."

"They're just fine. Pops is still preaching, and the farm is in good shape. They send their greetings," Gabe politely responded. "By the way, we will take the family up the line, moving them during the day. You won't have to get someone to take them."

"That's good," Mr. Hibben replied. "We weren't sure who we could find. That Fugitive Slave Law has people scared to help."

Marcus didn't say anything until his plate was clean, then asked if there was more.

"No," Mrs. Hibben said, looking down to avoid eye contact. "I'm sorry. That's all that's left."

Sensing that Marcus was about to complain, Gabe kicked him in the shin.

Marcus shot him a look that conveyed a clear message.

"You have a long day tomorrow," Mr. Hibben said, his eyes narrowing. "You'll need to start early. You can stop for a rest in Washington Court House, but the conductor there told us prolonging a stay is unsafe. He'll direct you to the next stop."

"Can we let the passengers ride in the open?" asked Gabe.

"You'll need to keep them hidden for a couple more stops," Mr. Hibben instructed. "Someone up the line will tell you when it's safe to let them out of the box."

Gabe heard the wind pick up, looked outside, and saw that the night sky was black as ink.

Later, Mrs. Hibben and Gabe checked in on the guests while Marcus remained in the small parlor reading a book. "I hope all of you are comfortable," Mrs. Hibben said.

"Yes, ma'am," Rose replied. "We's much obliged to you."

"We get joy helping people on their way to freedom," Mrs. Hibben said as she collected the licked-clean tin plates. "I wish we had more to eat and better accommodations."

"Everythin' is jus' fine," Hattie added, her stern countenance softening.

"We have to leave early tomorrow," Gabe explained. "Try to get some sleep."

"We will," Jasmine said.

"Good night, y'all," Mrs. Hibben said. They pulled the bookcase over the opening and joined Marcus in the parlor. "Let's get you two to bed," she said, leading Gabe and Marcus to a small room in the back of the house.

After Mrs. Hibben left the room, Marcus smacked Gabe on the arm. "Don't you ever kick me again."

Acting like he didn't feel the punch, Gabe sneered, "Just go to bed."

There was only one bed, and Marcus fell asleep as soon as he got under the covers. Gabe tossed and turned as the wind and rain blew against the window. He felt great trepidation for what lay ahead, but exhaustion eventually won out over his restless spirit, and his eyes closed.

Upon rising, the boys joined Mrs. Hibben at the table as she placed a small breakfast before them. Gabe had heard their hostess leave very early and assumed she was going to another house to obtain food for her guests.

After the travelers ate, Gabe hitched the horses to the wagon. Jasmine allowed Gabe to grasp her hand and elbow to help her into the cart. Her eyes fell on Gabe in admiration—a look not lost on Gabe. Or Marcus.

"Thank you for your hospitality," Gabe said to the Hibbens.

"You are most welcome. Here, take this blanket. It looks like you may need it," Mrs. Hibben said, looking up at the gray, overcast sky. "That cold north wind will be in your faces."

Mr. Hibben described how to get to the First Presbyterian Church in Washington C. H. "When you see the cupula of the courthouse, Marcus will need to ride ahead to let someone at the church, right down the street from the courthouse, know of your arrival."

Gabe's "hie" was not as bold as the day before, but the horses responded to his voice, and the wagon again lurched northward. The horses trudged along as the boys sat silently, huddled under the blanket. The weather continued to worsen, as did Marcus's mood. Rain pelted their faces with no relief in sight.

"I'm hungry," whined Marcus.

"So am I, and I'm sure they are, too," responded Gabe, gesturing with his thumb to the back of the wagon, "but there isn't anything we can do about it. We've already finished everything Mother packed." Trying to lighten the mood, he poked Marcus lightly in the stomach and teased, "Besides, you've got a little extra to keep you going."

Marcus wound up and slugged Gabe on the arm again. Despite every effort not to, Gabe yelped in pain and woke Benjamin, who coughed and cried.

"You'll have to keep him quiet," snapped Marcus over his shoulder to the concealed passengers, as if Rose had caused the baby's worsening condition.

Inside the box, Rose soothed Benjamin, and soon he was silent. Only the sound of hooves slopping through mud rose above the wind.

As they neared Washington C. H., Marcus mounted his horse and rode off for the church as instructed. Before reaching it, Marcus stopped at the general store and bought rations, which he hid in the horse's saddlebags. Eating a big piece of jerky, he made his way to the church and informed the caretaker of the approaching group.

As Gabe entered the little village, a man rode up to the wagon and ordered, "Stop them horses," ensuring Gabe could see the badge on his chest. "I'm Sheriff Jones. Whacha got in that there wagon?" He dismounted and started walking around the wagon like the bounty hunters had several nights before.

Gabe tried to stay calm. *I can't outrun the sheriff.* "I'm from Hillsboro and on my way to Williamsport to drop off supplies and pick up my brother."

Making a loop around the wagon, the sheriff stopped, crossed his arms, and looked Gabe up and down. *He's pretty young to be running slaves alone.* He stopped snooping and barked at Gabe, "Get along." Sheriff Jones seemed disappointed, as he had hoped to find some runaway slaves so he could claim his bounty and buy that iron bed his wife coveted and end her ceaseless nagging about it.

Gabe tipped his hat. "G-day, Sheriff," he said, flicking the reins. The baby whimpered as the wagon rolled down the street, but his mother quickly muffled the cries.

They approached the small church, and the caretaker was there to meet Gabe. "Take the wagon behind the church and under the porch."

Gabe brought the horses to a halt under a covered and partially concealed porch, generally used for funerals so that the deceased's family had privacy. It also hid the purpose of this visit.

Pastor Samuel Miller, an older man with short, white hair pushed back from a high forehead and wearing tiny glasses on the end of his nose, came out of the church. "We can unload here and get you some food. Rest for a little while, but then you'll need to be on your way. The sheriff has been nosing around and making things difficult. Not everyone in these parts shares our views."

It was still early in the afternoon but looked much later due to the dark clouds. "Where's the next stop?" Gabe asked, concerned. "I don't think the family can go much further. The baby seems to be getting worse."

"The Woods can provide some shelter in Williamsport—but that's fifteen miles away. You can still get there by sundown if you keep this rest short."

Gabe nodded his understanding and moved quickly to remove the cold crew from their cramped quarters. "We've only got about an hour to let the horses rest," he told them. "Then we have to move on."

Everyone but Gabe went inside seeking warmth and nourishment. The baby was noticeably ill. Rose did all she could to comfort him.

"I've got some paregoric in honey that you can give the baby," Pastor Miller said to Rose, handing her a small, dark brown bottle. "Give him five drops every couple of hours."

"Thank you. Dis will be a blessin'."

Marcus immediately plopped into a chair by the fire, chewing on large, torn pieces of bread and cheese he had taken from the table. The caretaker hid the fugitives in a closet under the stairs leading to the choir loft, lit a lamp, and left them with bread, cheese, jerky, and milk.

After attending to the horses and checking the wagon, Gabe joined the others in the closet to see how they were holding up, but with an ulterior motive. *I need a break from Marcus's surly attitude. I can't take it right now.* He sat down next to Jasmine so close he could smell her hair. Their knees touched when Gabe reached for a piece of cheese. She quickly turned her knee inward, away from the touch. Embarrassed by his naivete about how Jasmine might react to being touched by a white man, Gabe moved a few more inches away from her.

The hour of respite didn't seem that long. The paregoric had calmed the baby, who was asleep by the time the weary travelers returned to the wagon. The family piled into the false bottom. Marcus dragged his feet, upset they had to go back into the cold rain.

Gabe got directions to the next stop from Pastor Miller. With a "hie" and a slap of the reins, the wagon pitched forward again. The spitting rain turned into shards of pelting sleet. The cousins pulled the blanket tighter. The horses struggled as the road conditions worsened, and Gabe's worry increased.

About an hour after leaving the church, they came to a low spot in the road, and the wagon's wheels became mired in the muck.

"Damn," Marcus grumbled. "Why the hell did I agree to come on this blasted trip?"

Gabe climbed down to assess the situation. *I need to lighten the load so the horses can get the wagon out of this mud.* The escapees climbed out of the box, and Gabe led them into the trees and thick underbrush where they would be well hidden.

"Marcus, get over here and help unload the wagon," barked Gabe, no longer in the mood to appease his older cousin. "We gotta hurry."

Marcus begrudgingly lowered himself from the wagon and slowly began unloading the equipment.

They had no more begun their task when three burly men approached. Drenched from the rain, more space in their mouths than teeth and their faces heavily scarred, they looked like devils incarnate. Marcus reached for his rifle.

"I wouldn't do that, boy," snapped the oldest and most disgusting of the three as he pointed his rifle at Marcus. "We're just going to look around and relieve you of any contraband."

Gabe didn't know what contraband was, but he knew what the bounty hunters sought.

"Ain't got none of that," Gabe glibly replied, trying to sound like a country bumpkin. "Jus' headin' up t' Williamsport t' pick up more 'quipment. But the horses are havin' problems."

The boys had taken just enough out of the wagon to expose part of the unusual-looking box in the cart. One of the men poked at it with his rifle. Gabe quickly said, "Tha's whar ma puts the produce when she goes off to market. Keeps it fresh. And it's whar we sleep if we need to." *Even though it's wrong, I'm getting better at lying.*

One man used his rifle to open up the flap on the box. Seeing only what looked like bedding, he said, "Nuttin' here, Jed."

Just as they turned their horses to leave, the baby let out a raspy cough. Gabe began to cough to cover the sound that came from behind him. The bounty hunter next to the wagon dismounted and walked toward the bushes. Gabe's tension mounted as the man approached the shrubs where the fugitives were hiding. *At least the baby is quiet.* Gabe held his breath, breaking into a cold sweat.

The man poked around the bushes, then said, "Nuttin' here neither."

Instinct told the gang leader something didn't seem right, but the sleet had drained him of any desire to continue the investigation. Looking at the two skeptically, he said, "Looks like y'all will git that there wagon out all right and don't need us." He turned to his vigilantes and shouted, "Let's get outta here and git someplace warm an' dry." He and the men spurred their horses and galloped off.

Gabe exhaled, grabbed Nellie's bridle, and yanked her head. Nellie snorted. "Sorry, girl, I've reached the end of my patience."

Gabe looked at Marcus, who had not moved, and he felt some satisfaction when he noticed a dark, wet spot spreading downward from his cousin's crotch.

After leading the horses out of the mud and up the slope, Gabe went where the passengers hid. "All clear," he announced.

Sobbing, Rose came out of the bushes.

"Don't cry, Rose," Gabe said reassuringly. "It was a close call, but we're all right."

In response, Rose unwrapped her shawl and exposed the lifeless body of her baby. "I had t' keeps him quiet," she softly cried, kissing Benjamin's tiny lips.

Oh-my-God-oh-my-God-oh-my-God. Gabe was hardly able to breathe. *No! This couldn't have happened. NO! The baby can't be dead. OH MY GOD, what should I do?*

Jasmine and Levi, realizing their little brother wasn't moving, grabbed each other and began to cry. Hattie sank to her knees, her lips moving in prayer.

Rose walked slowly in circles, talking to herself, stroking Benjamin's beautiful, peaceful face.

Gabe dropped to his haunches. His head fell onto his knees, and he wrapped his arms around his shins, his shoulders heaving with each breath. After a few minutes, Gabe forced himself to stand and went to Rose. Gently, he reached for the baby. "We've got to go. I will give him a proper burial."

She turned away, not willing to relinquish Benjamin. Her face, wet with tears, had a far-off, blank look as if she was searching for the stairway to heaven. "If yu'se would dig a hole, I wants to hold him a bit longer."

"Bring me the shovel," Gabe snarled at Marcus, "and help me."

Marcus brought the shovel, walking stiff-legged, with his feet far out to each side due to the wet, cold fabric.

When the resting place was ready, Gabe again reached for the tiny body. This time, Rose allowed him to take the precious bundle.

Gabe wrapped Benjamin in the scarf his mother had given him. Jasmine and Levi, tears streaming down their faces, hugged the baby's body. As they kissed the baby's face, now wet from their tears, Gabe gently pulled him from their grasp. He laid little Benjamin to rest, and then he and Hattie both said a prayer. Rose hummed a deep, mournful song.

Once everyone and everything were back into the freed wagon, Gabe and Marcus took their seats on the bench. There was no "hie." No slap of the reins. The horses, sensing what was needed, pulled the wagon forward.

No sounds came from the box. Even Marcus had the decency to be still. There was nothing but silence.

FIVE

"Farewell, Ohio!"

October 21–26, 1853

Approaching Williamsport, the sleet began to let up, but Gabe's anguish did not. As the sun was setting, he and the bereaved family found their destination on the outskirts of town: a white clapboard, two-story farmhouse with a large wraparound porch and decorative gables above the upstairs windows and a sign arched over the path leading to the house: Woodland Farm. His apprehension grew as he approached the front door. He hadn't yet arrived at a station that was not expecting him. Knock, knock, knock. No answer. *Oh, no. What do I do if no one is home? I never stopped to think about that. Where would I go?* He rapped more assertively to calm his nerves. KNOCK. KNOCK. KNOCK.

A portly, stern-looking woman wearing a calico dress covered with a colorful apron came to the door. "Yes?" she asked, squinting at Gabe and then looking over his shoulder at the horses and wagon out front.

"Good evening. Are you Mrs. Wood?"

"Who wants to know?" the woman said, being cautious with the stranger on her doorstep.

"I'm Gabe Adams. Pastor Miller from Washington C. H. asked me to make a delivery."

"Yes, I am Mrs. Wood," she answered, her stiff demeanor softening. "How many boxes?"

"Two large and two small," Gabe replied. "Plus, my cousin, Marcus."

"Come in the gate and put the wagon next to the barn."

Gabe drove the horses up a curved gravel lane, lined on either side by late-blooming white chrysanthemums and red and purple cockscombs.

Hannah Ingham Wood ushered the noticeably somber group inside and led them to the milk room, which doubled as a hiding place. Not sure why the people seemed so sad and remained silent, she encouraged them to warm themselves by the fire and tried to lighten the mood. "I'm glad you made it," Hannah said, smiling. "The weather sure turned ugly."

"Is we safe here in dis room?" Hattie blurted, fear in her voice. "I means, shouldn't we be hid better?"

Gabe was surprised that Hattie, who normally was slow to speak, was so blunt.

"You're safe," Hannah replied without indicating that Hattie's question bothered her. "My husband's gone on business, but people leave us pretty much alone. Of course, that might be because I shot a bounty hunter who wouldn't get off the property!" she snickered. "Let's get you something to eat," and she headed for the kitchen, where she kept a pot of hot stew on an old woodstove for such occasions. She gave each person a bowlful, with bread baked that morning and fresh milk with a thick head of cream.

"While they are eating, may we talk with you alone?" Gabe asked, concerned she might continue with her light banter.

"Why, of course." Hannah led Gabe and Marcus to the kitchen. "Did I say something wrong?"

"No, it's not that," Gabe began softly with a hitch in his throat, as he told her what had happened with Benjamin.

"Oh, sweet Jesus," gasped Hannah, covering her mouth. "I'm so sorry. What can I do?"

"Will you come talk to them?" Gabe asked. "You might be able to give them some comfort."

"Of course I will."

"Marcus, would you please stay here while we go back to the others?" asked Gabe.

"I'll get you some food," Hannah offered.

"I'll stay. I'm hungry."

Rejoining the group, Hannah knelt before Rose and held her hands. "My dear, Gabe just told me what happened. I cannot begin to understand what you are going through. I wish I had been there. I would have shot the bastards."

"Thank you, Miss Hannah," Rose said, with a numb expression on her face. "Only thing dat bring me peace is dat my boy die free." Then, dropping her gaze to the floor, she said, "Gabe, I's needs new information 'bout your house. I done ate de paper yo' father gived me."

"Of course," Gabe replied, holding back tears. He looked at Jasmine with sad, knowing eyes, and she returned the gaze with the slightest nod of understanding. Not knowing what else to say, he excused himself, leaving Hannah with the family.

Despite stomachs being full, nothing could remove the pall that filled the room like fog. Hannah spoke to Rose quietly, then encouraged everyone to take a straw mat and a quilt from a pile in the corner. Hannah blew out the lantern and left the room. Blessed sleep came quickly to all but Rose.

Hannah found Gabe in the dark and quiet parlor. Marcus was asleep on a chair. "Is there anything I can do for you?"

"No, but thank you for all you've done. I'm wondering about how far along we are?"

"Well, you are about halfway between Ripley and Sandusky, and things do get better," Hannah reassured him. "If you make a long push tomorrow, you can get to my friend's house in Granville. I'll tell you a way around Columbus, where the road is better and reasonably flat. You shouldn't have any trouble. I believe your passengers can even ride in the open when you're not near the few towns you'll come to, but you need to be alert. Now it's time for you two to get to bed. She woke Marcus and led the boys to a small room with two rope beds.

Gabe rose early and readied the horses, while Marcus joined the group in front of the fire and waited for their host to bring him breakfast. The guests looked better after thawing out, getting some sleep, and refueling on hearty food, but Rose remained quiet, emotionally and physically removed from the others. No one wanted to leave, but Gabe knew they had to press on.

Hannah gave Gabe directions to her friends in Granville. "I'll get someone to ride into town and send a telegram to Newark. Someone there will get the message to the Linnells."

The ride to Granville was easier on everybody. The day was bright and warmer, and the road dried out as they went along. Following Hannah's directions, they headed east then curved north, bypassing Columbus. They didn't see much of anyone all day, and the passengers were able to spend time outside the box. Jasmine crouched behind the bench, centered between Gabe and Marcus. Rose and Hattie held each other and were very quiet while Levi dangled his feet over the end of the wagon with wide eyes, taking it all in. Marcus sat in stony silence, ignoring everyone.

"I'm so sorry about Benjamin," Gabe said to Jasmine. "And your father."

"I figgered dat once we gots 'crosst the river, we'd be safe," Jasmine said. "But it only gots worse."

"We'll get you to safety," Gabe said with more confidence than he felt.

"I knows you will," Jasmine replied.

Marcus had fallen asleep, slumped to the left with his head resting on a blanket atop the benchrail.

"I don't mean to make you uncomfortable, but will you tell me about yourself?" Gabe asked, turning toward Jasmine and looking into her dark eyes.

She returned his gaze and smiled. She began slowly, unsure what to say to a white person treating her respectfully and asking her questions. "I's borned and raised on de Murphy's place in

Jessamine County. Dat's how I gots my name," Jasmine started. "Mama want me to be a flower name, and she like the sound of Jasmine better dan the name of a slave county. She say dey are the same flower, anyway. Mama work in the kitchen. Auntie Hattie and Papa work in the field, growin' and beatin' hemp. I help cleanin' the main house, washin' and ironin' clothes, and servin' dinner. My Papa . . . ," her voice broke, "is a kind, gentle man, but de overseer had it out for him 'cause Mama went with Papa 'stead of him. I was comin' to dat age when Massa start looking at me diff'rently and tellin' me I was his property, and I needs to do whatever he want, whenever he say. Papa worry 'bout me." She saw that Marcus had awakened and was looking at her. She turned her shoulders more toward Gabe and softened her voice. "Papa was 'fraid he and Levi was goin' be sold to pay wha' Massa owes to others, so he takes us and 'scaped. I'm not sure wha' we'uns will do widout our Papa." She stopped talking and looked away.

Gabe didn't know what else to do, so he reached back and patted her on the head to comfort her. He had never felt a Black person's hair before. It was like soft and springy combed wool. He quickly took his hand back.

"Dat's all right. I don' mind," she said, again catching Marcus's sneer that gave her chills. It reminded her of owner's way of leering at her. "I's tired," she said, and crawled back into the box.

They made it to Joseph and Samantha Linnell's house at dusk. The Linnells were an older couple, ardent abolitionists, and leaders of Granville's anti-slavery society. Their house, about a mile east of Granville, was a frequent stop on the Underground Railroad.

The Linnells served their guests a meal of fried chicken, carrots, and peas. Gabe was tired, but his spirits were renewed having completed the long journey to Granville. The Linnells appeared to him to be generous, caring souls. "I'm surprised my friends don't have to be hidden in your house," Gabe told Mr. Linnell.

"Granville has many anti-abolitionists, but we've made sure bounty hunters know they are not welcome," Mr. Linnell said, emitting a chuckle that started deep in his ample belly.

Mrs. Linnell, who had a joyful laugh and eyes that twinkled, spent time with Rose and Hattie, showing them her quilts and exchanging tips on knitting. "Why, Rose, your knitting is exceptional. I've never seen hands move so effortlessly." Mr. Linnell taught Levi to play checkers. Jasmine helped Gabe with the horses in the barn. Marcus sat by himself, bored.

"Rose," Mrs. Linnell said, "Gabe told me about little Benjamin. I am so sorry."

"White folks been separatin' our families forever," Rose said ruefully. "I never 'magine I'd do whats I done."

"No one should have to endure that," Mrs. Linnell sighed.

"I guess you do most anythin' if'n you're a slave tryin' to get to freedom."

The Linnells asked their guests to stay an extra day and night to let the horses rest and give everyone a chance to recover from the events beginning with the family's escape. It didn't take a lot of convincing. Their taking the weight off his shoulders for a day brought Gabe relief.

That next morning, Mr. Linnell asked Gabe and Marcus, "Would you like to come into town and help me get provisions?" His soft and gentle voice belied his stern disposition.

"That would be nice," Gabe replied.

"No, thanks," Marcus moaned, sinking into a chair. "I'm tired."

Gabe was glad to leave Marcus behind, and he enjoyed the little town. Granville's main street, Broadway, was lined with elm trees, white-framed houses, small shops, a library, several churches with high steeples, and the Buxton Inn, an old wagon stop and watering hole with several rooms.

Passing multihued trees lining the way, Gabe said, "I remember hearing about a riot in Granville from my father's friend, Reverend John Rankin. Is this *that* Granville? Do you know anything about it?"

"You know John Rankin?" Mr. Linnell exclaimed in surprise. "There's no better man in the land."

"Reverend Rankin's family and ours spend time together," Gabe proudly replied. "Some of his boys are about my age. I picked up this load of passengers from his house just a few days ago."

"I'm sure he was talking about the Granville Riot of '36. Reverend Rankin led the first anniversary of the Ohio State Anti-Slavery Convention in Granville," Mr. Linnell said with admiration. "Granville and the area then, much as it is now, was equally divided between abolitionists and anti-abolitionists. The convention group met at Ashley Bancroft's barn, just north of the town. We called it 'The Hall of Freedom.' When the convention ended, a messenger warned us that a mob was forming in town. As a show of force, and to protect the women as we escorted them back to the Granville Female Academy, several hundred of us marched, four across, with the women in the middle, down Pearl Street, and onto Broadway. At first, the mob parted like the Red Sea and let us walk through. But the scum, who thought that Rankin, Judge J.G. Birney, and the rest of the group were a bunch of fanatics, started pelting us with rotten tomatoes and eggs, just as they had a few years earlier when they mocked and egged the great Theodore Weld. They call it 'the hen's argument against emancipation.'"

"What happened then?" Gabe asked.

"Well, someone yelled, 'Egg the squaws, too,'" and—fueled by copious amounts of whiskey—the mob closed in on us. There were fistfights, clubbings, and people got thrown into a ditch, but the melee ended without too many serious injuries. It was quite the event."

Upon returning to the Linnell house, Gabe began to check on the horses. When Jasmine walked into the barn, Gabe looked up and smiled.

Smiling back, Jasmine said, "You sure are good with horses. So was my Papa."

They talked, and as Jasmine opened up more and more Gabe relaxed, less afraid of doing or saying something offensive. Finally, feeling like he could delve into her feelings, Gabe asked, "What was it like being enslaved?"

"Der no way to describe it. Massa claim he was good to us 'cause he gave us food and some clothes and let us do wha' we wan' on Sunday, includin' goin' to church and visitin' folks we know'd from udder plantations. But none of dat matter. We was still slaves. We mean nothin' more to Massa than the money he cou' make off us. We'se not 'lowed to learn hows to read or write. Dey tears 'part families, rape de women, and whips or kill us'ens. Dey keep us in our place. If ya listen to white folk beat ya down day after day, month after month, and year after year, the beat-down part of you begin to believe ya ain't nothin.'"

"We never hear about that part of slavery," Gabe said, shaking his head.

"It get worse. Part of beatin' ya down is keepin' ebrybody toein' the line by whippin's and sellin' family."

"What do you mean?"

"Auntie Hattie's family was known to be folks tryin' to 'scape. 'Cept for her oldest, all eight of Auntie Hattie's children be sold or lost in a gamblin' bet, 'cludin' the ones who Massa was the father."

"What happened to the oldest?" Gabe asked innocently.

"He was hung in a tree for stealin' a piece of meat."

Gabe gasped, and Jasmine whispered, "Dat's not all. De ove'seer hated Mama for being with Papa. He once made Mama hug a tree an' he tied her han's and feets 'roun' it, then beat her wid iron rods he pull from de fire, 'til her back look like a piece a meat bein' cut from de bone. I's can't wait to be free. Ain't no one ever gonna sell or beat anyone in my family agin."

Both fell into silence, Gabe reflecting on the horrors of such unspeakable cruelty and Jasmine recalling the painful memories.

After the much-needed day of rest and emotional recovery, the band of souls loaded early and started toward the next station. Mr. Linnell told the group they could get to Mansfield that day and then to Oberlin the next. Gabe was feeling better, eagerly anticipating the reunion with his brother.

The refreshed horses had little trouble going up and down the undulating hills toward Mt. Vernon, and the well-maintained road flattened out after they passed the town. The passengers could ride in the open again, except when they came near a village or saw an approaching wagon.

Rose and Hattie spoke softly and spent time with Levi, who taught them to play checkers on the set Mr. Linnell had given him. It was the first object Levi ever called his own.

Jasmine continued to ride behind the bench seat. She wasn't as talkative when Marcus was awake, but she opened up when he appeared to be nodding off. "First thing I gonna do when we get to de Promise' Land is learn hows to write my name. We done got punish if dey saw us tryin' to learn. Mama always said dey goin' to keep us unlearned so's we cause less trouble an' keep us'ns from discoverin' what freedom mean."

"You don't have to wait. Come up here and I'll teach you now," exclaimed Gabe. "Move over, Marcus."

Awakened, Marcus looked at him with a deathly glare. "Next you'll want me to get in back with *them*."

Gabe reached under the bench and pulled out a well-used writing book and a pencil from his carrying bag. He showed Jasmine the words he had already written, pronouncing them and saying each letter, and then having her repeat how they sounded. "Let's spell 'Jasmine,'" he said, slowly pronouncing each letter and using the pencil to spell them. "Here, you try." He reached for her hand.

Jasmine saw him look with curiosity at her little finger, bent in an unusual way. "Miss Murphy broked my finger 'cause I dropped a dish," Jasmine said.

Gabe shook his head in disgust. "May I show you how to hold the pencil?"

"Course you can. How else you gonna teach me?" she teased.

Gabe curled his fingers around hers, positioning them around the pencil, and showed her how to make a J, an A, and the remaining letters.

Jasmine eagerly practiced for the rest of the dusty, daylong ride to Mansfield. As they approached Mansfield at dusk, the passengers reluctantly returned to their restricted confines. Climbing in, Jasmine clutched a piece of paper with one word written on it:

JASMINE

Following Mr. Linnell's directions, Gabe found the Jackson place in Mansfield. Edna Jackson was expecting them, having received a telegram from Mr. Linnell. Gabe was taken aback when Mrs.

Jackson came out to greet them: her skin was coal-black. Gabe had never met a Black conductor on the Railroad. Mrs. Jackson was of middle height and displayed an impish grin. Her hair, tinged with gray, was parted on the side, and she wore narrow, rimless glasses. The bodice of her coarse, drab brown dress tightly enveloped her bosom.

When the fugitives saw her, they lit up as bright as her smile. A Black woman helping them? She was the first free Black person Jasmine had ever met.

Like the others, Gabe had never been inside a Black person's home before. *Doesn't look any different than other houses I've been in.* The parlor contained a serpentine-backed sofa and two Hitchcock chairs with cane seats and tiny ball feet. A cast-iron cookstove and a large sawbuck table surrounded by several Windsor chairs filled the kitchen. Gabe closed his eyes and filled his lungs with the aromas of cooking and baking. *This reminds me of home.*

Mrs. Jackson had food ready, and the hungry group dug right in.

"How long you been free, Mrs. Jackson?" Hattie asked.

"Please, call me Aunty Jack like everybody else does," she chuckled. "My daddy bought me and my brother when I was a li'l girl in Kintuck. My mama died when she had my brother. Daddy brung us to this place. He dead now." Her mood changed. "He was hung in a tree by white men for tipping his hat to a white woman."

"I thought that only happened in the South," Gabe commented, his eyes downcast.

"I'm afraid lynching happens here, too."

"Wha's it like t' be free, Aunty Jack?" Jasmine asked.

"That depends on which side of the bed I get out of. Some days, I don't feel so free. Most whites in Ohio don't like us livin' here with dem. Though it's getting better, we's got no rights. Ohio has anti-Negro laws—dey call 'em Black Laws—we can't vote, we can't testify in court, we can't set on a jury, we got no schoolin', an' we can't go mos' places whites is allowed to go. I still am skeered about being taken up by slavers and sol' back into slavery, so I don't go out much. So, some days, dat's how I feel 'bout bein' free," Aunty Jack said, her voice bitter with anger. "But dis is alls I got. Dis is my home, so's I stay."

Those around the table fell silent, taking in the magnitude of the reality of a Black life in America—not just in the South they were escaping. Hattie was especially dumbstruck. She had dreamed of freedom since she was a little girl. It's all she ever wanted. She had tried to escape twice, but both times she was caught: one time she received a beating that disfigured her face, and the other, a whipping that stripped every bit of flesh off her back. She never imagined being free could be ugly, too.

"But," Aunty Jack continued, "dis here's de udder side of it. De most miserable day for us who be free ain't as miserable as de best day for the slave. Bein' free is what us humans was meant to be. Ain't no one gonna tell me what to do or how to live. I's learning how to read and write. Yes'm, being free is all dat matter. But, y'all needs to keep goin' to Canada, where Blacks are really free."

After dinner, sated and relaxed, Gabe fell asleep by the fire. When he awoke, Aunty Jack was in the parlor with Rose and Hattie, knitting and talking like they had known each other since birth. Levi was sound asleep at his mother's feet.

"Where are Marcus and Jasmine?" Gabe asked.

"Dey went to de barn to see how Nellie be doing," replied Aunty Jack.

That seemed odd. Gabe got up and headed toward the barn. When he entered, no one was with the horses. All he saw was the flickering glow from a lantern in the haymow. He heard an unfamiliar, low, grunting sound coming from above. He listened as he climbed the ladder into the loft.

His head poked through the opening, and as his eyes adjusted to the soft light, he saw Marcus on top of Jasmine, her legs splayed apart and Marcus between them. The bottom of her dress was up to her waist, and the top was pulled down and bunched below her small breasts. Marcus's pants were at his ankles. Gabe's eyes met Jasmine's. Tears were streaming down her cheeks as she silently resigned herself to each plunge into her body.

Gabe felt his stomach lurch and spasm into a sickening knot.

Marcus gave one final lunge and grunted as he pushed deeply into Jasmine.

Gabe was up the last few steps of the ladder in one motion, yanking Marcus's shoulders as he screamed, "Get OFF her, you FAT, RUTTING PIG! GET OFF HER!"

Startled, Marcus rolled onto his back, spewing the last of the residue from his vile behavior. Gabe looked back at Jasmine, and she just lay there, saying nothing, completely exposed and vulnerable. Her abused body glistened with her blood and Marcus's semen and sweat. Her dark eyes filled with rage.

"GET OUT OF HERE BEFORE I KILL YOU," Gabe threatened Marcus.

Marcus pulled up his pants, sardonically grinning at Gabe. "Bet you wish that was you, huh?" he taunted. "Don't fret, cuz. She doesn't mind. Slaves are used to letting anyone have their way with them."

In an instant, Gabe pounced on Marcus and began pummeling him with both fists. He managed a few good shots before Marcus's greater size and strength pushed him away. He was glad to see that Marcus's nose was bloody. As Jasmine scrambled down the ladder, Gabe and Marcus squared off, facing each other—but neither moved.

"Get your horse and get out of here," Gabe seethed. "Get out of my sight."

"I'll leave when I'm ready to leave," Marcus shot back, readying himself for another attack.

"You'll leave now, or I'll make you a gelding." Gabe turned and went down the ladder and into the night air. He paced up and down the length of the barn, trying to regain his composure. *What am I going to do now? I've let them down again. First the baby, now this.*

When Gabe returned to the house, Rose was tightly holding her abused and scarred daughter on her lap. Aunty Jack stood with her palm covering her mouth. Her feet appeared frozen to the floor.

Surveying the room, Gabe did not know the right words to express his shame and sorrow for what had just occurred. "I'm really sorry, Jasmine. Marcus is leaving tonight, and he won't ever hurt you again," Gabe said as he reached to pat her head.

Jasmine reared back and buried her head in her mother's bosom.

"I think it best to let her alone," Rose said to Gabe. "Nothin' you can do."

Gabe sank as low as he could on a chair before the fire. He heard a horse gallop off into the dark of the night. *Good riddance, you ass.*

That night, Gabe slept fitfully and often awoke, reliving Jasmine's traumatized glare. Tears like hot lead fell onto his pillow. *What must she be feeling? How did I let this happen?* His despair overwhelmed him. *I have to do something. But what?* The next thing Gabe felt was someone gently shaking him. As he opened his eyes, he saw Aunty Jack above him. "I'm sorry, but if you'se want to get to Oberlin, you'se needs to get goin'," she said. "Everyone is ready to go."

Stretching, trying to free the ache from his soul, Gabe dressed and headed for the barn. He hitched the horses to the wagon in silence as the fugitives climbed into their all-too-familiar place of confinement. Jasmine didn't look at him and crawled as far into the box as she could.

It was a quiet ride to Oberlin. The passengers in the box didn't come out. Instead of the thrill Gabe had anticipated at being reunited with his brother, he broke down when he saw him, a cascade of emotions overwhelming him.

"What's the matter? What happened?" Michael asked, his eyes squinched, his eyebrows nearly touching.

"All I can say is that I failed," Gabe blurted, his voice cracking. "They had a baby boy who died on the way north, and Marcus raped Jasmine yesterday. It's all been horrible."

Michael gave Gabe a brotherly hug. "You can tell me about it later. Everyone else is safe." Although shaken by the news, Michael took charge. "Hello, I'm Gabe's brother, Michael," he said, peering into the dark compartment. "We need to get you to a safe place." He reached in to help them out of the box.

Jasmine was the first out. She jerked her extended hand back and put it to her mouth. Tall and lanky, Michael reminded her of her former owner.

Michael assumed her reaction was because he was white. He extended his hand and said softly, "It's all right. I won't hurt you."

His gentle smile and warm, dark brown eyes overcame her initial reaction, and Jasmine took his hand and scooched off the wagon. The other passengers disembarked, and Michael led them into his house and hid them in a room below the floorboards.

After bringing the fugitives something to eat, Michael and Gabe went to the house of his fellow leader of the Young Men's Anti-Slavery Society, Professor Henry Peck. Michael and Henry discussed preparations to get the passengers on a steamer to Canada.

"How do we get them on board?" Gabe asked.

"Before daybreak, you'll go to Sandusky Harbor," Henry explained. "The *Arrow* is in port right now. Michael will talk to the captain, and he'll tell you how to sneak them on board."

"How will we pay for it?"

"I get donations for just this purpose." He gave twenty-five dollars to Michael. "That should be enough."

Before sunup the next morning, Michael and Gabe loaded the fugitives into the box one last time. "You'll have to stay inside," Michael told them. "There are many bounty hunters in these parts. Fortunately, it's not too far."

Relieved that Michael had taken command of the bruised and damaged group, Gabe gathered his composure, picked up the reins, and began the last leg of the journey. Gabe told Michael all that had happened since he picked up the escapees from the Rankins.

"Well, little brother, you've had quite a week," Michael mumbled, shaking his head in disbelief.

"They would have been better off making their way on their own."

"Horse manure! You crossed all of Ohio and managed to get them to freedom," Michael said, putting his arm around his little brother's shoulders. "You couldn't have stopped what happened to the baby or what Marcus did."

Gabe could not respond. He clenched his jaw and squeezed his eyes shut, hoping to extinguish the horrific images of the lifeless baby he had buried and Jasmine's abused body and tormented face. No matter how tightly he closed his eyes, the images and memories that anguished him continued.

When they arrived at the landing, the *Arrow* awaited to take them to their Promised Land. Michael went to talk with the captain. They were just a few hours from freedom.

Upon his return, Michael helped the passengers out of the wagon. Each of them, including Levi, was disguised with a large, floppy hat and a drab shawl. "Say your goodbyes. Hurry," Michael urged, looking around to see if anyone seemed to be watching.

In a motherly way, Rose took hold of Gabe's hands. "We's can't thank you enough. What happen to my baby an' Jasmine is not yo' fault. You done got us here. We is so grateful. We never forget you, Gabe."

Hattie chimed in. "She be right. Bad things happen, but you did alls you could. Alls I got to say is, farewell, Ohio! We're on our way to Canada, where colored folk are free! Thank you. God bless you."

Levi hugged Gabe tightly. "I hopes to see you again."

"We will," Gabe replied softly. "We've still got to find your father. Take care of your sister for me. Promise?"

"Promise," Levi said.

Jasmine approached Gabe. "I's not mad at you," she said.

"I feel horrible. I've let all of you down."

"No, you didn't. I hope you still want to be my friend," Jasmine said, looking deep into Gabe's eyes.

Unnerved by the tenderness in her eyes and unable to forgive himself for all that transpired, he stood in awkward and uncomfortable silence.

"Don' you want to be my friend?"

"Oh, Jasmine, of course I do. You'll always be my friend. I won't forget you." Gabe started to say more but realized he didn't know how to express his feelings. "Um . . . I . . . I guess it's time."

"Yes, it seems so."

"Better get aboard. You don't want to miss *this* boat."

"I'll miss you," she said, handing him the scrap of paper with her name printed on it. "Keep dis to remind you of me."

Michael escorted them up the gangplank as instructed. Gabe watched a deckhand lead them away, taking Jasmine out of his life—*forever?*

SIX

"If I had another face to wear, do you think I'd wear this one?"

October 26, 1853–August 3, 1855

Gabe and Michael turned back for Oberlin. They rode in silence, Gabe lulled into his thoughts by the rhythmic rocking of the wagon. The cloudy sky and the muskiness of the sweating horses covered them like fog, adding to Gabe's melancholy.

"Ya know," Michael said, ending the silence, "I have a break at school, and I'd like to see Mother and Pops. Besides, I don't think it's a good idea for you to be alone for the next few days. I'm coming with you."

"That would be great, Michael. It would be a sad and lonely trip going back by myself."

The brothers went to Oberlin, took the items for Michael out of the wagon, and headed south.

"Do you want to talk about all the things that happened?" Michael asked.

"Not right now. Maybe tomorrow. But I'll need your help when I tell Mother and Pops."

"I'll be there with you. They'll understand."

"I hope. Let's talk about you for a while. That will be better for me."

"Well, I do have some great things to share with you," Michael said as his voice went up a notch and his speech quickened. "I met a man named John Brown and several of his sons. He has some radical ideas about ending slavery and is willing to fight to end it."

"That'll be dangerous," Gabe said.

"Yes, it will. He says that blood will have to be shed." Michael's enthusiasm kept Gabe enrapt, and he spent much of the trip going into detail about what Brown had said and things he had learned from fellow abolitionists at Oberlin. "The Fugitive Slave Law has made abolitionists out of many Northerners and put the South in a defensive, defiant position," he expounded.

"I've been wondering—why won't judges stand up against that law? If they would do the right thing and not turn the slaves back over to the slave catchers, maybe the slavers would stop trying."

"Some judges hate the law and find it disgusting to enforce it. But they don't make the law. It would be against the judge's oath if he disregarded the law and took it into his own hands."

"Michael," Gabe wondered, "what will happen if slaves are freed? Where will they go? The North doesn't want them. Pops says the West is trying to keep them out, and they have no place to live in the South."

"I don't think anyone has an answer for that. Many folks like the idea of colonization, whether it's in Liberia, Cuba, or parts of the United States."

"But, from what I've read, Negroes don't want that," Gabe said. "Frederick Douglass rejects the notion of sending Blacks to Africa. Negroes no longer use their African language or know where their ancestors live. What about free Blacks who already live here? Would they have to colonize, too?"

"If everybody got sent back to where they came from, only the Indians would be allowed to stay," Michael replied, chuckling at the thought.

Without the extra weight in the wagon and by taking flat, well-traveled roads running through Columbus and southwest to Georgetown, they made fast progress, only stopping to sleep in the back of the wagon.

"Michael," Gabe said, getting anxious as they neared Georgetown, "I don't know what I'd do without you. Everyone looks up to you. I'm glad you'll be there when I talk with Mother and Pops. They're gonna be sorry they sent me."

"No, they won't," Michael tried to reassure him. "Rose did what she had to do by sacrificing Benjamin to save her other children. As for Marcus, Pops will figure out what is best."

Gabe turned the wagon onto the lane leading toward their house. Ailene shouted for joy when she saw them coming. "I'm so relieved you're home," she said, putting Gabe in a death grip, letting go only to wrap her arms just as tightly around Michael. "I'm so thrilled to see you, too!"

Gabe's heart quit pounding when he found out that Caroline, who was caring for an ill neighbor, and his father weren't home. *I'm not ready for whatever his reaction will be. Will Michael be right, or will Pops be angry at himself for letting me go, or blame me for all that went wrong?* He pondered as he brushed Nellie's coat. The horses' rhythmic breathing and the scents of the barn comforted Gabe and lessened his apprehension about the difficult conversation ahead.

When Atticus arrived, he reacted much as Ailene had. "It's so good to have both of you boys home," he said, leading them to the kitchen table. "I can't wait to hear about the trip."

"First, dinner's ready," Ailene interjected. "Let's say grace, then we can hear all about your journey."

The family sat down, and with Michael's support Gabe began to recount the trip from the beginning. His throat tightened, and his voice cracked as he told them what happened leading up to the first tragedy, finally exclaiming, "Rose smothered Benjamin to keep us from getting caught! He's dead."

"Oh no," his mother put her hand over her open mouth, her eyes wide.

His father put his hand on Gabe's shoulder. "What an ordeal. How were Rose and the children?"

"They were devastated, but Rose was thankful they weren't caught," Gabe said, choking on the words.

"How are you doing?" Ailene asked.

"Not great. I don't know what else I could have done. But there's more." He began to tell them about the trip through Granville and to Aunty Jack's house.

Ailene started to say something, but Gabe interrupted her, holding his hand up. "Wait. When we were at Aunty Jack's house in Mansfield, I fell asleep and . . . I can't."

"Go on," Michael encouraged.

"I don't know if I can tell Mother or whether she should hear this. It's just awful."

"Go on," Ailene said, putting her hand on Gabe's knee and squeezing it. "I need to hear whatever it is."

Gabe drank some milk and took another deep breath, exhaling slowly. "Well, when I woke up, Aunty Jack said Marcus and Jasmine went out to the barn. I went out to find them. They were in the haymow, and . . . I just can't say it," choking again.

"You can tell them," Michael encouraged.

"He . . . He . . . He was on top of her . . . and . . . and . . . was raping her." Gabe buried his face in his hands, sobbing.

Ailene rushed to Gabe's side and stroked the back of his neck. "Oh, poor Jasmine."

Atticus sat dumbstruck.

Ailene just kept repeating, "Oh, my poor dear. Poor Jasmine. How awful for you to see such a thing."

Regaining his voice, Atticus slammed his fist on the wooden table and said, "I would never have thought Marcus could do such a thing. I'll have a talk with Nathaniel."

"I don't know if that's a good idea," Gabe said, his eyes sparking like hot coals splashed with water. "Telling Uncle Nat won't change anything, and Marcus doesn't care. I never want to see him again."

"I agree. It wouldn't do any good," Ailene responded, shrugging her shoulders. "Neither he nor Rebecca would believe you."

Atticus considered what Ailene and Gabe had said. "I don't know what to do," he said, then nearly broke both his hands and the table by smashing it again.

Gabe finished the tale. "At least we think they are safe in Canada."

"We're proud of you," Atticus said, shifting his attention to his son. "You proved your mettle."

Gabe settled back into a routine, throwing himself into farm work with a vengeance. The mild fall allowed the Adamses to get all their corn and hay in. Ailene's garden overflowed with tomatoes, squash, cucumbers, and cauliflower. The apple trees sagged under the weight of ripening fruit. Caroline and Gabe spent evenings talking while they made applesauce and canned vegetables.

"Do you ever think of Jasmine?" Caroline asked.

"A lot," answered Gabe, turning as red as the tomato in his hand.

"I think she liked you," said Caroline, only half-teasing.

"I liked her, too." Gabe often confided in Caroline. "But we'll never see each other again, so it really doesn't matter."

"You never know."

One day, Gabe was reading in the parlor when there was a knock on the door.

"Why, hello, Mr. Bierbower," Gabe said, opening the door for his father's friend to enter.

"Hello, Gabriel. Is your father home? I have some information for him."

"He's in the barn. I'll go get him."

Gabe sprinted to the barn. "Pops. Pops. Come quick. Mr. Bierbower is here with some news."

They both ran back to the house.

"Hello, Jonathan. It's nice to see you," Atticus panted.

"I was in Ripley for business and thought I'd share my news about George in person."

"I appreciate that. What have you found out?" Atticus asked.

"A person by the name of Marie Haydel bought him. Her plantation, Habitation Haydel, is a large sugar cane plantation between Baton Rouge and New Orleans, built on the backs of slaves who are worked almost to death in the fields."

"While the owners sit on the porch sipping mint juleps and bragging about how the slaves love them and are part of their family," Atticus broke in with a sing-songy voice, the words dripping off his lips. "At least we know where he was taken. He doesn't have much of a chance. Thank you for bringing us that information. Won't you stay for dinner?"

"That's mighty nice. I'd enjoy that."

In the late summer of 1854, a letter addressed to Gabe came to the house. His heart skipped a beat when he realized who sent it.

Deer Gabe Mr and Mrs Adams and Caroline

I hope you get this leter. So much has hapen. I lernt how to rite som. I is so hapy. I no why massas would not let us lern to reed and rite. If we was smart, they cood not control us an more wood try to escap. Mama Hattie Levi and me are doing fine. But ther is one more person. Cause of what hapen on the way to canada, I had a baby. I love her so much. She is the first person in my famly to be born free. I name her Glory Gabriella. The midle name is after you. We go by the last name of French becuz that who help us when we first get here. We make bred and biscuts for the local market and are tryin to bild a litle howse. It sure is cold up here. I thot we wood all die las winner. Its nice now. The trees are so prety. Have you herd anything about my Papa? We miss him so much. Pleas rite back. We don has an adress but you can send a leter to the baptist church in Buxton Elgin setelment canada west. We all thank you agin with all our hart for all you did to get us free. You are spe-shel. Your frend,

Jasmine—and Glory!

Gabe immediately sat down and wrote her back:

Georgetown, Ohio, August 30, 1854

Dear Jasmine, Glory, Rose, Hattie, and Levi,

We were so excited to get your letter. We are glad things are working out for you. I don't know what to say about Glory. I am so sorry it happened, but I am happy for you that you have a little girl to love. I'm proud of you that you have learned how to read and write. Write me anytime. I have been reading a lot about getting rid of slavery. I might become a lawyer someday. Pops and Mother and Caroline are all good. We're glad you all are safe.

I don't know how to tell you this, but we did get some news about your father. He was sent to a plantation near New Orleans, Louisiana, called "Habitation Haydel." That's all we know. I promise I'll keep trying to find out more. I hope we will meet again.

Your friend,
Gabe

Gabe read whatever he could find about abolitionism. The invention of electrotyping made books readily available, and Gabe often accompanied his mother to the Georgetown library. One day, he checked out *The Narrative of Sojourner Truth*. Later, Gabe lay on the floor reading. "Mother, listen to this: Miss Truth says, 'Oh, Lord, what is this slavery that it can do such dreadful things? What evil can it not do? Oh, who has conceived the breadth and depth of this moral malaria, this putrescent plague spot?' Do you think slavery will ever go away?"

"For the sake of America, I certainly hope so."

After a pause, Gabe spoke with a resolve his mother had not heard before. "I hate slavery. We have to get rid of it. Words and speeches aren't enough. It will take action, and I'm willing to join the fight." Gabe cleared his throat and, trying to be casual, asked, "Have you ever heard of John Brown?"

Whatever pride Ailene felt due to her son's conviction turned into dread. "Yes, and I know Michael is intrigued by him and his cause, but I think he's trouble and a bit crazy," she warned, her voice quivering. "Although I like his views on the equality of races and women, I don't like him calling for violent action. He'll get himself and others killed. I prefer the nonviolent teachings of Frederick Douglass and William Garrison."

Gabe considered his mother's words. *I still prefer John Brown's thinking.* But he knew this moment was not the time to voice his opinion.

One afternoon in midsummer, Atticus said to Gabe, "Nathaniel and I need to go to Cincinnati. He's got a court case, and I need to go to the seminary. He wanted to know if you would like to go to court with him."

"As long as Marcus isn't going and you are, I'd enjoy it."

Gabe had the horses ready to go before dawn. Atticus and he went into town and picked up Nathaniel. As the sun rose and warmed their backs, his uncle said, "Gabe, there's something I've wondered about. What happened to you and Marcus when you two took those Negroes north? Ever since he returned, he doesn't seem to want to see you."

Gabe shot a glance over his shoulder at his father and swallowed hard. *I was afraid that would come up. I ought to tell him, but we agreed nothing good would come from it.* "I think that's a question you need to ask Marcus."

"Well, I don't like the tension, whatever caused it. I'd like you to try to work things out."

"We'll see."

Nathaniel looked at Atticus, who just shrugged his shoulders.

Avoiding the awkward silence, Nathaniel took out some papers to read. After a while, he put the pages back in his case, rubbed his eyes, and asked Gabe, "Your father says you want to become a lawyer. How come?"

Gabe thought for a few minutes. "I want to do something about getting rid of slavery. I figure if anyone can do anything significant, it will be lawyers. They have opportunities that many others don't. Lawyers are often elected to the legislature. They understand laws and can influence changing bad laws. Who else will help the minority preserve their rights and get equal justice?" Gabe said, realizing his voice had taken on a passion that surprised even himself.

"Well said, my boy," his uncle complimented him. "Lawyers have been the architects of society, and we need more lawyers with your ideals."

Gabe beamed at his uncle's words. "What do I have to do?" he inquired.

Nathaniel responded thoughtfully, "Going to college for a few years would be a good idea. Then you can study law in my office. Soon, Ohio may even require law school training, as some Eastern states have done. Regardless, you can always practice with me. You are a bright, energetic young man with a charming personality. You have your father's spirit and integrity. Being a lawyer is hard work, and you aren't afraid of that."

Atticus smiled proudly, "That's very nice of you to say."

When they arrived in Cincinnati, they went to the home of William Dickson, a friend of Nathaniel's. Dickson, handsome with dark hair and a full, flowing beard, had been the prosecuting attorney for Cincinnati's police court and now had a successful law practice. Dickson and his wife of three years, Annie, often invited out-of-town lawyers to stay at their house.

"Hello, Annie. It's good to see you," Nathaniel said as she opened the door and welcomed them. "Do you have room for us?"

"Of course," Annie said. Raised in Lexington, Kentucky, she was a genteel woman of refined manners, elegant dress, and gracious hospitality. As she led them into the foyer, she said, "There is someone I'd like you to meet. Oh, Abraham," she called out to a man sitting in the parlor, "would you be a dear and come over here?"

A man with big ears and nose, an odd complexion, and an angular face and body pushed himself out of a chair, rising to a great height. He strode, somewhat stoop shouldered and loose jointed, to where Gabe, Annie, and the others stood.

"I'd like you to meet my cousin Mary's husband, Abraham Lincoln. He's a lawyer from Illinois here on a case," Annie said.

"Nice to meet you, Mr. Lincoln," Nathaniel said with a slight bow. "This is my brother, Atticus, and my nephew, Gabriel."

"It is such a pleasure to meet you," the man said, dipping his chin and extending his hand. "But just call me Lincoln."

Gabe couldn't help but notice that, even with the long arms and tall body, Lincoln's large hands seemed out of proportion.

After a filling dinner of Cincinnati's finest pork chops with vegetables from Annie's garden, they spent the evening with the other gentlemen discussing law and politics. Gabe knew enough just to listen. He was surprised that, unlike the other men, Lincoln did not drink alcohol or smoke. He seemed to be a warm and considerate man who loved telling tales and anecdotes. At one point, the men traded stories about their conquests in court. Lincoln told a story of a not-so-likable braggart lawyer whom Lincoln encountered just after a verdict had come in on the lawyer's case. "I asked the man how the case turned out. He said, 'It's gone to hell.' I replied, 'Well then, you will see it again.'" The men guffawed.

The next day, Atticus went to the Lane Theological Seminary in Walnut Hills, and Gabe and his uncle walked to the courthouse. Gabe was excited for his inaugural visit to court—he always assumed going to court would be exciting, fast paced, and dramatic. Much to his dismay, it was none of those things.

The lawyers droned on incessantly using indecipherable words. Even the judge appeared to have trouble keeping his eyes open.

During a midmorning break, his uncle rescued Gabe: "This hearing isn't going well and will likely take the rest of the day." He handed him a handful of coins and said, "Get something to eat. Just be back here by the five o'clock bells."

"Thanks. I will." Gabe was out the door like a rabbit. Outside the courthouse, he saw Lincoln sitting by himself. Compared to what the other lawyers were wearing, Lincoln was poorly dressed, with ill-fitting, soiled clothes and a drab coat. The sleeves were short for his long arms, and his well-worn pants rode high above his ankles. His equally worn boots hadn't seen polish in a long while.

Recognizing Gabe, Lincoln greeted him in his rather high-pitched and squeaky voice. "Hello, son. It's nice to see you again."

"Hello, sir," Gabe greeted him. "Is your case done?"

"No," Lincoln replied with a hint of sadness. "I was hired on this case when it was set in Illinois. Now that it is here, the Eastern lawyers think they're smarter than me and can handle it without me. The judge and attorneys are having a closed conference, and they asked me not to attend. Why, one of the attorneys on *my* side of the case, a fella named William Seward, called me a 'damned, long-armed ape'!"

"That's plain old mean. What are you going to do?" Gabe inquired, feeling a sense of comfort with the man.

"I haven't decided," Lincoln drawled. "I reckon I'll head on back home in the next day or two. Today, maybe I'll walk around a bit and see the city. It's my first and probably only time in Cincinnati."

"Would you like some company?" Gabe offered, acknowledging Lincoln's hurt feelings. "I've been to Cincinnati lots of times and could show you around. I'm going to get something to eat."

"Sounds fine with me," Lincoln replied. "I'm hungry, too."

They walked from the courthouse south along Main Street to the waterfront, then followed the river upstream to escape the dank and noisy city, trying to ignore the eye-watering stench wafting from the nearby hog pens and slaughterhouses. The breeze coming off the river helped. They stepped into a little store to buy dried salami, cheese, and bread.

It was a typically muggy August day, and Lincoln slung his coat, which Gabe had noticed had a perspiration stain that looked like a map of Ohio, over his shoulder. As they walked, Lincoln regaled Gabe with quaint stories. Gabe enjoyed talking with Lincoln, who acted like he had known him for years. They climbed up the steep hill to the top of Mt. Adams, where the Cincinnati Observatory presided over the city. "The city renamed the hill when John Quincy Adams dedicated the observatory," Gabe said as they ate their lunch on a bench with an expansive view of the city and the Ohio River. "This is where my father proposed to my mother."

"Your father sounds like he's Mr. Romance," Lincoln laughed.

Soon, the talk turned to politics.

"There's something I don't understand. Can you explain the new Kansas-Nebraska Act to me?" Gabe asked. "Why would Congress change the Missouri Compromise after all these years?"

"Well, young Mr. Gabe," Lincoln laughed, "that's a good question. Settlers wanted to move into the western lands of the Louisiana Purchase, but it hadn't formed into territories. Southerners blocked adding new territories, which would eventually become new states, because the area was above the slave line established in the Missouri Compromise. Complicating the matter, a transcontinental rail line was planned, and Stephen Douglas, an important senator from my state of Illinois, wanted it to go on a northern route through Chicago. In a compromise with the Southerners, Douglas got them to agree to form the Kansas and Nebraska Territories. In return, he agreed that the people living there got to make the decision whether to be a free or slave state when they sought statehood, like what was done in the compromise when the Utah and New Mexico Territories were added. That's called popular sovereignty—I call it squatter sovereignty."

"What's wrong with that? Why shouldn't the people in the territory make the decision?"

"Look what's happening in Kansas Territory now," Lincoln said as he wiped his furrowed brow again. "Slaveholders moved in with their slaves. Now that the population is large enough to become a state, there will be a vote to see if Kansas will be slave or free. Here's the burr under that saddle: even if the people vote for Kansas to be a free state, how will the state get rid of the slaves already there? Tell them to pack up and leave? Free the Negro slaves, taking 'property' away from a person without compensation? Let the freed Negro live there? Even the Free-Soiler whites don't want that."

Gabe pondered Lincoln's words. Biting off a hunk of cheese, Gabe asked, "What do you think the answer for slavery is?"

"Son, if all earthly power were given me, I should not know what to do as to the existing institution. Slavery is a great and crying injustice and an enormous national crime, but I don't think there is much we can do about slavery where it exists, because the Constitution sanctions it. It may be that all we can do is prevent the spread of slavery."

"Why can't Southerners agree to keep slavery where it is?" Gabe asked.

"They believe the best way to protect slavery is to keep it spreading. If Congress limits slavery to where it is, the South knows that, as more states join the union, non-slave states would be in the majority. Those in control eventually would pass laws eliminating slavery."

"I just wish Congress had done away with the horrid Fugitive Slave Law. Pops calls it the sum of all villainies."

"Hmm, well, I'm not so sure it was wrong," Lincoln stammered. "The ability to recover escaped slave property is in the Constitution. I support the Fugitive Slave Law and would not interfere with it. Although I hate to see the poor creatures hunted down and carried back to the lash and unrewarded toil, I bite my lip and keep quiet."

"I mean no disrespect, Mr. Lincoln, but I can't bite my lip," Gabe shivered at the thought of the free man sold at the auction. "I think it's wrong that Northerners are required to assist in returning suspected fugitives. The government is on the side of the kidnappers."

"That's all true," Lincoln replied as the two got up from the bench. They walked down Mt. Adams's western slope, then continued across the valley and started up Mt. Auburn.

As they walked, Gabe saw a Black woman playing with her child and thought, *I wonder how Jasmine and Glory are?* He turned to Lincoln, "Do you think people will ever get over their prejudices and accept Negroes as equals?"

"There is as much prejudice in the North against the Black people as there is in the South—it just shows up in different ways. Half the country favors slavery, and most of the other half doesn't want to mix with Negroes. I don't think Negroes and whites will ever live with each other, due to their natural differences."

"Why can't we live with them? They're no different from us, except for the color of their skin," Gabe said, remembering the feel and look of Jasmine's hand in his as he helped her spell her name.

"Don't get me wrong. I abhor slavery. I hate it because of the monstrous injustice it is. I hate it because it deprives our republic of its just influence in the world, which taunts us as hypocrites. However, whites are the dominant and superior race. There is no question of Negro inferiority."

You're wrong, Gabe wanted to yell, feeling blood rushing to his head. "I don't think they are inferior, just uneducated. When they get an education, no one can doubt their abilities."

"Gabe, there is a natural disgust in the minds of nearly all white people to the idea of an indiscriminate mixture of the races. Even when the Northwest Ordinance passed excluding slavery in the Northwest Territory, Thomas Jefferson foresaw and intended a happy home of free, white, prosperous people, with no slave or Black person among them."

"Why should all that land be just for white people? Why couldn't free Negroes live in the territories?"

"Well, some did, but the settlers never welcomed them," Lincoln explained. "The settlers in the Western lands are also trying to get rid of the Indians. I agree with that philosophy. We want the territories for the homes and well-being of whites."

"Why? I learned in school that the Liberty Bell is inscribed, 'Proclaim liberty throughout *all* the land unto *all* the inhabitants.' What about the Declaration of Independence that '*All* men are created equal?" Gabe asked as they reached the top of Mt. Auburn and rested on another bench with a stunning view of the city and the river.

"The Declaration is the moral foundation of America, and I agree with you that slavery is a violation of that Declaration. Negroes should have the same freedoms and the right to try to make something of themselves, just like any other man. No man is good enough to govern another man without that other's consent. But, make them politically and socially our equals? My feelings will not admit of this, and if mine would not, I well know that those of the great mass of white people will not."

"Well, I think slavery should just be abolished now," Gabe nearly spat out the words.

"Whoa," Lincoln said, doffing his tall hat and wiping his forehead with his soiled handkerchief. "It's a complex problem. The Southern economy, and much of the North's, depends on what slaves produce. The immoral institution has become a 'sacred right' in the South and an economic necessity in the North."

They walked down the hill to the west. "They call this area Over-the-Rhine because of all the Germans who settled there," Gabe explained. "We can go to the new Findlay Market. After it opened last February, my aunt's father took us there to get carbonated sodas."

"Well, son, I could use something to drink."

As they enjoyed the cool refreshment, Gabe asked, "I don't understand. How can you hate slavery but not want to abolish it?"

"I struggle with that enigma. The nation wouldn't survive if we abolished slavery now. But, because Britain and much of the world have abolished slavery, and with slave importation banned, I believe it will gradually end on its own, as the Founders believed it would. Eventually, the best thing is either for Negroes to be shipped back to Africa, or Negroes can start colonies here or maybe in Central or South America."

"Will the South ever give up its slaves?"

"Not voluntarily, my young friend. The issue may very well divide the country, and that just can't be allowed to happen. Slavery will have to end gradually, or the nation itself could fail."

"Well, I think if it takes violence to abolish slavery, then so be it," Gabe stated defiantly.

"Ah, the undaunted courage of youth," chuckled the tall man. "I admire your passion."

They finished their drinks and began walking again. They passed a park with a clock tower, and Gabe said, "It's getting on towards five o'clock. My uncle wants me back at the courthouse."

When they neared the courthouse, Gabe saw Uncle Nathaniel waiting on its steps. "Why, hello, Lincoln," Nathaniel greeted him. "It appears Gabe found a friend."

"Yep," he laughed, "and he just about burned my ears off with his views toward slavery."

"He's got a lot of my brother in him," Nathaniel laughed. "He's a fine young man, but I'm trying to talk some sense into him."

"Don't break the spirit out of the horse," Lincoln cautioned Nathaniel. "He's got a lot more common sense and honest conviction than most people I've met—maybe even me. Why, people accuse me of being two-faced about a number of things. They can't be right. If I had another face to wear, do you think I'd wear this one?"

SEVEN

"FOR THE OLD MAN IS WAITING FOR TO CARRY YOU TO FREEDOM."

August 10, 1855–October 9, 1855

A week after the trip to Cincinnati, Gabe climbed the ladder to the bedroom he shared with Raphael, who had finished at Lane and was back helping on the farm. He waved a telegram from Michael that an agent just delivered. He read it aloud: "Raph Gabe. John B coming to Akron tomorrow night. Take train and meet me there. Michael."

"John Brown is coming to Akron!" Gabe said, grabbing his brother's shoulders and doing a little jig. "With Mother and Pops down at the Rankins', we can leave before they can stop us. Get ready. Let's go."

"I think that's a bad idea. Besides, I disagree with Brown's views."

"I'll go alone if I have to," Gabe said. He wished Raph's views on slavery, similar to what Gabe had just heard from Lincoln, were more like his and Michael's, but that didn't lessen his love and admiration for his brother.

"Pops will skin me alive if I let you go alone. I guess I have to go. At least I won't be the only one skinned when we get back."

"Get all the money you have. I'll get mine. I'll take the money Pops keeps in the old teapot on the buffet."

"That's stealing," Raphael admonished, still against going but not being given much choice.

"We may not have enough if we don't. Besides, we'll pay it back."

Gabe retrieved the money and put together a food basket while Raph wrote a note:

Pops and Mother: Michael invited us up to see him before school starts. We thought it would be fun. We're taking the train from Cincinnati. We'll be back in a couple of days.

Love, Raph and Gabe

"At least it's kinda true," Gabe said.

They saddled the horses and rode through the night to Cincinnati. They reached the riverfront railroad station just before dawn and stabled the horses there. Then they bought tickets, telegraphed their schedule to Michael, and caught the 6 a.m. Little Miami Railroad to Columbus, where they'd change trains for Akron.

The car's smooth sway and the wheels' rhythmic clacking soon put Raphael to sleep. Despite not having slept the night before, adrenaline and nerves kept Gabe awake. *I can't believe I'm on my way to see John Brown. What will he be like?* Gabe's mind wandered from John Brown to Jasmine. *Will I ever see Jasmine again, and meet Glory? I could go to Canada, and if slavery is abolished, Jasmine could travel to Ohio. But what if she doesn't want to see me?* The thoughts eventually morphed into dreams as he joined his brother in slumber.

Michael was waiting for his brothers with a wagon at the station. They fell into their usual banter of good-natured insults, headlocks, and laughter. "Let's get going," Michael said. "Brown is speaking tonight at the Town Hall and raising money."

"What for?" Gabe inquired.

"I think he's going to Kansas," Michael said. "He wants to stop the pro-slavery Missourians from coming into Kansas and illegally voting to sway the election and make Kansas a slave state."

When they arrived at the Town Hall, the room was already half full of mostly white men, a few white women, and even fewer Black men. *No Black women*, Gabe noted. As Gabe walked around, he overheard snippets of conversations that aroused his curiosity about Brown's mission.

"Ol' John goin' t' get hisself kilt," one man was saying.

"Not until he takes out more 'n a few slavers," countered another.

"He's looking for money and guns," said the first man. "I ain't got neither."

"I got a few dollars t' give 'im," the second man replied. "He wants men, too. I'd go with 'im if'n I could."

The man's comment about going with Brown got Gabe's mind spinning. *Would I go? Would he even take me?* Gabe noticed the room had become crowded. There was a stirring to the right of the stage, and Brown appeared. He was a bit hunched over, probably just under six feet tall, and thin and wiry. His coarse, bristly hair was brown with a hint of gray, and was combed back over his small head, accentuating vertical worry lines on his forehead between his deep-set eyes. As Brown stepped to the podium, electric energy filled the room. It was unlike anything Gabe had felt before. The hall went silent. When Brown began to speak, Gabe stepped forward into a slight opening between two men and leaned forward to better see the icon. Gabe took note of Brown's well-worn black frock coat and vest, black pants, and black slouch hat. Stains blotched his white collar. *He's certainly not spending the money he gets on clothes.*

"I am on my way to Kansas to join my sons and the local militia to stop the border ruffians from Missouri," Brown exclaimed with a stern and determined voice. After reading aloud a letter his sons had sent him about the problems in Kansas, Brown got more riled and heated. "Every slaveholding state is sending men and money to fasten slavery upon this glorious land, by means no matter how foul. The ruffians are harassing Free-Soilers and coming into Kansas, voting illegally to steal the election. Now is the time to act."

"Yeah, but them Free-Soilers don't want Blacks, neither," a Black man cried out. "They want Kansas to be free—and white."

"They are wrong about that," the intensity of Brown's face softened a bit, allowing Gabe to notice that Brown's left eye drooped a bit, and the right side of his mouth turned down. "I believe in the Golden Rule and the Declaration of Independence. They mean the same thing. But we have to stop the spread of the Satanic Institution first. Every day strengthens my belief that the sword, that final arbiter of all the great questions that have stirred mankind, will soon be called on to give its verdict."

Someone yelled, "Frederick Douglass thinks we need to be cautious and nonmilitant."

"Caution, sir! I am eternally tired of hearing the word *caution*! It is nothing but the word of *cowardice*!" Brown screamed, spittle flying from his mouth. His penetrating blue-gray eyes seemed to flash sparks like steel striking flint. "It is infinitely better that this generation should be swept away from the face of the earth than that slavery should continue to exist. I need men, money, and guns—I don't need cowards."

"What if we ain't got no guns?" a man called out.

"'He that hath no sword, let him sell his garment and buy one, sayeth the Lord.'"

"Slavery will die out," another countered. "Just give it time."

"Time?" thundered Brown in response, extending his arms over his head, his fingers outstretched. "The first slaves were brought to America in 1619. Isn't over two hundred and thirty-five years long enough? Slaveholders will never give up their slaves until they feel a big stick about their heads."

The speech ended with hurrahs and huzzahs throughout the hall. Brown circulated through the crowd, shaking hands and holding out his hat, which was not filling as fast as he wanted. Brown was not afraid to shove the hat into someone's belly if he thought the person could give more. He did not browbeat everyone, however. As Brown came within earshot, Gabe overheard him say to one of the women present, "Madam, your earnest and affectionate expressions of good wishes do me more good than money."

Gabe couldn't restrain himself. When Brown was an arm's length away, he impulsively grabbed the man's sleeve. "Mr. Brown, I don't have any money, but I'll come with you. I'm not a coward."

Brown's rough face, with its broad, granite-like chin and hawk-like nose, looked down at Gabe, and he snickered, "Fighting the border ruffians is going to be dangerous and nasty. I barely have enough money or food to get my men and me to Kansas, let alone a youngster like you. Why should I take *you*?"

"I can drive a wagon. I'm the best-darned teamster around," Gabe said defiantly, unwilling to be dismissed so quickly. "I'll outwork and outfight anybody."

Gabe's demeanor and passion intrigued Brown. "Stick around, and we'll talk," he murmured to Gabe before moving through the crowd to pry more money out of people's pockets. "Will some of you gentlemen or ladies take up my banner and collect contributions from counties, cities, towns, societies, churches, or in some other way?" Brown pleaded.

Michael grabbed Gabe by the shoulders and shook him. "You *can't* go with Brown. It would kill Mother."

"I'm not going to face Pops," Raphael frowned. "You're coming home with me."

As the crowd dwindled, the brothers continued to plead with Gabe, but his mind was set. He had made his vow when he saw George sold, and boasted to Jasmine that he would do his part to end slavery. "If he'll take me, I'm going. It's time for action," Gabe pledged, his lips firm and his face hard.

The crowd had thinned to just a few. Marching up to Brown, Gabe looked him in the eyes. "I want to go with you. I don't eat much and am not scared of any ruffian."

"Well, you should be," Brown said, softening his tone and pausing to take the measure of Gabe. "Once I get to Chicago, I'll buy a horse and wagon and pick up one of my sons, who is about your age. I could use someone to take care of the horse and accompany Oliver. But I don't know." Brown paused, taking his hat off and scratching his head. "You ever shoot a man?"

Taken aback, Gabe stammered, "Well, no, sir . . . but there's more than one slave catcher who came pretty close."

Brown chuckled at the young boy's bravado. "What's your name?"

"Gabriel Adams. Gabe."

"Well, Gabe, we will stay here tomorrow, getting more supplies. We're at that white house surrounded by a low picket fence," Brown said, pointing up the street. "Be there ready to help at first light, and if you're as good as you say, I might take you along."

"Yes, sir," Gabe said, puffing out his chest and almost saluting.

Michael and Raphael just stood there, mouths agape.

As the boys trudged back to the wagon, Raphael and Michael realized they could not dissuade Gabe from his foolishness.

"I'll be sorry I got you into this," Michael said, giving Gabe his coat, hat, and hunting knife. Putting his hand on Gabe's shoulder, he added, "Take care of yourself. Brown isn't going out there to talk—he's going to fight. People are going to get hurt."

Raphael gave him what little money he had left, saving just enough to buy a ticket home. "I'll have to put on an extra layer of clothing to withstand the switching I'll get. Be careful."

Gabe's backbone wasn't as stiff as before, but he tried not to show it. As the wagon pulled away, Gabe stood alone and anxious. His brothers turned to wave. Gabe raised his hand weakly in return.

Having no other place to go, Gabe went to the house where Mr. Brown was staying and crept into the carriage house. The horses neighed and pawed the ground expectantly. Gabe calmed them and made a straw bed, although sleep didn't come for a long time.

The creak of the carriage house door sliding open awakened Gabe. In the entrance stood John Brown and another man. "Well, well, my idealistic skinner, I didn't think you were serious." He introduced the man as his brother-in-law, Henry Thompson, then said, "Let's see if you can be of any help. We've got work to do."

"Yes, sir," Gabe said, again almost saluting.

The three went to Daniel Hadley's law office, where Hadley and E. C. Sackett waited. They had obtained money and other items for Brown, including several long, heavy boxes branded with the word "Bibles."

Hadley resolved Gabe's curiosity about why Brown was bringing Bibles. "The boxes marked 'Bibles' have the rifles from Mr. Beecher, and the other boxes have the swords Bierce gave you." Reverend Henry Ward Beecher, Lyman's son, provided Brown with the rifles, and Lucius Bierce, one of Brown's supporters, gave him the swords.

"I've got twenty-one revolvers and twenty-six rifles and muskets for you," Sackett offered.

Gabe's eyes got big. *Brown means business.*

"All I've got so far is a little under three hundred dollars," Hadley apologized, handing Brown a bag of coins.

"I'll take all I can get," Brown responded. "Thanks."

They boxed up the loose weapons, loaded all the boxes on a wagon, and headed to the railroad yard to have them transported to Chicago, where Brown would reclaim them.

After spending another day meeting with supporters and coaxing a few more dollars from them, Brown told Henry and Gabe he was leaving for Cleveland the following day.

Gabe's ears perked up, "So, are you taking me?"

Brown pondered for a moment. "You can come to Cleveland, then we'll see."

In Cleveland, Brown delivered another fiery speech about stopping the ruffians in Kansas and met with supporters. Brown took Henry aside. "What should I do about Gabe? Is it a mistake taking him?"

"I like his enthusiasm. He's been helpful and claims to be good with a horse and wagon. Besides, he'll be good company for Oliver."

Brown relented and told Gabe, "You can come. But I'm sending you home at your expense the first time you whine or complain."

"Oh, thank you. You won't be sorry," Gabe gushed.

"I might not be," Brown said, "but you might."

The trio made one more stop in Detroit before boarding the train to Chicago.

"Where are you from?" Brown inquired of Gabe as they started their journey.

"I'm from Georgetown, Ohio. It's down near Ripley."

"I know just where it is," Brown nodded. "Don't suppose you know my friend John Rankin?"

"I sure do. He and his family are good friends of our family."

"He's a good man. I also have an old friend who lives in Georgetown—Jesse Grant. Ol' man Grant used to work in my father's tannery in Hudson. He lived with us for a couple of years when I was about fifteen."

"Yes, I know him, too. My father works part-time at the tannery to earn extra money. My mother and Mrs. Grant are good friends."

"I greatly dislike the smell of a tannery," Brown snickered. "Even Grant's son, Ulyss, hated it. Jesse's a loquacious braggart, but he disdains slavery as much as I do. Is he still alive?"

"Yes, he's alive," Gabe replied, surprised by Brown's comment because he had never heard his father say anything disrespectful about Mr. Grant.

"So, why are you following me to Kansas?" Brown asked more seriously. Henry leaned toward the two to hear their conversation.

Gabe told him about his Underground Railroad activities, his feelings about the slave auction, little Benjamin's death, and all the reading he had been doing. "I promised myself I'd do whatever I could to end slavery, and you are just the person to take me on that mission," Gabe declared emphatically. He didn't feel the need to share with Brown: *I owe it to Jasmine and Glory.*

"You know, Gabe," Brown said, putting his arm around Gabe's shoulder, "sounds a bit like me. When I was about your age, I saw an enslaved friend of mine beaten with an iron shovel. I vowed to break the jaws of the wicked evil and pluck the spoil out of its teeth. After a pro-slavery mob murdered Elijah Lovejoy in 1837, I consecrated my life to the destruction of slavery. When the Fugitive Slave Act became law, I knew it was time to act."

"I despise that law."

"It's just the way it is," Brown said, gazing off to nowhere. "That's why it's going to take more than talk."

"Why don't the slaves revolt?" Gabe asked. "Aren't there more Negroes than whites in the South?"

"When someone has complete control over everything you do and can sell you like an animal, there's not much you can do. Enslaved people have tried. There were successful revolts in Haiti and on the *Amistad* slave ship. Nat Turner, Denmark Vesey, and Charles Deslondes led revolts that were failures, though, and disastrous for the enslaved. They each died a martyr's death by hanging or execution. I have no problem following them to the gallows if necessary. Regardless, Southerners live in constant fear and abiding dread of conspiracy and insurrection. So, they keep the enslaved uneducated and unarmed."

"Then, how will they ever get free?"

"They need a leader to take action. Just think what could happen on a larger, more organized scale than what they tried. My wife, Mary, and I prayed the night we got the letter I read in Akron and Cleveland, and just like God told Saul to slay the Philistines, I heard the voice of the Lord tell me, 'John Brown, go to Kansas and slay the border ruffians.'"

"*What?*" yelled Atticus. "He went *where* with *who*? You and Michael didn't stop him?" He paced the room like a caged tiger, his hands clasped behind his back.

"We tried, Pops," Raphael stammered, having never seen his father so angry. "He refused to listen."

Ailene buried her face in the towel she always carried on her shoulder. "I knew that child would do something foolhardy."

"You *lied* to us," Atticus said, slamming his fist into his other palm.

"We didn't lie. We just didn't tell you everything," Raphael said, dropping his chin and looking at the floor. "But I didn't think he'd do something crazy like run off with Brown."

"You need to go get him!" Ailene cried.

"I don't know where he is. Besides, I'd have to throw that boy over my shoulder and carry him back. I'm sure he'll write us. I'll figure out what to do then."

With each turn of the iron wheels, Gabe became more excited yet anxious. *I wonder what it will be like in Kansas. I still don't understand what we will do or how we'll do it.*

Along the way, Brown talked—more like delivering a sermon with frequent biblical references and quotations—about the evils of slavery and the obligation for action, including military-type efforts to stop the spread of the "devilish institution."

"Squatter sovereignty is an idiot's solution, and Stephen Douglas is the head idiot," Brown snapped, as Gabe and Henry hung on every word. "We must stop those damned slavery-loving ruffians *now*. We've got to fight," he said as he smacked his thigh with an open hand. "I am determined to defeat Satan and his legions."

"As am I," Henry added.

"Why is force the only way to get rid of slavery? My mother agrees with Garrison that nonviolence has a better chance of success."

"Garrison is nothing but a milk and water pacifist," Brown spat out the words. "He's been writing his form of abolitionism for ten years, and nothing has changed. He'd rather see the North secede than take action. I'll hear nothing more of that."

They arrived in Chicago. Lake Michigan sparkled, reflecting the bright blue sky. *It's even prettier than Lake Erie.* This caused his thoughts to drift. *I wonder how Jasmine is doing. What will she think when I tell her I'm off to fight with John Brown?*

That night, he wrote the first of many letters he would write home and to Jasmine.

> *Chicago, Illinois, August 20, 1855*
>
> *Dear Pops, Mother, Raph, and Caroline,*
>
> *I am fine. I am sorry I ran off, but I knew you would keep me from going. I'm with Mr. Brown and his brother-in-law, Henry. We're in Chicago but will be heading to Kansas to join some of Mr. Brown's children.*
>
> *I just had to go with Mr. Brown to act on my belief that slavery has to end. Please don't be mad. I need to do this. I trust Mr. Brown. You'd like him too if you got to know him. I'll be all right. Try not to worry.*
>
> *I'll write every opportunity I can. I'll send the information where you can write to me as soon as I know.*
>
> *Love,*
> *Gabe*

Gabe wrote a similar letter to Jasmine but started it with a longer description of Brown's mission. He added to the letter, "I hope I can make a difference so that no one ever goes through what you and your family have endured. If I survive this trip to Kansas, would you mind if I came to Canada to see you and Glory? I don't know how long I'll be with Mr. Brown. He thinks it could be years."

Brown purchased a stout horse for $120, a sturdy wagon for $40, and surveying instruments, which Brown planned on using to earn money. They retrieved the boxes shipped from Akron and loaded them onto the wagon.

Oliver, Brown's son, who had been working on a relative's farm in Rockford, Illinois, joined them. Oliver was a year younger than Gabe, all sinew and bones. His face was softer than his father's, and his bushy brown hair was not as wiry. While Brown and Henry were getting food and supplies for the trip, Gabe and Oliver guarded the wagon. They sat under it for shade, chewing on long pieces of grass and exchanging their mutual desire to abolish slavery. "You're amazing," Oliver said to Gabe. "Our family pledged that we would follow Father through thick and thin, but you don't have to do this."

"I think God meant me to meet your father and follow him."

The four left Chicago on August 23. Gabe and Oliver quickly became friends, exchanging stories about family, childhood experiences, and hopes for the future. They found their backgrounds were similar. Both were raised in strict but loving, devoutly religious homes. Neither family had material riches. Although Gabe always believed his family was poor because he compared their situation to his uncle's, he came to understand what poor really meant when Oliver openly talked about Brown's failed business ventures and the spartan living conditions in which he and his ten living brothers and sisters had grown up.

One day, when they were deep in conversation, Oliver asked, "Are you afraid of dying?"

"I guess I'm not afraid to die, but I'd rather not," Gabe responded. "Do you think it could come to that?"

"It could. Father isn't afraid to die, so I have to face that possibility."

> *Scott Co., Iowa, September 4, 1855*
>
> *Dear Pops, Mother, Raph, and Caroline,*
>
> *I am fine. We left Chicago, heading for Kansas. We're walking most of the time because the wagon is full of supplies, and it's hard on the horse if we're riding. Mr. Brown's son, Oliver, who is my age, joined us in Chicago. We've become great friends. It's hot, dry, and windy. The land is flat as a pancake, and the roads are mostly good. We eat enough, but as Oliver says, "We have nothing but beans and johnny cake, and for variety, johnny cake and beans." I would love some of your cooking, Mother! I love and miss you all.*
>
> *Your son, Gabe*

Gabe's letter to Jasmine had more details about his growing friendship with Oliver and Brown's mission. He closed the letter to Jasmine, "Oliver tells me that Blacks and whites live together in his town of North Elba. I wonder if that will ever occur in other places, like Ohio. Your friend, Gabe."

Each night, Brown preached and prayed, always importuning God to give them David's courage when they fight their Goliath. Other times, Brown spoke wistfully as if speaking to the wind. The power and fervor with which Brown spoke kept Gabe riveted. "Even with people in my life like Pops and Reverend Rankin, I have never met anyone so passionate about his calling," he told Oliver.

"We need fundamental reforms in America," Brown lamented. "There are infinite wrongs to right before society mirrors Christ, but number one is slavery. If the abomination of slavery continues, the United States might just as well disappear."

"Even if slavery ended," Gabe asked, his head cocked to the side, "will Negroes ever be considered equal to whites?"

"Enslavement must end before equality comes," Brown counseled. "My prayer is that soon, Negroes *and women* will have the same equal rights and treatment as white men."

"My mother would love your prayers to be answered," Gabe said with his palms pressed against each other in front of his chest.

One night, while looking at the starry firmament and admiring the Big Dipper, Gabe began to sing a song Jasmine had taught him on the way north. "She told me that slaves learned many songs to help them find their way to freedom," Gabe said to the others. He was surprised when Brown joined in with a rich, deep, and haunting voice:

Follow the Drinking Gourd.

Follow the Drinking Gourd.

For the old man is waiting for to carry you to freedom,

If you follow the Drinking Gourd.

When the great big river meets the little river,

Follow the Drinking Gourd.

For the old man is waiting for to carry you to freedom,

If you follow the Drinking Gourd.

"The symmetry of God's plan is evident in the heavens," Brown said softly. "The wind on the prairie is full of voices, which inspire me. Everything moves in sublime harmony in the government of God."

I'll follow this man anywhere, thought Gabe, crawling into his bedroll and slipping into a deep sleep.

After several days of traveling through northern Missouri, the party came to the Missouri River. As Gabe and the others waited for the ferry across the river, a nosy local man menacingly approached the wagon.

"Where ya' goin'?" the man asked as he started eyeing the wagon's contents.

"Kansas," Brown said defiantly.

"Where ya' from?"

"New York."

"Where do you stand on the goose?" the man inquired.

"If 'the goose' means slavery," Brown replied, "I'm here to kill the goose—and the gander."

"You won't live to get there," the man declared as he stared down the leader of the beleaguered group. "We don't like your kind and your ideas about slave rebellion or race mixing. Take a look at this." He handed Brown a crumpled, torn piece of newspaper.

Brown read it aloud: "'We go in for a war of extermination against the lawless nullifiers and Negro-stealers now infesting this Territory, and when occasion offers, we will show our love for Northern blood by causing it to flow in profusion to enrich our soil.'"

Brown's steely eyes bore a hole through the man, "We are prepared not to die alone."

As they neared Waverly, a small town on the southern bank of the Missouri River, Brown told his companions, "We're getting close to where Jason buried Austin. No Brown should lie to rest in the soil of a slave state. We will disinter my grandson and provide for a proper burial."

"Jason is my eldest brother," Oliver explained to Gabe. "His four-year-old son, Austin, died from cholera on their way to Kansas."

Following Jason's directions, they located Austin's grave, disinterred him, wrapped his body, and placed him in a box they built in the wagon. With little weight added to the wagon but a significant weight added to their hearts, they trudged toward Kansas.

After almost two months on the trail and with only sixty cents left between them, the tired, hungry, and bedraggled band turned onto the small lane leading to Brown's sons' homestead.

"Brown's Station" was located on the bank of North Middle Creek, near Osawatomie, on the eastern Kansas border. Jason had told his father in a letter that they had purchased a rich and bountiful land claim, and Brown assumed they would have houses built and the land cultivated. To Brown's great dismay, the families were still living in tents and wagons, mired in mud and facing a cutting, cold wind. They had no corn or hay fodder laid up for the winter, and the fields appeared untended, with what few cows they had roaming freely.

Gabe heard Brown mutter, "This is *not* altogether paradise."

Brown's sons, John Jr., Jason, Owen, Frederick, and Salmon, and their wives and children, except for John Jr.'s wife, Wealthy, were all suffering mightily from the flu, malaria, or some other malady. Regardless, they greeted the arriving group with as much glee and excitement as their ailing conditions allowed. Gabe was warmly received and immediately felt like part of the family.

"Gabe and Oliver," Brown commanded, "get wood. Build the fire up. Glean the fields for anything edible. I'll take what we have left in the wagon and make what dinner I can."

The next day, the weather brightened, as did everyone's spirits because of the new arrivals. Gabe, Oliver, and Henry spent the day building the rudiments of a shelter and a corral for the stock.

"Boys, we need to unload the wagon. I want to share with you what we brought. First, our most important item." Brown choked as he and Henry lifted the makeshift coffin they had built for Austin.

Weeping, Jason and his wife took the little box containing Austin's remains and went near the creek to mourn. The others hauled the large, heavy boxes to a lean-to shed, where John opened one. "These are 'Beecher's Bibles,'" Brown said, sounding to Gabe as Moses must have sounded when he presented the Ten Commandments to his people. Brown picked up one of the rifles. "I spoke with Reverend Beecher before I left for Kansas, and he told me, 'There is more moral power in one gun than in a hundred Bibles. You might just as well read the Good Book to buffaloes as to the pro-slavery fellas. The only thing those people have supreme respect for is the logic that a Sharp's rifle embodies.'" Brown opened another box, displaying Bierce's short, heavy broadswords. Gabe could see an ornamental eagle stamped on the lustrous silver blade.

"These broadswords are hollow and loaded with quicksilver that slides from the hilt to the tip when swung," Brown explained through clenched teeth, "to add force to the message." Brown brandished one and demonstrated a fierce, downward hack.

Gabe's heart nearly stopped as he heard the whistling sound of the quicksilver moving through the broadsword. *Those swords only have one purpose.*

The other boxes Brown opened contained knives, pistols, and ammunition.

That evening, Brown announced that all would join him on a hill overlooking the creek among a stand of cottonwood trees. Standing at one end of the hole dug for Austin's coffin, he prayed, "Our dear Heavenly Father, thank you for getting us here safely and reuniting this part of the family. We come to remember and bless little Austin." Jason and his brothers gently lowered the coffin into the ground as Brown continued, "We are here to continue the struggle he was part of but knew nothing about. We may join him in heaven for doing so, but he will not die in vain."

The following day, Gabe, Oliver, and Henry continued building log shelters and preparing for winter while Wealthy cared for her sick husband and in-laws. Brown, exhausted from the long trip, watched Gabe work. *He's a great lad. But can he fight?* He fell asleep singing to himself:

> Follow the Drinking Gourd.
> Follow the Drinking Gourd.

> For the old man is waiting for to carry you to freedom,
> If you follow . . .

EIGHT

"Trust in God, men, and keep your powder dry!"

October 10, 1855–August 30, 1856

The ailing Browns began to recover. Soon they were able to help the newcomers start building a cabin and barn. They cut and sold wood to earn money or to trade for food and supplies, and despite a cold and windy fall, their lives improved.

About a month after Gabe and the others arrived in Kansas, the group huddled under blankets around the woodstove in the unfinished cabin, now three logs high, chinked and mudded with a tent for a roof, eating a sparse dinner of beans and cornbread. Their nightly discussions, including Brown's sermons and prayers, were met with a sobering warning. John Jr.—Junior to his family, and the eldest of Brown's living children—read from a local newspaper column: "'We will tar and feather, drown, lynch, and hang every white-livered abolitionist who dares pollute our soil.'"

"Right now," explained Jason, the second eldest, "the anti-slavery folks outnumber the slavery folks in Kansas, so the only way the pro-slavers can gain ground is through force, with help from the Missouri border ruffians. They are well organized, well armed, and filled with corn-liquor courage."

"The election was a fraud," Junior steamed. "The bogus legislature enacted draconian pro-slavery laws. It's a crime for anyone to express anti-slavery views, and just having *Uncle Tom's Cabin* in your possession carries a death sentence!"

"They aim to drive every Free-Soiler into submission," Frederick, fourth in line, added.

"As long as I live, we will *not* be stopped!" exploded Brown. "*Slavery* will stop, but not *us*!"

"It's hard to organize resistance, because the anti-slavery group is not all fighting for the same cause," sighed Salmon, a few years older than Oliver.

"What do you mean?" Gabe asked.

"White bigots from the East stir the pot to keep Kansas and Nebraska for white settlers only, while others, like us, don't mind if free Negroes settle here," Salmon explained. "On the other side, the pro-slavery force is united."

In early December, a neighbor rode into Brown's Station, exclaiming, "The sheriff's massing the militia and Missourians to destroy Lawrence."

"Why destroy Lawrence?" Gabe asked Junior.

"Because it's the free state stronghold," Junior explained. "If they raze Lawrence, the resistance might be over."

Brown quickly mobilized Henry, Gabe, his sons, and about a dozen other men from Osawatomie. They named themselves the "Liberty Guards" and elected Brown as their captain, a title he would never relinquish. They loaded a wagon with what food each person could gather, blankets, cooking utensils, and some of the firearms and broadswords from Ohio. They also secured poles upright around the wagon with bayonets lashed to the end of each one. Junior tossed a rifle to Gabe and teased, "Do you know which end to hold?"

Although a crack shot when it came to squirrels, prairie chickens, and wild turkeys, Gabe was shaking as he took the gun, wondering, *Will I be able to shoot a man?*

They began a thirty-five-mile march to Lawrence through the dark, cold, and windy December night. As dawn broke, the frozen and footsore men approached Blanton's Bridge, a log structure spanning the Wakarusa River. A border ruffian camp with upwards of one hundred men blocked their way. Gabe noticed that many men were sleeping on the ground around dead campfires, with bottles littered about. *They don't look very organized, and I think they had too much to drink.*

"I want you men to line up on each side of the wagon," Brown commanded, "with a broadsword strapped to your chest, a Sharps in your hands, two pistols in your belt, and one in your pocket. Do not fire unless fired upon first. If they do, shoot as speedily as possible, make a breastwork of the horse and wagon, empty the rifles, then the revolvers."

Brown led the horse by the bit and walked toward the bridge, armed as he had instructed the others. As Brown flanked the camp, a disheveled ruffian wearing an untucked shirt under a dirty coat with makeshift captain's bars on the shoulders stepped in front of Brown. "On your way to Lawrence?" he slurred.

"That's our business." Brown looked the ruffians' leader in the eye. "Your men will suffer greatly if you block our path."

Gabe clutched his rifle, but his palms were so wet he could barely hold it. With each step, he feared, *Will this be my last?* Although barely sixteen and still sporting peach fuzz, he firmly set his lips and squinted his eyes at the ruffians. No one uttered a sound. By then, the men in the camp were standing, holding their weapons across their chests and watching Brown's men closely. *I think they're supposed to be guarding the bridge. What are they waiting for?* Gabe kept his eye on the lead ruffian to see if he signaled his men to fire. Cold sweat soaked through Gabe's coat. He glanced at Oliver, also covered in sweat, and shrugged. He gripped his rifle tighter and ran his hand along the thick blade of the sword.

Brown continued to stare down the captain as he stopped at the edge of the bridge. He told Gabe to lead the horse, and his men filed across the bridge. When they made it across, Brown followed.

Gabe let out an audible sigh, puzzled that the men at the bridge didn't resist. Gabe noted that Brown's expression hadn't changed.

The Liberty Guards arrived at the Free-Soilers' camp at Mt. Oread and joined a growing number of men forming into militia regiments. Brown was named Captain of the Fifth Regiment of Kansas Volunteers. The ruffians massed south of Lawrence along the Wakarusa River.

Captain Brown joined a meeting of the leaders at the Free-State Hotel. His blood reached the boiling point when he saw, lying on a table for all to see, the body of a Free-Soiler killed the night before by a roaming band of drunk ruffians. "It's time to take a stand and fight and *die* if that's what it takes to stop slavery in Kansas," Captain Brown ranted. Returning to his regiment at Mt. Oread, Brown incited them to act. "We must show that there are two sides to this fight, and that they cannot go on killing without revenge. Trust in God, men, and keep your powder dry!"

But they didn't get a chance to stand or fight. While Brown was training the loosely organized unit to defend its position, the Free-Soil leaders reached a truce with the band of border ruffians. To Brown's disappointment, the Wakarusa War ended before it began. Brown's gang trekked back to Osawatomie.

The winter was not kind to the family. Snow piled high, driven like dry sand by the fierce Kansas winds. The thermometer bottomed out at twenty-eight below zero. Captain Brown had to sell the horse and wagon for food and supplies.

Despite the conditions, Gabe continued to impress Brown with his hard work, without complaint, to make the homestead livable. Gabe missed his family and wrote them and Jasmine whenever he could. Gabe relished the letters he received from his mother and father, although his mother begged him to come home and his father threatened to come and get him. Gabe's letters tried to convince his father that such an action would be futile. He especially enjoyed letters from Jasmine and her stories about Glory.

As spring approached, both the weather and the political situation heated up. "That dough-faced Pierce has recognized the bogus pro-slavery government and declared the Free-Soilers' government illegal," an exasperated Brown announced to the group sitting at the table, reading Lawrence's newspaper, the *Herald of Freedom*. "It's time for action—without truces."

"What do you mean?" Junior asked.

"We have to rise, take control, and oust the ruffians despite President Pierce's support." He grabbed his well-worn Bible, opened it to Deuteronomy, and read out loud: "'To me belongeth vengeance and recompense; their foot shall slide in due time; for the day of their calamity is at hand.' This is the day I have lived for."

Only a few days later, a winded rider rode furiously into Brown's Station, jumped off his horse, and approached Brown. "Cap'n Brown, are you any relation to Reese Brown?"

"No, why?"

"He's been slaughtered in Leavenworth by ruffians. They hacked him to death with hatchets." He handed Brown a broadsheet he had ripped from the side of a building. It read:

Free State men who fail to leave the Territory within 30 days will have their throats cut.

Signed: Law and Order

"People are fleeing to Lawrence, and the ruffians are threatening an attack there."

"Should that take place, there can be no truce. We will have to fight," Brown said, crumpling the sheet and throwing it to the ground. "We will buckle on our armor, and with the help of God, there will be hell to pay."

The ruffians' raid did not take place, and the Captain continued to wait.

A month later, Brown, Gabe, Henry, and several of Brown's sons headed into Osawatomie for a meeting regarding President Pierce's declarations.

Reverend Martin White, a fiery, slaveholding Baptist minister, rose to present President Pierce's and the pro-slavery position. At the end of his comments, he said, "Anyone who declines to follow the law should be charged with treason for insurrection."

Brown could not remain composed, and his reptilian eyes blazed as he declared, "I would rather see the Union dissolve and the country drenched with blood than obey Pierce's abominable edict."

Another Free-Soiler argued, "Kansas should be a free state, but lazy, worthless, vagabond Negroes should not be allowed. If they can be here, I prefer they be under a master's control."

Brown went apoplectic. Veins stood out on his neck. His face, looking much thinner, older, and more worn after the severe winter, turned beet red. "NEGROES are my BROTHERS and my EQUALS! The humanness of the Negro should NEVER be questioned! They should be able to go as FREE men wherever ANY white man can go!"

Gabe shook his head in silence as bigoted Free-Soilers heckled in protest, and Reverend White and the other pro-enslavers walked out.

With nothing resolved, a disgusted Brown and his outfit returned to their homestead.

Not long after the meeting, the group at Brown's Station received word the ruffians were again massing to attack Lawrence. Junior assembled his militia group—the Pottawatomie Rifles—and Brown mobilized what was left of the Liberty Guards. A total of thirty-four men began the march to Lawrence.

They got only halfway there before a messenger's horse slid to a stop in front of Brown's band. "The ruffians are burning Lawrence to the ground. There was no resistance. The Free State Hotel is nothing but ash."

"What can we do?" Brown asked, holding the reins to calm the horse, its sides heaving.

"Nothing. They have taken the city and are parading with banners saying, 'Supremacy of the White Race.' The fight is over."

"It's not over until we say it's over," Brown vowed. "We'll set up camp here and await additional news before determining our next step."

Two days later, another rider came into their camp at Middle Ottawa Creek. Breathless and speaking rapidly, he said, "We just got word from Washington that Representative Preston Brooks savagely beat Senator Charles Sumner about his head with a cane—right on the Senate floor. Sumner had insulted Brooks's cousin, Senator Andrew Butler, by saying Butler 'was in love with a harlot called slavery.' He might not live."

Brown went into a frenzy. "Something is going to be done *now*! It's time to STRIKE! I know what to do and where to do it. It's time to show these barbarians they cannot go on with impunity! We'll dispose of these Philistines in a way that causes a restraining fear amongst them all! It is ordained by the Almighty God, ordained from eternity, that I should make an example of these men!"

Gabe felt his innards clench and growl. He tried to read Oliver's expression, which seemed to mirror his own. *I wonder what that means?*

Brown put a number of the broadswords and a few rifles and revolvers into a borrowed wagon and climbed on. Jason and Junior were ill, and Brown instructed them to return to the Station to protect the property and women in case of trouble. Henry Thompson, Frederick, Salmon, and Owen joined him in the wagon. Captain Brown looked over his shoulder at Gabe and Oliver, who had not moved, and shouted, "Are you coming with us?"

Without hesitation, they both ran and jumped into the wagon. Trying not to notice the knot in his belly, Gabe picked up one of the broadswords and, following the lead of the others, began sharpening it. *I've got to prove to Captain Brown I'm a soldier ready to fight.*

Several miles later, nearing Dutch Henry's tiny settlement of pro-slavery rabble-rousers who had previously clashed with the Browns at various meetings, Brown announced, "We'll walk from here." He strode in the lead with resolve, his head pitched forward and his right shoulder slightly ahead of the left. The band passed Pottawatomie Creek before stopping and waiting for the cover of darkness on a very still, hot, and humid night, fighting a multitude of bugs at aptly named Mosquito Creek.

"We will strike these men down," Brown told the nervous crew, each sweating from more than just the heat. "Let my raised sword be the signal for all to engage, and when engaged, do not do your work by halves. Do not delay one moment. You will lose all your resolution if you do."

Gabe watched as the men buckled on the broadswords and tucked a pistol into their waistbands, and he did the same. His courage abated. He could not keep his legs from shaking.

"Follow me," Brown said.

They silently descended on the small settlement with a few houses spaced far apart. As they approached the first cabin, a large dog bounded toward the group, growling and snarling. Frederick unsheathed his saber. In one blow, the dog lay motionless and silent.

"Henry, Salmon, and Owen—come with me," Brown whispered. "You others stay here and keep guard. Take anyone who approaches the cabin a prisoner."

Gabe and Oliver looked at each other with eyes wide. Gabe had no idea how to take someone as a prisoner.

Brown pounded on the cabin door. A voice from within asked, "Who is it, and what do you want?"

"I'm looking for the Wilkinson place," Brown answered.

The door opened a crack.

Brown kicked it fully open. *"We're the Northern Army.* Get your devilish hides ready to face your Maker."

Brown and the three men burst into the house. They handcuffed an older man and three younger men at gunpoint as a woman screamed in terror.

Brown looked at the horrified faces in the cabin and said calmly yet sternly, "Haven't you been warned what you were going to get for the course you have been taking?"

"Oh, please. Don't take my husband and boys," the woman pled through sobs and tears.

Brown released the youngest boy as a show of mercy and ordered him, "Light the lantern and give it to me." Gabe watched the men drag the three prisoners out of the doorway and away from the cabin. *Oh my God. That's the way the slave-handler ripped the two boys away from their mother at the slave auction.* He shook his head as if to rid himself of the ugly memory.

The Brown gang prodded the men like cattle, poking them with the swords' tips or slapping them with their sides to keep them moving. A hundred feet from the cabin where Oliver and Gabe waited, Brown, in a normal tone with no inflection in his voice, ordered the group to stop. Henry and Owen unceremoniously pushed the three captives to the ground.

Still not grasping the magnitude of what was about to happen, Gabe stood still, tensing every muscle.

Brown raised his sword, gleaming in the candlelight, above his head. Gabe gasped as Salmon violently swung his broadsword into the body of James Doyle, the quicksilver whistling through the hollow canal. *Swishh.* His son, William, tried to run, but Owen brought him down, slashing his legs. *Swishh.* Henry opened a gash on Drury Doyle's neck. *Swishh. Swishh.*

The moment became surreal for Gabe. The men on the ground cried in anguish; screams came from the woman in the cabin. Gabe's boasts about ending slavery transformed into a feral rage. He joined the melee. *This is for Jasmine. Swishh.* Blood splattered on Gabe's face. *George being sold. Swishh.* It dripped off his chin, arms, and hands. *The red-hot rod used on Hattie. SWISHH.* He could smell and taste it.

"At ease," Brown commanded in an inflectionless voice.

Caked in blood, the party left the three victims' dismembered remains and moved down the road to the next house. They announced themselves in the same manner as before, kicked the door in, and dragged Allen Wilkinson, barefoot and still in his bedclothes, out of the house. Brown gave his signal. The fanatical group took little time hacking and mutilating their enemy.

They went searching for Dutch Henry Sherman. The party was disappointed to learn from the occupants of his house that he wasn't in the vicinity. Instead, they yanked his brother, Dutch Bill, outside and slaughtered him in the same fashion as the others, his brains spilling into the creek.

"Enough," Brown said.

Gabe was in a daze. *Did that really just happen? Did I just help massacre unarmed men? Me? Gabriel Adams? Son of Atticus and Ailene? Is that what fighting against slavery looks like?*

Noticing his discomfort, Oliver, also shaking, put his arm around Gabe's shoulder. "It'll be all right," he said, not believing his words.

"Take their horses, saddles, and supplies as bounty," Brown demanded. He climbed onto Dutch Henry's prize gray stallion, and they headed back to Brown's Station.

When Junior and Jason saw the bloodied group and were told of the massacre, they uncharacteristically challenged their father, "You are a man of God. How could you order such ungodly actions? It was an uncalled-for, wicked act."

"God is my judge," Brown defiantly stated. "We were justified under the circumstances. It was absolutely necessary for the defense of others."

"Why did you steal their property?" Junior asked.

"As is said in Exodus 12:36," Brown preached, "'And the Lord gave the people favor in the sight of the Egyptians so that they lent unto them such things as they required. And they spoiled the Egyptians.'"

"What does that mean?" Jason asked.

"The Lord looked favorably on the Israelites and allowed them to take the Egyptians' gold, silver, jewels, and fine clothing."

"It was a just action," Salmon snapped back at his brothers. "The ruffians have been slaughtering our people. It's time they got a dose of their own medicine."

Pale and sweating profusely, Owen said to no one in particular, "I will do no more work such as that."

Sensing Brown wanted no more discussion, each person
drifted off alone or in pairs to deal with the aftermath.

Gabe went down to the water to wash the blood off his body
and face. By lamplight, he saw his eerie reflection in the water
and vomited, purging himself until nothing was left. Throughout
the night, he continued to convulse and heave from the taste of
blood and the visions of mutilated bodies.

News traveled fast. The authorities pieced together what had
happened and came to the conclusion that Captain Brown was
the leader of the massacre. As a result, the marshal issued arrest
warrants, and Brown and his men became outlaws. Word came
from the town that a marauding, sixty-man force of ruffians led
by Henry Pate was assembling to find them and bring them to
justice—dead or alive.

Now fugitives, the small band left Brown's Station, and for a
little over a week, kept on the move, hiding in swampy areas or
thick woods, eating gooseberries, bran flour, and, when lucky,
wild game. One night, Brown mused, "We, like David of old,
dwell with the serpents of the rock and the wild beasts of the
wilderness."

Oliver and Gabe spent time with each other processing the
events at the Pottawatomie settlement. One night, Brown joined
them. "Sons, I know this is hard on you. I've had a lifetime to
think about what this action would be like. I tried to prepare
you for battle but failed. Sometimes, in war, you must strike first
and hard to let the enemy know you mean business. This is the

first time these inhuman swine have felt the wrath of God for their sins. We've put the war against slavery in motion."

"But they were unarmed, Father."

"So were the enslaved they have brutally treated and murdered without recourse for over two hundred years."

"Will we ever have to do that again?" Gabe asked.

"If God wills it."

I hope He doesn't. I'm not sure I'll be able to do His will.

While in hiding, they learned of Junior and Jason's arrest for attempting to help two young slaves escape and on the assumption they were involved in the killings. They also were told that Pate's posse had torched Brown's Station and destroyed the crops. Brown decided the band needed to act again, perhaps capture prisoners with whom to bargain for the release of his sons. That night, he concocted the next plan in his crusade.

The following day, Brown, along with his band of six fugitives, went into Osawatomie and convinced twenty men to come with them to fulfill the plan Brown laid out. Brown's small army marched through the scrub blackjack oak toward Pate's camp. Sentries heard them coming and rushed back to warn the others, vastly overestimating the size of the approaching force.

Brown split his men into two groups. A group of nine engaged Pate's troops in an open field. Brown spread the others out in a ravine that curved like a banana around Pate's position.

The two sides fired upon each other for several hours, with few casualties. Henry Thompson was hit. A number of the ruffians had gotten more than they bargained for and took off for Missouri. Neither side was making much headway when, out of nowhere, Frederick, who had an intellectual disability and was usually quite timid, rode out between the fighting groups and yelled, "Father, we have them surrounded and have cut off their escape."

Hearing this and believing his sentries' estimate of the enemy's size, Pate raised a white flag and marched his men out to surrender—only to discover it was the infamous John Brown pointing a gun at him. Adding insult to injury, Pate soon realized that Brown and his smaller force had outsmarted him.

Despite his hands being tied behind his back and rifles aimed at his chest, Pate brazenly declared, "United States Marshal Donaldson has deputized me, and I am duty-bound to fulfill my obligation to bring you to justice."

"I know who you are and why you are here," Brown replied haughtily.

"I am here to take you . . ."

"SILENCE!" roared Brown. "Here's my only proposition to you. You must surrender unconditionally."

Pate said nothing.

"Give the order of surrender," Brown commanded. "My brother-in-law lies wounded from the battle. I have no problem shooting you."

"We don't surrender unless our captain gives the order," Pate's second-in-command replied, aiming his gun at Brown, as did the other Missourians.

"Put a dozen balls through the first man that shoots," Brown commanded his troops, aiming his revolver directly at Pate's heart. "Give the order!"

"Men," Pate said just above a whisper, his shoulders and head slumping, "lay down your arms." The Battle of Black Jack was over.

Three days later, as Brown plotted their next move, a squad of the United States Cavalry came across the Brown band and their prisoners.

"Well, well, what have we here?" the officer in charge asked as he looked down at the motley crew.

"I'm Captain John Brown of the Northern Army, and these are my prisoners of war," he said with his hands on his hips and head and shoulders rigidly upright. "Pate and I have signed a treaty that I will release his men and him in exchange for the release of my two innocent sons."

"I'm Colonel Edwin Sumner, commander at Fort Leavenworth, and this is my lieutenant, Jeb Stuart. Pate has no authority to agree to an exchange. We have an arrest warrant with your name on it."

"My fight isn't with you, sir," parried Brown. "Please don't make it so."

Gabe had never seen soldiers except in a parade, and he feared that he and the Browns would lose if the troops started shooting. His pulse raced; his breathing was like a dog panting.

Not wanting to make a martyr of the unpredictable Brown and fearful that his arrest would incite the Free-Soilers to greater violence, Colonel Sumner told Brown, "My advice is that you best leave the state."

"I'll leave when the ruffians leave," Brown blasted. "I have only a short time to live—only one death to die, and I will die fighting for this cause. There will be no more peace in this land until slavery is done for. I will give the ruffians something else to do rather than extend slave territory."

"The next time I see you, I'll have the United States marshal with me, and I'll have you taken," the colonel stated angrily.

"If the United States marshal attempts to serve the writ, I'll shoot him dead on the spot," Brown spat in response.

"I'll take these men off your hands," said the colonel, pointing at Pate and his men.

Not knowing how he could keep the prisoners from being taken, Brown asked, "When will my boys be released?"

"When I'm ready to release them," Colonel Sumner said, waiting to see if Captain Brown would try to prevent Pate's troops from leaving. When Brown didn't move, Sumner ordered Pate's men to "Fall in." Sumner jerked the reins, and his chestnut mare turned sharply.

After that incident, Brown's gang dwindled in size, but those who remained continued to hide and wait for opportunities to strike. It was a miserable existence, but Brown didn't seem to notice. Each day began and ended with their leader's fervent prayers, sometimes lasting an hour. Speaking with his eyes closed, Brown quoted at length from scripture and prayed, "We beg for God's blessing and recount the sufferings of his colored children," going on in great detail about their adversity. "May this meager meal give us the strength to help relieve their agony and lead them to freedom."

The gang hid without shelter. Their clothes were torn and threadbare; their toes protruded through worn-out boots. They kept multiple pistols stuck in their belts, and had horses and rifles at the ready. Meals were pan-bread, gooseberries, and creek water flavored with molasses and ginger. But for the charity of John Tecumseh "Ottawa" Jones, a Native American whom Brown had befriended, they might have perished. He brought wild pigs, root vegetables, berries, and molasses to the outlaws several times over the ensuing month. Brown would roast the whole pig, and then the men greedily devoured the meat like a lion eating its prey.

Ottawa was the first American Indian Gabe had ever met. He was far from the kind of blood-thirsty renegade he had read about; instead, he was a gentle and intelligent man. Gabe enjoyed talking with him and discussing the Indian's plight.

"It's not good," Ottawa said, drawing circles in the dirt with a stick. "My people have been displaced by white expansion since the first Europeans came to America. President Jackson's Relocation Act forced tribes to move from the southern Appalachians to Indian Territory west of the Mississippi River." Ottawa stopped to compose himself. He wiped his eyes. "Thousands died on the long trek. We call it the Trail of Tears. Jackson's policy was assimilation or annihilation."

"Where will all the Indians go, with all the settlers heading west?"

"The white man is trying to confine us on reservations. They call it 'Manifest Destiny,' their God-given right to expand into territory occupied by Indians and own and possess that land to the exclusion of those of us who were there first. Being sent to a reservation will kill our culture if not our people."

"Why don't the treaties I've read about help?"

"Your government exploits my brothers. Treaties reduce the land available. Then the white men repeatedly break the treaties as they discover gold or as settlers move west. Being forced into smaller regions leads us to protect our way of life and what little land we have left."

"And we seem surprised or angry when the Indians fight back," Gabe scoffed.

"You're right. I like this quote from Shakespeare's *The Merchant of Venice*," Ottawa said, and recited:

> If you prick us, do we not bleed?
> If you tickle us, do we not laugh?
> If you poison us, do we not die?
> And if you wrong us, shall we not revenge?

"That makes me think," Gabe said. "The government's treatment of the Indian is as despicable as the slaveholder's treatment of the Negro."

"What do you mean?" Ottawa asked.

"Well, the Indians and the slaves don't own land, but they belong to it, yet the government deprives them of it. Manifest Destiny forces Indians onto reservations and restricts their freedoms, and enslavement does the same on plantations and farms. Indians are taken from their ancestral homes, just as the enslaved were forcibly taken from their native homes."

"That's very wise," Ottawa said, his eyes looking down. He dug deeper into the dirt.

One evening, when Ottawa brought them food, he informed Brown of Junior's and Jason's release from jail and of the Territorial governor's request for Brown to meet him in Lawrence with the promise he'd forget the past. "Don't do it," Ottawa warned. "Stay hidden. If you come, they'll arrest you."

In late August, the Free-Soilers began getting the upper hand. Despite his outlaw status, Brown had again amassed a band of about forty men. His small group, along with other Free-Soil militias, routed several pro-slavery strongholds. In retaliation, the ruffians assembled a significant force for a final push to besiege Kansas. Word spread that their mission was to scare off abolitionists with attacks on Free-Soil strongholds in Osawatomie and Lawrence.

"We'll go to Osawatomie to head them off," Brown said, mustering his troops. "We'll stay the night and head out tomorrow."

At dawn the following day, Frederick walked down the lane toward the house of Brown's half-sister and Frederick's aunt, Florella Adair, and her husband, Samuel, just a few miles from where Brown and his men were encamped, intending to care for the horses the band had stolen and stabled there. A small group of men on horseback came over a rise and drew to a halt in front of him.

"I know you. You are Reverend Martin White," Frederick said.

"And I know you." White leveled his pistol and fired a bullet through Frederick's heart.

The Adairs heard the shot, ran out onto their front porch, and saw a man, whom they didn't recognize from a distance, lying in the lane. At that moment, a much larger group of over two hundred men came into view. Figuring they were aiming for Osawatomie, Samuel told his son to go out the back door and warn the town that a large band of ruffians was heading their way.

Charles Adair, only thirteen, took off bareback like he was shot out of a cannon. He crossed the Osage River and, before getting to town, came across Brown and his outfit. Recognizing his Uncle John and some of his cousins, Charles blurted out, "The ruffians just kil't a man, and lots of them are headin' toward town."

Knowing Frederick had left that morning to go to the Adairs' house, Brown asked, "What happened? Who'd they kill?"

"I don't know who he was. They shot him in the lane in front of our house. All I saw was a man lying on the ground wearing brown pants and a red plaid shirt."

Brown fell to his knees and began sobbing, "Frederick! Not Frederick. Oh dear God, not Frederick!"

Oliver and Jason rushed to Brown's side to console him. It was the first time Gabe had seen Brown lose his composure. Gabe stood there, helpless.

After a few minutes, Brown rose, his eyes flashing with anger. Regaining his iron will, he told Charles to warn the town and firmly stated in a voice that would freeze hell, "Men, let's go. We must meet them before they get to town."

Brown positioned the men quickly, hiding in trees along the Osage Road between the invading force and the town. "Keep your wits," he commanded. "Aim low. Be sure to see both sides of your gun. Remember, take more care to end life well than to live long."

The band of raggedy men didn't have to wait long. The small army, led by Martin and John Reid, advanced on horseback, with two brass cannons at the rear.

Gabe put a "Beecher Bible" to his shoulder. His composure had caught up to his resolve. He had to avenge Frederick's death. He no longer felt fear. His hands were steady and dry.

Brown raised his sword, and the well-hidden guerillas fired. Gabe's first shot hit its mark, knocking the lead rider off his horse onto the dusty road. The ruffians dismounted, took cover, and returned fire. Gabe fired rapidly with his breech-loading Sharps rifle until the barrel was red hot.

Gabe ran for another tree to get a better angle to fire. He felt a sharp, searing pain like the sting of a mad hornet on his side. The woods went silent. Gabe felt like he was floating. He glanced down and saw his shirt turning bright red, but he no longer felt anything. He looked up and saw Oliver running toward him, mouth open and face contorted, but Gabe heard no sound. His knees buckled, and darkness came over him.

NINE

"AND THE WIND WHISPERS DEATH AS OVER THEM SWEEPING."

August 30, 1856–January 15, 1857

Oliver cradled Gabe's head as the red stain spread on Gabe's shirt.

"Is he alive?" Brown yelled to Oliver.

"Barely!" Oliver called back. "His breathing is shallow. I can't feel a pulse! Oh, God, we can't lose him."

Brown ran to the unresponsive Gabe and knelt next to him. He yanked open Gabe's shirt and saw a hole six inches to the right of his naval. Brown rolled Gabe onto his side and discovered another hole in his lower back. He ripped Gabe's shirt off, wadding two pieces into balls and pressing them over each hole to staunch the flow of blood. Brown took off his shirt and tied it tightly around Gabe to hold the two wads in place.

Bullets continued to zing around them. A shot hit one of Brown's men, who fell motionless.

"We've got to move," Brown commanded.

Brown picked Gabe up under his armpits, and Oliver grabbed him by the knees. They crossed the Marais des Cygnes River, climbed a small hill, and laid Gabe down.

"I don't think he made it," Oliver cried.

"No, he's still breathing," Brown said, lightly slapping Gabe's cheeks. "Gabe. Gabe. Are you with us?"

Gabe's eyes opened, fluttered, then shut again.

Brown slapped him again. "Gabe. C'mon, Gabe."

His eyes opened again and stayed open. "Where am I? What happened?"

"You were shot," Brown said, exhaling a deep "phew." "I think the bullet went right through. I pray it didn't do too much damage."

The firing stopped. Rather than chase the beaten band, the ruffians regrouped and headed for nearby Osawatomie. Within minutes, the men could see smoke rising over Osawatomie.

"They're sacking the town," Brown declared, his voice clear and resonant but tears streaming down his face. "God sees it! There will be no peace in this land until slavery is done for. I will carry this war into Africa."

Oliver had told Gabe that "Africa" was Brown's code name for the Southern states.

Brown's band hid during the day and moved at night until they reached Ottawa Jones's ranch. Henry was already there, still recovering from his wounds from Black Jack Creek. Ottawa tended to Gabe, cleaning the wounds and putting a poultice of finely chopped yarrow, dogwood, and lavender on the bullet holes. Ottawa's wife, Jane, spoon-fed Gabe her chicken soup.

A week later, Brown said, "We've got more to do here. But, Gabe, it's time you and Henry went home."

Still weak and hurting, Gabe didn't argue.

"The closest railroad station is in Iowa City, about six days' travel," Brown explained. "Pro-slavery Missourians block the Kansas-Missouri border, so Oliver will take you north along Lane's trail into Nebraska, then east to Iowa City."

The following day, Oliver and Brown placed Henry in the back of the wagon, laying him on a straw bed. Brown gave Oliver the money Ottawa had given him.

Now as tall as Captain Brown, Gabe looked him in the eyes, "I hate leaving you."

Brown's eyes glistened. He put his hands on Gabe's shoulders. "We will see each other again. You have become another son. Godspeed, Gabriel."

Gabe crawled into the wagon and lay down next to Henry. Oliver took the reins, and the wagon rolled north. Gabe returned Brown's wave with a salute.

Along the way, whenever he felt strong enough, Gabe moved onto the bench next to Oliver.

"I wonder what your father has in store for the future?" Gabe asked.

"He wants to strike them in the heart. He'll go into the South. He admired Nat Turner's rebellion and believes it would have succeeded with better organization."

"Will you join him if he does?"

"I don't know," Oliver replied. "I pledged to follow him, but I'm still messed up after Pottawatomie. What about you?"

"I don't know, either. I'm not done fighting to end slavery, but I'm not sure I can do it with a gun and sword."

When they arrived in Iowa City, Henry chose to recuperate there before returning to New York. Gabe bid Oliver and Henry goodbye at the railroad station to begin his solitary trek home.

Gabe took trains through Chicago and Dayton to Cincinnati, then a coach to Georgetown. He began the mile walk to his house with a spring in his step, eager to be home, stopping now and then to absorb the familiar countryside. Spooked from its perch, an owl took flight. As if seeing an owl in the daytime wasn't ominous enough, the *whoosh* of its wings sounded like the quicksilver swishing through the broadswords. Gabe's heart stopped, and he began trembling. He fell to his hands and knees on the dusty path, his head almost touching the ground, until his heartbeat returned to normal and the sweating subsided. He started up again, slower and less confident, fearing his parents' reception. *Will they know about the massacres? How will they react?*

Gabe's mother was hanging laundry on the line when she saw him approaching. She dropped a wet towel in the dirt and ran toward him, rejoicing, "GABRIEL! GABRIEL! Atticus! Children! Come! Gabriel's home!"

Caroline and Raphael rushed from the house. *"Son!"* was all Atticus could choke out as he came out of the barn and joined in the race to Gabe.

Caroline got to him first. "I prayed for you every day. We were afraid you were killed, but I knew you'd come home." She wrapped her arms around his waist and squeezed.

"Oooooooof," Gabe winced and grimaced, holding his side. "Not so hard. I'm a little sore."

Caroline released her grip and backed off. His mother saw the exchange. "Oh, Gabriel, what's the matter?"

"Mother, I guess I can't hide it. I got shot, but I'm all right."

"What? How did that happen?" she gasped.

"We can talk about that later," Atticus cut in, putting his arm around Gabe's shoulder. "Let's just all get inside and get some food in him."

"You need it. You're as thin as a rail," Raph teased, punching him on the arm, although he was a little upset that his younger brother was getting a hero's welcome. *I've been home the whole time doing the work of three, and they treat the wounded vigilante like royalty.*

"Yes," his mother agreed. She held Gabe's hands as she stepped back to look at her son from head to toe. "You've grown, but you *are* skinny."

"I've dreamt about your cooking for a year. I will never eat another gooseberry or prairie chicken as long as I live," he said as they all headed to the house.

Caroline couldn't take her eyes off her brother. *He looks older, and more handsome.* "I missed you so much," Caroline gushed before blurting, "Tell us about your adventures! We haven't heard from you in so long. Were you with Captain Brown when the people were hacked to death?"

"Caroline, hush!" her mother scolded.

Gabe couldn't believe how cavalier Caroline's comment was. He broke out in a cold sweat and felt bile rise in his throat as the room began to spin. He held onto the table to steady himself.

"Are you all right?" his mother asked, frowning, her forehead scrunched.

"Yes," Gabe feebly replied. "I'm sorry. I guess you already know some of what happened."

"It was in all the newspapers," Atticus told Gabe with grave seriousness. "They never mentioned you by name, but the U.S. marshal wants John Brown and his gang. We won't talk about it now, and I suggest you never tell anyone about whatever role you played."

"Yes, sir."

Everyone fell silent. Caroline, feeling rebuked, went to tend the fire in the stove. Gabe broke the tension: "This past year had been quite an experience," he began. "I tried to put a lot of it down in my letters. Despite all the difficulties, I think we made a difference in preventing the spread of slavery."

"We're proud of you for that," Atticus said. "Although we are concerned about the reports we have heard. I'm afraid the events in Kansas have only made the South angrier and more defensive."

"Speaking of letters," Ailene broke in, "you've got two from Jasmine."

Gabe grabbed the envelopes and ripped into the first one.

> Elgin Settlement Canada West, July 4, 1856
> Dear Gabe,
>
> I hope you are doing okay. I havent heard from you in a long time. You might not be in kansas so I am sending this to your house. Did I say something rong? Glory will be 2 this month. All she does is talk and laff. Levi is working at the new sawmil in town. He talks nonsense about leaving and trying to find Papa. Have you heard anything more about Papa? We miss him so much.
>
> Today is indipendence day for you but my indipendence day is in October when we arrived in Canada. Here I am treated like a real person. I've read about what is happening in kansas and it looks like there will never be a real indipendence day in the US. Slavery wont end.
>
> > Come visit us,
> > Jasmine

The second letter was not as cheerful and depressed Gabe:

> Elgin Settlement Canada West, August 25, 1856
> Dear Gabe,
>
> Because you have not wrote I guess you dont want me to write you anymore. I dont understand except maybe you are like others we have met. You want to help free slaves but you dont want to associate with a negro. It makes me sad to see how the north copies the prejadaces of the south. Because of the fugitiv law even the

north has let loose the bloodhounds and snakes. I hope
you and your family are doing good.
                              Still grateful,
                              Jasmine

As soon as he could get to his room, Gabe wrote Jasmine:

Georgetown, September 11, 1856

Dear Jasmine,

*   I got your letters. I assure you I want to stay
in contact with you. You may have read about
things that happened with Captain Brown in
Kansas. Because of that, we were on the run, and
I wasn't able to write. All I can say for now is
that I fought to end the spread of slavery just like
I told you I would. I'm home now. I don't know
what I'm going to do next. Maybe I will come to
Canada. I'm eager to see you and everyone else
and to meet Glory. Please write again soon.*
                              Fondly,
                              Gabe

The next day, Gabe went into town to mail the letter to
Jasmine and telegram Michael, letting him know he was home
safe. He ran into Zeb Runyan, his best friend from school. Zeb
was nearly twice his size but as gentle as could be. He was always
looking for ways to get into trouble and always had a big smile
and a hearty laugh.

"Gabe!" Zeb yelled as he reached out to embrace him, "Where've you been? Nobody would tell us where you disappeared. We couldn't figure out what happened."

"It's a long story, but please don't give me one of your bear hugs," Gabe responded, pulling back. "Pops warned me not to tell anyone, but I can't keep secrets from you. You have to promise not to say anything. Promise?"

"Promise," Zeb said with emphasis.

"I was in Kansas with Captain John Brown. I was part of his militia. I got shot, see?" he said, lifting his shirt and exposing the healing wounds.

Zeb was stunned. "*You?*"

"Yep," Gabe said, straightening his shoulders.

"Holy cow!" Zeb shook his head. "Tell me all about it."

"I can't right now, but someday," Gabe said, shaking his head. Changing the subject, he asked, "What are you up to?"

"Well, I'm gettin' ready to go to Miami College," Zeb said, although he wanted to know more about Gabe getting shot. "You should come with me. I'm going to stay with Zach. You could live with us."

Gabe had always liked Zeb's brother, Zach, who was a year older than Zeb. "I don't know," Gabe replied. "We don't have any money. I've been out of school for a year. If I go to college, I'm sure my parents want me to go to Oberlin. I'd get in free because Michael teaches there, and I could stay with him."

"Well, think about it," Zeb smiled. "We'd have a great time. Zach tells me there are a lot of pretty girls at the women's college nearby!"

Gabe laughed. "I may have to change my parents' minds."

When Gabe got home, he broached the subject with his parents.

"You aren't going anywhere!" Ailene reprimanded, her hands on her hips.

"Your mother's right. We don't oppose you going to school, but you just got home. Maybe next year," Atticus reflected.

"You're probably right, but talking with Zeb got me excited."

"We'll talk about it later," Atticus mused, glancing toward Ailene.

Less than two weeks later, Gabe received a letter from Jasmine, who insisted he come to Canada to see everybody. He showed the letter to his mother and father. "I really want to go. I am eager to see Jasmine again and meet Glory. I can stop in Oberlin and see Michael."

"At least you're telling us," Atticus said gruffly. "That's an improvement."

"And you're not going off to get yourself killed," Ailene added. "Regardless, I wish you'd stay home and help your father."

"I wouldn't be gone long. Just a couple of days."

"You've been gone for a year. Raph, Caroline, and I can manage a bit longer."

His mother shook her head in resignation.

"Pops, could I borrow a little money?" Gabe asked sheepishly.

Two days later, Gabe repeated the trip toward Akron, but he disembarked at the LaGrange station, where Michael met him. They spent the evening together, talking well into the morning about Gabe's adventures in Kansas and Michael's activities at

Oberlin. "I couldn't be more proud of you," Michael said, dropping off Gabe at the train station after just a few hours of sleep.

Gabe took the train into Cleveland and caught the morning ferry to Canada, then the coach to Buxton. When leaving Georgetown, he was excited to be heading north but became more disquieted the closer he got to his destination. *Maybe I should have told them I was coming. I'm not sure surprising them was a good idea.*

By late morning, Gabe was walking up Buxton's Main Street toward the center of the small town. The houses were just as Jasmine had described: twelve feet high and set back from the dirt road about thirty feet. Each had a stoop running the eighteen-foot length of the house, a white picket fence, and a flower garden in front. Unlike his fast-beating heart and fluttering stomach, the pretty little town was calm and quiet.

He stopped abruptly. The bakery and home before him were precisely as detailed in Jasmine's letters. He looked to the heavens, said a quick prayer, and took a deep, deep breath to steel himself for whatever the reunion would be. He went inside. The smell of baking bread was as powerful as sweet lilacs in spring.

"Anybody here?" Gabe asked as calmly as he could, trying to control the excitement exploding within him.

Rose's head popped out from behind a bakery rack. The screech that followed brought the household running. Rose danced toward Gabe. Hattie came crashing through a door at the back of the store and, upon recognizing Gabe, let out a yelp of her own. Jasmine, close behind with a little girl clutching her hand, froze as if she couldn't believe what she was seeing.

"GABE!" Jasmine screamed with delight.

Gabe's mouth had gone dry, and suddenly it felt like every nerve was being pricked with a pin. "Hello," was all he could choke out, spellbound at how beautiful Jasmine had become.

Suddenly everyone was motionless, not knowing what to do or say.

Gabe made the first move, getting down on one knee to be at eye level with the little girl. Regaining his voice, he said with an ear-to-ear smile, "And I'll bet you're Glory," and reached for her.

Glory jumped back and hid behind her mother's leg, whimpering.

Surprised, Gabe quickly stood up and stepped back.

"It's all right: she's been taught not to trust a white man," Jasmine said. She gently pulled Glory out from behind her and knelt down. "Glory Gabriella," Jasmine began in a soft, sweet voice, "this is Gabriel Adams—the man who brought us to freedom, and who I named you after."

"Hello, Glory," Gabe said, dropping back to one knee, now with an apple-size lump in his throat. "I've wanted to meet you for so long."

Glory stood like a stone statue with a blank expression, her arms around Jasmine's neck for protection.

"Oh my Lawd, dis is a heavenly day!" Hattie proclaimed, regaining her composure. Now everyone started laughing and talking at the same time. Jasmine hushed the others so Gabe could hear her: "You shoulda let us know you was coming! I woulda dressed up and had some food for you."

Dress up? You look just fine. "I wanted to surprise you. But I can't believe I'm here."

"Come. Sit down," Rose said. "Hattie, go fetch Levi. Tells him to come right quick."

Rose brought Gabe a muffin fresh out of the oven and a mug of apple cider. Glory sat on her mother's lap and wouldn't stop staring at Gabe. She didn't return Gabe's smile, but her big brown eyes seemed to absorb all that was happening. Her skin was the color of coffee with milk, and her dark, curly hair shone in the light. Jasmine stroked her hair and whispered in her ear. The corners of Glory's lips moved ever so slightly upward.

"Oh, Gabe, I'm so happy to see you," Jasmine began, speaking rapidly and high-pitched. "I've thought of you every day since we said goodbye at the ferry."

"I'm so glad to see all of you," Gabe said, leaning toward Glory and smiling.

The corners of Glory's lips moved up again.

Hearing heavy footsteps running on the plank walkway, Gabe turned as Levi burst through the door. *Whoa! He's over six feet tall, and solid muscle!*

"Gabe!" Levi yelled, stepping forward to hug him.

Gabe held his hands up in self-defense. "A horse kicked me in the ribs, and I'm pretty sore," he lied.

Levi tapped him lightly on the shoulder as if Gabe were fragile, and teased, "If'n you had a bit more meat on them bones, a kick wouldn't hurt so much."

"Oh, shush," Jasmine scolded. "He look just fine."

They spent the next few days sharing stories, laughing, and eating Rose and Hattie's delicious fare. Gabe held nothing back, including retracting the horse-kicking story. Each detail of his time with John Brown enraptured them. Likewise, to Gabe's great pleasure, Jasmine and the family shared their experiences and stories about their new life.

Jasmine and Gabe took walks into the heavily wooded countryside. Once, Jasmine slipped, and Gabe grabbed her hand to keep her from falling. Even after regaining her balance, she didn't let go. "It's so nice to have you here," she said. "What you did for us cannot be measured."

"You've done more for me than I did for you. You've given me meaning and purpose in life. Before I met you, abolitionism was an abstract concept. Now, it's real and tangible. I have a couple of bullet holes to prove it."

After being in Buxton for three days, Gabe sadly announced, "I think it's time to head home. I'll be leaving in the morning."

Even Glory was sorry to see Gabe leave. She had finally warmed up to him and now loved sitting on his lap while he read or told her stories. She was a soft and gentle little girl, full of spunk, with an infectious giggle and smile.

"I'll see you again, my little friend," Gabe quietly told her. "I will always be there for you."

Rose and Hattie used their matching aprons to wipe away tears as they said their goodbyes. Jasmine, Levi, and Gabe walked to the lumber mill.

"We'd be much obliged for anything you can find out about whether Papa is still alive and where he is," Levi said, finishing a conversation they had had throughout Gabe's visit.

"If he's alive, I'll find him," Gabe said, unsure how to back up those words. The two shook hands.

Jasmine walked with Gabe in silence to the station, from which he would take a coach six miles to the coast and the ferry across Lake Erie. "Please come back. I'll miss you."

"I'll miss you, too," Gabe said. "Jasmine, um . . . would it be . . . May I give you a hug before I leave?"

"I thought you'd never ask," she said as she put her arms around his neck. He wrapped his around her slim waist as she kissed his cheek.

Gabe didn't want to let go.

After some time, Jasmine said, "You better go. The coach is about to leave."

Reluctantly, Gabe released her and turned for the four-horse-drawn carriage. He stopped, turned back toward Jasmine, and waved before stepping inside.

Gabe began reliving each moment of his reunion with Jasmine with a smile. Then the smile faded into a frown. *Why do I have so much conflict between my brain and heart?*

Several days after returning to Georgetown, Gabe sat down for breakfast with his parents. "Have you thought more about me going to Miami with Zeb?"

"Son," Atticus began, "we were afraid you'd bring this up. After what you've been through, maybe being home doesn't seem as exciting to you. We'd prefer you stay for a while, but Raphael wants to stay home and work the farm. As long as Caroline is here, we can make do."

"We would feel better if you were with your brother at Oberlin," Ailene added. "But you can make your own choice. We don't want to hold you back from your ambitions."

"I'm not sure how we could afford it. You'll have to help pay for it, and we may have to borrow some money from my brother."

"Thanks," Gabe nodded, acknowledging his parents' sacrifice. "I'll help all I can, and I won't spend a half-cent more than I need. I'll work for Uncle Nat and pay him back when I finish."

Two days later, as Gabe and Raphael were chopping and splitting wood, Gabe tried to appease his brother, who had been quiet and withdrawn. "I know I just got back, and I should stick around and help you. I missed you, but I want to go to college."

"Don't worry about me," Raph replied, covering up his jealousy. "Now that you've seen half the country as a rebel, you won't like being in Georgetown as a farmer."

The following week, Gabe took the Georgetown coach to Cincinnati, stayed overnight at the Dicksons', then took the Cincinnati-Hamilton-Dayton Railroad to Hamilton. From there, he hitched a ride on a wagon to Miami College in Oxford, a small, pastoral town on the western edge of Ohio, north of Cincinnati. As the wagon rolled into town, Gabe saw expansive oak trees dotting a campus square with several buildings along its perimeter. Oxford's red brick High Street matched the two-story buildings that lined it.

Having received a telegram from Gabe, Zeb was waiting for him at the house where he and Zach lived. Zeb's welcoming slap on the back knocked Gabe's apprehension out of him. Gabe put his meager belongings in the little room next to a bed Zeb had borrowed for him. "Let's go to the dean's office and get you registered," Zeb said with his usual enthusiasm. "It's so good to have you here." Meeting with the dean, Gabe registered for classes in literature, logic, moral philosophy, and Latin. His college days began.

Moral philosophy, which dealt mainly with the current political climate, was exciting and challenging. The 1856 presidential election was approaching, and Bleeding Kansas, as it was called, was still in the news. The daily debates in the class were intellectually challenging. Although Gabe was careful not to talk about his own experiences, he was active in the discussions and enthralled by the class's energy and the exchange of ideas.

Professor Jackson Smythe, a tall, distinguished attorney with close-cropped hair, graying at the temples, told the class several weeks after Gabe arrived, "The Secretary of War, Jefferson Davis, said that the next presidential election will probably bring the South to the alternative of resistance rather than surrender their birthright. What do you think?"

"If Buchanan wins," James Caldwell, a Southern sympathizer from Ohio, said, "he'll make sure the Southerners keep their slaves."

"Buchanan's an idiot," chimed in Gabe's new friend, Benjamin Runkle. "He'll help the South. I'm for 'Free soil, free men, and Frémont.'"

"There's nothing wrong with being behind the Southern states," countered James, only fifteen with a handsome, almost effeminate face and build. Despite their differences, James's intellect impressed Gabe.

"I think Millard Fillmore is the best," another chimed in. "I agree with his American Party that *true* Americans are anti-foreigners, anti-Catholics, and anti-Whigs."

Ben, tall with a slight build, bushy brown hair, and an expressive face, threw a wad of paper at the Fillmore supporter, "You're the idiot. Their anti-everybody position is why people call the party 'The Know-Nothings.'"

"We need a president who will support the Kansas-Nebraska Act and Senator Douglas's ideas about popular sovereignty. Buchanan will make a great president," countered James.

"Letting people decide whether to allow slavery in a new state or territory is wrong," Gabe interjected. "Pro-slavery forces push their way in and vote even if they don't live there. Frémont and this new Republican Party are right: there should be *no* expansion of slavery."

"Slavery is here to stay," argued James. "It's part of the Constitution and part of America. Negroes are ignorant and lazy. That's why God made them slaves."

Gabe tried to control himself but couldn't. His voice went up an octave. "Slavery is wrong. Negroes aren't lazy, and it's white men who have kept them ignorant. Slavery must end, even if the South resists."

"It'll take more than John Brown and his gang to end slavery," James said, smirking, not knowing anything of Gabe's relationship with Brown.

Gabe slumped in his chair. He buried his head between his knees, his heart pumping so hard he felt like it would come out of his chest. He began shaking and sweating profusely and was having trouble breathing.

"Are you all right?" Ben asked, alarmed.

"No, and yes," Gabe weakly replied. "Just let me be for a minute."

After class, Gabe went up to James and extended his hand. "I'm sorry, but I'm opposed to slavery and am willing to fight for its abolition."

"Well, we're just going to disagree," James responded, refusing the outstretched hand. "I see nothing wrong with slavery. Even the Bible supports the Southern views towards the darkies, as do most people in the North."

Gabe, disgusted, turned to walk away from the group, but Ben stopped him. "Hey, Gabe, a group of us are meeting in my room. We formed a fraternity. We named it Sigma Chi. Want to come over? One of the guys has some beer!"

"After that class, I could use a beer," Gabe replied, trying to sound like drinking beer was something he regularly enjoyed—although he had drank beer only once, when Raph gave him one in the barn, and he disliked the taste.

They went to High Street and up to the second floor of a narrow brick building called the Crystal Palace. Ben's tight quarters contained two small rope beds, several hard-backed chairs, and a desk.

"Brother Dan, please give my friend a beer."

"Sure thing," Dan replied as he opened an Eagle Brewery lager and handed it to Gabe with his left hand while extending his right. "I'm Dan Cooper. Just call me Ol' Dan like everybody else."

Before Gabe had taken his second swallow, James from class walked through the door. Gabe was dismayed to see him, and crestfallen when he found out James was Ben's roommate. By that time, seven people, plus Gabe, were crowded into the room.

The debate over the presidential candidates started again, although the beer helped Gabe control his temper and dampened his intolerance of what he thought were ignorant, hate-filled opinions. *They all seem to get along. Can I be friends with someone who thinks so differently from me?*

As the term sped along, Gabe found himself enjoying his literature class—the next book he had to read was Homer's *Iliad*. He thought of himself as a modern-day Achilles and saw the Trojan War as akin to the battle against slavery. He was not doing well in Latin, however, and intensely disliked the teacher, whose high-and-mighty attitude reminded him of Marcus.

The moral philosophy class continued to provide an opportunity for lively discourse about the election. The North had split its votes between Frémont and Fillmore, but Buchanan easily won the South. He had fallen short of 50 percent of the popular vote but won the election in the Electoral College—which triggered a debate about abolishing the Electoral College. Discussion in class often turned toward Buchanan's election's effect on slavery.

"It's a good thing Frémont didn't win," Ben said. "If he had, the South would have seceded."

"But Buchanan winning just kicks the problem down the road," Gabe said. "His support of the Fugitive Slave Law and popular sovereignty will create more tension between the North and South."

"I'm not sure why following the Constitution creates more tension in the North," James countered.

"I've read that there are many more claims of free Negroes being captured and taken south because of that law," Ben added. "That's why."

"Well, that shouldn't happen," James concurred.

"Popular sovereignty isn't in the Constitution," one student challenged.

"In a way, it is," said James. "The Tenth Amendment says that if the Constitution doesn't delegate a power to the federal government, then it's left to the states and the people of those states to decide."

"You make a good point," Gabe conceded, finding that he could better listen to another person's position without anger with each debate or argument.

As much as he enjoyed school, Zeb, and other friends, Gabe sorely missed his family and was glad to go home when the winter break arrived. He was happiest sleeping in his old bed next to Raph's, talking long into each night about what both were experiencing in this new stage of life.

"How are you managing with Mother and Pops, the farm, and everything?" Gabe asked, leaning on an elbow in bed.

"I'm fine. I miss you. Caroline and I are getting closer than we ever have. She's a very gentle, warm, and caring person. But Pops criticizes how I do things—he doesn't think I pay attention to details."

"It's just that you don't do things his way."

"I get frustrated that I'm slower at doing things than Pops. Plus, he gets up way too early!"

Gabe laughed. "Maybe you can do more with the fruit trees. Pops never did like trimming and cleaning up. He won't be so critical."

"Not a bad idea."

"Caroline told me you go with her when she goes to care for Mrs. Abernathy so you can see her daughter, Sherry," Gabe said, smiling.

"Well, that's true. If you can have a girlfriend, so can I."

"I don't have a girlfriend," Gabe said innocently.

"What would you call Jasmine?"

"A dilemma!"

Both boys broke out laughing.

"What do you think will happen if the slavery question doesn't get resolved?" Gabe asked, getting serious.

"I don't know. Pops thinks it might mean war if the South secedes."

"Would you join the fight if it came to that?"

"Not unless I had to," Raph replied. "Slavery isn't a cause I'm willing to die for."

"I wouldn't want to die, but I'd join if it meant ending slavery."

The second term began, and Gabe continued his classes. *Walden,* a new book by Henry David Thoreau, was the first book of the semester in literature class, and Gabe absorbed Thoreau's views on a simple life.

Moral philosophy took on a new excitement. "We are waiting for an opinion from the United States Supreme Court on the *Dred Scott* case," Professor Smythe announced. "The case is about whether an enslaved person taken to a free state or territory becomes free or remains a slave," he noted. "Depending on its outcome, it could have important ramifications on the nation."

"I read something about it," Gabe chimed in. "But I don't remember the details. Can you give them to us?"

"It's a bit confusing. A Missourian, John Emerson, owned a man named Dred Scott. Emerson took Scott to his army assignment in Illinois, then to a part of the Louisiana Territory where slavery was not allowed, and finally back to St. Louis. Scott sued Emerson for his freedom, claiming that his time in Illinois and the non-slave part of the Louisiana Territory rendered him a free man. At least eight times, Missouri courts have held that, if an enslaved person is taken to a free state or territory, he becomes emancipated. Eventually, the case went to trial in 1850, and Scott won. He was free!"

"Why wasn't that the end of the case?" Gabe inquired.

"Well, Missouri politics changed. In 1852, to protect Missouri's slave owners, newly elected state Supreme Court judges took the unprecedented action of reversing the *Scott* verdict—they declared that he was still a slave. The Missouri Supreme Court sent the case back to the trial court. In the meantime, Emerson died, and Scott became the property of John Sanford. The case again went to trial, and this time the judge instructed the jury that Scott had never been free and was a slave. To no one's surprise, the jury found for Sanford and against Scott."

"That doesn't sound right," Ben interjected.

"It gets more complicated," Smythe went on. "Sanford also argued that, because Scott was still a slave, he wasn't a citizen, and therefore he could not bring the action in federal court. The case is on appeal to the United States Supreme Court, which has four Northern justices, including Justice John McLean from Ohio. Chief Justice Roger Taney"—he precisely pronounced the name, "Taw-ney"—and four other justices are Southerners. "Taney is a slaveholder, a rabid pro-Southerner angry with what he calls Northern aggression, and, interestingly, the brother-in-law of Francis Scott Key, who wrote the lyrics to *The Star-Spangled Banner*. It will be important to see how they vote. It could have grave consequences for the country."

"England abolished slavery in the 1830s," Whitelaw Reid, who had become a friend of Gabe's, said. "If a slave is taken to England, the slave is declared free. Why isn't it the same here?"

"That's right," Professor Smythe replied, "but this isn't England."

That night, Gabe lay in bed reading *The Tyrant's Jubilee!*, a newly published poem by Frederick Douglass, who had written it after the recent slave-insurrection panic in the South that had fueled lynchings, murders, and lashes beyond anyone's ability to count.

> The fire thus kindled, may be revived again;
> The flames are extinguished, but the embers remain;
> One terrible blast may produce an ignition
> Which shall wrap the whole South in
>   wild conflagration.
>
> The pathway of tyrants lies over volcanoes;
> The very air they breathe is heavy with sorrows;
> Agonizing heart-throbs convulse them
>   while sleeping,
> And the wind whispers Death as over
>   them sweeping.

Now, I understand Captain Brown's vow to carry the war into Africa.

TEN

"THE NEGRO HAS NO RIGHTS THE WHITE MAN MUST RESPECT."

March 5, 1857–October 7, 1858

Almost two months later, a puzzled Professor Smythe addressed his class, his head tilting to one side. "In his inaugural speech yesterday, President Buchanan made a peculiar statement: that the Supreme Court will settle the question of popular sovereignty, and that he would cheerfully submit to the decision. Someone must have given him a tip about the *Dred Scott* case, which would be improper. A Supreme Court justice should never give advance notice to anyone, including the president, about how the Court will rule."

The next day, the Court orally issued nine separate opinions in *Dred Scott v. Sandford*. Chief Justice Taney read the lengthy majority opinion, six justices read concurring opinions, and two dissented. Although it would be several months before the Court released official written opinions, lengthy summaries and editorials about the oral opinions appeared in newspapers.

"Taney has made this a complicated mess with a disgustingly pro-white opinion," Professor Smythe said a week after the oral ruling, when the newspaper reported more information about how the separate opinions came about. "At first, the justices voted 7 to 2 to say that the question of Negro citizenship was not properly before the Court, and therefore the Court did not have jurisdiction to decide the case. They voted not to address other issues raised. That should have been the end of the matter, with a short opinion that the lower court's decision stood. However, before the Court gave its oral opinions, Chief Justice Taney was told that Justices McLean and Curtis intended to issue a dissent that opined on all of the arguments before the Court, including whether the Missouri Compromise was constitutional. So, the seven in the majority voted to address all of the issues. Taney, as he had wanted to do from the beginning, wrote an emphatic, lengthy opinion going far beyond what was necessary in order to support his Southern sympathies."

"I don't understand. Why is it a mess?" Zeb asked.

"It's not easy to determine which of his conclusions have a five-person majority. What is clear is that the case has declared Scott is still a slave, Negroes cannot be citizens of any state, and they declared the Missouri Compromise unconstitutional, with each justice giving separate reasoning on that issue."

"What about free Negroes?" Gabe asked. "They aren't citizens, either?"

"That's right," Professor Smythe answered. "Chief Justice Taney said that Scott and *all* persons of African descent, free or slave, were not citizens when the Constitution was written and, therefore, cannot be citizens now. I can't tell if four others agreed with that opinion. Two did for sure, and two or three others may have accepted that position without actually saying it."

Gabe was dumbfounded and indignant. "How could our United States Supreme Court say that?"

"He was just following what the Constitution says," James retorted. "Show me in the Constitution where it says a darkey is a citizen? I think Taney is correct when he says Negroes can't claim any rights or privileges of citizenship."

"If you look at it from a neutral standpoint, you may be correct," replied Professor Smythe. "It does follow the Constitution. Even though the importation of slaves had to end, nothing in the Constitution said slavery itself had to end or that the government had the right to stop it from spreading or eliminate it. Counting a slave as three-fifths of a person for Congressional representation purposes hasn't changed. Taney also said that the framers understood the meaning of their language and that indelible marks separated the unhappy Black race from the white. In the Constitution they were never considered or spoken of except as property. For the same reason, they may be legally correct that banning slavery in the territories was unconstitutional."

"Does that mean slaveholders can take their slaves anywhere, even if a state is a free state?" Gabe asked incredulously.

"I think that's correct," Professor Smythe exhaled slowly.

"The Court was right," James said with a smug smirk. "If a person can take his horse anywhere, he should be able to take his slave anywhere. The Constitution does not permit the limitation of slavery."

"What does this do to Douglas's notion of popular sovereignty?" Ben asked.

"Popular sovereignty appears to be dead," Professor Smythe stated as he contemplated the question. "*Dred Scott* condones and nationalizes slavery. The *Cincinnati Gazette* urges the North to secede from the Union because free states will not be able to keep slavery out. It even implies a civil war could result.

For the next few days, newspapers continued to predict dire consequences due to the different opinions. Southerners, as a whole, and Northern anti-abolitionist pundits applauded the majority opinions and agreed with their conclusions. Commentaries from abolitionists argued that Chief Justice Taney's opinion was an abomination and a disgrace. The *Gazette* said, "Taney's opinion is a burlesque on judicial opinions."

"We'll continue our discussion when the written opinions come out," Professor Smythe told everyone.

In late May, the Court issued the written opinions. Professor Smythe told his class the day after newspapers published them, "The *Dred Scott* case just got stranger. McLean and Curtis are accusing Taney of adding new arguments to his oral pronouncement in his written ruling to rebut their dissent. They're in the so-called majority opinion, but no other justice saw or voted on his additions. That's unheard of."

"Taney's opinion is just wrong," Gabe said, his voice rising. "I can't even imagine the wicked consequences of it. It's an outrage the way Taney dehumanizes Negroes, calling them 'the unfortunate race,' 'inferior,' and 'unfit to associate with the white race.'"

"And what he says about Indians," Harold Widepath, whose mother was an Indigenous Miamian who had lived on the Miami Indian Reservation in Indiana before marrying a white man and moving to Fort Wayne. When Harold's father died, she was forced back onto the reservation, where she raised Harold and his brothers. Harold's soft demeanor and quiet strength reminded Gabe of Ottawa Jones and the kind-hearted assistance he had provided. "Taney calls us 'uncivilized, untutored, and savages,' 'under the subjection of the white race,' and 'in a state of pupilage' for *our* sake. Am *I* uncivilized? Am *I* a savage? I was forced to live on a reservation for *my* sake?"

"The Court was just stating what most Americans believe," James shot back at Gabe and Harold.

Harold's fists clenched, and he started to rise to confront James. Gabe grabbed his arm, pulled him back to his seat, and said to James, "It's still nothing but whites claiming superiority. The Supreme Court should protect the minority's rights, not just agree with the majority of the population."

"Whether it's right or wrong," Ben chimed in, "it's the law of the land. We gotta accept whatever the Supreme Court says, whether we like it or not."

Professor Smythe said, "To a legal scholar, including Northern scholars who believe in the Founding Fathers' original intent, it is arguably a correct interpretation of the Constitution. Remember, several Northern justices agreed with Taney.

"So, the *Scott* opinion may be legally correct, but it goes too far?" asked Zeb.

"That's a better way of putting it," Smythe nodded.

"Well, I'm upset," Gabe retorted. "The Supreme Court should take the lead in social change. If people are supposed to follow a holding like *Dred Scott*, wouldn't they also have to follow the opposite holding if the Supreme Court had gone the way of the dissent? Rather than countenance bias and prejudice, why not rebuke it?"

"The role of the Supreme Court is to interpret the laws," James countered. "They aren't there to put a moral stamp on the Constitution or to worry about what people think."

"I disagree. Maybe if the Supreme Court upheld people's basic civil rights, some prejudice against non-whites and women would erode. The part that is most offensive to me is when Taney says that Negroes are an inferior order, unfit to associate with the white race, and that 'they had no rights which the white man was bound to respect.'" Taney's words had troubled his soul. *I never thought what happened at Pottawatomie was the answer. But maybe Captain Brown is right. Only guns and knives will settle this.*

Summer break came, and once again Gabe relished being home and spending time with his family. At the same time, life as he knew it was changing rapidly. Because of the *Dred Scott* decision, Northerners continued to threaten secession. Speculators and

Northern financiers who had bet heavily on Western Expansion of the railroads had been losing vast sums of money because whites found it risky to invest in the West's development, now that slavery could extend into new territories. Banks collapsed, and lenders called in their loans, setting off the Panic of 1857.

One night, while Gabe sat on the front porch with his father, Atticus said with a heavy sigh, "I'm really sorry to tell you this, Gabriel, but it doesn't look like we can afford to send you back to school. We have no cash left, with the Georgetown Bank closing its doors."

"How about I see if Mr. Grant will hire me to work in his tannery?" Gabe asked. "I could make enough to pay for at least one term."

"That's nasty work."

"I can take it," Gabe boasted.

The next day, Gabe went to see Jesse Grant, a stern, hard-working man who was known not to tolerate laziness. Jesse knew the Adamses' work ethic and hired Gabe on the spot. Gabe quickly realized why Captain Brown disliked the tannery business and its backbreaking work. The hot and humid days of summer intensified the pungent, penetrating, and nauseating odors of the urine and manure used to treat the hides and the rotting flesh scraped from them before being burned.

"How's school going?" Jesse inquired one day during a break. "What do you think you might study?"

"School is excellent, sir," Gabe said, looking at the flushed face of the six-foot-tall, broad-shouldered man. "I want to be a lawyer. I especially enjoy the philosophy class. Next year, I might take a geology class Miami is offering.”

“Ulyss liked geology at West Point,” Jesse said, speaking of his son, whom Atticus and Ailene knew well but Gabe had never met because Ulyss left for West Point the same year Gabe was born. “You remind me of him a bit. You both love horses, have abolitionist views, and dislike the tanning business,” he chuckled.

“Oh, I don’t mind. I appreciate your hiring me,” Gabe politely replied.

After a slight pause, Jesse said, squinting, “I hear rumors you were in Kansas with John Brown.”

“Uh, yes,” Gabe said, taken aback. “I was for a time.” Trying to change the direction of the conversation, Gabe said, “He told me that he lived with you years ago. He wanted me to give you his regards.” *I won’t mention what he really said about you.*

“That crazy ol’ coot,” Jesse snorted. “He could have gotten you and a lot of other people killed. I’ll bet we haven’t heard the last of him.”

“No, sir. He’s passionate about his ideals.”

“Well, get back to work.” Then, shaking his finger in Gabe’s face, Jesse said in his usual brusque way, “Stay away from Osawatomie Brown!”

The summer flew by. When school started again, it didn’t seem quite as much fun, because Ben Runkle and Dan Cooper had graduated. Gabe sought solace by joining a debating club: the Miami Union Literary Society. The debating club competed weekly against other teams from Miami and other schools to debate the day's issues. Gabe was always amazed that bright, knowledgeable students could dramatically disagree on a subject. *I learn so much from these discussions*, he thought as he finished preparing for that week's debate: "Who is a Negro?"

Billy Ray Anderson, from Tennessee and a member of Miami's snobbish rival, Erodelphian Literary Society, started off the debate. He gave an impassioned talk, then ended his argument, "If a person has even one drop of Black blood, that person is a Negro. A person is either white or Black. There has to be a way to keep the races separate and preserve the white race's purity and sanctity, to keep us from becoming a mongrel race."

Gabe had to stifle his anger and regain his composure before speaking. His position became more passionate as he went along, ending his remarks, "The one-drop rule is nothing more than bigotry and prejudice. 'Who is a Negro?' really *is* simple. The Declaration of Independence says, 'All men are created equal.' A Negro is a man, and endowed by the Creator with unalienable rights to life, liberty, and the pursuit of happiness."

Some in the audience roared their approval. Some hissed and booed.

"You know, Zeb," Gabe said over a beer after the debate, "I'm scared. I felt the uncontrollable rage I had at Pottawatomie coming on tonight. I wanted to bust Billy Ray."

"That's not a good thing," Zeb said, lowering his voice. "Where do you think that comes from?"

Gabe paused and thought. He said, "When I feel that rage building, I relive the slave auction and Marcus raping Jasmine," experiences he had discussed at length with his friend.

"You'll need to find a way to control your anger," Zeb cautioned.

"You're right. But it's not easy."

Gabe's love for learning continued to grow during the second semester, although he was happy that it would be his last semester of Latin. He found Guizot's *The History of Civilization in Europe* remarkable and read everything he could by Thoreau, Ralph Waldo Emerson, and Walt Whitman. One day, when Gabe returned to his room, he found a letter from Jasmine waiting for him.

North Buxton, Canada West, May 10, 1858

Dear Gabe,

I hope this letter finds you doing fine. I think of you often and look forward to a time when we can be together. Mama and Hattie are doing fine and have expanded the bakery. Levi is still working at the lumber mill. He looks just like I remember Daddy. Glory is getting better at reading and is learning to write. She's so smart and precious. She sings like a nightingale.

I have to tell you where I've been the last 2 days—Chatham, in Canada West, just a few miles from where we live. Guess who I met? John Brown!!! He was in town raising money and men for his next mission and called this his Chatham Convention. There were about

50 people, most of them colored. He didn't go into detail about his plans, except to say he was going to go into the South, free slaves, and send them north. He wants men from Canada to go with him, but it sounds risky. He even talked about a new country with its own Constitution where Black men and women would be equal to whites and could vote, testify, own property, and sit on juries. Can you imagine such things?

He seemed to know all about Glory and me. Captain Brown was just as you described. No wonder you admire him so. Several of his sons, including Oliver, were there. Oliver asked how his "brother" was! They all wanted to know everything I knew about what you were doing.

I sure hope you can come and visit. We all miss you and want to see you again.

With fondness,
Jasmine

Gabe smiled at his memories of his time with her as he wrote her a long reply. *To think that the Browns and Jasmine got to meet each other. That's exciting.*

Gabe worked at Grant's tannery again during the summer of 1858 to enable him to return to Miami. He made another trip to Buxton. The walks with Jasmine got longer, and their deep conversations, including discussing the society's debate topics and arguments and her time with Brown and his sons, lasted well into the night. He was forging a strong emotional bond with Glory.

Upon his return to Miami, he was eager to begin the semester in another philosophy class with Professor Smythe. He hurried to class on a crisp fall morning.

"Welcome, gentlemen. There is so much to discuss and do this fall," Professor Smythe began his first lecture. "The rising tension in the West with the 'Indian problem,' the events in Kansas, and the political intrigue are all happening at the same time. We will take a field trip to Galesburg, Illinois, to attend a debate between two candidates running for the Senate in Illinois. You've all heard of the 'Little Giant,' Stephen Douglas. His opponent is Abraham Lincoln, a lawyer from Springfield, who isn't well known outside of Illinois, but his views against the expansion of slavery and pro-unionism are catching on."

"When do we go?" Gabe asked, his voice rising, not disclosing his relationship with Lincoln after being ridiculed for claiming he knew John Brown.

"The debate is on October seventh," Professor Smythe replied. "We'll leave the day before."

After weeks of building excitement, the day to leave arrived. Gabe joined five other students and Professor Smythe on the train ride to Galesburg.

"Nobody's ever heard of Lincoln. Douglas is bound to win the Senate seat. Why are these debates so important?" Whitelaw asked.

"Whether slavery is going to spread or not is coming to a head, and these debates are directly on that point," the professor answered. "Douglas's Democratic Party is losing support in the South because it won't adopt a strict, pro-slavery platform. Douglas won't budge from his popular sovereignty stance. Lincoln is a growing voice of the new Republican Party. If the Democrats can't rally the South, the Republicans could win the 1860 presidential election. That means that Seward or Chase will probably be our next president—and the South won't stand for that."

"Back to the secession threat," Gabe added.

"Correct. Because of that threat," Professor Smythe continued, "these debates are catching attention nationwide. The Chicago newspapers send shorthand reporters to take down every word, and then the newspapers print the debates within a day or two."

They arrived in Galesburg amid a hard, cold rain and were soaked and nearly hypothermic when they reached the Knox College dormitory where Professor Smythe had arranged for them to stay.

The following day dawned bright but cold, with a biting wind. To shield the debaters as much as possible from the elements, a group of men dragged the debate platform from the open town square to the protected east side of Old Main, a three-story, red brick building on Knox's campus.

"As I told you on the train, I met Mr. Lincoln several years ago," Gabe said to his teacher. "I doubt he'll remember me, but I'm going to try to see him before the debate begins."

"I'll come with you," Professor Smythe enthusiastically replied, despite giving up a great vantage point on a dormitory roof east of Old Main.

Thousands of people crowded the area, and Gabe and Professor Smythe had difficulty pushing their way toward the door of Old Main, where they were sure Lincoln and Douglas would appear before the debate. Banners hung everywhere supporting or vilifying each candidate: one showing Douglas slashing a Kansas Constitution with a pen, another with Lincoln cavorting with Black women. Several women had "White Men or None" embroidered on their aprons to support Douglas. The anticipation became palpable as Galesburg residents, college students, and out-of-towners continued to assemble.

Gabe's eyes scanned the large crowd, looking for some sign of the debaters. *This is as exciting as when I first saw Captain Brown in Akron. It's hard to believe the man I showed around Cincinnati is getting this much attention.*

"There's some commotion over there," Professor Smythe said, pointing away from Old Main.

"*Look*, there he is," Gabe yelled, jabbing his index finger back and forth toward the tall man sporting a stovepipe hat and working his way out of a carriage.

ELEVEN

"A HOUSE DIVIDED AGAINST ITSELF CANNOT STAND."

October 7, 1858–August 10, 1859

Douglas's four-horse carriage arrived at almost the same time as Lincoln's. A great stirring occurred as the crowd parted like the Red Sea at Moses' command, allowing Lincoln and Douglas, each surrounded by a throng of supporters, to approach Old Main. Lincoln, towering over the crowd, waved to the cheering masses.

As Gabe had hoped, Lincoln had to pass directly in front of them. Lincoln carried an old cotton umbrella in one hand and a well-worn black case in the other, which matched his scuffed and unpolished boots and the battered stovepipe hat sitting high atop his head. He wore a long, dirty, light-colored duster to ward off the chill.

Lincoln's and Gabe's eyes made contact. Gabe waved and shouted above the din of the multitude, "Mr. Lincoln! Mr. Lincoln!"

Lincoln's eyes lit up. "Why, young Mr. Gabe, my abolitionist tour guide," he said as he draped his arm over Gabe's shoulder and yelled in his ear. "How are you, my friend? It's nice to see a friendly face—even one who might not agree with everything I have to say," he laughed.

Professor Smythe was dumbstruck.

Looking at Smythe's face, Gabe thought, *I don't think he believed I knew Lincoln.* "Mr. Lincoln, I'd like you to meet Professor Jackson Smythe."

"Glad to meet you," Lincoln replied. "Men, I could use a little help. Would you be my seconds in this duel? Keep Douglas to his time, get me water, that sort of thing."

Now, Gabe was as stunned as his professor. "Of course," he stammered. "We'd be honored to assist."

With that, an official escorted Lincoln and Douglas into Old Main and through an opening where workers had removed a window so they could access the recently moved platform. Lincoln towered over the short and stocky Douglas by a foot, but it appeared to be more, with his long legs and tall hat. *Douglas is more handsome and well dressed, but he has stumps for legs and is all paunch*, Gabe observed.

To the utter amazement of their fellow Miami students on the dormitory rooftop, Gabe and Professor Smythe came through the window opening, and a marshal ushered them to a seat on the side of the platform with other dignitaries.

Lincoln removed the duster, exposing threadbare pants and a black coat, both too short for his long legs and arms. Underneath the coat, he wore a white shirt with its collar turned down over a thin black tie. Handing the cloak to Gabe, Lincoln said, "Please hold this. I've got to go stone Stephen!"

As Lincoln walked past Douglas, Gabe heard Douglas say, "How long, O Lord, how long?" which Gabe recognized from the Book of Psalms.

Lincoln looked down at Douglas and retorted with a quote Gabe knew was from Proverbs, "The days and years of the wicked are short."

Before their first debate, the candidates had agreed on a format. In the odd-numbered debates, Douglas would go first for an hour, Lincoln would follow for an hour and a half, and Douglas had thirty minutes to rebut, and vice versa in the even-numbered debates. This being the fifth debate, Douglas went first.

Three tremendous cheers greeted Douglas. "Ladies and Gentlemen," he began with his typical bluster, "as you know, I support the compromise measures of 1850 and the Kansas-Nebraska bill that rest on the great fundamental principle of popular sovereignty. I carried the banner of that cause aloft and never allowed it to trail in the dust nor lowered my flag until victory perched upon our arms."

Cheers erupted, "That's so!" "You did all that!"

I've read about Douglas's legendary oratory skills, Gabe thought. *The papers say he speaks with a deep, precise, and clear voice. But today, he sounds raspy and hoarse.*

Douglas continued his criticism of the Republican Party, pacing the platform like a caged animal: "It is a sectional organization which appeals to the passion, pride, ambition, and prejudices of the Northern section of the Union and is against

Southern people, states, and institutions. No political creed is sound which a person cannot proclaim fearlessly in every state of this Union."

"Hear, hear!" reacted the crowd. "Give it to him!"

His voice was weakening, despite the Smith Brothers cough drops he periodically popped into his mouth. Changing course toward *Dred Scott*, he continued, "Unlike Mr. Lincoln, I support the *Dred Scott* decision. The Declaration of Independence's signers never dreamed of the Negro as a man or equal when writing the document. Under our Constitution, the Negro is not a citizen, cannot be a citizen, and ought not to be a citizen. The Black race is indisputably incapable of self-government and enslaved naturally. Lincoln and the Black Republicans want to free the slaves, make them citizens with the right to vote, hold office, become legislators, jurors, and judges, and ultimately marry your daughters."

"NO!" "We won't let them!"

When the crowd quieted, Douglas said, smirking, "So, if you want Sambo riding in a carriage with your wife and daughter whilst you drive the team, then vote for Mr. Lincoln!"

Gales of laughter swept across the grassy square in front of the platform. Gabe was incensed at his fellow Americans. *How can so many people agree with that bigoted and prejudiced statement?*

Douglas scanned the crowd, smiling at the reaction he was getting. Puffing out his chest, he continued, "Here in Illinois, we rightfully deprive the Negro of political rights and correctly refuse to put him into equality with white men."

Gabe desperately wanted to speak out against Douglas's words. He made eye contact with a Black man near the front who was shaking his head, his eyes flashing.

After going on for his allotted hour, Douglas, pointing his index finger into the air and raising his voice as best he could, finished, "If we administer this government as our fathers made it and every state minds her own business, there will be peace between the North and the South."

And there will still be the enslaved, Gabe wanted to scream.

The crowd tripled the three cheers they had given at the beginning, and Douglas sat down with a wave and a satisfied look.

The crowd cheered wildly as Lincoln approached the platform, chanting, "Lincoln! "Lincoln! Lincoln!" *I'm glad he's getting as much support as Douglas.* He removed his tall hat, pulled notes from it, and returned it atop his unkempt hair. Then he cleared his throat, put one arm behind his back, and began: "Senator Douglas accuses me of 'wishing' that slavery would die, but I don't 'wish' for slavery to die any more than I 'wish' to die; however, I do expect it to die just as I expect someday, I will die."

Parts of the crowd erupted in laughter, yelling, "You got him on that one!"

Despite the shrillness of Lincoln's voice and its backwoods twang, Gabe enjoyed the measured pace and timely pauses as Lincoln addressed the multitude.

"Dred Scott and Mr. Douglas are wrong," Lincoln continued, bending his knees then rising on his toes to tower over the crowd even more. "The Declaration may be searched in vain for one

single affirmation that the Negro was not included within its meaning."

"That's right!" half the crowd yelled. "Hurrah for Lincoln!"

"I do not believe the Negro is entitled to equal civil rights with the white race," Lincoln said as he became more animated, raising his arms at an angle above his head, his fingers outstretched. "I have all the while maintained that social and political equality between the Black and white races is impossible. I am in favor of the race to which I belong having the superior position. But I firmly believe the Negro is entitled to his natural rights; however, just because I do not want a Negro woman for a slave does not mean I must necessarily want her for a wife."

Cheers and laughter resounded. "Hit him again!"

"*Dred Scott*, taken to its logical and legitimate consequences, will allow all states to establish slavery. I have no purpose to interfere with the institution of slavery in the states where it exists, but it should not be extended into new areas."

Lincoln was interrupted by an extended loud cheer. He turned to Gabe and Smythe, gave them a wink, and motioned for something to drink. Gabe jumped up, handed him a glass of water, and nodded in support and encouragement. Lincoln wiped his brow despite the unpleasant temperature and grabbed his lapel with his left hand. "My greatest trouble with Senator Douglas's position," Lincoln continued, pointing a long, bony forefinger in the Little Giant's direction, "is that every sentiment he utters discards the idea that there is anything morally wrong with slavery."

"You got him!" supporters yelled amid tremendous applause. "That's the doctrine!"

"I believe," Lincoln went on, "that Douglas and whoever like him teaches that the Negro has no share, humble though it may be, in the Declaration of Independence, is muzzling the cannon that thunders its annual joyous return. He is blowing out the moral lights around us when he maintains that anyone who wants slaves has a right to hold them."

"Bravo!" "That's so!"

"My time is almost up," Lincoln said. "This slavery question has been the only issue that ever endangered our republican institutions. It's a problem that threatens, menaces, and disturbs us in such a way as to make us fear for the perpetuity of our liberty and our Union." Quoting from the Bible, Lincoln concluded, his voice rising several notches both in tone and volume. "'A house divided against itself cannot stand.' The country cannot survive half-free and half-slave. I do not expect the Union to dissolve, but I do expect it will cease being divided. It will become all one thing or all the other. Allowing the expansion of slavery by any means will add to the disturbance between us and threaten the perpetuity of our Union."

Thunderous cheers arose as Lincoln tipped his hat to the crowd and took his seat, smiling and nodding at Gabe and Professor Smythe.

Douglas charged to the front of the platform to respond in his remaining thirty minutes. Some in the crowd called for six cheers. "There is no moral question involved," Douglas feverishly argued in rebuttal, white foam appearing on the corners of his mouth, his voice harsh and rough. "Lincoln himself acknowledges the inferiority of the Negro and the impossibility of that race being socially or politically equal to whites. It is only a question of degree, not a question of right."

"That's correct!" "You got 'em on that!" many in the crowd shouted, so loud that Douglas had to quiet them before he could continue.

"Mr. Lincoln attacks the *Dred Scott* opinion," Douglas heated up, shaking his fist. "Suppose he succeeds in destroying public confidence in the Court so that the people will not respect its decisions but feel at liberty to disregard them and resist the laws of the land? What will he have gained?"

"Nothing!" "Anarchy!" the gallery chanted.

"My friends, Mr. Lincoln's 'house divided' comment is an open invitation for war. Our founders divided this government into free and slave states and left each state to have its say on the subject of slavery. Why can't this country exist on the same principles our forefathers believed?"

Douglas wiped his forehead and thanked the gathering. The crowd roared, "Hoorah!" "Huzzah!" each side trying to outshout the other.

Lincoln and Douglas shook hands, then separated to celebrate with their respective supporters. Gabe handed the coat back to Mr. Lincoln. "My friend," Lincoln said to Gabe, "Did I manage to change your views on immediate emancipation?"

"Uh, no, sir," Gabe shouted over the crowd's raucous noise. "The Negro should be free immediately, even if it takes force. But I sure like your position a lot better than his."

"Well, Son," Lincoln said with admiration in his voice and laying a large hand on Gabe's shoulder, "I pray you are wrong about the force part." Lincoln turned away and began mixing with the crowd, shaking hands and enjoying an abundance of backslaps and "atta-boys."

As the Miami crew headed toward the train station and their return to Oxford, Gabe was practically glowing. "We were part of history," he said. "Will the powers of slavery or the hosts of freedom prevail?"

Professor Smythe added, "I think the questions and answers put forth in these debates will determine our next president and the future of our country."

The rest of the year passed quickly and uneventfully. Graduation was a jubilant scene. Gabe could see his father, mother, Raphael, and Caroline beaming with pride as he gave them a little wave. *I wish Jasmine could be here.*

Upon his return to Georgetown, Gabe began his apprenticeship with Uncle Nathaniel. On his first day in the office, Gabe rubbed his eyes, leaned back in his chair, and clasped his hands behind his head: *Uncle Nat thinks after three years of reading the law, I'll be ready to be tested and become a lawyer. I can't wait.*

In early August, however, a telegraph messenger announced, "Telegram for Gabriel Adams."

Gabe's heart pounded, and his breath became labored.

Post Office Department

TELEGRAM

Gabe. I need your teamster assistance. Going
into Africa is imminent. If you are able, meet
Jr in Cleveland and pick up wagon full of supplies and bring them to me. Need them soon. Jr
has rest of information. JB

"What does he mean?' Raph asked Gabe that night as they lay in bed.

"He's going into the South. He threatened this action in Kansas and during the Chatham Convention."

"Does he really expect slaves to revolt with him?"

"He believes they will."

"This will be far riskier and more dangerous than Kansas," Raph said, trying to talk sense into his little brother. "Those were skirmishes; this would be war."

"How can I tell him no? But I don't know if I'm brave enough to tell him yes. I didn't hesitate to go to Kansas. I've wanted to fight for this cause since I was thirteen, and here's my chance. So why am I hesitating now?"

"Maybe because you are scared just like you ought to be. I couldn't talk you out of going to Kansas, but I've got to stop you from doing this."

"Raph, I have to put my words into action. How can I let the Captain down by not going?" *And Jasmine.*

"Who would you rather let down—John Brown or Pops and Mother?"

Gabe tossed and turned all night. Thoughts returned of sev-ered arms, brains on the ground, and his body sprayed with blood. As dawn broke, he made the decision: *I can't do it. I'm not going.*

At work the next day, Gabe remained troubled. Then, his worst nightmare appeared in the doorway: Marcus.

"Hey, cuz, it's been a long time. Are you still mad at me?"

"Get out of my sight, you ass."

"Aw, c'mon, grow up and get over it. I understand you wouldn't tell my father what happened. If it was such a big deal, why not tell him and get it off your chest?"

"If it's not a big deal, why don't *you* tell him?" Gabe said, his words dripping with venom.

Marcus waved him off. "So, do you still think you are Don Quixote and can do anything to end slavery?

"Damn right, I do."

"Good luck with that," Marcus snickered, then turned on his heel and went to ask his father for money.

Gabe's mind flashed to Marcus raping Jasmine, the fighting in Kansas, the long talks with Jasmine. His thoughts became a discussion with Jasmine. *What should I do, Jasmine? [I can't tell you.] Would you be disappointed in me if I didn't help? [I'm not sure I'd be disappointed, but not going isn't the Gabriel I know.] What if I am killed? [What if you stay home and live?]*

He knew what he had to do. His friend and mentor—and the cause—needed him. *What am I going to tell Pops and Mother?* Gabe pondered. *Do I dare reveal the truth? Even if I tell the truth, I won't let them stop me.*

That night at dinner, Gabe took a long drink of milk, swallowed hard, inhaled a deep breath, and began: "Pops and

Mother, something has come up, and I'm going to leave for a while," he began.

"Are you off to see Jasmine?" Pops teased.

Gabe blushed at his father's suggestion. He had been thinking about going to Canada, but now he had a different mission.

"No, a friend . . . ," and at that instant, Gabe decided he could tell the whole truth. "John Brown needs my help. He's asked me to bring supplies to him. I have to meet Junior in Cleveland to find out where," he said boldly, trying not to sound defiant.

Ailene gasped, her eyes widened, and she put her hands on her cheeks. "You are not going with that madman again. He almost got you killed in Kansas. He's willing to lose his children as part of his insanity. I will not let him take mine."

"Son, this is *not* a good idea," Atticus said, thoughts swirling in his head and a huge knot forming in his stomach.

"I've made up my mind. This is my time," Gabe quietly replied as he looked deep into his mother's eyes. "This isn't just John Brown's fight, and he is not insane. I'm almost twenty, and I can make my own decisions. If I die for this noble cause, then so be it."

Shocked by the callousness in his tone, Atticus scolded Gabe in a way he had rarely done before, "How *dare* you say such a thing to your mother?"

"I'm sorry, Mother. You know how much this cause means to me."

Atticus took Ailene's hand, caressed it, and asked Gabe, "What else can you tell us?"

"All I know is what I've told you," Gabe said, looking at his father intently. "I'm guessing he is planning a raid to free slaves—kind of a Nat Turner type of rebellion."

"No one will come back alive from such foolishness!" Atticus warned with great alarm. "The day may come when there will be fighting over the enslaved, and everyone must decide where they stand. But following this crazy idea is not the way."

"Pops, you always said ending slavery is your life's dream. It is mine, too. It's time to take a stand."

Atticus looked at Ailene, then back to Gabe. "We cannot stop you from doing what you think is right. You do *not* have our blessing or encouragement, but you *do* have our prayers. We love you and have faith in you."

Tears fell from Ailene's eyes. She knew she could not change Atticus's or Gabe's mind.

"When are you leaving?" Atticus asked.

"Tomorrow."

Ailene stumbled to her feet and went behind Gabe's chair. Putting her arms around his neck, she whispered, "Please don't do this. My children are what makes my life worth living. I love you too much to lose you."

"Mother, I love you more than anything, but I know you want me to stand up for what I believe in."

Holding a towel over her mouth, she ran to the kitchen.

That night, Gabe asked Raph, "What would you do if you were in my shoes?"

"I have no idea what it's like to be in your shoes, but I know you'll kick yourself with them if you *don't* go."

The next day, Ailene packed some food for Gabe, convinced in her heart that this would be the last time she would provide for him. Her tearful goodbye melted Gabe's heart and nearly his resolve.

Atticus and Gabe rode silently into Georgetown.

Upon arrival, Atticus said, choking back his emotions, "Son, be careful. Do what you must, but please come back, for your mother's sake."

"I will, Pops," Gabe said with false bravado. Overcome, Gabe grabbed his father tightly. Atticus squeezed as if his life depended on it. Only the sound of the arrival of the horses and coach broke their embrace.

Gabe boarded the coach. He did not look back or wave. He might have gotten off if he had.

Part II

Righteous Hope

TWELVE

"Let disunion come."

August 10, 1859–October 20, 1859

Gabe's hand jerked to a stop, his knuckles inches from Junior's door. *What's in store for me? Jasmine and Glory deserve to have me take action, but is this suicide? The Captain needs me . . . Oh, the hell with it.* He rapped with conviction.

"Ah, Gabe, it's nice to see you again," Junior said with a broad smile as he opened the door. "I didn't know if you'd come. I'm not sure if I would have if I were you. Come on in."

Junior beckoned Gabe to a seat in the sparsely furnished parlor. Only a few rays of sun found their way through the drawn curtains. Junior poured two fingers of Old Crow bourbon into tumblers and asked, "How are you doing?"

"Fine. I finished school and am reading the law with my uncle."

"No. How are you *doing*?" he said, handing a glass to Gabe.

"Not too bad," Gabe replied, swirling the liquid gold and inhaling the stinging fumes before taking a small sip, holding it in his mouth a moment before swallowing. "I still get awful flashbacks, but they come less often and don't seem to rattle me as much. How about you?"

"I'm not doing well after Frederick's death and all the killing in Kansas. I drink too much, which, as you know, Father disapproves of. Instead of joining him, I will try to raise money and recruits."

"I'm sorry you can't go, but I understand."

Over dinner, Junior outlined what he knew about his father's undertaking and his request of Gabe. "If you agree to do this, you'll be hauling a load of weapons to a place in Virginia near Harper's Ferry, where my brothers and others are gathering. I don't know his exact plans, but I know he's taking the battle into Africa."

"The least I can do is deliver the goods, but I don't know if I'll join up after that."

"Father hoped he could count on you, especially since I let him down," Junior said. "A recruit, Dangerfield Newby, will be going with you."

The following morning, Gabe met Dangerfield. In his mid-thirties, he stood ramrod erect, with his broad shoulders pulled back in dignity. His tired and worn face had bags under his otherwise alert, clear eyes. Dangerfield was eager to get going.

"You're going into Virginia to join John Brown?" Gabe asked incredulously, admiring the risk this man was taking for the cause.

"Yes. I was freed last year by my former massa," Dangerfield said. "But my wife an' six chillen are in Virginia and their massa won't free 'em an' may even be gettin' ready to sell 'em. Not only is I going to help Cap'n Brown," he added, his voice cracking, "I's going to rescue my fam'ly."

Junior, Dangerfield, and Gabe hitched two horses to a wagon Junior had purchased, then they rode to a furniture warehouse in nearby Ashtabula. Hidden below a pile of coffins were long boxes similar to those taken to Kansas. They loaded the wagon and covered the boxes with hay for the horses and other supplies Brown had requested. Gabe and Dangerfield said goodbye to Junior and headed southeast toward Pittsburg. It was odd to have a Black man riding openly in the wagon with him, but Gabe enjoyed his company, and they exchanged stories about their backgrounds, dreams, and fears about what lay ahead.

"I's got nothing to lose," Dangerfield confided. "I's free, but 'til my wife and chillen are free, I's got nothing. B'sides, my friend Cap'n Brown have bigger plans for my people. He need my help."

"I hope he has more people with your enthusiasm helping him."

"If I has anythin' to do wid it, he will."

The journey was the opposite of the hot, dusty, slow venture to Kansas. Despite the wagon's load, they made good time across Pennsylvania on the well-traveled Pittsburgh Pike, a twenty-five-foot-wide macadam road made of small pieces of broken, angular rock compressed into a smooth, hard surface by the wagon traffic. Arched stone bridges crossed the creeks and streams. *Little Benjamin would still be alive if there had been bridges like these on the way to Canada.*

On the third day of the trip, they were beginning Sideling Hill's steep ascent. Dangerfield was asleep and Gabe was daydreaming, when three men on horses bounded out of the trees bordering the road, galloped straight at them, and slid to a stop, all before Gabe could grab his rifle. The eldest of the three, a plug-ugly man with a pockmarked face and two kinds of teeth—rotten and gone—grabbed the reins from Gabe. The other two lowlifes leveled guns at Gabe and Dangerfield, who had jerked upright in his seat.

"Where's ya goin' wid Sambo?" demanded the poor excuse for a man holding the reins.

"It's none of your business," Gabe snapped. "'Sides, he's a free man. Show 'em your papers."

"We're makin' it our bizness," one of the riflemen said as he snatched the papers out of Dangerfield's hand. After examining the papers, the man said, "Well, Hank, it 'pears he's free. These here his . . . what they called? . . . man-ee-mission papers."

"Guess'n if'n we burn these papers up, we could turn you in and make us some money."

"You do, and I'll have half of Pennsylvania on you faster than greased lightnin'," Gabe sneered as he glared back. "Ever'body between here and Bedford love this man."

"Big talk, Nancy-boy. I'll whup yo' ass," the youngest said.

"Let 'em go," the leader said. "Mo' problem than they's wu'th. Give 'em back his papers."

Dangerfield found sleep hard to come by after that.

It took another day to get to Chambersburg. There, they headed south toward Harper's Ferry through Maryland. It was risky for Dangerfield to ride in the open through a slave state, but bounty hunters weren't all that suspicious about a Black man driving a wagon loaded with supplies heading south with a white man by his side.

A few miles past Sharpsburg, they came to an old red barn with "Africa" painted on its side. "This is the turn," Gabe said, following Junior's directions. "We go about a mile and look for a farmhouse with a blue star quilt hanging on the porch."

They found the run-down farmhouse and a log cabin, which Brown had rented from a man named Kennedy, set back from the road about fifty yards, partially hidden by thick underbrush and surrounded by trees. As they turned off the main road, a brown and white mongrel puppy romped toward them, raising a storm of barking. Brown came out on the front porch to check on the commotion. Seeing the wagon, Brown yelled at the yapping dog, "Cuff, enough!" then ran to meet the newcomers. "Welcome to the Kennedy Farm."

Gabe sarcastically greeted his hero as he climbed down from the wagon, "This is some place you got here, Cap'n!"

"If you don't like it, then unload this wagon, turn your sorry fanny around, and go back to Ohio," Brown teased, then embraced Gabe, whom he had not seen since Kansas. "Son, I'm sorry to drag you into this business, but there was no one else I could trust other than my boys. Junior sent a telegram when you left, but we didn't expect you for another day or two."

"It's good to get here and to see you. It helped that we had good weather." Gabe turned toward his passenger and said, "Captain Brown, this is Dangerfield Newby."

"Such a pleasure to meet you," Brown said. "Junior speaks very highly of you. Welcome to the farm. Y'all need to come inside and meet the gang. They stay out of sight, so the neighbors won't see how many folks we've got here."

Oliver, Watson, and Owen Brown were eager to see Gabe, and all the other "soldiers" were happy to meet him. Everyone was pleased to meet Dangerfield, the first Black man to join their force. Oliver threw his arm around Gabe's shoulders and teased him about Jasmine's gushing about Gabe when the Browns met her in Chatham. Gabe was jealous that Oliver, not he, had seen her.

"This is my wife, Martha," Oliver said, introducing one of two women in the entryway. Martha was petite, with short-cropped pale brown hair and blue-gray eyes. Gabe guessed she was about sixteen, and he noticed a distinctive bump under her apron. Motioning to the other woman, who appeared a bit younger than Martha, Oliver continued, "This is my sister, Annie." She was rather plain looking, her brown hair pulled back tightly into a bun, but she flashed a big smile. "They came to cook and clean for us," Oliver explained.

The new arrivals went up the stairs to the attic, a large room with a low, slanted ceiling and no furniture or any place to sit except on boxes that were marked "mining tools" and "hardware and castings" but which really contained rifles, ammunition, and black powder. The men spent the evening getting to know one another and exchanged stories about how they had met Brown and why they were on this mission.

Martha and Annie had the run of the house, which included a basement storeroom, a kitchen, a parlor where Brown slept, and a small bedroom that Annie, Oliver, and Martha shared.

The women called the men in the attic "The Invisibles," although the men called themselves "The Prisoners."

Several days after his arrival, Brown told Gabe to get the wagon ready for a trip to Chambersburg to meet someone important as well as John Kagi, his second-in-command, who had left the Kennedy Farm a month earlier to procure men, supplies, and money. Gabe looked forward to the trip with Brown, much like he enjoyed trips with his father.

Along the way, Brown told Gabe who they were meeting and the purpose of the trip. Despite knowing those things, Gabe was in awe when he saw the great Frederick Douglass awaiting them in an abandoned quarry. Douglass had an impressive mane of curly dark hair framing his face, and flashing, piercing eyes. He was well dressed in a blue coat, white silk shirt, gold tie, and vest. He carried himself with a dignified air. Brown introduced Gabe to Kagi and Douglass, and Douglass introduced Shields Green, a Black man who was with him.

"I need you to join us, Frederick," Brown pleaded, wearing an old, storm-beaten hat and drab clothing and carrying a fishing rod to disguise the real purpose of the meeting. Gabe was struck by the reversal of stereotypes between the way the two men, leaders in the fight for the same cause, dressed.

With urgent determination, Brown described his plan to Douglass.

"Why not go straight to the hills and raid plantations?" Douglass inquired, his square jaw and firm-set mouth magnifying his serious demeanor. "Running off the enslaved is one thing. Trying to take the armory could startle the nation and turn people against our cause."

"Seems that something startling is just what the nation needs. I drew my sword in Kansas and will not sheathe it until this war is over."

"Attacking the arsenal is a steel trap," Douglass warned him. "Once in, escape will be impossible. You will never get out alive."

Brown dismissed Douglass's logic as if swatting away a fly. "Remember the trumpets of Jericho? Harper's Ferry will be mine. The news of its capture will be the horn's blast that will rally the enslaved to my standard from miles around." He put his hand over his heart. "But I need you for a special purpose. The bees will swarm when I strike, and I shall want you to help hive them. Together, we will bring slavery down. I will defend you with my life."

"When you are captured or killed, it will be worse for those in bondage than before," Douglass said, shaking his head.

"We will take captives," Brown continued. "The best citizens in the neighborhood, the descendants of presidents. If we cannot cut our way out, we will use our hostages to dictate the terms of our release."

"No, I will not go. Virginians will blow you and your hostages sky-high rather than let you hold Harper's Ferry for an hour." Despite his decision not to join Brown, Douglass turned to Shields and asked, "What do you want to do? Go back with me or stay with Captain Brown?"

"I b'lieve I'll go wid de ol' man," Shields replied. "If dis white man is willing to die for de Black man, I's willing to die wid him."

They loaded the wagon with the supplies Kagi had brought, then shook hands. Douglass rode north with Kagi, who would continue his quest for recruits and money.

Brown's shoulders slumped more than usual, and he rubbed his head with both hands as he watched his friend depart.

He looks like he feels abandoned, Gabe thought.

Recovering his stoicism, Brown said, "Let's go, men. Don't tell the others the plans I discussed with Douglass. I'm not ready to reveal the details until I work out a few things." Brown, Shields, and Gabe got into the wagon and headed back to the farm.

With the addition of Shields, eighteen men crammed into the two farmhouses on the Kennedy Farm. So as not to arouse the suspicion of their few neighbors, the small army remained hidden throughout the day in the large attic of one house. Martha often sat as a sentry on the front porch, enjoying the katydids and whippoorwills. At her signal that someone was approaching the house, the men in the attic went silent. One neighbor, Elizabeth Huffmaster, an incredibly nosy busybody, frequently made unannounced visits to the farm, trailed by her four dirty, barefoot, and practically naked children—"a worse plague and torment than fleas," Annie complained.

The days were tedious and repetitious. Each morning began with Captain Brown reading from his Bible and praying for the mission and the deliverance of the enslaved. Gabe and the men passed the time in the loft, bronzing their guns, practicing loading them, and learning hand-to-hand combat under the tutelage of one of their members, Captain Aaron Stevens. Several men couldn't read, so Gabe read newspapers and books aloud, including Thomas Paine's *The Age of Reason* and the Forbes *Manual of the Patriotic Volunteer.* They fashioned leather into belts and pouches, played cards, debated religion and politics, and exchanged life stories. Captain Stevens led them with a fine baritone voice as they softly sang songs, including Gabe's favorites, "Nearer My God to Thee" and "Faded Flowers."

Only at night did they dare venture outside to exercise and breathe fresh air. Some of the men, unbeknownst to Brown, risked discovery by sneaking into town, although Gabe and Brown's sons declined their invitations to go along.

Buying food and supplies in Harper's Ferry for so many men would raise eyebrows, so Brown sent Gabe to Chambersburg once a week, which was a blessing to Gabe, as it got him away from the stench of unbathed and gassy men and out of the cramped attic.

One day toward the end of September, Brown sent Gabe to Chambersburg to pick up a load of freight and another man. A man with a handsome face, deep, dark, penetrating eyes, and close-cropped hair and beard was waiting for Gabe at a prearranged rendezvous location. Like Dangerfield, he had come from a land of freedom to join Brown in the South.

"Hello, suh, I am Osborne Anderson from Chatham, Canada West," he said, extending his hand. "I signed up to be with the Captain at the Chatham Convention. Junior told me it was time I got down here."

"So pleased to meet you. I am Gabriel Adams from Ohio. I must ask: if you were at the Chatham Convention, perhaps you met a friend of mine, Miss Jasmine French."

"Why, suh, of course I know Miss Jasmine. And you must be the Mr. Adams she talked about. I tried courtin' her, but she never seemed interested. I think she has more feelings for you than just as a friend. She's a special woman."

Gabe turned his eyes away, blushed, and toed the ground, unsure how to respond to such a comment. After briefly pausing, he said, "Yes, she is." He paused again. "It's good to have you here."

They went to the railyard, loaded the wagon with long crates, square wooden boxes, and heavy canvas bags, then began the trip south.

The Prisoners, especially Dangerfield and Shields, welcomed Osborne into their clan. When they unloaded the wagon, Gabe saw that the crates from the railyard were filled with hundreds of six-foot-long ash shafts. The boxes had a similar number of two-edged, ten-inch-long dirks, and the bags contained metal collars to attach the two pieces. Everyone spent several days attaching the blades to the poles. "I designed these pikes," Brown said proudly. "The dirk is modeled after the bowie knife I took from Henry Pate at Black Jack. I paid a blacksmith in Connecticut one dollar apiece to make them. I plan to arm the freed slaves with the pikes until each learns how to fire a gun."

"Those pikes are no match for rifles," Captain Stevens challenged.

"They'll know how to use a pike. Give one to a slave, and you make him a man," Brown told him.

Brown was making final plans, which he hoped to implement within a month. "Men," Brown began when he finally laid out his strategy, "We'll split into teams. One team will cut the telegraph lines, take command of the railroad, and capture the Federal Armory at the Ferry. Another team will take our guns and pikes to Loudoun Heights. After we take the Armory, a team will go out and capture hostages from nearby plantations, convincing the slaves to flee or join us. We'll meet at Loudoun Heights, get up into the hills, and begin our mission to free the enslaved and give them a choice to either head north or join our army."

"Why the Armory?" one of the men, William Leeman, asked. "Won't that be well guarded?"

"Actually, it's not guarded much at all," said John Cook, Brown's spy who had spent a year snooping around Harper's Ferry and, much to Brown's disgust, managed to impregnate a local teenager while doing so. "No one would ever suspect an assault on it."

"Not only will taking the Armory let them know we mean business," Brown elaborated, "but we can use the guns and ammunition for our fight."

"What is Loudoun Heights?" Gabe asked.

"It's the gateway to what I call the Great Black Way. The Appalachians' rugged, forested ridges and valleys, angling from Georgia into Pennsylvania and beyond, provide a natural, secluded 'highway' from the South to the North," Brown explained, his excitement rising as he explained each step of the plan.

"Why not wait for the presidential election and see if there is a political compromise?" asked Barclay Coppoc, a once-pacifist

Quaker who had met Brown in Iowa when Brown was leading a group of slaves he had captured in Missouri to freedom.

"Talk, talk, talk! Talk is the national institution, but it doesn't help the enslaved. What is needed is ACTION, ACTION, ACTION!" thundered Brown. "Gradual termination will never occur. We must strike the head of the snake."

Brown sent Annie and Martha back to New York at the end of September. The men serenaded their departure with "Home Again," lamenting that the cooking and cleaning chores were now theirs.

Gabe took the women to the train station in Chambersburg. "We may never see any of you again," Martha said, choking on her tears and holding her growing abdomen. "Please watch over my Oliver. Our child needs a father."

"I'll do what I can," Gabe said, knowing he had little control over the events about to unfold. He waved as the train pulled away from the station. *She's right. I may never see them again— or, for that matter, my family . . . or Jasmine.*

Several days after the women left, Brown told Gabe, "I need you to come with me to Philadelphia. Junior and some others are meeting us there with more supplies."

On the first night away from the Kennedy Farm, the two men camped outside Gettysburg, a small Pennsylvania town. On the cool autumn night, Gabe leaned back and gazed at the Great Dipper, Orion, and the Pleiades. Brown joined him when Gabe began humming "Follow the Drinking Gourd." The smoke from the fire stung his eyes, but its earthy, pungent odor brought back a flood of memories. "This is like sitting around the fire on the way to Kansas," Gabe reminisced.

"The trip on the way to Kansas," Brown smiled, looking far off into the distance, "was the most peaceful time of my life. Those days are over."

"I imagine that's true," Gabe said, swatting away another mosquito.

"I'm getting eaten, too. There are enough mosquitoes here to make a pie. They are worse than at Mosquito Creek."

Brown's comment shattered Gabe's pleasant revelry. He broke out into a sweat, his heart raced, and his breaths became gasps.

"Oh, Gabe, I'm sorry. I shouldn't have said that."

Trying to get the vision of dismembered limbs out of his head, Gabe got up and walked in tight circles, clutching himself. "I've got Junior's problem. Sometimes, I can't shake the memories."

Brown went to his side and held his shoulders. "I know it's difficult fighting for a noble cause. It brings pain and suffering, but it's the right thing to do."

"I know," Gabe said, turning and looking into Brown's steel gray eyes.

Brown guided Gabe back to the fire and gave him a tin cup of water. After a few minutes of silence, Gabe's breathing returned to normal. Brown pulled a dirty, worn roll of paper from his carpetbag. "I haven't shared this with many people, but I thought you'd like to read it. I started it in Chatham, and I've been working on it all summer."

By the light of the fire, Gabe untied the string holding the roll together. He read the large, printed words from the foolscap, which Brown had pasted onto white cloth:

_____ *4*[th]*, 1859*

A DECLARATION OF LIBERTY BY THE REPRESENTATIVES OF THE SLAVE POPULATION OF THE UNITED STATES OF AMERICA

When in the course of human events, it becomes nec-essary for an oppressed People to Rise, and assert their Natural Rights, as Human Beings, as Native and Mutual Citizens of a free Republic, and break that odious yoke of oppression, which is so unjustly laid upon them by their fellow countrymen, and to assume among the powers of Earth the same equal privileges to which the Laws of Nature, and nature's God entitle them . . . Slavery is a history of injustice and cruelties inflicted upon the Slave in every conceivable way . . . it is the embodiment of all that is evil, and ruinous to a nation, and SUBVERSIVE to all Good . . . We will obtain these rights or die in the struggle to obtain them. We make war on oppression.

Gabe read the remainder of the manifesto and handed it back to Brown. "This is powerful."

"Writing it was easy," Brown responded. "Putting it into action will not be. Gabe, I'm concerned Douglass is right that my plan is too risky and has little chance of success. I don't want to put anyone unnecessarily at grave risk."

I don't know what to say. I've never heard the Captain doubt himself.

Brown continued, "I'm ready to die for the cause, but I wonder if it is too much to ask of all of you."

Gabe summoned up the nerve to say what was in his heart. "Captain, we wouldn't be here if we didn't believe in you and the cause. You seem to think it will work. That's enough for me. But, what will happen to your wife and children if something happens to you?"

"That's a good question. Mary has been a saint," Brown replied with a sigh and his hand over his heart. "I haven't been home much for three or four years, and I left her with the worries of lack of money and taking care of our daughters. When I last saw her in June, she was hopping mad that I talked Owen, Oliver, and Watson into joining me here. I'd hate for that to be her last memory of me." He paused, contemplating Gabe's concerns. "I guess my supporters will see she's taken care of."

On that sobering note, they stretched out for the night, leaving Gabe alone with his thoughts. *Will anyone know or remember Captain Brown's sacrifice for the cause? Will whatever we accomplish be worth the bloodshed? Are we walking into the Valley of Death?* Gabe looked at Brown in amazement. *He's already asleep! And his face is at peace.*

When they arrived in Philadelphia, Brown and Gabe met with Junior, Kagi, and Francis Meriam, a one-eyed, scar-faced, physically frail abolitionist from a wealthy family. Francis idolized

Captain Brown and wanted to join his "army." Although Brown was skeptical of Francis's ability to fight due to his poor condition, he couldn't decline Francis's offer of money and munitions as a bribe to take him along.

Several days after their return to the Kennedy Farm, two additional Black men arrived. Sporting a thin mustache and a stiff-brimmed felt hat, Lewis Leary introduced himself and his twenty-five-year-old nephew, John Copeland, and told them that Junior had recruited them at Oberlin. Gabe was pleased to find out they knew Michael and had been part of the Anti-Slavery Society. Copeland told Gabe, "I'm ready to dig coal. Just give me the tools. I'll fight this evil blight even if it takes me to the gallows."

A day later, Francis arrived at the farm after going to Baltimore to procure the weaponry he had promised Brown in Philadelphia. He brought a slew of rifles, 40,000 Sharps primers and percussion caps, and $250 in gold, the remainder of the money he had borrowed from his uncle to fund the incentive for Brown to let him join.

What Brown called the Provisional Army of the United States was now complete: eighteen white men and five Black men.

That night, Brown announced, "We begin our mission three days hence, on October 16."

The next day, Gabe began feeling like he was coming down with a fever. He decided to say nothing, hoping it would pass. It didn't. He started sweating, aching all over, and had the chills. As he moaned and groaned, his compatriots called for Brown.

Brown took one look and said, "Damnation, he's got marsh fever. Must have got it when we were on the way to Philadelphia."

The next day was worse, with Gabe going in and out of delirium.

Brown couldn't change the overall plans, but he had to shift them due to Gabe's incapacity. Originally, Gabe was to accompany Brown and most of the others into Harper's Ferry. After capturing the Armory, Gabe was to load a wagon with arms from the arsenal and take them across the Shenandoah Bridge to a schoolhouse on Loudoun Heights, where all the men would rendevous.

Owen took Gabe's place. Brown left Gabe with Francis and Barclay, who were assigned to guard the Kennedy Farm until the main group captured the Armory, at which time they were to take the pikes to the schoolhouse.

A deep solemnity pervaded the farmhouse as everyone realized that the long-awaited moment was at hand. As Gabe went in and out of consciousness, Brown read a passage from Isaiah, offering a fervent prayer to God for His assistance in liberating the bondsmen. Captain Stevens read the Provisional Constitution aloud, the first time many of the men had heard it. Each took a loyalty oath. Brown closed, saying, "You all know how dear life is to you and your friends. Do not, therefore, take the life of anyone if you can possibly avoid it. But, if it's necessary to take life in order to save your own, then make sure work of it."

Gabe slipped back into delirium. He woke up at eight o'clock in the evening amid much hustle and bustle, and heard Brown proclaim, "Men, get on your arms. We will proceed to the Ferry."

Gabe tried to get up. *I don't want to be left behind.* But he fell back on his mat in a cold sweat. Almost inaudibly, he pleaded. "Put me in the wagon. I'll get better. I can help."

"Son, you can catch up to us in the mountains," Brown calmly said, stroking Gabe's forehead. He bent and kissed Gabe where his hand had been.

"Don't leave me," Gabe pleaded before slipping out of consciousness.

Three days later, Gabe stirred. Through bleary eyes, he could see he was in a small room with a portly woman taking a cloth from a pail of cold water and wringing it before placing it on his forehead. "Glory be!" she exclaimed, "Jus' like Laz'rus. You done come back from de dead."

Still not alert, Gabe looked at the woman and said, "*Rose?* Where am I?"

"No, chile, I's Iris—you has got yo' flowers mixed up," she answered, letting out a raw, hearty chuckle. "Now, rest. I's tell you everythin' later."

When he awoke, Iris told him, "You is hidden in de slave house at de Wellington Farm. Yo' frien's ask me t' keep you safe. You is going t' be all right."

Gabe's head was clearing as the fever broke, and the broth Iris fed him began restoring his strength. "I've got to leave and find the Captain," he rasped, trying to regain his voice.

"No use in talking 'bout it. Nothing you kin do ta help. De raid fail."

"What happened?"

"All I hear was dat Cap'n Brown capture de arsenal, but de army came an' caught 'em or kilt 'em 'fore he could free us'ns."

"I should have been there to help," Gabe said, shaking his head to clear the fog between his ears. "I've got to get into town."

"Not for another couple o' days, but soon you be strong 'nuff t' leave," Iris reassured him, softly pushing him back onto the mat.

Gabe mumbled, "I've got to go. Please help me get out of here tonight."

Later that night, against her better judgment, Iris helped Gabe out of the quarters, giving him directions to the Harper's Ferry road. Gabe made his way to it and stumbled along. Once he recognized where he was, he got to the farm, which was deserted, the still-smoldering cabin burned to the ground and the farmhouse pillaged. He checked a secret cache the men had dug, where they hid food, water, blankets, and guns. To his relief, it had not been discovered. He sat down, biting off a piece of jerky, and tried to digest all Iris had told him.

Feeling stronger the following morning, Gabe wrapped a revolver, ammunition, and food in a blanket, slung a canteen filled with water over his shoulder, and began the five-mile walk to Harper's Ferry. *I never went into town, so I'm pretty sure no one will recognize me as being with the Captain.* Taking confidence in that thought, he pressed on.

Arriving at the Potomac River across from Harper's Ferry, Gabe walked into the small town through the dark tunnel of the covered bridge. The aftermath of the battle was still evident. People were milling around as if they were at a carnival—pointing out bullet holes in homes and businesses and telling each other the bits and pieces of what they knew.

Glancing down an alleyway, Gabe reeled in horror. Pigs were routing and dogs were sniffing a purplish mass in a pool of coagulated blood. Within the horrific mutilation, Gabe recognized the clothing of Dangerfield Newby. Gabe disgorged his breakfast into a bush. He turned toward the Potomac. He saw two bodies lying amidst the rocks in the shallow water. Townspeople were using them for target practice.

Gathering himself, Gabe went into the crowded Gault House Saloon to discover whatever he could. He overheard that Oliver and Watson were among the dead and that John Brown, although badly injured, was alive and, along with a few other survivors, had been taken to the jail in Charlestown, Virginia, the county seat about seven miles away. The army was combing the area for escapees.

Needing air, he went outside. He looked across the Shenandoah River to Loudoun Heights, where he should have been, and shook his head in frustration. His eyes dropped to the water level. He recognized Lewis Leary's and John Kagi's clothing, their bodies face down in the river.

Gabe found the telegraph station, but the lines were still not operational, having been cut as part of the raid. He needed to get to Charlestown to find out what he could and notify his parents that he was alive.

About a mile out of town, a horse and buggy approached Gabe from behind. As the wagon came alongside him, a well-dressed man called, "Hey, can I give you a ride? I'm heading to Charlestown."

Hoping it would not be a wrong decision but not knowing how to refuse, Gabe accepted the ride. "Much obliged," he said, throwing his blanket roll into the back of the buggy and hopping onto the bench.

"My name's Theophilus Packinfish. But that's the awfulist name to have, so just call me Theo," the man chuckled at his play on words.

"Nice to meet you. I'm Gabe Adams.

"What brings you to this area?" the white-haired man asked with a gentle voice and demeanor.

"I was in Washington," Gabe said, trying to develop a good story quickly. "The work I was doing ended, and then I got robbed. I started back to Ohio, where I'm from, figuring I'd stop in towns and work to earn enough to get further along. I did some odd jobs in Leesburg, and a man told me there might be work in Charlestown." Wanting to change the topic away from him, Gabe asked, "What do you do?"

"I'm a lawyer."

"I want to be a lawyer. I was reading the law with my uncle before I went to Washington."

"Y'know what? I might have some work you could do around the office."

"That would be very nice of you and would help me out. By the way," Gabe asked, "What happened in town? I saw bullet holes everywhere and a lot of dead bodies. I haven't seen a newspaper in days."

"I'm not entirely sure," Theo began. "Have you ever heard of John 'Osawatomie' Brown? It seems Kansas wasn't enough for the lunatic. He brought his battle to Virginia but got himself badly injured and some of his boys and men killed. The state will charge him with murder, but he needs a head doctor more than he needs a lawyer."

"Yes, I've heard of him," Gabe answered, trying not to react to Brown's fate or sound too eager to hear more. "What did he do?"

"Best anyone can tell is that he and about fifteen to twenty men came into town late Sunday night and broke into the main arsenal building. The reports are that they planned to take the rifles, go into the Blue Ridges, and start freeing slaves."

"What happened?" Gabe ventured innocently.

"For some reason, they stayed in the arsenal and took hostages, which gave the town militia time to form and call for the army led by Colonel Robert Lee. My son, Victor, was part of his troops. From what I've heard, they'd still be up there creating havoc if they had grabbed the weapons and headed for the hills right away."

"Sounds like it's a good thing they didn't make it."

"Yes, it is. Anyway, the townspeople spent most of Saturday shooting at the arsenal and Brown's men shooting up the town. Once the army arrived the next day, they stormed the arsenal and took it back, killing many of the insurrectionists. Apparently, some escaped. Brown and a few others were captured and taken to Charlestown."

"It all sounds pretty crazy."

"It is. According to the papers, the rogue band had a place outside of town, but the army found it deserted. There were many weapons, including long wooden poles with large blades attached, ammunition, and sufficient supplies to sustain them for a long time. They also found an old carpetbag with Brown's papers, including a printed Constitution for a new country, a manifesto like the Declaration of Independence, and letters from Frederick Douglass and Gerrit Smith—who may have been conspirators. What a fool. Stealing valuable property and a way of life from the South will take more than a zealot like John Brown and a few men."

Gabe fell silent, trying to take it all in. He feigned sleep.

When the two arrived in Charlestown, Theo invited Gabe to his house for supper and to spend the night. Hungry, tired, and still recovering from the past few days, Gabe couldn't refuse the kind invitation.

"I won't be much company, I'm afraid," Gabe said, making excuses. "I'm recovering from the ague and still don't feel so good."

"Well, let's get some food in you. My wife, Louisa, is a great cook. Maybe that will help," Theo said as they arrived at the Packinfish home, a pristine, white, two-story house with a broad wraparound porch.

Gabe helped take care of the horse, put the buggy in the carriage house, and then they went inside.

"Louisa, I've brought a guest for dinner and told him he could stay the night," Theo announced. "This is Gabe."

"Nice to meet you, Gabe," Louisa said, wiping her hands on a towel as she came out of the kitchen. She reminded him of his mother, her hair askew and with bright, sparkly eyes. "It's always a pleasure to have people join us. The room you'll be in is to the left at the top of the stairs. I'll get you a pitcher of water so you can clean up. Then we'll get you something to eat."

Gabe knew he would be questioned at dinner—not out of malice but curiosity. In response to Louisa's questions, he built on the story he had told Theo, ending with, "Sorry to intrude on you folks. I'll find a place to stay tomorrow."

"No reason you can't stay here until you get your bearings," Louisa said. "Besides, I'll bet Theo has work you can do around the house, too. There are many things to be done with our son, Victor, away in the army."

"Louisa is from Pennsylvania and won't allow us to have a darkie, so there are always chores," Theo responded. "But you don't need to call me 'mister,' except in court." He turned to his wife, "Guess what? I saw Victor in Harper's Ferry. He's with Colonel Robert Lee's unit. They were there to quell the disturbance at the arsenal. He said he enjoyed seeing ol' man Brown lying in a pool of blood. He might even be able to get home for a couple of days once they round up those who escaped."

Gabe almost choked, afraid to take another bite out of fear the result would not be pleasant.

Louisa noticed his reaction. "Is everything all right?" she asked.

"Yes, but I saw some grisly scenes in Harper's Ferry," Gabe managed to say. "I don't mean to be rude, but I'm tired and ought to head toward bed. Thank you so much for dinner. Theo, may I take the newspaper to read the accounts?"

"Of course," Theo responded, handing him the *Republican Citizen* he had picked up in Frederick, Maryland, where he had been in court.

"Good night. See you in the morning," Gabe said softly. Gabe read the paper by candlelight. The account went into great detail, including listing those who had died or been taken prisoner. Brown was apparently near death. Several had escaped and were believed to be heading north, with Lee's lieutenant, Jeb Stuart, in pursuit. *That can't be the same Lieutenant Stuart who was with Colonel Sumner after Black Jack, could it?* The news of his friends caused Gabe to be distraught beyond measure, but the editorial chilled his blood:

> The Harper's Ferry invasion has advanced the cause of disunion more than any other event that has happened since the formation of the Government; it has rallied to the standard men who formerly looked upon it with horror; it has revived, with tenfold strength, the desire of a Southern Confederacy. Our peace is disturbed, our State invaded, and our peaceful citizens cruelly murdered. We say, *let disunion come.*

"It seems the raid lit the fuse," Gabe said aloud to himself softly, shivering. "This is just the beginning."

THIRTEEN

"Blow ye the trumpet, blow!"

October 21, 1859–November 2, 1859

When Gabe descended the stairs the following day, Theo was reading the local newspaper, *Spirit of Jefferson.* "Look at this headline," he said, handing Gabe the paper.

Gabe read to himself: "The infernal desperadoes caught and the vengeance of an outraged community about to be appeased." He tried not to react, but his eyes gave him away.

Theo looked at Gabe and said gently, "Parts of your story about why you were in Harper's Ferry don't make sense to me. Your look just now was like what I saw last night when I mentioned Victor's comment about Brown. Do you know the man?"

"I can't answer that," Gabe gulped.

"Yes, you can. You may be in trouble if you know Brown and were with him. I can act as your attorney; anything you tell me is confidential. I may be a Southerner, but you'll have to trust me."

Gabe's eyes darted around the room, looking for a way to escape, and his feet shifted uneasily. He realized how Jasmine and the other fugitives must have felt when they first met

Atticus, and had to have faith that they would be helped, not harmed.

"Please, Gabe, I need to know."

Cornered, Gabe gave a halting response. "Yes, I know him. He asked me to bring him some supplies from Ohio. I didn't know his plans until I got to the farm. But I got sick and wasn't at the raid."

"I'm sorry you were with that madman. Stick with your other story with Louisa," Theo cautioned. "What you tell her isn't privileged."

"I won't involve you or her. I'll find someplace to stay."

"Jeb Stuart is still hunting for the men who escaped. Who knows what anyone knows about you. It's best to stay here where you'll be safe."

"I've got to see Captain Brown," Gabe said, his mind spinning as fast as his stomach.

Theo's calm demeanor was some relief to Gabe. "I can get in to see Brown. I'll figure out what I can do for you."

"I also need to telegraph my parents and tell them I'm alive."

"Charlestown doesn't have a telegraph yet. In the meantime, write them a letter, and I'll post it today. Remain at the house until I get into town and find out what I can."

Theo left for town to investigate Brown's status and whether Brown's documents or anyone's statements had implicated Gabe. To keep his mind off Brown, Gabe began on some requested chores.

A few hours later, Theo returned from town. "I have some news, Gabe. The judge asked me if I'd represent Brown. Now

I have an excuse to meet with him. I nosed around some, but no authority seems to know your name. Also, they've put in a telegraph line because of the massive interest in this case, so you'll be able to get a telegram to your parents."

"That's a relief. Will I be able to see him?"

"I think so. We'll go tomorrow."

Theo handed Gabe the day's newspaper and saw Gabe blanche at an advertisement: "Cash for Negroes—Men, Women, Boys, Girls, and Families."

"This your first time in the South?" Theo asked. "It's ironic that the slave dealer running this ad is also the jailer in charge of Brown.

"I don't see how one human can sell another."

"That's just the way it is here."

The morning could not come soon enough. Gabe and Theo went into town, and after sending a telegram to Gabe's parents, they headed straight for the jail.

"I will talk with Brown," Theo said. "If I can get you in, be careful what you say around the jailer. He's no friend to Brown, and he can't find out about your relationship with him."

Gabe nodded and waited outside.

"Hello, my friend," Theo said, greeting the jailer, John Avis, with a smile and a slap on his back. Avis was an older man with sunken cheeks and dark eyes that exuded anger and disdain, as if they had never experienced joy. "Judge Parker wants to know if I'll be part of Brown's defense team. I need to meet the old man."

"I don't know why anybody would represent that lunatic," Avis responded, shaking his head.

"He needs representation. That's my job. How's he doing?"

"I thought he was a goner yesterday, but he's doing better today. If you ask me, he got what he deserved. Come on back." He led Theo to Brown's cell. "Brown," rousing his prisoner gruffly, "someone here to see you."

"Who and why?" Brown responded groggily, his hair matted and tangled with blood and his face, hands, and clothes all caked with it.

"A lawyer," Avis said, leaving the two men to talk confidentially.

"Mr. Brown, I am Theo Packinfish, a lawyer in town," he said, kneeling down to face Brown, whose injuries prevented him from sitting up. "The judge asked if I would represent you. I'm willing to, but I need you to make the decision. But first, how are you feeling—anything I can get for you?"

"Nice to meet you, Lawyer Packinfish, and thanks for asking, but considering everything, I'm fine enough," Brown answered, grimacing from the pain caused by merely talking. "The blow to my head and the bayonet stab in my side shoulda killed me, but I'm still here."

"Before we can go on, I need to know if you want me to represent you so that everything we discuss is private and confidential."

"I'm hoping friends will get me a lawyer, but until they do, I wouldn't mind having somebody on my side. I'd appreciate your help."

"Good. I have some information for you."

Brown's bloody eyebrows drew together, and he turned his head slightly, looking skeptically out of the corners of his squinting eyes. "What?"

"There's a young man named Gabriel Adams waiting outside. He wants to see you."

Brown flinched. "How do you know Gabe?"

"I met him near Harper's Ferry. With quite a bit of prodding and a promise of confidentiality, he told me about his involvement with you. From what I can tell, he hasn't been implicated yet."

Brown dropped his eyes and sighed. "Two of my boys are dead. I can't take the chance of anything happening to Gabe."

"I've got an idea. I'll bring Gabe on as my law clerk to assist with the case, and no one will suspect he knows you in any other way."

"If you think that will work," Brown replied as the worry lines on his forehead deepened. "I'll have to trust you. Please bring him in. It'll warm my heart to see him."

"Just don't act like you know him."

Theo introduced Gabe to Avis as his new law clerk. Avis led them to Brown's cell, then left them alone. Brown's injuries and Theo's warning prevented the greeting both desired. "Captain, what can I do for you?" Gabe pleaded, trying not to react to the sight of Brown. *He's lucky to be alive.*

"Just seeing you is all I need."

"We don't have much time right now," Theo interrupted them. "We'll be going to court Monday. I'm sure that Judge Parker will want to move fast on this case. The judge's session ends in a few weeks, and if he doesn't wrap this up, it will have to wait for spring—and he won't allow that. Hey, John," Theo yelled to the jailer, "mind if I introduce myself and my clerk to the other prisoners so they know who we are?"

"Sure, not a problem," the jailer yelled back.

The real purpose of introducing himself was for each of the men to see Gabe so as not to show surprise when they saw him in the jail or court. They were thrilled to see him and seemed less anxious, knowing Gabe was okay and helping.

On Monday, October 24, 1859, the jailers brought Brown, Aaron Stevens, Barclay Coppic's brother Edwin, John Copeland, and Shields Green into the courtroom. It occupied most of the first floor of the Georgian-style, two-story red-brick courthouse, its four Doric columns standing guard beneath a triangular facade and a square clock tower.

All but Brown, who lay on a cot in the middle of the courtroom, rose to their feet as Judge Richard Parker took the bench. The judge was a stern, stoop-shouldered, heavyset man. He commanded respect and smiled about as often as a chicken.

The hearing started immediately. Judge Parker and the prosecutors, Charles Harding and Andrew Hunter, promised the case would proceed "double-quick," despite claiming they would give Brown—they refused to call him Captain—and the other prisoners a fair trial.

Hunter was a distinguished Southerner with long, flowing hair, alert eyes, and a vigorous and deliberate courtroom style. On the other hand, Harding was obese, unkempt, and sporting several days of scraggly stubble on a chin that merged into his neck. He was prone to eat and smoke at the counsel table and was better known for his vulgar, stammering speeches and love of whiskey than his legal acumen.

Outside, people gathered, chanting vile rhetoric and venting their anger. "Shoot the Nigger stealers." "Hang 'em first, then try 'em!"

"You will present the case for a preliminary examination before the magistrate panel," Judge Parker ordered the prosecutors. "Due to other cases already on the docket, that inquiry will take place tomorrow."

Judge Parker assigned Theo and two local attorneys, Lawson Botts and Charles Faulkner, to Brown's defense. Botts and Faulkner were slaveholders and reluctant to serve as counsel. Faulkner was related to Colonel Lewis Washington, a great-grandnephew of George Washington, who was taken hostage during the Harper's Ferry raid and would be a witness. Faulkner also took part in storming the armory and was present when Virginia Governor Henry Wise and, ironically, Henry Pate, the infamous leader captured by Brown at Black Jack, interrogated Brown on the day of his capture. Judge Parker didn't seem concerned when Theo expressed his belief that Faulkner had an ethical conflict. "The case will proceed tomorrow," Parker barked.

After the court recessed, Theo and Gabe met with Brown. They spent several hours in the cell, with Brown alternately telling his story and sleeping. Before they left, Theo gave Gabe some time alone with Brown, telling Avis he was finishing the interview, which gave them privacy.

"I'm so sorry for what has happened to you, your boys, and the other men," Gabe said, choking back his emotions.

"Don't cry for me," Brown said tenderly, only able to elevate his head a little on a pillow. "I knew this might be the result of my mission. I have beat the drum against slavery and injustice for most of my life. You need to carry on with the mission."

"I'll do what I can," Gabe assured him, "but I may do it as a lawyer, not a warrior."

"You might have no choice," Brown predicted with an emphatic nod and a firm voice. "The end of slavery won't happen without a fight and more spilled blood. One more thing," Brown whispered. "Be careful. If you sense that the authorities suspect you in any way, get out of town immediately. Do *not* delay a minute. Head south along the Blue Ridge. They won't look in that direction. Then, cross western Virginia into Ohio. I can't bear the thought of you being in this cell with me as a prisoner."

Colonel Lee's division, including Victor, arrived to guard the courthouse and jail to prevent anyone from attempting to help the prisoners escape. Victor had to stay with his unit, but Lee, who knew Theo, granted Victor permission to have dinner with his parents. That evening, Victor made little effort to hide his disdain for Brown. "It would have been a lot easier if we had killed Brown and all of his insurrectionists. We'd be rid of those piles of dung."

"Oh, Victor," Louisa scolded, "don't say that with your father representing him."

"I don't care. We'll be better off when the traitors are all hanged."

Gabe flinched, and regurgitated bile into his mouth. He kept his eyes fixed on his plate and said nothing.

The next day, a perfunctory preliminary inquiry began with Colonel Braxton Davenport presiding over a panel of eight magistrates. Brown was carried by jailers into the courtroom on a cot, followed by the other prisoners. He looked haggard, his eyes swollen from the wounds to his head. Aaron, with near-mortal injuries, was encrusted in blood, and Avis wasn't sure he would live long enough to be hung. Edwin sat bewildered, his eyes darting around the unfamiliar surroundings. Neither the court nor the prosecutors addressed the two captured Black insurgents, Copeland and Shields, or acknowledged their presence.

"Are the defendants ready to proceed?" Magistrate Davenport inquired.

Brown raised himself on an elbow and said, "If you seek my blood, you can have it at any moment without the mockery of a trial."

Magistrate Davenport waved him off, slammed his gavel, and began the preliminary hearing. After taking testimony from a few witnesses, the magistrate's court found probable cause.

In the afternoon, Judge Parker convened the grand jury and instructed them: "Gentleman of the grand jury: in the state of excitement into which our whole community has been thrown, I need to remind you that, however guilty the unfortunate men who are now in the hands of justice may prove to be, they cannot be called upon to answer to the offended laws of our

Commonwealth for any of the multifarious crimes with which they are charged, until the grand jury, after diligent inquiry, shall decide whether for those offenses they should be put on trial. I will not permit myself to give expression to any of those feelings, which at once spring up in every breast when one reflects upon the enormity of the *guilt* of those involved. I speak from no evidence but upon vague rumors which have reached me. They invaded a peaceful, unsuspecting portion of our common country, raised the standard of insurrection amongst them, and shot down Virginia citizens without mercy."

Gabe sat in amazement as the judge continued his inflammatory commentary:

"These men who have lately thrown themselves upon us, confidently expected to be joined by our slave and free Negroes. They unfurled the banner of insurrection and invited this class of our citizens to rally under it. And yet, I am told, they were unable to obtain a single recruit. Regardless, they are to have a fair and impartial trial."

Fair and impartial? With that speech? Gabe shook his head in disbelief.

The magistrate's court reported its finding, and the grand jury took evidence. Then, the following morning, it heard from several more witnesses, retired to deliberate, and at noon it returned a True Bill of Indictment. Judge Parker announced, "The defendants are hereby charged with first-degree murder, conspiracy with Negroes to cause insurrection against others, and treason against the Commonwealth of Virginia."

Faulkner claimed illness before the morning session ended, and the judge excused him. Judge Parker immediately ordered Thomas Green, Charlestown's mayor, who was sitting in the gallery, to come to the table and assist Theo and Botts. Green did so reluctantly.

Judge Parker made Brown and Aaron stand, both needing assistance, while Hunter read the indictment. The other prisoners stood in silence behind them. It took Hunter twenty minutes to read the entire indictment.

"Your honor," Theo said as he rose, "my client pleads not guilty but demands a separate trial. He also requests a continuance to recover from his wounds and participate fully. Attorneys of his choosing are on their way to represent him."

Hunter replied, "With all due respect, your Honor, there is no need for a continuance. But we agree to try Mr. Brown alone—and first."

"Motion for a delay is denied," snarled Judge Parker. "Sheriff, round up a jury panel. Let's get the jury selected."

Even Theo was shocked at the judge's decision to start the trial immediately.

The courtroom brimmed with people cursing at the defendants. People in the gallery ate peanuts and chestnuts, throwing the shells on the floor. The men spit tobacco at small spittoons, the juice often missing the target. Judge Parker reclined in his chair, his feet resting on his elevated bench cluttered with books, papers, and inkstands. Newspaper reporters moved about without restraint, their shoes crunching nutshells, which sounded like someone trampling broken glass. A militia officer, Colonel

J. Lewis Davis, his hair braided into two rows and tied with a bow knot over his forehead, strutted about the courtroom like a peacock. Ostensibly to keep order, he brandished one of the Sharps rifles he had looted from the stash of weapons seized. No Blacks, other than defendants Copeland and Shields, were allowed to attend. All the while, Brown lay on a cot with a blanket covering his battered, bruised, and bloody body.

"This is more like a circus than a courtroom," Gabe whispered to Theo.

The bailiff led the jury panel, consisting of white, male, and, for the most part, slaveholding farmers, into the courtroom. Judge Parker asked each one a series of ten questions, including, "Are you sure that you can try this case impartially from the evidence alone?" If any answer was "no," the judge simply rephrased the question until he got a "yes."

It took less than an hour to select the jury, with Judge Parker limiting the lawyers to one or two questions per juror and giving no consideration to their challenges other than the eight strikes each side was allowed.

Theo whispered sarcastically in Gabe's ear, "This *fair* trial is off to a great start."

The court recessed for the night.

The next morning, Gabe met with Brown and his attorneys.

Botts had received a telegram informing him that insanity ran in the Brown family. He told Brown emphatically, "I think the best thing for you to do is plead insanity,"

"I agree," said Green.

"Never!" Brown cut them off. "Insanity is a miserable artifice and pretext. I view it with contempt. I'm perfectly unconscious of insanity, and I reject any attempt to interfere in my behalf on that score."

Gabe smiled in admiration. *Mr. Grant was right. You really are a stubborn old coot!*

After opening statements, the prosecutors called witnesses to prove Brown and his men captured the armory and killed several people during the shoot-out. Several witnesses testified about the seizure of all the weapons, including the pikes and the other items found at the Kennedy Farm. Governor Wise described Brown's plans, which he had learned from interrogating Brown.

Theo cross-examined several witnesses whom Brown had held hostage inside the armory, including Colonel Washington. They admitted that Brown insisted his men not intentionally harm innocent people and that any shooting—and killing— would be done only in self-defense. They all agreed that Brown treated them well, was not rude or insulting, and made efforts to make them comfortable even though his sons were dying of their wounds by his side. Colonel Washington, however, was incensed when he described the dishonor of having President Washington's ceremonial sword stolen from his house by a Black man when the insurgents kidnapped him.

The jurors looked bored; some slept. The judge fidgeted as if annoyed when the defense asked questions. As witnesses described the death of Oliver Brown, Gabe almost broke down.

"Don't show any emotion," Theo whispered.

But the admonition may have been too late. Gabe saw one of the jailers look quizzically at his reaction. *Does he suspect I'm involved in some way?*

When the court recessed after the first day of evidence, they went to Theo's office to prepare. Gabe asked Theo, "What can I do to assist?"

"Now that we have the indictment, start with the law," Theo instructed. "Look at the crimes charged, which are made up of elements, kind of like a recipe. The prosecution must prove each element beyond a reasonable doubt. We have a chance if we can cast doubt on any of them. That's why I asked questions about Brown's intent not to harm anyone except in self-defense. They have to prove he *intended* to kill people."

While researching the treason charge, Gabe excitedly told Theo, "Treason can be committed only by a citizen of the state. Because neither Brown nor his men are citizens of Virginia, they can't be guilty."

"You've got something there," Theo complimented Gabe, impressed by his quick mind.

The second day of taking evidence went much the same as the first, except that George Hoyt, a twenty-one-year-old lawyer from Boston, arrived. He was an inexperienced lawyer sent by Brown's friends, more to consult on plans and methods for Brown's escape than to act as his counsel. Judge Parker dismissed both Botts and Green.

The prosecution called a few more witnesses. "We rest our case," Harding announced. Theo rose to his feet to argue for a judgment of acquittal at the close of the prosecution's case. He made a grand speech about how the prosecution had not proved the counts of the indictment, stressing Gabe's treason argument and demanding the dismissal of all charges.

"Your motion to dismiss the treason charge is denied," said Judge Parker, totally rejecting Theo's argument and waving his hand as if to bat it away. "Even a non-Virginian owes some allegiance to the sanctity of the Commonwealth. The motion to dismiss the other charges is also denied."

Brown slowly and gingerly rose from his cot to address the court: "I discover that nothing like a fair trial is to be given me, notwithstanding all of your assurances. I ask for more time for my attorneys to arrive and subpoena witnesses in my defense."

"Denied!" bellowed Judge Parker. "Do not challenge me or my ability to assure you a fair trial. Let's *proceed*."

Gabe bristled and whispered to Theo, "Wouldn't it be nice to have a judge who is even remotely interested in a fair trial?"

"He actually is, and thinks that's what he's affording Brown," Theo replied with a hint of sadness due to the obvious rush to justice. "But, first and foremost, he's a Southerner. Nothing runs deeper in the South than the fear of a slave insurrection."

Theo had several witnesses testify for the defense about Brown's humane treatment of them and his instructions not to shoot except in self-defense. The jury wasn't paying attention.

Avis came into Brown's cool, damp cell that evening, just as Theo and Gabe were about to leave. "I've got some news you'll want to hear. One of your accomplices, John Cook, was arrested and was just brought to Charlestown. He's given a lengthy confession, naming names of those involved, including your wealthy supporters, and blaming you for everything, hoping to save his skin and beat the gallows."

After Avis left, Brown said to Theo, "You've got to get that traitor's statement. We must know if Cook named or implicated Gabe." Turning to Gabe, he asked, "Has anyone said anything to you, or looked at you suspiciously?"

"I feel like everyone is giving me the eye."

"Cook's duplicity is disturbing. I always asked for loyalty and that my followers stand by one another while a drop of blood remained in their veins. You heard me say it was better to be hanged than betray one of your own."

"It's never surprising what a person will do to save their neck," Theo said.

"Cook's a loud-mouthed braggart and turncoat, full of falsehood and cowardice. I should have sent him home when he got that girl pregnant."

"Speaking of going home, I hear there's a growing movement to break you out of here," Gabe said in a low tone.

"I won't allow it. Despite my utter disgust at his other job as a slave-trader, I promised Avis I would not try to escape if he allowed visitors. Besides, I am worth inconceivably more hanging than for any other purpose. To seal my fate with my blood will do vastly more toward advancing our cause than all I have done in my life before, or could do later."

The trial became even more bizarre on Saturday, October 29. Hiram Griswald and Samuel Chilton, lawyers hired by Brown's supporters, had appeared and were attempting to take over his defense.

Judge Parker gave the new attorneys five minutes to discuss the case with Theo in a small room next to the courtroom.

"Please let me continue. You haven't even read the indictment or heard the testimony," Theo pleaded with dismay. "How can you do anything more for him than what I am doing?"

"Don't worry. It's Saturday. We'll get a continuance and have time to prepare," Chilton said with confidence.

While the men were away, Gabe tried to convince Brown to allow Theo to continue taking the lead.

"It's not going to matter," Brown said. "I have nothing against Theo. He's done a fine job. But I think I should go with the lawyers my friends paid for and sent."

The attorneys returned, and Chilton made his motion to delay the trial.

"Denied," Judge Parker ruled. "Call your witnesses."

On Brown's behalf, Griswald called several witnesses with whom he hadn't even spoken to prove that Brown had not hurt any of the hostages. The jury paid little or no attention to what they had to say. The defense rested.

Judge Parker asked, "Mr. Hunter, are you ready for closing arguments?"

"Yes, your Honor," Hunter answered as he coolly looked at the defense, then gave an impassioned speech about Brown's guilt.

The court adjourned.

That night, Gabe joined Brown in the cell. Brown could now sit up enough to lean his back against the cell wall, and Gabe handed him a delicacy he had brought from the bakery.

"So, this is Charlestown's famous lemon pie," Brown said, savoring the moment as well as the bite. "It soothes all asperities, and overcomes all crustiness but its own."

How can he be so calm and at ease? Gabe wondered.

Theo interrupted the enjoyment of the moment, entering Brown's cell with a sense of urgency, holding a sheaf of paper. "I just got Cook's statement."

Gabe's heart leapt into his throat. His stomach churned, and his breathing became more and more rapid and labored as Brown scoured the twenty-five-page document, reading off names as he came to them in the narrative.

"Neither you nor Osborne are named," Brown said, letting out a long, loud sigh. "That seems odd, but I won't complain. But, damn him, that turncoat described Owen and others who escaped, and implicated Douglass and other supporters."

"Not naming Gabe might not last, once Cook sees him," Theo warned.

"Get in to see him and give him a message," Brown seethed and said uncharacteristically, "He can say what he wants about me. But I will see to it that his wife and child suffer if he implicates Gabe."

On Monday, Theo yielded the closing argument to Griswald, who had very little to say.

The jury left the courtroom to deliberate. Forty-five minutes later, they informed the bailiff they had reached a verdict.

The jailers again brought Brown into the courtroom on his cot. He reached his hand out and held Gabe's forearm. "We know what the result will be. Be strong, and show the world they can convict the man but not the spirit."

"Yes, sir, but I still have hope."

The crowded gallery watched with intense anticipation. Judge Parker asked, "Gentlemen of the jury, what say you? Is the prisoner at bar, John Brown, guilty or not guilty?"

"Guilty," said the foreman.

"Guilty of treason, conspiring with slaves to rebel against their owners, and murder in the first degree?"

"Yes."

Hunter slapped Harding on his back, causing a large, well-chewed lump of tobacco to shoot from his mouth and into his lap.

Brown pulled himself up to sit as erectly as possible and squeezed Gabe's hand. "I'm all right. Part of the fight is facing the opposition with dignity."

Astonishingly, the gallery, which had treated Brown crudely throughout the trial, was silent, apparently in respect of the stoic Brown.

"Sentencing is set for the day after tomorrow," Judge Parker announced, slamming his gavel and leaving the bench. The guards lifted Brown's cot and carried him back to his cell.

Sentencing day came. Jailers brought Brown into court on his cot. The courtroom had a palpable tension, with the gallery murmuring threateningly, ready to react if the sentence was anything other than death. Brown softly sang his favorite hymm:

Blow ye the trumpet, blow!
The gladly solemn sound
Let all the nations know,
To earth's remotest bound.

The year of jubilee is come!
The year of jubilee is come!
Return, ye ransomed sinners, home.

Judge Parker took the bench and pounded the gavel for quiet. He turned his attention to Brown. "Mr. Brown, do you have anything to say before I pronounce your sentence?" he barked.

Brown mustered his strength and rose from his cot with Gabe's assistance. The gallery became as silent as a tomb. Brown spoke to the court in a clear and distinctive voice: "I deny everything except a design to free slaves. I never intended murder or treason. I have done these things on behalf of His despised poor, which is not wrong, but is right. Now, if it is deemed necessary that I should forfeit my life for the furtherance of the ends of justice and mingle my blood further with the blood of my children and with the blood of millions in this slave country whose rights are disregarded by wicked, cruel, and unjust enactments, I say let it be done."

Judge Parker left no question as to how little moved he was by Brown's speech. "No reasonable doubt exists of your guilt. I sentence you to hang in public on Friday, the second of December. Court is adjourned."

Brown stood with complete composure as long as he could. One man clapped, apparently thinking others would rejoice with him, but disapproving glances from others in the gallery, apparently moved by Brown's stoicism, quickly silenced his celebration.

Brown was removed from the courtroom. Gabe was gathering his papers when he felt fingers and a thumb tightening on his shoulder. He turned to see who was holding him, and he looked into the eyes of John Avis.

Oh my God. They figured out who I am?

FOURTEEN

"He that is slow to anger is better than the mighty."

November 2, 1859–December 2, 1859

Avis loosened his grip and patted Gabe's shoulder. "You and Theo did a fine job for the old man. I respect you for that."

"Thanks," Gabe replied, exhaling a sigh of relief, "but it wasn't good enough."

"Theo, I've been with Brown for over a week now," Avis said, softening his gruff demeanor. "He has treated me with nothing but kindness. I don't agree with him or what he did, but he truly believes he was doing the right thing in God's eyes. I find myself actually respecting him some."

"Yes," Theo replied, "I've come to the same conclusion."

Gabe knew he couldn't leave Charlestown as long as Brown was alive. The Packinfishes graciously extended their hospitality, although Gabe avoided Victor whenever he could. The pallor of the upcoming execution hung over Gabe's visits with Brown like a heavy curtain. Gabe spent hours pouring out his distress in letters to Jasmine, and his main source of buoyancy was her return letters.

Brown's friends in Boston sent another Northern lawyer, George Sennott, to represent Shields and Copeland. Sennott was a very large, disheveled man. The local press derided his massive girth, brought on, they said, by the consumption of too much lager. The neophyte, Hoyt, represented Edwin. The three went to trial the day after Brown's sentencing. Hunter was particularly hostile to the two Black defendants for their part in killing whites.

Sennott provided a fascinating legal twist in defense of Shields and Copeland. "According to *Dred Scott v. Sandford*," he argued, "the Negro defendants are not citizens of any state or the United States. They can have no allegiance to a state or country. Thus, Virginia cannot charge them with treason."

To Gabe's surprise, in Judge Parker's only ruling in favor of the defense in any of the trials, he said, "Well, Mr. Sennott, I've got to agree with you on that. The treason charges against Green and Copeland are dismissed."

"Unfortunately," Sennott said to Gabe, "his ruling won't do them much good. They can't testify, and no Negroes were allowed on the jury. Only on a jury does a white man claim to be a Black man's peer."

The jury convicted Edwin on all charges and Shields and Copeland on the murder charges. Judge Parker sentenced all to hang. Without stating why, he delayed Aaron's trial until February.

Cook's trial started the next day. "I wonder what his statement will do for him?" Gabe pondered aloud.

"Probably save him from hanging. Prosecutors love cooperation and confessions," Theo replied.

As Cook's trial progressed, Brown became furious at Cook's attorney, Ashbel Willard, a doughface Southern sympathizer who was Cook's brother-in-law and also the governor of Indiana, with close political connections to Governor Wise. Willard condemned and denounced Brown to curry favor and relieve Cook of responsibility for his actions.

Despite his cooperation and Willard's efforts, the jury convicted Cook, and Judge Parker was unmoved. In a slow, methodical voice at sentencing, Judge Parker said, "John E. Cook, you are to be hanged by the neck until you are dead."

As he did each morning, Gabe arrived at the jail. Theo had told Avis that Brown wanted Gabe to act as his valet, help him with letters, take care of other needs in preparation for his execution, and provide assistance. Avis, who had come to enjoy Gabe's presence, saw nothing unusual about that request and greeted him warmly. "Take these letters and some coffee for Brown," Avis said as if he cared about Brown's comfort.

"You better be careful, Mr. Avis," Gabe teased. "You're softening up. People will begin to think you like Captain Brown."

"Your captain may be an abolitionist zealot, but he's righteous and treats me with dignity and respect. I still am incensed by what he did, but I find it hard to treat him differently than he treats me."

As Gabe entered Brown's cell, Brown greeted him cheerfully. "Good morning, my son."

"Good morning. How're you feeling today?" Gabe asked, noting Brown was getting stronger each day, most of the cuts and bruises had healed, and the swelling around his eyes had disappeared.

"Doing better," as he rose and walked gingerly the few steps to a chair.

"Good. You'll see in the papers that Ralph Waldo Emerson gave a speech about you," Gabe told Brown. "Did you know him well?"

"Yes," Brown replied. "I spent many a pleasant evening with Emerson, Thoreau, Melville, Whitman, and others who were not shy about writing on the evils of slavery. What did he have to say?"

"He called his talk 'Courage,'" Gabe said, then began reading it aloud, ending with, "'Brown is the new saint awaiting his martyrdom, and who will make the gallows glorious like the cross.'"

"Oh, Waldo always talks with too much hyperbole. I'm not a saint. I'm a sinner. But the greater sin is slavery. Everyone's fate—in the North and South—is tied to the fate of the Negro. If my death hastens the day of freedom for the enslaved, I will not have died in vain."

"I don't know how you have such peace within you. I'm scared for you."

"I'm an old man. They can dispose of me very easily. I am nearly disposed of now. One should not be afraid to die. Death is harder on those left behind than it is on the one doing the dying. You'll find that out one day."

After a pause to reflect on Brown's words, Gabe asked, "What do you think is in store for me?"

"You have to follow your path and passions," Brown said, gazing deep into Gabe's eyes. "I can't tell you what or how to do it. You have a moral and worthy character. Surround yourself with people like yourself, and you can oppose a multitude of oppressors."

"But helping slaves escape doesn't end slavery," Gabe said.

"Helping them to escape was *my* mission. You need to find *yours*."

The days passed slowly, and the agony of waiting weighed heavily on Gabe. He had trouble sleeping and lost his appetite. On the other hand, Brown calmly accepted his impending fate, spending his time putting his affairs in order, writing letters, and welcoming visitors, including newspaper reporters and clergymen—but only Northern men of the cloth. "There are no ministers of Christ in the South," Brown told Avis. "My knees will not bend in prayer with a minister who professes to be a Christian while he stains his hands with the blood of souls."

The day of the execution approached, and Brown was most distressed at the thought of never seeing his beloved wife again. "Please allow Mary to see me before I am hung," Brown pleaded with Avis.

"With your execution scheduled for tomorrow, I'll see what I can do. Until now, we could not permit a visit because we couldn't take the risk that seeing her might impel you to try to escape."

Later that afternoon, Colonel Lee, who was in charge of the execution, gave Avis permission to allow Mary to see Brown. Avis arranged to bring Mary from Harper's Ferry, where she was staying in hopes of setting eyes on her husband one last time. Before ushering her to the cell, Avis cautioned her, "Don't try anything foolish."

Brown's emotions overcame his remaining frailty, and he embraced his bride. "My dear Mary, seeing you is good for my soul."

There was a precious silence as Mary rested her head upon his chest and clasped her arms gently around his waist.

Breaking the silence, Mary said, "My dear husband, our life has been hard." Her typically solemn and dour face softened. "We've faced poverty, separation, and the death of most of our children. I worried myself asleep many nights for fear of the danger you were in. But I know your heart. Over twenty years ago, I pledged my love to you and my devotion to slavery's defeat. I wouldn't change a thing."

"You have always been my rock. You've endured our losses with courage. You are a godly woman with a strong-minded devotion to me and the cause. I regret that my manner has been rough, harsh, and not as kind and affectionate as you deserve."

"You always came back. Even your letters from the Kansas swamps cared more about me than your plight. How will I go on when you don't come home and your letters are no more?"

"We must all bear life in whatever manner we can. I believe it is all for the best. Tell our children their father died without a single regret for the course he has pursued—that he is satisfied he is right in the eyes of God and of all just men." He gently led her to the chair and pulled a crate from the corner for himself. "Sit. Tell me about each child. How's the farm?"

Mary gave him an update on each of their surviving children and grandchildren and the difficulties with the farm. "All is well but difficult. We manage."

"You are a good woman. A true Proverbs 31 woman."

Uncomfortable with compliments, Mary blushed and changed the subject. "Your speech to the court is a topic of discussion and was well received. Even the preachers are quoting from it."

"I always thought I'd be a minister."

"If you had, you could never have done as much in ten lives' worth of sermons as what you said on behalf of those poor souls."

Brown shrugged his shoulders and nodded in resigned agreement. He handed her a piece of paper and said, "Here is my will. I just finished it this morning."

"I hate to interrupt," Avis said as he entered the cell. "You don't have much more time. My wife brought dinner, and we'd like you to join us." As a testament to Brown's effect on even those who opposed him, they enjoyed each other's company and the food Avis's wife had made, almost forgetting their surroundings and the event set to happen the next day.

"I'm afraid it is time to go," Avis informed Mary after her longer-than-authorized four-hour visit.

For the first time since Brown had been brought to jail, Avis saw him lose his composure.

"No," Brown pleaded, rising from his chair. "Please let Mary stay with me on my last night. I beg of you."

"As much as I'd like, I cannot, sir," Avis responded. "Rules is rules."

"Damn the rules," Brown said, his voice rising, pleading for mercy. "Cannot you show compassion and grace to this fine woman?"

"I'm sorry, I can't. Mrs. Brown, you'll need to return to Harper's Ferry. A carriage is here to take you."

Brown tenderly held Mary's hands, regaining his composure. "You have blessed my life, my dear Mary. May God Almighty bless, save, comfort, guide, and keep you to the end."

"Goodbye, may Heaven have mercy on you."

They embraced, kissed, and began to part, Brown still holding her hands. He pulled her toward him. Mary buried her face in Brown's chest. His arms enveloped her.

Avis reached for her elbow, and she yanked it away. "Leave. Me. Be."

"I'm sorry, ma'am. You do need to go."

Brown released his hold on Mary, kissed her forehead, and gave her up to the jailer.

The second of December arrived, and Gabe was as depressed as a person could be. *I don't know if God is playing a joke or is*

honoring Captain Brown, Gabe thought as he looked up into a bright sky and felt a warm day that would have been beautiful in May but was almost unheard of in December.

"Farewell, Son," Brown said as he hugged Gabe. "Pick up my drum and carry my field flag into battle." He gave Gabe a folded piece of paper and a quarter.

At first, the quarter seemed odd, but Gabe quickly realized that Brown was giving away all he had left. Avis allowed Gabe to accompany Brown to see his comrades.

As they went from cell to cell, the jail eerily silent and still, Brown gave a quarter to each of his men, telling them, "Stand up like men—no flinching now—and do not betray your friends." He did not speak to John Cook.

Copeland and Brown put their hands on each other's shoulders, looking intensely into one another's eyes. Copeland said, "I could not die in a better cause. I would rather die than be a slave."

Brown gave Avis two notes. One read:

I, John Brown, am now quite certain that the crimes of this guilty land will never be purged away, but with Blood. I had, as I now think vainly, flattered myself that without very much bloodshed it might be done.

The other was an instruction to Colonel Lee to sell the pikes, guns, and belongings confiscated from the Kennedy Farm and give the money to Mary. He never did.

For his execution, Brown dressed in a worn and wrinkled black suit, a clean white shirt Mrs. Avis provided him, blood red slippers, and a black, slouchy hat. He remained calm, almost cheerful, as they tied his hands behind his back and seated him atop his own coffin in a wagon. A military escort led the wagon to the edge of town. "This is beautiful countryside. I never had the pleasure of seeing it before," Brown said to Avis. "I thank you for all your kind treatment."

Avis shook his head in amazement at Brown's demeanor. The guards stood at attention.

Gabe noticed a man standing by himself, well behind the rings of red-flannel-shirted cadets and other military units guarding the gallows against any attempt to kidnap Brown. The man wore a waist-length, gray wool uniform partially covered by an elbow-length cape hanging on his shoulders and a gray kepi hat. He was about Gabe's age and size, with jet black hair curling out from under the cap, dark eyes, a mustache drooping over the corners of his mouth, and a smooth, handsome face. Because the man was standing away from the drama being played out on the field in front of them, Gabe thought he might share Gabe's feelings. Gabe approached him and asked, "How come you're not up with your unit?"

"I'm not part of the Richmond Grays. I borrowed this uniform so I could get close to see the old man hang. I couldn't be happier," was the harsh reply as the man took a long pull on a hand-rolled cigarette.

Gabe tensed, and his fists clenched. "All these slaveholders are the ones who ought to be hung," Gabe said through bared teeth.

"He's a traitor and terrorizer," the man said, spitting the words at Gabe. "I have unlimited contempt for him."

Gabe started moving toward the man, but the thought of Brown's serenity stopped him. Giving the man an evil stare, he began to walk away.

"Hey, tough guy, what's your name?"

"Gabriel Samuel Adams," he said defiantly. "What's yours?"

"John Wilkes Booth."

Recognizing the name, Gabe stopped, turned back toward Booth, and asked, "Are you the actor?"

"Yep."

"Well, break a leg," meaning it literally, not how he knew actors used it. His gaze returned to the wooden weapon of death, where Avis was escorting Brown up the steps. Nothing felt quite real to Gabe. The gallows and Brown were on a small hill, silhouetted by the peaceful and idyllic backdrop of the Blue Ridge Mountains and Shenandoah Valley.

A slight breeze ruffled Gabe's hair. He reached into his pocket and took out the quarter and the piece of paper Brown had given him. Holding the quarter tightly, he read the note softly aloud: "May you ever prove yourself equal to the high estimate I have placed on you. Pure and undefiled religion before God and the Father is an *active* (not a dormant) *principle*." The note ended with a quote from Proverbs that Brown often recited: "He that is slow to anger is better than the mighty; and he that ruleth his spirit than he that taketh a city."

Gabe felt faint as the executioner placed the noose over Brown's head and pulled on the rope to slide the thirteen coils tight around his neck like a buttoned collar. When Avis put the white linen hood over Brown's head, Gabe felt a pain in his chest he had never experienced, caused by a mixture of rage and sadness. There was a profound stillness in the field. Gabe couldn't watch. To keep from screaming, he turned and ran toward the mountains for solace.

FIFTEEN

"Bury me not in a land of slaves."

December 2, 1859–December 16, 1859

Gabe's heart cracked with every step. His soul felt the trapdoor snap open, and he fell to his knees, broken in body and spirit.

He remained motionless, his head bowed. Time stood still. He reflected on the long walk to Kansas and his time with Brown there. The days since he left Ohio to bring the supplies to Brown in Virginia were a blur, but he tried to focus on each moment. He slowly returned to reality. *I've got to go back. I've promised Mary I'd take charge of the Captain's body and belongings and bring them to her.*

He arrived at the foot of the gallows just as the guards were placing the long, newly made pine box into the wagon. Theo and Louisa were standing near the wagon, surrounded by the Richmond Grays, without Booth in sight.

"I'm glad you are here," Gabe said. "I needed to see friendly faces."

"We couldn't let you leave without saying goodbye," Theo said.

"Thank you so much for your kindness."

"You are a fine young man," Louisa said softly and gently, "and are welcome at our house anytime."

"Please stay in touch," Theo requested. He placed a carpetbag with Gabe's meager possessions in the wagon.

Gabe boarded the wagon and sat next to the coffin. With its military escort, the wagon began the trip to Harper's Ferry.

Gabe pulled a well-worn piece of paper from his pocket. On it was a poem by Brown's favorite poet, Frances Harper, which the Captain shared with his army while on the Kennedy Farm. Gabe read to himself:

> Make me a grave where'er you will,
> In a lowly plain, or a lofty hill;
> Make it among earth's humblest graves,
> But not in a land where men are slaves.

Gabe turned his eyes from the paper to the mountains, which blended from a deep green to deep blue the farther he looked south along the ridge. *How can this beautiful country harbor such evil?* He wiped a tear from his cheek and returned to reading the poem.

> I could not rest if I heard the tread
> Of a coffle gang to the shambles led,
> And the mother's shriek of wild despair
> Rise like a curse on the trembling air.

I could not sleep if I saw the lash
Drinking her blood at each fearful gash,
And I saw her babes torn from her breast,
Like trembling doves from their parent nest.

His thoughts shot to the slave market outside of Maysville. A whiff of wind cooled his damp cheeks.

If I saw young girls from their mother's arms
Bartered and sold for their youthful charms,
My eye would flash with a mournful flame,
My death-paled cheek grow red with shame.

He thought of Jasmine running from her enslaver only to be taken by Marcus.

I ask no monument, proud and high,
To arrest the gaze of the passers-by;
All that my yearning spirit craves,
Is bury me not in a land of slaves.

Gabe silently vowed, *That's a promise, Captain.* He dropped his chin in prayer. The sun's rays warmed his back and magnified the fresh scent of pine.

Mary was waiting at the Harper's Ferry train station. With the assistance of several soldiers, Gabe moved the casket to a specially arranged train. They proceeded to New York City, where an undertaker transferred the body into a walnut coffin made in the North, and reduced the Southern-made casket to ash and charred nails. The mourners traveled north by coach, took a boat across Lake Champlain, and rode a covered carriage through the slush to North Elba, New York.

Gabe and Mary joined the newly widowed wife of William Thompson, Henry's brother who had joined Brown at Harper's Ferry and was killed, and the wives of Oliver and Watson as they interred Brown in a private ceremony. The abolitionist Wendell Phillips ended his eulogy: "John Brown has loosened the roots of the slave system. It does not live hereafter. He put his foot on the neck of the accursed system of slavery."

"The cause has taken most of my family from me," Mary lamented softly to those gathered around the mound of fresh dirt. "If I am to witness the ruin of my house, I cannot but hope that Providence may bring out of it some benefit to the poor slaves."

As the group dispersed, they sang, "Blow ye the trumpet, blow!"

Needing Jasmine's comfort in person rather than through letters, Gabe left North Elba and traveled north into Canada. He went west on the Canadian Great Western Railroad to Chatham, and by coach to Buxton. Gabe entered the bakery. Seeing no one, he called out, "Anybody here?"

Rose stuck her head out from behind a bread cart and whooped, followed by her loud, contagious laughter. "Gabriel Adams, how many times are you gonna sneak in here and give me such a fright?"

Gabe rushed to her and embraced her, lifting her off the ground. "How are you, Rose?"

"I'm doing as well as can be expected for an old lady."

"You aren't old, but you *are* a lady," Gabe laughed, letting her feet find the ground. "Where is everybody?"

"Hattie is in bed with rheumatism. Levi is at the mill. Jasmine and Glory are at the school. Why don't you run down there and surprise them? We'll see you back here after school for dinner."

"I'm all for that!"

Gabe made his way to the schoolhouse near the town square. He looked through the window. Jasmine had her back to him. The ribbon tied in a bow around the waist of her high-collared, light blue smock accentuated her slim figure. A few strands of hair escaped from the bun on her head, loosened by the day's toil. He almost felt guilty watching her in such an unguarded and innocent pose, but he could not take his eyes off the vision he had longed to see.

One of the young girls saw him, pointed, and covered her gasp with her other hand.

All the other students snapped their heads toward the window. Jasmine turned and let out a shriek.

"Sorry, I didn't mean to startle you," Gabe apologized to Jasmine when she came out to meet him. Her face was aglow, and her eyes sparkled.

"Oh, Gabe, it's so good to see you. Come in and meet the children."

Other than Reverend King, the founder of the Elgin Colony and of Buxton, the school didn't have many white visitors, and all the students were wide-eyed and silent as Gabe and Jasmine walked into the room.

Gabe instantly recognized the prettiest little girl in the class, who was looking at him suspiciously.

"Glory, do you remember Mr. Adams coming to visit several years ago?" Jasmine asked.

Glory shrugged her shoulders.

"Class, this is Gabriel Adams. He is the friend I've told you about who brought my family to freedom."

The class erupted in cheers, with everyone talking at once.

"Quiet, everyone. It's the end of the day. Perhaps Mr. Adams will be here for a few days and can visit us again. Maybe he'll even tell all of you some of his stories."

Gabe, Jasmine, and Glory, who kept close to her mother, walked the short distance to the house. Gabe visited with Hattie, eagerly awaiting Levi's arrival. Hattie gushed, "My, my, Gabriel. You have grown into one handsome man!"

Embarrassed, Gabe laughed, "Oh, Auntie Hattie, your eyes are as bad as your rheumatism."

Levi arrived, bear-hugging Gabe with excitement.

At dinner, Gabe was thrilled to hear how well they were doing, especially Glory, who was as bright as a full moon on a cloudless night. Just five and a half years old, she was reading, writing, and learning her multiplication table. Levi told Gabe that he had become the foreman of the sawmill. Rose was still as healthy as a horse, and blue ribbons from fairs and cooking contests plastered the bakery's walls.

After dinner, the family and Gabe gathered around a square piano made of burled walnut with carved, curved legs, an ornate front, and brass pedals. Jasmine sat down to play, and Glory crawled onto the bench beside her. After Jasmine played the opening movement of Beethoven's Fifth Symphony, she asked, "Would you like to hear Glory sing?"

"Of course. Will you sing for me, Glory?"

Looking up at her mama for reassurance, she said shyly, "Yes."

"Do you know 'Follow the Drinking Gourd?'" Gabe inquired. "Your mother taught it to me on the way north."

"Yes."

When she finished the song, Gabe praised her, "No one can sing it any more beautifully than that."

Jasmine and Glory played the piano for over an hour while everyone sang, talked, and laughed, then it was time for Glory to go to bed.

"Glory, would you like me to read you a story?" Gabe asked.

"Would that be okay, Mama? Will you come with us?"

"Yes. Of course."

They went to the small bedroom Glory shared with Jasmine. Glory brought her favorite book, *Flower Fables* by Louisa May Alcott, for Gabe to read.

When they returned to the parlor, Levi was sitting on a chair with tight lips and eyes focused. "Gabe, I have to find Papa, and buy or rescue him. Will you help me?"

"Of course," Gabe replied, not knowing whether there was any chance of success—assuming George was even still alive.

"You can travel in the South. If you find him, I can plan how to get him out."

Later that night, Gabe and Jasmine were alone in the parlor. They sat close to each other, talking softly.

"I've wanted to ask but have been afraid to," Jasmine said, gazing directly into Gabe's eyes. "Is there someone special in your life?"

Taken aback, Gabe said, "No." Then teased, "No one wants a vagabond like me." Gabe returned the question with trepidation, afraid of her answer: "And what about you? Do you have a special somebody?"

"No," she replied. "Several men have come a-courtin', but no one has caught my fancy."

"No one?" Gabe paused and studied Jasmine's face, with her clear skin, full, soft lips, and large brown eyes. It was as if he could look into her soul and see her strength, dignity, and wisdom.

Jasmine fixed her eyes on Gabe. "Well, there is someone. No one makes my heart beat fast like you do. And I don't think of you as a vagabond."

They clasped and clumsily kissed. Just as quickly as the kissing began, Jasmine pushed away but didn't completely let go.

What do I do now? Why is she hesitating? I've wanted to hold and kiss her for a long time. He threw caution to the wind and enveloped her in a passionate embrace.

Jasmine pushed away again. "No," her demeanor changed as if a candle were blown out. "I can't, Gabe. Not now, not here."

"What is it? Did I do something wrong?"

"It's not you . . . it's *him.*"

"Who? I don't understand." Then, Gabe recognized an anger in Jasmine's eyes that he had only seen once before. "Oh, yes. I do."

Jasmine started to cry. "My heart and memories fight each other. I want to be with you, but my mind flashes to you looking at me when he was on top of me, and when you touch me, all I feel . . . "

"Shh," putting his finger to her lips. "My God, Jasmine, I should have realized. I'm so sorry." Fearful to touch her, Gabe looked into her eyes and said, "I want to be with you, but I'll let you determine the time."

"Thank you." She briefly touched his lips lightly with hers. Hearing movement in the house, she put space between them as Levi entered the room.

"Hope I'm not interruptin' anythin'," he chuckled.

Her cheeks burning, Jasmine replied, "I think it's time for bed."

A few days later, a great commotion arose as everyone sat down for dinner. A bell began pealing, and Gabe could hear doors slamming and people talking rapidly and loudly in the street.

Glory yelled, "Hooray! Somebody is free!"

Jasmine explained, "Freed slaves in Pittsburgh put their money together, bought a 500-pound bell, and sent it here. Every time a new person arrives, townspeople ring the bell."

Gabe looked outside, and it seemed everyone was running toward the town courtyard. "Let's go!" yelled Glory above the growing din.

As they reached the courtyard, a hundred or more people gathered in a tight knot. "Let 'em breathe!" someone yelled.

The cluster loosened, and Gabe saw two people on their knees, their arms raised and looking at the heavens. A man, maybe in his late twenties, dressed in tattered clothes and with bloody bare feet, dropped his arms and fell into the bosom of a woman about the same age. The woman's face had dried blood tracing multiple scratches. She wore a muddy, ripped, and tattered dress. She wrapped her arms around the man's neck. A mud-covered little girl, maybe five, seemed frozen in place. Only the whites of her eyes were visible as she looked at the crowd.

"*We's free!*" the woman screamed over and over. "*We's free!*"

"Yes, you are," a townswoman yelled back. "Welcome to Buxton!"

The crowd led the newcomers to the bell tower's ladder, where the man and the woman climbed to the top and rubbed the bell with their left hands—the hand closest to the heart. The brass was shiny at that spot from all the touching.

Although he appreciated the profound impact of this moment, seeing the ecstasy in Jasmine's face as she danced around the newly freed family made him realize that the privilege of being *born* free prevented him from experiencing the exhilaration of *gained* freedom.

Once again, the time came for Gabe to leave. "I haven't been home since August," he said to the Frenches at dinner. "I'm always eager to go home after being away for so long."

"We understand," said Rose.

On the day of Gabe's departure, Glory became withdrawn and quiet. She wouldn't come out of her room.

"Come say goodbye to Gabe," Jasmine pleaded, standing next to the front door.

"I don't want to," Glory said, stomping her foot. "I want him to stay."

"I would like that too," Gabe said, "but I must go back home to see my mother and father. I'll be back. I promise. Please come out so I can say goodbye."

Glory slowly emerged.

Gabe knelt to give Glory a hug, which she feebly returned. "Glory, you and your mama's happiness is all that matters to me, but I've got things I must do, including trying to find your grandpapa."

Glory nodded as if she understood.

"I'll write as soon as I find out anything about George," Gabe told Levi. "Take care of Jasmine—don't let anyone run off with her," he warned with a wink and a smile.

"I don't know how long I can hold 'em off," Levi teased.

Jasmine shook her head. "I can take care of myself."

As they walked to the carriage station, Jasmine said, "I feel the same as Glory. I don't want you to leave."

"Come visit," Gabe pleaded. "My folks would be so happy to see you."

"You know I can't. Traveling is too dangerous, with all those pattyrollers still out there like buzzards, looking for any Black meat they can find."

Gabe realized he had selfishly ignored the sharp truth of Jasmine's words. "I'm going to change things, I promise. I'll be back."

They embraced, the passion between them aching for more. "You've got to go," she said softly, pushing him away, "before I won't let you go."

"I'll miss you more than you know." He entered the coach, leaned out of the opening, and waved. *Will we ever be together?*

SIXTEEN

"Beat! Beat! Drums!"

December 16, 1859–April 15, 1861

"Don't you *ever* run off on a death mission again," Ailene scolded Gabe upon his return. Because his parents already knew he was alive, their welcome home was less hospitable than his return from Kansas. "I can't take it."

"I know you felt you were doing what you had to," Atticus added. "But staying out there another month after the failed raid and then going to Canada crushed your mother. Are we no longer important to you?"

"You're right," Gabe responded, hurt by the rebuke. "Of course, both of you are everything to me. You're right, Pops. Mother, I'm sorry I disappointed you."

"If I'm a bit distant, I'm sorry," Ailene added, crossing her arms and clutching her shoulders. "You can't imagine what your disregard for me and putting yourself in such harm's way does to me. I was worried sick every moment you were gone. Carrying out your mission with such violence and danger is not how we raised you."

"I'm not sure what else to say," answered Gabe. "Talking about ending slavery isn't going to accomplish anything. I've committed to Jasmine and Glory to do what I can."

"I appreciate that, but it doesn't make it any easier," Ailene said, shaking her head.

Gabe reimmersed himself in the study of law. Uncle Nathaniel was a patient teacher, and Gabe was a fast learner. He took a part-time job at Grant's tannery to repay his parents the money they had lent him, and he pitched in at the farm to help Raph and his father as much as possible.

Right after the first of the year, a cannon boomed, then boomed again. A group of Georgetown abolitionists had a notification system to inform them that bounty hunters had captured a fugitive and were headed for Kentucky. Ohio was teeming with slave catchers looking for quick rewards, and they patrolled the area around Georgetown nightly. They didn't need to go before a constable or judge if they could get the fugitive across the Ohio River.

For such an occasion, a local farmer was notified. He fired two shots from an old twelve-pound cannon he had retrieved after fighting in the Mexican-American War. Within minutes, whoever could respond rushed to a prechosen meeting place, a junction on the way to Ripley. On this occasion, Gabe and four others met at the crossroads and then galloped at full speed to the river's winter crossing, about two miles west of Ripley, to keep the bounty hunters from leaving Ohio.

Gabe and the others caught up to the band with the fugitive only a short distance from the river. The captured man was gagged, with his hands tied to the saddle horn and his feet to the stirrups. Gabe pulled his pistol and shot it into the air. "Stop, or I won't waste another bullet."

The posse got in front of the kidnappers, jerking their horses back and forth, keeping the men from moving toward the river like a sheepdog weaves in front of a flock of sheep. The bounty hunters had pulled their weapons, but they knew better than to shoot a white man in Ohio.

Gabe quickly identified the gang leader and confronted him. "You know the law. You can't just take this man. You have to take him to the constable. You will come with us back to Georgetown."

"Over my dead body," barked the leader, much older and larger than Gabe, in a low, scorched voice.

"If you wish," Gabe replied, leveling his pistol. "When you are on this side of the Ohio River, I got the law on my side. I'd be glad to rid the state of one more loathsome swine. If we shot a few of you, I'm guessing others would stay away."

The leader backed down. "Doesn't matter," he sneered. "You've wasted your time. When we win in court, we'll expect an escort back to Kentucky."

Both groups of men headed north to turn the fugitive over to the sheriff in Georgetown.

The following day, Gabe appeared in court for the constable's hearing. One of Georgetown's anti-abolitionist lawyers, Thomas Hamer, blocked his path. "I understand there's been some coon hunting," Hamer chortled. "You aren't thinking of trying to stop them, are you?"

"Please, get out of my way, Mr. Hamer," Gabe tried to say respectfully when in reality he detested the man. "I've got work to do."

He pushed his way past Hamer, who smiled dismissively.

The bailiff hauled the prisoner before the constable. "I demand a hearing before a judge," Gabe said, citing the law in Ohio affording the accused escapee at least that much due process.

"Fine, the matter is set before Judge Warden this afternoon at three o'clock."

Unfortunately for the fugitive, the bounty hunters had done their job. They knew who they had caught and had telegraphed the owner, who was on his way to Georgetown. It wouldn't have mattered much, even if the escapee was a free man. By Ohio law, a Black man could not testify, and the judge, who was a retired part-time judge substituting for the regular judge, did not care. There were no penalties for false claims or the wrongful return to slavery, and the judge would get paid if he turned the slave over to the purported owner. Contrary to the presumption of innocence, there was a presumption that *any* Black person was a fugitive slave.

At the hearing, the owner snarled, "This here is my Nigra, and I got the paper to prove it. He 'scaped from my land with one of my horses. That's theft. He's got my brand on his left arm, a half-circle above a star. Show 'em, boy. Pull up your sleeve."

"Your Honor," Gabe pleaded, "the bounty hunters had no right to enter the Stevenses' house. The Stevenses are law-abiding folk who can have visitors in their house whenever they like. It was an illegal entry into the home, and they improperly seized the property, if you want to call this person property."

"Where'd you learn the law?" said Mr. Hamer, who was representing the purported owner of the fugitive, rolling his eyes. "If a man has stolen property inside his house, the law allows using force to retrieve it. Stevens knew this darkie was the property of another, so he knew he had stolen goods on his hands."

"Mr. Adams," Judge Warden drawled as he leaned back in his chair, "Mr. Hamer is correct. Boy, show us your arm."

His eyes seared with fear, the young Black man pulled up his sleeve, revealing a scar precisely as the owner described.

"I conclude Mr. Rutledge has proven the man is his property," Judge Warden stated sanctimoniously. "Your writ of release is denied. The prisoner will be turned over to Mr. Rutledge tomorrow after I get the paperwork completed. Case closed." The bailiff took the captive back to his cell.

Gabe was stunned. He thought he had proved the man should be released. He trudged across the street to his uncle's office and told him what had happened.

"There's nothing you could do," Nathaniel said, trying to comfort Gabe. "The judge was right because they had the right proof. That's the Fugitive Slave Law in action."

"Bad men make bad laws," Gabe defiantly replied. "It's up to good men to do something about it."

That night was one of the coldest nights anyone could remember. Gabe walked into the jail, bundled up in his heaviest coat, a wide-brimmed slouch hat, a thick scarf his mother had knitted, and large boots. The jailer glanced his way with a start, not recognizing Gabe because he was so heavily attired.

"Evening, Fred. Gabe Adams here. I need to see my client. I'll only be a few minutes."

"Hey, Gabe. I didn't recognize you. Go on in. The key is hanging inside the door. Sorry that you're out on a night like tonight," Fred replied, not looking up as he warmed his hands in front of the fire. "Take him some hot water from the stove. It's plenty cold in there."

The man, about Gabe's age and size, was curled up in a corner, shivering as much from fright as the cold. Gabe removed his outer clothes. The fugitive recognized Gabe from court.

"I'm going to get you out of here. I need you to put on these things," Gabe whispered.

Bewildered by what he was hearing, the fugitive did as told.

Wrapping the thick scarf around the man's neck, Gabe said, "Now, just walk out, hang these keys on that hook over there, and say, 'Night, Fred.' Keep walking out the door and across the street to the office with a candle burning and a big star on the window. A person there will take you to a safe place. Got it? Now, what do you say as you leave?"

"Ni', Fre'"

"No, listen: NighT, FreD."

"Night, Fred."

"Great, where do you go?"

"'Cross de stree'. Look fors a candle an' a star in de window."

"That's right. Now go."

Bundled beyond recognition, the fugitive walked out of the cell and hung the keys. "Night, Fred," he said with as much confidence as he could muster.

"G'night, Gabe," answered Fred, without looking up, continuing to warm by the fire.

An hour or so later, Fred went to check on his inmate. Sitting there wasn't the person he expected. "Jesus, Gabe," he said with dismay. "You can get in a lot of trouble for this, and I could get fired."

"Fred, let me tie you up, and you can say you didn't recognize who came in the door. That would be the truth," Gabe suggested, hoping his concocted plan would satisfy Fred.

"Better than the alternative," Fred agreed. "But leave me near the fire."

When Fred was discovered the next morning, Gabe's client was on his way to Canada.

Several months later, Gabe, Raph, and their father were drinking coffee at the kitchen table, entranced with the news from the Democratic Presidential Convention in Charleston, South Carolina. Ailene and Caroline were in an extension of the kitchen area, darning socks and repairing frayed quilts and linens.

"This is good," Atticus said, pinching the skin on his throat. "The Southern Democrats may be trashing any Democrat's chances of winning the presidency. They walked out of the convention."

"Why?" asked Raph.

"Southern Democrats want a candidate who will enforce *Dred Scott*, but Northern Democrats support Douglas's popular sovereignty. If they split the vote, the new Republican Party will win, and the South will have an excuse to secede," Atticus explained.

"Oh, I get it," Raph said, stroking his cheek. "If slavery can't be allowed everywhere and slaves can't be taken, at will, to other states, Southerners want no part of it."

"That's right," Atticus answered. "They'd rather have their own country where Northerners can't interfere."

"Do you think the threat of secession is real?" Ailene asked. "What would that mean for the country—and us?"

"I doubt much would change," Raph said. "Who cares what the South does? We'll just go on farming and doing the things we do. Factories like Aunt Rebecca's family's could still buy Southern cotton and make thread and cloth."

"Yes, but at a huge cost," Atticus argued. "The South will control the supply—and cost—of cotton and sugar, and the North will control investments, banks, and finished products. The two parts of America could kill each other with tariffs and the like."

"I have a hard time imagining what the country would be like if split in two," Caroline said. "But a Northern country wouldn't have to allow slavery and could invalidate *Dred Scott*."

"That's a good point," Gabe said. "Amendments and laws could be passed eliminating the three-fifths clause, Southern compromises, and the Fugitive Slave Act."

"But what happens in the Western Territories?" Raph asked. "We'll have to fight for control."

"It's a real uncertainty," Atticus offered, shrugging his shoulders. "But I promise you it will not be good for anybody."

Several days later, Gabe sat down with his mother and father at breakfast, looking like he had something to say.

Ailene glanced at Atticus with raised eyebrows. Atticus shrugged his shoulders.

"Pops. Mother," Gabe began, confirming Ailene's fearful intuition. "With the unknown about what the South might do, I better go now to fulfill my promise to Levi and Jasmine and see if I can find George. We've done the planting, and there's a bit of a break here."

"I knew something like this was coming," Ailene moaned. "Keeping still is not in your nature."

Atticus frowned. "How do you propose to do that?"

"I don't know. I'll probably nose around the Haydel plantation and go from there."

"What excuse are you going to give for snooping around?" Atticus inquired.

"I don't know yet. I'll think of something. I want to see if George is still alive and where he is."

"As long as you don't try to bring him out yourself," Ailene said, trying to convince herself this adventure would not be like Kansas or Harper's Ferry.

A week later, Gabe stood on the lane facing Haydel's massive plantation home, which he had no trouble finding. Halfway between New Orleans and Baton Rouge, covering 1,800 acres fronting the Mississippi River, Habitation Haydel was one of the most extensive sugar cane plantations in Louisiana. The two-story raised Creole cottage had a high roof adorned by two gabled windows. Nine white columns held up the roof and the second story, and a broad, whitewashed porch and railing ran the length of the cypress and brick house.

Dressed in black pants, polished boots, white shirt, black bow tie, gold brocaded vest, and black coat—all purchased in Lexington, Kentucky, on his way to Louisiana—Gabe approached the front door with trepidation. Adjusting his vest, he knocked with emphasis.

An older woman opened the door. "Yes, suh, wha' can I help you wid?"

"Is your master or the lady of the house at home? I have some business to discuss."

"Come in. Massa pass away years ago. I'll get de Mrs." She left Gabe standing in the foyer of the richly furnished home with its decorative murals and went to inform her owner of the visitor.

"Hello, sir, I am Marie Azélie Haydel." An elegant older woman wearing a steel blue, silk, crinoline dress that shimmered in the light approached him. The fabric barely moved as she glided toward Gabe. "I go by Azélie. And you are?"

"Hello, Ma'am. I am Gabriel Murphy, from outside Lexington, Kentucky. May I take your time to discuss a possible business opportunity?"

"Why, of course," Azélie replied, intrigued by the unannounced appearance of the handsome and dignified stranger.

"Please have a seat," she said as they entered the parlor. Gabe obliged. "Would you like some lemonade?"

"That would be very nice. I am a bit parched."

"Sally, please bring us some lemonade and some of your crumpets."

"Yes, Miss Azélie."

"Mrs. Haydel," Gabe began, speaking with a slight Southern accent as he recited the story he had concocted on his way to Louisiana, "about six years ago, a slave, George, ran away with his wife and children from our farm in Kentucky. He was captured. My father knew he'd run again, so he had him sold at an auction. George is a large, very dark, and muscular man. When sold, he had a recent injury to his right shoulder from where a bounty hunter winged him. A man named Dan purchased him, and we were told he sold him to your plantation."

"Why, yes, I know about whom you are speaking. Why do you ask about him?"

"George was the best buck my father ever had. He sired our top hands and domestic help. My father requested that I come here and try to buy him back to keep our plantation well supplied. We can keep him ball-and-chained to keep him from running."

"Well, well, Mr. Murphy, your proposition is rather unusual. However, you're right. He is a runner. He ran and was caught several years ago, and we cut off his toes. Apparently, that wasn't enough because he escaped again several days ago. Our overseer, Ursin, bounty hunters, and dogs are searching for him as we speak. We can't break him. Besides, he hasn't gotten anyone pregnant since he got here. You still want him?" she chuckled.

"Maybe not. I'll have to check with my father. So that I can tell him, what's your price?"

"Let me check my book," Azélie said, rising and walking into a small room adjacent to the parlor.

Bringing back a large, leather-bound ledger, she flipped through the pages, which Gabe could see contained columns of writing and dollar amounts. She saw the look of surprise upon seeing the enormous book. "Ever since my husband passed away, I've been running the plantation. I keep meticulous records."

"You've done a wonderful job. You have a beautiful place. The frescos and murals are very unusual."

"Why, thank you. I commissioned those by Dominici Canova," she said as if Gabe would know who that was. "Ah, here it is. I paid Dan one thousand two hundred and fifty dollars for him. If they catch him, I'll owe the bounty hunters two hundred dollars. I'll sell him to you for fifteen hundred."

"My father might still be interested. If you would be so kind as to inform us if George is apprehended?"

"Of course. Please leave me your address?"

Gabe gulped. *That was stupid. I didn't think of that.* His mind racing, Gabe said, "My father is ill and, at this time, is staying with his cousin, Jonathan Bierbower, in Maysville. I will be traveling in the East until spring. I'll give you Mr. Bierbower's address, and you can contact my father through him."

"I will do so."

"Thank you, Mrs. Haydel. I've taken enough of your time. I bid you goodbye."

"Goodbye, Mr. Murphy. It was a pleasure speaking with you."

"The pleasure was all mine, Mrs. Haydel."

"Sally, please show Mr. Murphy out."

"What a nice young man," Gabe heard Azélie say to Sally as the heavy door closed behind him.

Kentucky, February 18, 1860

Dear Rose, Hattie, Jasmine, Levi, and Glory,

I'm on a train somewhere in Kentucky, heading back to Ohio from Louisiana. I have uncertain news about George. I did not see him, but he may be alive. He's been at the Haydel plantation all this time but escaped last week and is on the run. The owner agreed to contact me and sell him for $1,500 if they catch him. If she knows she can sell him, she may not have him harmed.

If he doesn't get caught, we can pray he makes it to the Ohio River and remembers where he was when you separated. He may remember our name, or I'm sure someone will direct him to Mr. Bierbower, Mr. Rankin, or Mr. Parker, who will get him to us.

*Despite this news, I hope you are all well. I am
busy studying the law and helping with the farm.
I'll try to get to Canada when time allows.
        My best to all of you. Your friend,
        Gabe*

The day after he arrived back in Georgetown, Gabe went with Raph and their father into town to pick up supplies and mail the letter to Jasmine and her family. Atticus said, "We ought to go to Nathanial's office and see if he is back from the Chicago convention."

Nathaniel was there, and they all greeted each other as the three entered the office. "It's good to see you," Nathaniel said. "We don't seem to get together as often as we should."

Atticus shot a glance toward Gabe. "Yes, with your boys and Michael living all over the state and life so busy, we don't. Let's plan something soon."

"Uncle Nat, tell us about the convention," Gabe said. "What happened to Mr. Seward and Mr. Chase? I didn't think Mr. Lincoln had a chance."

"Seward was the best known and the favorite," Nathaniel said. "But he was just an opportunist who said whatever he thought would get him nominated. I went as a Chase delegate, but part of my duty was ensuring Seward didn't get the nomination."

"So, what happened?" Raph asked.

"As expected, Seward and Chase were the front-runners, but neither could gain a majority. Lincoln's strategy was to be the compromise candidate. When we saw Seward gaining momentum, we switched our votes to Lincoln. Seward's backers wouldn't support Chase, and they also threw their support behind Lincoln. He's quite a rube and unsightly, but everyone settled on Lincoln because of the debates with Douglas, the Cooper Union speech, and his stance on keeping the Union together. He received the nomination on the third ballot. Marcus was very disappointed."

"Why is that?" Raph asked.

"He's been wooing Chase's daughter, Kate, and was hoping to be the president's son-in-law," Nathaniel chuckled.

Oh, sweet Jesus, wouldn't that have been something, Gabe thought.

"Well, Gabe," Atticus said, laughing at Nathaniel's comment, "Marcus may have lost out, but unless the Democrats pull together, your friend Abe Lincoln will be our next president!"

One month later, the Democrats held their second convention in Baltimore, which many Southern Democrats boycotted. "Pops, it looks like Lincoln will do it," Gabe said, talking rapidly, his voice rising as he ran toward his father, who was hoeing a section of the field behind the house. "The Democrats still can't agree. The Southern Democrats nominated Breckinridge, and the Northern Democrats nominated Douglas."

"It's Lincoln's election to lose," Atticus said, bringing the hoe down on a pesky weed.

"South Carolina and Alabama have already said they'll secede if Lincoln wins," Gabe said, shaking his head. "All Mr. Lincoln wants is to keep the Union together."

Atticus gave Gabe a disapproving glance, "The mess at Harper's Ferry didn't help with that. But if you're just going to stand there gabbing, grab a hoe and help me," he teased.

"Yes, sir," Gabe replied, going to the shed to retrieve another hoe, wondering what the future held.

A short time later, a letter came to Gabe. Seeing it was from Jonathan Bierbower, he didn't even sit down before eagerly ripping it open:

> *Maysville, March 10, 1860*
>
> *Dear Gabe,*
>
> *I am enclosing a letter from Marie Azélie Haydel regarding George. Thank you for letting me know to expect such a letter. I'm sorry the news is not better. I hope you are doing well. Give my regards to your father.*
>
> > *Most sincerely,*
> > *Jonathan Bierbower*

With shaking hands and trepidation because of Bierbower's comment, Gabe unfolded the letter from Azélie:

> *Habitation Haydel, March 2, 1860*
>
> *Dear Mr. Murphy,*
>
> *I write to inform you that George was captured. He was in bad shape because a gator got a piece of his leg, and the dogs tore him up. The bounty hunters who caught him were rounding*

*up some stock to sell to mine owners in the bayou
and were willing to waive their fee if I sold him
to them. I didn't need the problem of caring
for George until he recovered and wasn't sure
you would still want to buy him, so I accepted
their offer.*

I wish you and your father the best.
Regards,
Marie Azélie Haydel

Gabe crumpled the letter in his hand. Writing a letter to inform George's family was the most difficult thing he had ever done. His hand shook as he wrote that he had no other ideas about how to find George. Although he was sorry he couldn't tell them in person, Gabe was relieved he wouldn't be there to see their reaction. He wept when he mailed the letter.

In November, Gabe and the family sat around the dinner table after the presidential election. "Can you believe Lincoln won the popular vote without getting a single vote in the Southern states?" Gabe said in wonderment. "He easily won the Electoral College."

"Douglas was second in the popular vote," Atticus chimed in. "Breckinridge was second in the Electoral College, taking every slave state in the deep South, but he was third in the popular vote."

"Now that he is president-elect," Caroline asked, reaching for the bowl of carrots, "what happens next?"

Raph said, "I think some of the Southern states will secede."

"I agree with William Garrison that we should let the South go," Ailene said, her eyes narrowing and mouth firm. "The free states get nothing from the slave states we couldn't get anyway, even if it were another country."

"I agree with you and Wendell Phillips," Raph added. "Let them secede so the world would understand they rebelled to save slavery. No one would recognize them as a country. I would be glad to see them go."

"A country with slavery separated by an imaginary line from a country without slavery," Gabe said, leaning back in his chair with his hands clasped behind his head. "A Northern legislature will repeal the Fugitive Slave Law, and nothing can stop slaves from escaping. The North would keep bounty hunters out. We could make owning slaves a risky business."

"I think the South will try to conquer Cuba, Mexico, and Central America to spread slavery in that direction," Caroline predicted, taking a bite of her mother's savory meatloaf.

"Maybe so," Atticus said, nodding his head in agreement.

"Can't Buchanan stop it?" Ailene questioned.

"Buchanan will try to keep secession to a minimum, but he's so feeble and timid, he won't do anything else," Atticus bemoaned. "He doesn't think states have the right to secede, but he doesn't believe the government has the right to prevent it."

"How will that change with Lincoln?" Caroline asked.

"He also thinks states do not have the right to secede," Gabe said, wiping gravy from his lips, "but he believes the government can prevent them from doing so."

"Won't keeping the Union together take force?" Ailene asked, her voice suddenly quivering.

"I don't know, my dear," Atticus said softly, reaching to hold her hand. "I don't know if he can keep the country together without a fight."

By February 15, 1861, seven states had seceded and were threatening to overtake federal forts in the South.

In March, speaking rapidly, Gabe said to Raph, "Lincoln's train is coming through Cincinnati on his way to Washington. And to think I know him! I wonder if I could get close enough for him to see me?"

"Maybe you'd get invited onto the train's platform, like at the debate," Raph teased.

"I doubt that, but it would be fun to see him. Caroline and Raph, come with me!"

"I'm with you," Raph said.

"Let's go!" Caroline exclaimed.

It was a triumphant sight to see Lincoln standing on the back of a train, waving to the crowd as the next president of the United States!

Gabe, Caroline, and Raph pushed their way through the cheering crowd until they were within earshot. "President

Lincoln! President Lincoln!" Gabe shouted as loud as he could, jumping up and down and waving wildly.

The tall man, looking tired and thinner than at the debate in Galesburg, turned his eyes toward Gabe in recognition. Lincoln's taut face softened, and he smiled as if the troubles he faced had disappeared for just that moment. Lincoln waved with one hand and tipped his hat with the other.

"You really are something!" Raph yelled at Gabe, slapping him on the back with brotherly love and respect.

Gabe laughed, puffing his chest out. The sting on his back felt like Raph had bestowed an award on him.

Lincoln's comments, hard to hear above the huzzahs and hurrahs, were aimed at the Kentuckians, not the Ohioans. Lincoln held out an olive branch in his usual shrill but clear voice: "We mean to treat you, as near as we possibly can, as Washington, Jefferson, and Madison treated you. We mean to leave you alone and in no way to interfere with your institutions where they exist."

Although Gabe still didn't agree with that position, he joined the others with a rousing three cheers.

Several days later, Atticus told his family at dinner, "News coming out of Washington is troubling. Southern delegates and their supporters threaten to forcefully take over the Capitol and prevent Vice President Breckinridge from counting Lincoln's electoral votes."

"How can they do that?" Gabe asked, knowing that counting the electoral votes was a ministerial task.

"Ironically, if their threat works, Breckinridge would make himself president because he would then have the most electoral votes."

The day before the electoral votes were to be counted, Vice President Breckinridge, showing his statesmanlike qualities, made it clear he would not go along with the unconstitutional plan, and the threat fizzled.

On March 4, 1861, the day after Lincoln's inauguration, the newspaper printed his inaugural address. Atticus read aloud to his family: "'Apprehension seems to exist among the people of the Southern States, that by the accession of a Republican administration, their property, and their peace, and personal security, are to be endangered. There has never been any reasonable cause for such apprehension.'"

"Pops, does he say anything about slavery and the Fugitive Slave Law?" Gabe asked. "Maybe he has changed his position."

"He hasn't," Atticus said, skimming the speech. "He's still saying he won't interfere where slavery is, and he still supports the law."

"I'm sorry to hear that," Gabe said, shaking his head from side to side. "I was hoping he'd come to his senses."

"He's more sensible than you," Raph mocked, punching Gabe's shoulder.

"Stop it," Atticus scolded. "Listen to these words: 'I hold the Union of these States is perpetual. It follows that no State, upon its own mere motion, can lawfully get out of the Union. Acts of violence within any state against the authority of the United States are insurrectionary or revolutionary.' However, he also says, 'There needs to be no bloodshed or violence; and there shall be none unless it be forced upon the national authority. The power confided to me will be used to hold, occupy, and possess the property and places belonging to the government. The central idea of secession is the essence of anarchy.'"

Atticus paused to let that comment sink in.

"Those are fighting words to the South," Gabe said.

Atticus continued to read from Lincoln's address: "'In your hands, my dissatisfied fellow countrymen, and not in mine, is the momentous issue of civil war. The government will not assail you. You can have no conflict without being the aggressors. You have no oath registered in Heaven to destroy the government, while I shall have the most solemn one to preserve, protect, and defend it.'"

Gabe started to interrupt, but Atticus waved him silent, saying, "Wait—here is his conclusion: 'We are not enemies, but friends. Though passion may have strained, it must not break our bonds of affection. The mystic chords of memory, stretching from every battlefield, and patriot grave, to every living heart and hearthstone, all over this broad land, will yet swell the chorus of the Union, when again touched, as surely they will be, by the better angels of our nature.'"

Ailene's eyes gleamed from the tears she choked back. More beautiful words she had never heard, but she also knew they meant war, and that Gabriel, Raphael, and Michael would patriotically join the fight to keep the Union together. Like any mother, she trembled in fear at the thought of the possible results.

Shortly after taking the oath as president, Lincoln sent reinforcements to the besieged Fort Sumter as promised. On April 12, 1861, Southerners turned the Charleston, South Carolina, batteries against the ships, forcing the reinforcements to retreat out of range. Barraged by cannon fire, Fort Sumter surrendered on April 13. The Civil War had begun. On April 15, 1861, Gabe read Lincoln's executive order calling forth 75,000 men to form militias in their states.

"I think we ought to go," Raph said. But he wasn't sure if his rapid, thumping heartbeat was from false bravado or patriotism.

"Don't be rash," Ailene said, trying to dissuade her boys from going to war.

Gabe's pulse raced.

War changes everything, Gabe thought the next day as he read Walt Whitman's new poem.

> Beat! beat! drums!—blow! bugles! blow!
> Through the windows—through doors—burst like a
>   ruthless force,
> Into the solemn church, and scatter
>   the congregation,
> Into the school where the scholar is studying,
> Leave not the bridegroom quiet—no happiness must
>   he have now with his bride,
> Nor the peaceful farmer any peace, ploughing his
>   field or gathering his grain,
> So fierce you whirr and pound you drums—so shrill
>   you bugles blow.

Beat! beat! drums!—blow! bugles! blow!
Make no parley—stop for no expostulation,
Mind not the timid—mind not the weeper or prayer,
Mind not the old man beseeching the young man,
Let not the child's voice be heard, nor the
    mother's entreaties,
Make even the trestles to shake the dead where they
    lie awaiting the hearses,
So strong you thump O terrible drums—so loud you
    bugles blow.

Gabe put down the poem. *This is my call to action.*

"I'M HERE TO SAVE THE UNION, NOT FREE THE SLAVES."

April 18, 1861–September 11, 1861

"Aw, c'mon, Gabe," Raph pleaded as they sat on the farmhouse's front porch two days after Lincoln's call for troops, "join Marcus's company with me."

"Uncle Nathaniel can buy Marcus an officer's title," Gabe spat back, "but I wouldn't go with Marcus if his company were the only one from Ohio."

"What will you do?" Raph challenged. "Enlist and be a buck private?"

"If that's my option, yes," Gabe said defiantly. "Zeb said some of our buddies from Miami are starting a company in the Ohio militia. I'll go there and join them."

"What are you two quarreling about?" Ailene asked, insinuating herself into the conversation.

"I'm trying to get Gabe to quit being stubborn and enlist with the Georgetown Company Uncle Nat is raising. Governor

Dennison offered Uncle Nat the rank of colonel if he filled a company and paid for their arms and uniforms. Marcus will be the captain, and I will be his lieutenant."

"Lieutenant?" Gabe chided. "You'll be his lackey. He'll take all the credit and blame you when things go wrong."

"What could go wrong?" Raph laughed. "This fight will be over in three months. Why else would Lincoln ask the states to supply volunteers only for three-month enlistments? I'm enlisting to get the hundred-dollar bounty the government is offering."

"I watched Southerners fight for slavery in Kansas," Gabe said through clenched teeth. "My friends were killed in Virginia by people preventing the slaves from being freed. Southerners won't stop fighting until the last of them is dead."

"That won't take long—they're soft," Raph countered. "Slaves have done all the work while the masters enjoyed the good life."

"*Stop it*," their mother said with hands together as if in prayer. "Raphael, you act like this is a game. It's not. Your father and I don't want either of you to enlist until we know more about what will happen. I will worry every day to the core of my soul about the two of you. Now stop this foolish talk."

"Mother," Gabe said quietly, "I'm leaving tomorrow to enlist. The final battle to end slavery has come, and I must do my part. Besides, if I had a thousand lives and laying them down would free a thousand slaves, I would give them."

"Everything is always about slavery to you," Raph berated his younger brother. "But this rebellion isn't about slavery. You heard President Lincoln say if he could save the Union without ending slavery he would. I'm going with Marcus, and I'll be back before the corn is knee-high."

Joining them on the porch, Atticus interrupted with a raised voice. "You two have done a fine job upsetting your mother. We can't stop you from enlisting—everyone has patriot's fever—but would you please respect us enough to treat each other like brothers before you go?"

"Sorry, Pops. Sorry, Mother," Gabe said.

"When I was in town this morning, Nathaniel told me about his commission," Atticus said. "He would like both of you to join his company. He's got connections and will be able to keep the men out of harm's way. Guard duty or something similar."

"Pops, you know that's not what I want," Gabe said. "I'm not looking to be a hero, but I'm not a coward."

"Who are you calling a coward?" Raph shot back.

"Be quiet, you two," Atticus's eyes narrowed, and the creases in his forehead deepened.

"Pops, can I talk to you—in private?" Gabe asked.

"Private? *Private* Adams is exactly what you will be," mocked Raph.

"*Enough*," Atticus snapped, glaring at Raph. "Boys, this is a war, not some spat. The day of reckoning has come."

Wringing her hands, Ailene went back inside to keep herself busy. Atticus sat down next to Gabe.

"Pops, I'm leaving with Zeb for Oxford in the morning to enlist there. I'd like your permission to take Sugar and the old wagon. The newspaper said the army needs wagon masters to haul supplies."

"Gabe," Atticus said with resignation, "you can take Sugar and the *new* wagon. You—and our country—need it more than we do. If this rebellion succeeds, it will ruin the nation, and a wagon won't mean much."

"That's why I have to go."

"It takes a toll on your mother—and me—every time you go off to fight the Devil. We want you back home—alive."

Gabe met his father's eyes and saw his tender love and worry. Gabe nodded his head, resolving to do as his father pleaded.

The following morning, the goodbyes were agonizing for everyone. Ailene's and Caroline's sobs did not make it any easier. Atticus had a far-off look in his eyes, and Raph continued to beg Gabe to go with Marcus's regiment. "I've got to go," Gabe said quietly and gently. "I love you all."

Ailene buried her head in Atticus's chest, unable to watch Gabe as he wheeled away.

The scene was repeated when Gabe picked up Zeb. "I'm sorry, but we need to leave," Gabe finally told him.

Zeb climbed into the wagon, his cheeks wet from his mother's tears and kisses. He turned toward her and waved.

When Gabe looked at Zeb's mother's feeble waves and woeful demeanor, he felt like a hungry dog was chewing on his heart. *Now I understand Mother's anguish.*

Contemplating the future, the boys didn't talk as much as usual on the two-day trip to Oxford. It was an unnerving scene when they arrived in Oxford on a warm spring day. A bell rang from the platform roof of Old Main. A sparrow trilled its song in a budding oak tree. However, no students were playing on the quad or studying under a tree.

Instead, on one side of the central square, Gabe saw a group of young men marching, one waving the Stars and Stripes with its thirty-tree stars, still including those representing the seceded states. They shouldered wood slats like little boys playing soldier.

Approaching the person holding the American flag, Gabe inquired, "Where do we sign up?"

"You enlist over there," the man answered, pointing toward a large tent.

After signing the enlistment form on which he had written his height, weight, complexion, and next of kin, Gabe took the Oath of Muster:

> I, Gabriel Samuel Adams, do solemnly swear that I will bear true allegiance to the United States of America, and that I will serve them honestly and faithfully against all their enemies and opposers whatsoever, and observe and obey the orders of the President of the United States, and the orders of the officers appointed over me according to the rules and articles for the government of the armies of the United States.

"You're leaving for Columbus tomorrow," the enlistment agent instructed. "You three-month men are part of the University Rifles." With nothing else to do, Gabe sat down to write Jasmine.

Oxford, Ohio, April 20, 1861

Dear Jasmine,

*I just enlisted in the army and will be sent
to a camp in Columbus tomorrow. After that,
I have no idea. I'm going to do what I told you
I'd do—I'm going to fight for freedom. Nothing
matters to me anymore except ending slavery.
It makes me sad to think I'll be fighting against
other Americans, but I look at the Rebels as traitors. I disagree with Lincoln. I don't want to
fight to keep the Union together if it means continuing slavery. I want a Union without slavery.
If this battle doesn't end slavery, maybe nothing
will. I won't rest until you can come to Ohio as a
free person. If I die trying, at least you'll know
I tried. Be with me in spirit. I'll write as often
as I can. You can write me at the Ohio Volunteer
Infantry University Rifles. How they'll find me,
I don't know, but that's what we were told.*

Fondly,
Gabe

The next day, 120 young men milled around aimlessly, all clad in bright red flannel shirts that students from the three women's colleges in Oxford had quickly sewn.

"Men, fall in," Captain Ozra Dodds yelled.

"What does that mean?" one would-be soldier asked Gabe.

"I think we're supposed to get in a line."

Realizing the raw, young troops had little understanding of what to do, Captain Dodds gave more explicit instructions, and the men did as told, although there was nothing straight or orderly in their formation.

The townswomen presented the University Rifles with a company flag and a pocket New Testament for each soldier. Miami's President Hall made a farewell speech. Led by the Oxford brass band and cheered by townspeople, the company marched down High Street to the train station, singing "Red, White, and Blue" and "Yankee Doodle."

Gabe trailed behind in the wagon, filled with the men's gear he had offered to transport. The marching men chattered with bravado.

"Can't wait to kill my first Reb," bragged one.

When the train arrived, the new soldiers boarded. Twelve miles later, at the railroad junction in Hamilton, they changed trains for Columbus. After midnight, Captain Dodds marched his University Rifles through the dark Columbus streets to Goodale Park, where sentries allowed their passage into Camp Jackson. They broke ranks and slept on the ground.

Kicking Gabe's foot to rouse him from sleep the following day, a soldier wearing sergeant stripes grunted at him, "That your wagon and horse?"

"Yes, Sir," Gabe replied, rubbing the sleep from his eyes. "I want to be a teamster."

"We call 'em quartermasters in the army," the sergeant said, spitting out his words and a wad of tobacco juice. "Why would you want that? The army gives QMs the dirtiest, hardest, and nastiest work. When people aren't shooting, you're moving tons of supplies and digging latrines; when people are shooting, you're moving bodies."

"Working a horse and wagon is what I do best," Gabe responded, getting to his feet. "I'll be better at that than shooting someone."

"You may have to do that, too," the sergeant replied matter-of-factly. "You're part of Company B in the Twentieth Regiment of the Ohio Volunteer Infantry—infantry means front lines. Understand, Sonny?"

"Yes, Sir."

"Go see Lieutenant McIntosh. He's in charge of QMs," the sergeant said, jerking his thumb toward the right side of the camp by the Olentangy River.

Gabe led Sugar and the wagon to the river and located Lieutenant Patrick McIntosh, a short, husky man with bushy hair and a mustache drooping over his top lip. He barked at Gabe, "Take care of your horse, then go to that big tent for your body exam."

After unhitching the wagon and hobbling Sugar, Gabe went to the designated tent and stood in line with hundreds of men, all naked as newborns. Each was required to jump twice, bend over, touch toes, and kick each leg higher than his waist. The doctor thumped Gabe's chest several times in several spots, pinched his collarbone, and peered at his teeth the same way a veterinarian would examine a horse.

This is the stupidest thing I've ever had to do, to prove I'm fit to drive a wagon, Gabe chuckled to himself.

"You have pretty good health, do you?" the doctor asked.

"Yes," Gabe responded. "I mean, yes, Sir."

"Fine. Go get your uniform."

The sergeant handing out the uniforms sized up Gabe and tossed him a pair of bluish wool pants.

"These are too big in the waist and too short in the legs," Gabe said, trying them on.

"That's as close as I can get. Here's a belt to hold 'em up," the sergeant muttered, handing him a wide, black strap. "And here's your bloomer shirt, wool coat, and stupidest looking hat in the world."

Gabe looked at the kepi hat. *This is the same type of hat that jerk Booth was wearing.*

Several days later, the novelty of camp life had run its course. It was raining, and the troops, confined to their small tents, were bored and miserable. Gabe opened his rucksack, retrieved a pen, ink, and paper, and penned the first of what he hoped would be just a few letters home.

Camp Jackson, May 5, 1861

Dear Mother, Pops, and Caroline,

As we are idle this morning, I figured I could do as much good writing as anything else. Camp life in Columbus is dreary. I'm guessing you're getting as much rain as we are.

We got our rifles—Springfield muzzleloader muskets—they didn't give us good Sharps like we had in Kansas or Burnside's Breeches used by the cavalry. They take a .58 caliber minié ball, and they have rifling to make them more accurate. Of all places, the rifles are from the Harper's Ferry armory. But I like my squirrel gun better than this long, heavy, slow-to-load relic.

I'm glad I'm a QM—that's what us quartermasters are called. The soldiers march and drill, then drill and march some more. Zeb thinks it's stupid. I have to drill some but spend most of the day moving things around. Sometimes, Lt. McIntosh orders me to move stuff just to look busy. I bet I've moved the same sack of potatoes five times. Speaking of potatoes, the food, especially the hard-as-rock pilot bread, called hardtack, is awful, but there's plenty of it so far. We also have rice, hominy, and bacon to go with whatever meat the army can find (usually salt pork—sowbelly, we call it—but probably mule the rest of the time), with rations of sugar, coffee, and salt. At least I'll get paid $11 a month with a promise of more money and maybe some land at the end of the fighting.

We sleep in long, canvas tents, about 100 men to a tent, 2 to a bunk, and about 24 inches between bunks. It helps to be skinny. The tents have sides that go up about 2 yards, then angle to a peak about 3 yards high. The floor is dirt, and the tents are only marginally adequate at keeping

out rain, so everything is muddy. We cut brush
to put on the ground inside the tent. That helps
some. You can't imagine the vile stench inside,
especially if you aren't near an opening.

It looks like we will be moving soon. Lt.
McIntosh says we're taking a train to western
Virginia. I'm not sure what's going on there. I
heard Raph's regiment was sent to Washington
to guard it. That'll be easy duty—just the kind
Marcus wanted and all he's good for. Has Michael
decided what he's going to do? We read that
Lincoln suspended the writ of habeas corpus
in Maryland and is arresting people who are
threatening to breach the peace. A few of us who
have some legal training wonder whether that's
even constitutional.

Write often. Mail gets here fairly quickly—
usually about 6 days. Send newspapers, too.
Everybody shares all the information they can
get. Please send me some stamps.

I miss you terribly. Your obedient son,
Gabe

Georgetown, May 15, 1861

My dear son,

We received your letter with pleasure. I read
it aloud to remind me of reading to you when you
were little. Yes, it's raining here, too. It seems

like God is sad that this war is going on. Michael will finish teaching this term and summer, but then the 90-day muster will be done, so he's not enlisting. I'm happy about that. Raphael thinks the Rebs will run the first time the Yanks come at them. I hope so, but I know you disagree.

England's "Proclamation of Neutrality" is going to hurt our cause. Your father thinks that's the same as recognizing the rebel South as legitimate. I hope France doesn't support them. I don't want anything to happen that puts you in greater danger.

Your father got the corn planted with Caroline's help. She's a sturdy girl! We all miss you and Raphael so much, although I'm a little more accustomed to your absence, not that I like it, than I am with Raphael's. I want you both back home safe—and soon.

> *Believe me, your most affectionate,*
> *Mother*

"All we do is march, drill, and practice loading our rifles," Zeb grumbled to Gabe as they sat around a fire after another day of boredom, along with Luther Yenski, a well-built, blond-haired farmer from Pennsylvania.

"I'm getting better at loading and shooting," Luther replied. "I can usually get off two shots in about a minute."

"Sometimes, I can even get three," Zeb said.

"I wish we had the Sharps breech loaders," Gabe added. "They are so much faster."

"It's hard enough practicing. How will we fare in battle when getting shot at?" Luther asked.

"I don't know," Zeb answered. "But maybe if we were shooting Rebs instead of targets, we could go home."

"I sure miss home," Luther sighed.

"Me, too," Zeb said, dropping his head.

"As if that isn't enough," Luther added, "did you hear that another man in our company died from dysentery? I wonder what causes it."

"There's been at least one death a day due to sickness," Gabe responded, shaking his head. "They think maybe it's due to bad water and our waste. We won't have anyone left to fight if this keeps up."

"It's so sad," Luther said. "These men knew a bullet might kill them, but who woulda thought they'd die from the trots?"

"You sure know how to cheer a guy up," Zeb said.

Clarksburg, Virginia, June 1, 1861

Dear Mother, Pops, and Caroline,

Yours of May 15 was received with great gladness. We're near Clarksburg, Virginia, guarding the Baltimore & Ohio Railroad and the people in this part of western Virginia who refused to secede.

They made me a corporal. I think that's because I have some education. I'm in charge of three wagons. I have an assistant, who's a private, for my wagon. His name is Luther. He's shy and quiet but strong as an ox and willing to do anything asked of him. I'm teaching him how to read and write. He doesn't even know how to boil water, so I've got some work to do!

There isn't much to do except march and drill, so we have lots of free time. Many of us play the new game called baseball. It's great fun, and I'm actually pretty good at it. The men also box, wrestle, and footrace. We spend time playing cards and games like checkers and backgammon. Most everyone smokes, but I don't. We're not supposed to, but there is a lot of alcohol in camp, which causes fights, shirking responsibilities, and disobeying orders. At night, we have a tattoo—that's what they call it when a band plays and the men march past a review stand. I'm not sure why we do it. I guess it teaches discipline and makes it look like we're all the same. No one is better than anyone else (except the officers). After that, we sit around the campfire, talk about home, and sing songs. Every outfit seems to have several soldiers with a banjo, fiddle, and mouth harp.

I miss and love you. Happy Birthday to Pops!
Gabe

Gabe's unit didn't have to wait much longer to "see the elephant," what experienced soldiers called being in a battle. "Look at those Rebs run!" one soldier yelled to another as Gabe watched the action near Philippi, Virginia, from his wagon, soaking wet in the unpleasant downpour.

"It's the Philippi races," another responded, firing another shot at the backsides of the fleeing men.

"Yee-haw! Look at 'em go!" Luther exalted.

"I hope they run all the way to Richmond," Gabe added. *Maybe Raph is right. That took all of twenty minutes.*

Gabe's revelry was disturbed by Lieutenant McIntosh commanding, "QMs, get out into that field and retrieve the wounded."

Startled and unsure of what to do, Gabe and Luther headed to the battlefield.

"There's a wounded man over there," Luther said, pointing to a man with his bloody shirt wrapped around his head, assisted by two other soldiers.

"Let's get him," Gabe said to Luther. "See any others?"

"I don't. It looks like they've all been picked up," Luther said as the wounded man and his comrades climbed into the wagon. "Let's head back to camp and get dry."

Western Virginia, August 1, 1861
Dear Mother, Pops, and Caroline,
*   I rec'd letters today from you, Michael,*
Caroline, and Jasmine. I assure you that I was
very glad to hear from all of you! I realize you

won't be happy, but you need to know that I reenlisted. It's what I had to do.

Gen'l McClellan took most of the 20th OVI to
Manassas, including Zeb, who went with Captain
Dodd's regiment. Several thousand of us were
left behind to guard the railroads and bridges.
We've had a few skirmishes, but nothing to worry
about. The Rebs turn heel as soon as the shoot-
ing starts. I don't understand what happened at
Bull Run.

Love to all,
Gabe

Georgetown, August 8, 1861

Dearest Son,

We received your most heartily welcomed
letter. We assumed that you reenlisted and
understand. Now that the school year is over
and another call went out for enlistees, Michael
signed up, too. Three boys in the war is more
than my nerves and heart can handle. Michael's
heading to an assignment in Illinois as an aide
to our friend Jesse Grant's son, Ulysses. Jesse
got it arranged. You and Raphael didn't know
Ulyss, but he watched and played with Michael
during church.

It's hard to believe that my boys are out fighting in this crazy war, yet life goes on here as if

nothing else is happening. The corn is growing very well—we're told we have to sell most of the crop to the army. The wheat isn't doing well, but Father thinks it will be adequate. Caroline is teaching local Negroes how to read and write. Church has a peculiar feel. Nothing but women, girls, and either young boys or old men are in the pews. It's not the same without you boys sitting next to me.

I've been feeling melancholy lately. Ever since Michael was born, taking care of my children was my life's purpose. Now, I sit by the window and worry about you and whether you will come home alive. I held my babies close, protecting them with every fiber of my being. It's not easy letting go.

The Confederate victory at Wilson's Creek in Missouri is troubling. After five months of war, the North has nothing to show. We worry about you boys and pray for your safety every day.

With love,
Mother

A general malaise blanketed the camp. Gabe's regiment was still guarding the junction of the Baltimore and Ohio and the Parkersburg-Grafton railroads at Grafton, Virginia, with nothing to do. There were skirmishes elsewhere in western Virginia, but none involved Gabe's regiment. It had been a cold and rainy summer, and the Union defeats ended any hope of a short war.

"No one even knows why we're fighting this stupid war," Luther griped as rain pelted the canvas.

"We know why the South is fighting," Gabe answered. "The vice president of the Confederacy made it clear that preserving slavery *is* the reason for the war. He said the cornerstone of the South is that the Negro is not equal to the white man and that slavery is his natural and normal condition."

"Yeah, but Lincoln claims the war is only about saving the Union," Luther said as he pulled a blanket around himself tighter to ward off the chill.

"Well," Gabe replied, "Douglass and Garrison claim the war must be about abolishing slavery and that the North must allow Blacks to join the army and fight; otherwise, the South will win."

"Nigras in the army? Never!" declared Wesley Wagner, an older soldier from Dayton, who shared the same view as many of the white soldiers.

"Who better to fight for freedom?" Gabe retorted. "Would you rather lose the war without their help?"

"We can win without them."

"I disagree," Gabe said, pounding his fist into his open palm. "Look at those Negroes digging trenches in the rain. They're not even allowed in the army, but they work harder than any of us. The army gives them all the nasty jobs and pays them only a pittance. Douglass says that if four million Negroes were freed, they would be available as an asset for the North, and not the South."

"Congress's First Confiscation Act frees any slave the Confederates use to further the war. Why isn't that enough?" Wesley asked.

"They aren't free until they get behind our lines, and maybe only while the war lasts. Besides, they are considered confiscated *property*, not men," Gabe countered angrily. "They aren't allowed to be armed or fight. We need the Negroes coming into our camps to do more than just dig latrines and trenches."

"I ain't going into battle with no Negro. I won't risk my life standing next to a person who won't fight," Wesley swore. "I'm here to save the Union, not free the slaves."

"To win this war, we may need them," Gabe countered. "I know they will fight. Imagine how hard you'd fight for your freedom."

"Well, I sure don't want them sleeping in my tent."

"I wouldn't mind at all," Gabe retorted.

"You act like you know some nigras and actually like them," Wesley challenged.

"Matter of fact, I do," Gabe said.

The bugle call for "extinguish lights" sounded, ending the spat.

His tentmates had no trouble falling asleep, but Gabe did. He listened to the rhythmic breathing and snoring. *I have to fight the bigots in my tent with words as much as across the line with bullets. Either way, I seem to be losing. If they could only meet Jasmine and Levi, they'd feel different.* The thought of Jasmine made him smile, and he drifted off to sleep.

The next morning, the men were milling around the campsite. Lieutenant McIntosh ordered everyone to fall in.

"Men, we move out tomorrow. The army is transporting us by train to Camp Dennison, near Cincinnati."

Gabe's ears perked up at the thought of being so close to home.

"Those who reenlisted will be reassigned into new units once you arrive. Get your bags and equipment packed."

Gabe didn't need to be told twice.

EIGHTEEN

"HIS SOUL IS MARCHING ON."

September 12, 1861–April 11, 1862

Camp Dennison, located a few miles northeast of Cincinnati along the banks of the Little Miami River, was bustling with activity as hundreds of men arrived each day.

Gabe had been there a week when Captain Rich Ritner barked, "Adams, somebody's here to see you."

"Who, Sir?"

"Over there. That colored boy says he knows you."

Gabe almost fell over. "Levi! What are you doing here?" he said, running to him with arms outstretched.

"Hello, Gabe! I finally found you. I'm here to join you, fight to free my people, and find my Papa."

"You're not serious! The army's not letting Negroes fight. It's risky for you to go into the South. If they capture you, they'll send you back into slavery—or worse."

"I may end up dead, but they won't capture me. I'm here to stay."

"How'd you find me?"

"In your last letter to Jasmine, you said you were moving to Camp Dennison. When I got here, I asked where your unit was."

"Well, I am glad to see you," Gabe said. Then, turning to Ritner, he asked, "Captain, can this man be assigned to me?"

"Don't see why not. You'll be responsible for him."

"Men, this is Levi. He's joining us," Gabe said, slapping Levi on the back. "We've got another group coming tomorrow. We've got to set up their tents and prepare their camp. Let's move."

As the men sat around the campfire that evening, Gabe and Levi told their story before turning to other topics. "Gabe," Luther asked, "what do you think of Lincoln getting mad and removing General Frémont for freeing the slaves in Missouri?" Frémont, the former presidential candidate, had shed his political garb for a uniform. Known as the "Pathfinder" due to his Western military and exploration exploits, Lincoln gave him command of the Department of the West. Frémont immediately issued a proclamation emancipating the enslaved. Lincoln ordered him to rescind it. When he didn't, Lincoln relieved him of his duties for insubordination.

"I thought Frémont's emancipation order was courageous and the right thing to do," Gabe answered, staring into the glowing coals. "President Lincoln will have to face the same issue sometime soon. What will he do with all of the Negroes coming into camp? Most of them aren't freed by the Confiscation Act because they weren't being used to further the Confederate war effort."

"Just don't make us go back," said Billy White, an escapee from Kentucky, about eighteen and willing to take on any task. "I'll dig a trench all de way to Richmond if'n it keep me free."

"Why doesn't dey give us'ns rifles?" asked Malachi Lassey, a short, stocky man in his twenties and an escapee from Tennessee. "I's only got one time t' die, migh' as well be shootin' for my freedom."

"I know Generals Grant and Sherman are pushing Lincoln to let Negroes enlist in the army," Gabe said. "Frederick Douglass says we can't win unless they do."

"Well, I'm ready to fight," Levi said. "That's what I came to do."

"I just wish the soldiers would treat us the way you and Luther do," Billy said.

Camp Dennison, Ohio, September 23, 1861

Dear Mama, Auntie, and Jas,

I found Gabe and his unit. I am safe. We're in southern Ohio but may be going into Kentucky. I'm scared to go back into the South, but I'm determined to find Papa.

Gabe says hello and that he misses you. Gabe wanted to know all about what all of you are doing—especially Jas. Don't worry, Jas. I left out that you're seeing someone. Gabe's a bit thinner but in good spirits. He has many escapees under his command. We do all sorts of chores around the camp. I just wish they'd give me a gun instead of a shovel. I'll write again soon.

Love you all,
Levi

Camp Dennison, September 23, 1861

Dear Mother, Pops, and Caroline,

I received the scarf and woolen socks. What a welcome present. Guess who showed up in camp? Levi French! He wants to go find his Papa. It's doubtful he'll be successful, but trying will make him feel better. He said Jasmine is doing well.

I'm no longer with the quartermasters. When I returned, they made me a sergeant in an infantry division under Gen'l Sherman. I'm in charge of a crew of about 50 Negroes setting up tents, digging latrines, and readying camps for recruits. Some of my men are free Blacks from the Cincinnati area, and some are recent escapees, who the army calls "contraband of war."

How the army treats them is not fair. They aren't allowed to be soldiers or carry guns. They only get paid a few dollars a day for their hard work. They often get spoiled food and fewer rations than the soldiers. 20 of them use old, leaky Sibley tents that look like tepees which were made to hold 12 to 15 men. It's just not right. I've complained to the captain in charge of the contrabands, but he hasn't been able to do anything about it.

> I miss all of you. Your loving son,
> Gabriel

Georgetown, October 2, 1861

Dearest SERGEANT Adams!,

We received several letters from you and were delighted to hear about your promotion and that you're well. It sounds like you've got your hands full watching over all those Negroes. We're proud of you. That's such exciting news about Levi.

Rumors about the war have people on edge. It's hard to know what to believe. Many are clamoring for a truce, but Lincoln won't budge from his stance that the South must agree not to expand slavery. Everything is very discouraging. Prices are low for what I can sell and high for what I buy. I need help getting the hay in, but hired hands are hard to come by. Otherwise, things are normal. We had an excellent rain, and I think we shall commence sowing winter wheat tomorrow.

Your mother is melancholy worrying about you boys. I miss doing daily tasks with you.

Take good care of yourself, and try to do right in all things as we've tried to instill in you, and you will meet your reward.

All my love,
Pops

"Sergeant Adams, get your men together," Captain Ritner ordered. The miserable, cold rain that had pelted the camp for two straight days had stopped, and a bright sun appeared, lifting the men's spirits. Once Gabe assembled the men, Ritner announced, "We're about to move out of Ohio and into battle. We've got new assignments for you."

Gabe shared the men's anticipation as they all looked at each other, shrugging their shoulders.

"Sergeant Adams will put you into teams of two. Each team will have a wagon and two horses. When we move, the soldiers will mark anything they can't carry and have it ready to move. You will pick up anything that remains in your assigned camp area, move it to wherever we stop, and help unload the wagons. You'll also transport sick soldiers not sent north."

"Yes, Sir," Gabe saluted.

"That's not all," Ritner went on. "Each wagon will have a stretcher," he said, holding up a seven-foot-long by three-foot-wide piece of thick canvas with two poles inserted in loops sewn into the long sides of the rectangle. "During battles, you will wait for soldiers helping the wounded off the battleground, get the wounded into your wagons, and transport them to a field hospital nearby. After battles, you will go onto the battlefield, help pick up the wounded, and bring them in."

Wide-eyed, the men looked at each other.

"There's more. Once you've recovered all the wounded, you'll glean the fields for any items that can be saved, such as guns, ammunition, boots, canteens, and the like, help bury the dead, and be available to assist wherever needed. Any questions?"

"Yes, Sir," Gabe answered. "What are we going to do in our spare time?"

Even Captain Ritner broke out laughing.

"That'll be a lot of work," Levi said that evening. "But we'll get it done."

"You all work so hard," Gabe said. "How absurd that Southerners believe Black men are lazy workers unless prodded with the whip."

"We aren't lazy, but if we worked hard, they would've made us work harder," Levi said, reminding Gabe of the life Levi, Jasmine, and their parents lived. "We worked just enough to avoid the lash. I can still hear the whip hissing through the air like cold water hitting a hot iron, then cracking like thunder. I only felt the sting once, when I told the overseer I was tired. Papa got the lash more cause the overseer didn't like him."

Gabe fell silent for a few minutes, contemplating Levi's words. Wanting to know more about Jasmine, he asked, "Did Jasmine ever get punished like that?"

"Other than her busted finger, not as far as I know. I think Massa wanted to keep her skin unblemished."

The slaveholder's reasoning made Gabe shudder. "I can't imagine what you all went through."

Two days later, the army broke camp and headed to the Ohio River docks in Cincinnati.

"Where do you think we're going?" Levi asked.

"I hear we're headed downriver to a camp in Paducah, Kentucky."

Levi blanched. The reality of entering Kentucky made him shake. "I'm not gonna leave your side."

"You'll be all right in camp surrounded by soldiers." *I hope.*

Paducah, Kentucky, January 21, 1862

Dear Mother, Pops, and Caroline,

We've been in Paducah for a month. Michael has come over from Cairo twice to see me. He told me that Pops broke his arm when he got bucked off Buster. I guess you didn't tell me because you didn't want me to worry. I hope the arm heals well. I should have taught you how to ride a horse better! Ha ha.

Camp life is pretty dull. We do endless drilling and eat terrible food—unless you like hardtack crackers. Some call them "teeth dullers" or "worm castles." The only way to eat them is to smash them to bits with a rock or butt of the rifle and put it in bark tea or coffee—but then you have to skim the worms off the top—unless you want a little bit of meat! Sometimes, we fry the soaked hardtack crumbs in bacon grease. We call that concoction skillygalee. If we add bacon or some sort of meat, beans, and anything else we've got, we get a stew called lobscouse (rhymes with house).

We all want to move south, destroy the Rebs, and get this war over with.

My love to all,
Gabe

Several days later, Gabe's unit was on the move again. "Where are we headed now?" Levi asked, after the army, led by General Ulysses S. Grant, boarded steamships going south on the Tennessee River.

"I've heard that the Rebs are massing their forces to move into Kentucky. I think we're going into Tennessee to head them off," Gabe said.

"The boys are itching for a fight, and most think one good rout will end it all."

"I don't share their confidence, but I sure hope they're right."

Georgetown, January 30, 1862

Dear Gabe,

We hope you are doing well. Your father's arm is healing, but he still can't straighten it. It's not easy to be one-armed. Some good folks from church are stepping in to help. Caroline is still teaching, assisting several elderly women, and helping me at church and your father in the fields.

It's a great relief for Michael to be close to you. I'm sure you know that Raphael reenlisted and that his regiment joined General Don Carlos Buell. I'm so fearful that all of you are in such danger.

I am saddened the war drags on with no success. Supplies like sugar, beans, and rice are running low, and meat is scarce. It doesn't really

matter because we don't feel like eating much
anyway. It's been cold and rainy, which makes
my arthritis act up. But don't worry about us.
Nothing compares to what you are going through.

I'll finish, as I want to get this posted today.
We love and miss you.

Your Mother

Grant's army massed near the border of Kentucky and Tennessee, a few miles north of Fort Henry. Union gunboats on the Tennessee River began bombarding the fort.

"How can anything stand up to that shelling?" Gabe shouted at Levi.

"I'm nearly deaf!" Levi yelled.

The blasts suddenly ended, and Gabe heard a wild celebration in the distance.

"The Rebs gave up the fort without a fight!" came the report from runners returning from the front. "They abandoned it and retreated to Fort Donelson!"

Days later, Captain Ritner yelled, "Men, we're movin' on to Donelson! We've got twelve miles of muddy road ahead of us."

"I hope Fort Donelson is taken as easy as Fort Henry," Gabe said to Levi. Hours later, Gabe could hear the gunboats open fire.

There was no letup with the bombardment, which was even fiercer than at Fort Henry. As they neared the fort, Gabe's men found themselves on the edge of the battlefield. Trees splintered and burst into flames around Gabe as cannonballs rained down.

He and Levi took cover behind several downed trees, bullets whizzing overhead.

"I've never heard anything like it!" Levi shouted.

"I can't see a thing through the smoke! It smells terrible!" Gabe yelled back.

After two hours, the unnerving din stopped, replaced by the guttural sounds of anguish from wounded and dying men. The weather had turned freezing cold, adding to the misery.

"Sergeant Adams, take your men and get the wounded to the field hospital. NOW!" Captain Ritner ordered.

"Men, let's go!" Gabe ordered his contingent of contraband.

"HELP! WATER! HELP!" could be heard from all parts of the battlefield.

Gabe didn't make it past the first few dead soldiers lying in disfigured positions—some without arms, legs, or heads, their innards spilling out like pus from a sore—before he fell to his knees, convulsing and vomiting. Levi ran to his side, gave him water, and helped him to his feet.

"I'll be all right," Gabe said before retching again.

Working in teams, Gabe's men carried wounded soldiers to the wagon and the waiting doctors and nurses.

"HELP!" wailed a man missing a leg, but he expired before Levi could get to him.

"Help me with dis man!" Billy cried to Malachi. "We can save him."

"My legs are giving out," Malachi answered. "I's don't know how many more trips I's can make."

"Well, at least you'se got legs," Billy shot back. "If we don' get dese men to de tent, dey'se gonna freeze to death."

Several hours later, shivering from the cold, Gabe said, "We've saved all we can."

"Sergeant Adams," the captain at the field hospital barked, "get your men and haul these amputated parts to the ravine, then glean the fields for anything salvageable."

Well past midnight, Gabe and Levi collapsed. "I'll never get used to it," Levi said.

"Me, either. I just hope I don't get sick every time."

The battle raged for three days. Each night, Gabe and his men repeated their gruesome duties. A few feet away during an unstated truce, the Rebels did the same thing, although it seemed the Rebs needed the haversacks with provisions more than the ammunition. Quiet finally overtook the field, and a messenger exalted that the Secesh—what soldiers called the secessionist Rebels—had surrendered to Grant. Unconditionally.

Several nights later, Gabe found Michael with John Rawlins, Grant's aide-de-camp, near Grant's tent. "Michael," Gabe said, "can you get away for a walk?"

Michael looked at Rawlins, who gave him a nod of approval.

"What's up, little brother? You don't look well."

"I'm having trouble coping with what happened taking Donelson. I can't get the death, injuries, and amputated limbs out of my mind. They bring back the Pottawatomie memories. I don't know if I can do my job."

"You're seeing the worst of it, that's for sure. Soldiers who have gone through other battles say what you are experiencing is normal. As awful as it sounds, you'll get used to it."

"On the one hand, I hope not. But on the other hand, I have to. When I described to Raph what I saw at Fort Donelson, Marcus wrote a note in the margin of Raph's letter to me to 'Grow up and be a man. That's war.' Maybe he's right."

"What a jackass. He hasn't even seen any action. How would he know?"

"Our soldiers must feel the same way I do," Gabe said. "Some who stand their ground get so scared they don't fire their rifles. They just reload. We find rifles with multiple balls in the barrel."

"I've heard that, too. According to Grant, they'll get less frightened as they get battle-hardened," Michael said.

"They better. Speaking of General Grant, I hear rumors that he was drunk during the battle. Is that true?"

"No!" Michael said emphatically. "I was with him. His tactics won the battle. You should have seen him riding all over the battlefield, urging the soldiers on. General Halleck and his bootlickers are jealous and encourage those rumors that come out of Grant's past."

"Have you heard from Raph?" Gabe asked. "Where is he?"

"His regiment is with Buell. They are supposed to meet up with us somewhere in Tennessee."

Almost back to Michael's tent, Gabe stopped walking and looked his brother in the eye. "I'm concerned about Mother. She sounds very depressed in her last few letters."

"I know. I've been sending letters with news of things other than battles to reduce her fears. She just wants us home."

"Maybe I'll try that," Gabe sighed. "Thanks for listening. I needed that."

Michael watched as Gabe trudged away. *So did I.*

Two weeks later, the army was again heading south. "Watching this army move sho' is something," Levi said, sitting next to Gabe on the wagon bench.

"Yep. Twenty-five thousand men, marching to cadence and song. There seem to be more support troops than fighting men. Wagons filled with tents, food, supplies, ammunition, uniforms, forage for thousands of horses and mules, and everything else the army needs stretch for miles." Gabe snapped back to his surroundings when he heard soldiers singing a marching song that made him smile and his pulse race.

John Brown's body lies a'moldering in the grave,
While weep the sons of bondage whom he ventured all to save;
But tho he lost his life while struggling for the slave,
His soul is marching on.

Glory, Glory, Hallelujah,
Glory, Glory, Hallelujah,
Glory, Glory, Hallelujah,
His soul is marching on!

"Old Osawatomie is leading the army!" Gabe exclaimed.

Pittsburg Landing, Tenn., March 20, 1862
Dear Mother, Pops, and Caroline,

We remain encamped at a place called Pittsburg Landing on the Tennessee River, waiting for Buell's army—and Raph—to join us. It's a lovely and serene place. The soldiers pass the time by playing cards, horseshoes, or writing letters. Levi and I are busy helping in the hospital.

I think you'd like to hear about our drummer boys. Each regiment has a drummer (some also have a bugler and a fifer). Our drummer, Charlie Robinson, joined us at Camp Dennison. He's from a farm near Hamilton and ran away to join the army. He's 14 and tall for his age but skinny as a fence rail. I don't think a comb has ever touched his hair or a bar of soap his body. He loves playing practical jokes on us. Most drummers are in their early teens and are too young to fight. They wear red caps, and their uniforms have red trim. The drummers beat different cadences to "instruct" soldiers on what to do during marches and battles. Most nights, the drummers accompany the music and singing. They also help my men retrieve the wounded, bury the dead, and glean the battlefield.

We're not doing much of anything. I'll try to get a furlough and come home if it is in any way consistent with my duty to my Country—you can depend on it.

> *With love to you all,*
> *Gabe*

Gabe and the men in his detail were up early tending to the horses. Most of the soldiers were still in their tents or sitting under tarps by fires, trying to warm up with a cup of coffee. Cardinals chirped their morning song.

From the other side of camp, half a mile away, they heard a god-awful scream from the throats of thousands of men. It sounded as if it was coming from the bowels of hell. The crackle of rifle fire punctuated the morning stillness.

"Get those wagons hitched and ready to move!" Gabe yelled over the growing sounds of battle.

"The Rebs overran our outposts, and our men are retreating," drummer Charlie breathlessly reported.

He had no sooner told Gabe and his men this news when retreating Union soldiers came running toward them.

"Stop the retreat!" General Sherman yelled, yanking his horse back and forth before the fleeing men. "Drummer! Sound *advance*. Corporal!" he screamed at his orderly, "Tell General Grant that I need any men he can spare. Tell him we'll hold as long as we can. Drummer—*Advance*."

Gabe's anxiety lessened only a bit as the chaos abated and the Union lines held then slowly advanced. The pungent smell of gunpowder overpowered him, and the thunderous clangor of muskets and cannons sounded like thousands of men beating empty barrels with iron hammers.

What seemed like an eternity later, the zinging hot lead stopped flying, and the booming cannons went silent.

"Stretcher-men, let's go," Gabe commanded, growing nauseous at the sight of the ground, red with blood. "Get the wounded to the landing!"

"This is awful. We can't walk without stepping on the dead," Levi moaned.

"Oh God. Look at those bodies," Gabe said, pointing at a gruesome pile. "They have been stacked like bags of dirt and used for defensive cover."

"I can't bear the screams. Men are burning alive in the woods."

"I know, but many are behind Rebel lines, and we can't get to them," Gabe answered.

Finally, their work for the day ended, but the situation barely improved. A torrential cold rain fell throughout the night. Most of the troops were without shelter, having left everything behind in the camps during the initial assault. Two gunboats, the *Lexington* and the *Tyler*, restarted bombarding the Confederate positions, and the Rebel artillery answered.

Whissssh. "I can hear the fuse," Gabe heard Levi say before his voice was drowned out by a shell exploding a few yards away, spewing dirt and debris into the air above the protected men who were cowering in the bomb-proofs—trenches they had just dug and covered with logs and dirt.

"We should've built these shelters last week when we had nothing to do," Levi said, shoving his shovel into the mud and throwing it on a growing mound of dirt.

"The rumor is that Grant didn't believe the picket's concerns that skirmishes were portending a battle. He was waiting for Buell so he could move on Corinth," Gabe said.

"Did you see Grant at the hospital?" Levi asked. "He had to leave because he couldn't stand the sight of the surgeons standing up to their ankles in blood and amputating so many limbs."

"It was the worst I've seen," Gabe said, shaking his head. "My heart aches for the injured when the ether ran out, and surgeons were amputating without anything except whiskey and leather straps to bite on. I wish there was something I could have done for them."

The second day at Pittsburg Landing, also called Shiloh due to a small log church in the middle of the battlefield, was worse than the first, but the Union forces got the upper hand.

Buell's troops arrived and were able to push the Rebs back. As the Union troops advanced, the Reb's dead and dying were under their feet. Their screams for help were no different than Union soldiers' screams. At last, the Rebs had had enough and retreated toward Corinth. The battle at Shiloh, which means "Tranquil Place," was over. Bodies were strewn over several square miles, and it took hours to transport the wounded to the field hospitals.

"The gut wounds are the worst," Luther said, gagging slightly. "The minié balls and cannon shot blow such a big hole. Soldiers who cling to life pray to die."

"Doctors can't seem to save them, and amputating a limb to save others is horrifying," Gabe said with tears in his eyes.

> *Pittsburg Landing, April 8, 1862*
>
> *Dear Mother, Pops, and Caroline,*
>
> *I only have a few minutes to write. I survived a horrendous battle at Shiloh Church. I'm sure you read my friend Whitelaw Reid's account of the battle in the Cincinnati Gazette (he writes under the name of Agate). He got some things wrong and was very unfair to Gen'l Grant. Believe it or not, I also saw my Sigma Chi and Miami buddy, Ben Runkle. His face was wounded, but the nurses said he'd live. He still has his sense of humor, telling me, "Now I will look like you!" It's nice to see people I know, even under these brutal circumstances.*
>
> *I'll find Raph's unit as soon as I can, as I am sure he arrived with Buell. I can't wait to see him, but it will be several days before I can get away from the hospital. Too many injured and sick to even count.*
>
> *I'm weary and homesick. Love,*
> *Gabe*

Late that night, Gabe and Levi were gleaning the field. "Halt! Who is that, and what are you doing?" Gabe called out to a figure with a lantern moving slowly along a line of trees, stopping and stooping every few feet.

"I'm Union nurse Mary Ann Bickerdyke," a portly woman said, straightening up to her full height and smoothing her muddy and frayed calico dress. "I can't rest thinking anyone still living has been overlooked."

"Sorry, ma'am. We thought you might be looting the bodies. I'm Sergeant Gabe Adams, and this is Levi French. We're doing the same thing."

After searching the field for some time without finding anybody alive, Gabe said, "I think we've done all we can. Let's head back to camp." As they returned to camp, Gabe asked, "Mrs. Bickerdyke, what brought you here?"

"Please call me Mother Bickerdyke like everyone else does. I couldn't sit at home knowing these boys needed me. I figured my married friends could stay at the hearthstone and prepare bandages and lint for the soldiers while I bound the wounds of the suffering in the field. I was assigned the field hospital under General Sherman's command."

"We're with Sherman, too. Where do you hail from?" Gabe asked.

"I grew up near Mt. Vernon, Ohio, went to college at Oberlin, then did nursing training in Cincinnati."

Gabe exchanged glances with Levi. "I helped Levi escape with his family through Mt. Vernon and Oberlin, and my brother taught at Oberlin before the war."

"You don't say! Where are you from?"

"I grew up in a small town near Cincinnati—Georgetown— and went to school at Miami."

"It's a small world," Mother Bickerdyke said, brushing a few stray strands of gray hair back into a bun, tightly wound like a cinnamon roll. She had a narrow nose, and her dark blue eyes sparkled as she turned to Levi. "And how about you?"

Still startled when a white person spoke to him, Levi stammered, "Um, I was born in Kentucky and, thanks to Gabe, escaped to Canada with my sister, mama, and auntie. I'm working with the contraband unit under Sergeant Adams."

"I work with many contraband women," Mother Bickerdyke said. "They are wonderful people. We clean and scrub the hospital, wash and mend the cast-off uniforms, or cut them up for bandages. Unfortunately, bandages are in short supply these days, with all the amputations and such."

They arrived at camp and went to the hospital to help.

Gabe had already seen the gut-wrenching process of amputations more times than he could count. He watched as Major Hill went about his tasks. Like all surgeons, soldiers called him "Doc Butcher" or "Sawbones." He rolled up his sleeves and took a swig from a flask to settle his nerves. The nurse gave the patient ether. Major Hill held the appendage just above where he began the cut, and the aide held the end. He cut through skin and muscle to the bone and pulled the muscle back to expose the bone. Clamping the knife in his teeth, he grabbed the amputating saw and cut through the bone as quickly as possible, throwing the severed limb onto a gruesome pile. He stretched the loose skin over the wound, sutured the skin, and left the nurse to clean the wound. Wiping the knife and saw on his apron, he moved to the next patient.

After the surgeons finished the last amputation for the night, Gabe and Levi sat with Major Hill. "Why do you amputate rather than try to save the limb?" Gabe asked.

"We don't have time," the surgeon responded, shaking his head, "and the damage done by a minié ball, which splinters the bone and shreds the muscle and tissue, causes irreparable damage. Besides, if not amputated, gangrene can set in and kill the patient."

"Sacrificing a limb to save a life is a grisly business," Gabe said softly. He turned to Levi. "Let's get to bed. We've done enough for one day. Hopefully, we'll be done with this tomorrow. I need to find Raph."

The following morning, a sergeant from Raph's regiment whom Gabe knew from Georgetown stuck his head into Gabe's tent. "Gabe, I've got some news," and told Gabe what he never wanted to hear. They sprinted to Buell's troop encampment, and the sergeant led Gabe to the tent he sought.

Gabe ripped open the flaps on Captain Marcus Adams's field tent and burst inside. "*You son of a bitch,*" he showered spittle onto his cousin's face. "*You killed my brother!*"

"Back off, or I'll have you court-martialed," Captain Adams sneered, trying to sound tough, but his eyes belied his false bravado.

"I'll take you down with me, *you foul piece of used asswipe,*" Gabe threatened, stepping forward. "*You shitfaced coward. You ran and left him to die.*"

Marcus stepped back and put his hands up in a defensive position, realizing Gabe was now big enough to back his words with action.

"Sergeant! Stand down, or I'll arrest you for insubordination," an aide ordered as he put his arm between Gabe and Marcus.

"You can hide behind your rank, you smug dung beetle, but *never* expect me to call you anything but Captain *Asshole*," Gabe said, clenching his fists and taking another step forward.

"Enough, Sergeant," the aide again interjected. "Dismissed, or I'll have you arrested."

"If you weren't my cousin, you'd be dead right now. I never want to see you again, *Captain Asshole*." Gabe mockingly saluted with such a jerk that Marcus almost fell, reeling from the anticipated blow. Gabe did an about-face, leaving Marcus and the aide with mouths agape and bodies rigid.

Gabe went to a secluded spot on the river bank, put his head between his knees, and wept. Finally able to compose himself, Gabe had the sergeant from Raph's regiment lead him to where they had laid Raph's body. Gabe arranged with the company undertaker to prepare the body for burial and construct a long, wooden box lined with zinc. Gabe went to Captain Ritner's tent and found him poring over camp diagrams with his lieutenants. "Captain Ritner," Gabe said as he snapped to attention with a proper salute, "may I have a word?"

"At ease, Adams," Ritner replied. "What's on your mind?"

Gabe told him about his brother. "I'd like permission for a furlough to take my brother's body home to Ohio."

"Your loss grieves me," Ritner said softly. "Although we could use your help in the hospital with all the casualties, we're waiting for our next orders and probably won't move for a while. Request granted."

In the meantime, Atticus and Ailene received the letter no parent of a soldier ever wants to receive:

THE WHITE HOUSE

April 11, 1862

To the Father and Mother of Lt. Raphael Nathaniel Adams:

My dear Sir and Madam, it is with extreme regret that I inform you of the untimely loss of your noble son during the conflict at Shiloh Church. Our affliction here is scarcely less than your own. I have heard from others that Lt. Adams was just like his brother and my friend, Gabriel. So much promised usefulness to one's Country, and of bright hopes for one's self and friends, have rarely been so suddenly dashed, as in his fall. In size, in years, and in youthful appearance, a boy only, his power to command men was surpassingly great. This power, combined with a fine intellect, an indomitable energy, and a taste altogether military, constituted in him the best natural talent in that department. The honors he labored for so laudably, and, in the sad end, so gallantly gave his life, he meant for them no less than for himself.

In the hope that it may be no intrusion upon the sacredness of your sorrow, I have ventured to address you this tribute to the memory of your brave and early fallen child.

May God give you that consolation which is beyond all earthly power.

Sincerely, your friend in a common affliction—

A. Lincoln

NINETEEN

"Too
BEAUTIFUL TO BURN"

April 11, 1862–May 16, 1863

Gabe didn't leave the pine box's side, taking what seemed an endless route aboard a troop transport steamer going north on the Tennessee and Mississippi Rivers, then transferring to a ferry up the Ohio River. His emotions vacillated with every bend in the river. He'd laugh at all the funny and stupid things he had done with Raph, then weep from the unbearable grief at the loss of his brother and best friend. *Jasmine never got to meet Raph. They would have liked each other*. Overriding all emotions was an unmitigated anger at Marcus.

Having received a telegram from Gabe, his mother, father, and Caroline met him at the riverfront wharf in Ripley. Ailene embraced Gabe like a velvet vise. "Oh, Gabe," she sobbed in his ear. "I'm so relieved you are safe. But *why* did Raphael have to die?" Atticus gently pulled her away from Gabe, and she dropped to her knees, throwing her body across the casket, draping her arms down the back side and digging her fingernails into the soft wood. Atticus knelt next to her and gently rubbed her back and neck.

Caroline buried her head into Gabe's chest, wrapping her arms around him even tighter than his mother had.

After some time, Atticus said without inflection, "We better get going." Gabe and his father loaded the coffin into the wagon. Atticus helped Ailene and Caroline into the wagon's bed, where they sat on a bench Atticus had built behind the driver's bench.

"Do you want to drive?" Gabe asked his father.

"Not really."

Gabe climbed onto the seat and slapped the reins. "Hie!" Nellie and the family's new horse, Little Guy, jerked the wagon forward.

After leaving Ripley and turning on the well-traveled road toward Georgetown, Ailene asked, "Do you know what happened?" Atticus winced, not feeling capable of hearing the response.

"Here's what I could piece together after talking with some men in Raph's company," Gabe began, speaking slowly to avoid complete collapse. "Marcus always kept his regiment near the rear of any action. Thinking they were still away from the fighting, the regiment advanced and marched into a Rebel position. When the shooting began, Marcus ordered a retreat and took off like a scared rabbit. Raph took control, rallied the men, and counterattacked. The Rebs held their position, firing away. Raph was hit . . . " Gabe's voice trailed off.

Caroline buried her head in her mother's bosom.

After a long silence, his father began, "It's hard to believe that Marcus would . . . "

"Dammit, Atticus," Ailene snapped in a way she had never spoken before to her husband. "I don't care if he is your brother's son. You know this is not the first time he's been dishonorable. By all that is Holy, *enough*. It's time to listen to *our* son."

Three days later, the First Presbyterian Church in Georgetown was filled to capacity. A friend spoke about Raph's courageous spirit, bright smile, quick wit, and generous heart. Gabe fought back tears as he related Raph's life in a eulogy, blending in some personal stories. "Raph once saved . . . " Gabe's voice cracked and became high-pitched. He drank water, blew his nose, and continued as best he could: " . . . saved me from drowning when I fell through the ice after he told me not to go on it." He took another drink of water. "Many nights, we talked and talked until one of us fell asleep. We used to go hunting and on adventures, thinking we were early explorers." He paused, chuckled, and told the crowd, "On one hunt, I missed a rabbit three times. Raph rolled his eyes at me and said, 'I can do better than that with a rock.' He picked up a nice-sized stone, flung it sidearm," with Gabe mimicking that motion, "and knocked the rabbit silly." As the laughter subsided, Gabe finished the eulogy, "He died a hero. He'll be missed. Oh, so surely, brother, I will miss you. Rest in peace."

A captain and a three-man unit from Camp Dennison stood by. "Arms, ready!" ordered the captain. "Fire!" BOOM, all three guns responded. "Ready. Fire!" Another blast. "Ready. Fire!" a third time. The captain presented Ailene with the flag that had draped the casket. Despite their loving efforts, Atticus and her friends could not console her.

The day after the funeral, the family gathered around the kitchen table. "My furlough is almost over. I have to head back tomorrow," Gabe said, his shoulders and voice slumping as if in pain.

"I cannot bear the thought of you going back," Ailene wept, covering her face with her apron.

Caroline looked into her brother's sad eyes and reached her hand out to touch his.

Atticus pushed back from the table and said to Gabe, "Let's go for a walk."

Chester, the mutt Gabe had raised from a puppy, came bounding up as they left the house as if to cheer them, and ran alongside as they walked. "Son, I don't know how you can do it, but you've got to stay out of harm's way. Your mother's heart cannot take another loss. Michael isn't on the front line and is as safe as possible. We thought Raph was protected. It was you we worried about."

"Pops, I'm usually not in on the fighting. I spend most of my time at the field hospitals. We haven't lost any men in my unit due to fighting."

"Whatever it takes. For God's and your mother's sake, come home."

"I always do."

On the way back to Tennessee, Gabe wrote an agonizing letter to Jasmine as he related Raph's death and funeral. "It'll be good to be back with Levi," he finished the letter. "I enjoy talking to him like I did with Raph. I've learned so much about you and your family. I miss you. Fondly, Gabe."

Gabe returned to his unit amid a flurry of activity.

"Men," Captain Ritner announced, "we begin our move on Corinth tomorrow. They say the Rebs are dug in and about the same size as our force. If so, it could be worse than Shiloh."

Gabe's unit and the troops inched their way to Corinth. Because of their failure to fortify the lines at Shiloh or to anticipate an attack, the troops moved less than a mile each day before stopping so that the men could dig trenches and erect defensive earthworks. It took six weeks to move the twenty-two miles to the outskirts of Corinth, where they again dug in their defensive breastworks. They were close enough to the Rebel position that they could hear train whistles and the Rebs yelling "Huzzah!" and "Hurrah!" amid the drone of a band playing "Dixie" each time a whistle blew.

"Listen," Gabe quieted the group. "They must be reinforcing."

"I wonder how many men are on each train?" Luther asked, his voice shaky.

"Probably too many. We better brace for the worst," Gabe whispered to Luther. "It looks like it could be bad."

"Huzzah!" came the cheers as another whistle sounded. "Hurrah!"

"Fill your canteens," Captain Ritner instructed. "Put a full load of bullets, cartridges, and caps in your cartridge box and sack, and fill your pockets with hardtack. We move at first light. We'll be going at it hammer and tongs. Better be ready."

> Corinth, June 1, 1862
>
> Dear Mother, Pops, and Caroline,
>
> I have good news. We were spared a terrible battle at Corinth. All the reports were that the Rebs were reinforcing and dug in, but when we stormed the city and breached the redoubts, we discovered the Secesh tricked us. No one was there! They weren't reinforcing; they were moving out! They fooled us with "Quaker cannons"—tree trunks painted to look like cannons—and "men" made of straw in gray uniforms lining the ramparts. We didn't care. Not a man lost in battle, and a critical railroad crossroads now in our hands!
>
> I know you worry about us. I wish I could ease your pain, Mother. Raph died a hero for his country. Michael and I are doing what every American must do. I understand your agony. I promise you I'll come home.
>
> I am respectfully and affectionately,
>> Your son,
>> Gabe

"Now that the Union has taken New Orleans, more Negroes are escaping and coming behind our lines every day," Captain Ritner said to Gabe, Levi, and several of his men sitting around the campfire on a pleasant, warm, and largely bug-free spring evening. "With the Second Confiscation Act, any slave owned by a person in a state that seceded is free, and we don't have to send them back, even if their master claims them. But what are we going to do with them?"

"The Act says Lincoln is going to send them off to some tropical place and colonize them," Gabe said.

"We don't want that. We want to be free here. This is our home," Levi said, his arms outstretched.

"Well, until then, we have to feed them and take care of them," Ritner added. "It's getting beyond our ability. Many can't work because of sickness or age."

"General Dodge has hired the able-bodied as cooks, teamsters, and laborers," Levi said, "but the men say they want to fight."

"I hear Lincoln is thinking about freeing slaves who have not escaped," Gabe said.

"How can he do dat?" Billy asked. "De only way a Negro knows he be free is when he be behind our lines, and we protect him. De Act don't change nothin'."

"Douglass says that the rebellion and slavery are twin monsters, and they must fall or flourish together," Gabe added.

"But what does freeing the slaves mean?" Luther asked. "Where will they go? How will they live without money, education, or skills?"

"They did it in Canada," Gabe said. "They can do it here."

"I hears General Grant want to put us'ns in the army and maybe even give us guns," Malachi interjected.

"No way our troops will allow them to be armed," Wesley Wagner predicted self-righteously. "They'll refuse to bring Negroes into their regiments. You don't know how to fight."

"You're being stupid," Gabe said, his nostrils flaring. "Blacks are eager to fight. But they want the war's aim to be about ending enslavement."

"Dat's right," Billy agreed. "Why shoul' I fight if de goal is to reunite de Union and den return me to slavery? But," turning to Wesley, "give me a gun, and I'll shows you I kin fight."

"I say it's not safe to arm them. If we give them arms, they may even turn on us," Wesley added.

"Why would we turn on you?" Billy challenged, his voice rising.

"Because we're white," Wesley said. "You'll want revenge for all the years of slavery."

"If I wanted revenge, you woulda been dead long ago," Billy said, his fists clenched and muscles bulging.

"Settle down, you two," Captain Ritner interjected. "Wesley, even soldiers who don't seem to care about ending slavery realize that the Negroes help the war effort and might speed up the day the soldiers can go home."

Georgetown, August 20, 1862

Dear Gabriel,

Another hot, dry summer. Even the corn is suffering. It's supposed to be "knee high by the 4th of July," but it didn't make it. It's just a bit taller than that now. I am quite concerned that your mother remains depressed. It makes me sad to see her this way.

Caroline left for Washington to work with a woman named Clara Barton, who started an organization to care for the wounded. Miss Barton sounds like your Mother Bickerdyke. Now Caroline is near the fighting. We worry every day about whether any of you will survive.

The news is bad everywhere. It's dreadful in the West. I know the Indians are unjustly treated and suffering, but why do both sides slaughter the other? It's awful. In the East, Gen'l McClellan is stalled after the near disaster during the battles in the Virginia Peninsula. Envoys from the Confederacy are in Washington, working toward a truce. France might recognize the South. Will the North capitulate? If so, no one wins, and I fear Raphael's death will be for naught.

Despite the war, the government and life go on. We paid the new 3% income tax. It's quite a bit of money for us, but we pay without complaint if it helps the soldiers in the field. To top it off, I've got a jury summons for next week.

Please be safe.

Love,
Your father

The summer ended with little action. Buell's forces were in Eastern Tennessee chasing the Secesh, and General Halleck sent

Grant and his troops to stop another Rebel force from invading Kentucky.

After a day's work in the field hospital, Gabe, Luther, Levi, and several of the unit gathered around the evening fire, cooking a meager meal of lobscouse and coffee.

"President Lincoln issued an order threatening the South that he will emancipate the slaves if they don't stop the rebellion by January first," Gabe crowed.

"I've heard that Lincoln is doing it only for military and political reasons, and it won't mean a thing when the war ends," Levi said. "Besides, Lincoln said that Negroes can dig trenches and drive mules, but he doesn't think we are fit to be soldiers."

"Well, I's guess he be comin' around to de truth," Malachi said, puffing out his chest.

"Michael told me Lincoln was waiting for a victory before announcing his plan so it wouldn't appear as a desperation tactic," Gabe told the men. "Antietam was as close to a victory as he has seen in the East."

"Finally, the goal of the war will be what it should have been from the beginning—abolishing slavery!" Levi said.

"I think this might keep England and France from recognizing the South as legitimate," Gabe added. "Neither country will support the South if it means maintaining slavery."

Captain Ritner interrupted their discussion. "Men, General Price and the Secesh circled back to Corinth. We'll be double-timing it back there first thing tomorrow."

By the time Grant's troops got to Corinth, the Rebs had pushed the garrison left to guard the city back to the city's center. Grant's troops met severe fighting as they entered the city.

"This is the battle we expected in May!" Gabe yelled at Luther. "Our men are being mowed down!"

"Good God, I have never seen anything like it!" Luther screamed back.

"Gabe, take your men to the Academy building on the edge of town," Captain Ritner ordered. "Mother Bickerdyke has set up a hospital and needs help."

As they pulled up to the large brick building, Gabe could see Mother Bickerdyke standing in the road as a regiment hurried toward the battle.

Gabe drove his team next to her.

"What are you doing?" Gabe asked Mother Bickerdyke.

"I'm stopping this regiment. I'm not letting them go into battle without some food, water, and a little rest."

"You can't stop a regiment."

"What do you mean I can't?" Mother Bickerdyke responded with her hands on her hips. "Watch me."

The regiment approached the Academy. She stepped in front of the captain leading the men.

"HALT!" she shouted as she planted her feet on the road, blocking their way.

"Out of my way!" the captain yelled back.

"You've got to let your men rest and get some food and water before going into battle," Mother Bickerdyke said, raising her voice. "One of your advance scouts came by begging for water and something to eat. He told me you were coming through and that your men have been marching since morning without stopping or eating."

"You have no authority to stop us!" the captain yelled. "Move, or you'll hear from General Sherman."

"You tell Cump hello," Mother Bickerdyke smirked, calling Sherman by the nickname used only by those who knew him well. "My authority comes from the Lord God Almighty. Do you have anybody who ranks higher? Your men aren't moving until they get some food and a little rest."

Knowing he was bested by the person he had heard of—the Cyclone in Calico—the captain ordered, "Men, at ease." They collapsed.

"Ladies," Mother Bickerdyke instructed the band of Black women helping her, "see that every man gets cups of soup, coffee, and a loaf of bread. Fill their canteens."

In short order, the women completed their tasks. "May we go now?" the captain asked.

"Give them another five minutes," Mother Bickerdyke ordered, giving Gabe a wink.

After fearsome fighting, the Union forces chased the Rebs out of Corinth. That night, the full moon cast a ghostly light on the dead and simultaneously sparkled upon the gun barrels and bayonets scattered around the battleground. In the bushes and brambles, bodies were entwined, lapped, and twisted together in dreadful poses of death. The desperate nature of the struggle was unmistakable.

> *Georgetown, December 28, 1862*
>
> *Dear Gabriel,*
>
> *The Emancipation Proclamation goes into effect in a few days. While we anticipate such a momentous occasion, we read in today's newspaper that 38 Indians in Minnesota were hanged on Lincoln's order for their part in the Dakota uprising last fall. These are the same group of Indians about whom Gen'l John Pope said, "It is my purpose to exterminate the Sioux. They are to be treated as maniacs and wild beasts." Admittedly, the killings of settlers were random and gruesome, but they executed the Indians for protecting their land. There seems to be a contradiction between Lincoln's Proclamation freeing enslaved people and his order to execute free people trying to remain that way.*
>
> *It is cold and snowy. We've been indoors in front of the fire for a week! We've missed having you home for Christmas for the second year in a row.*
>
> *With love and affection,*
> *Your Mother and Father*

"Explain de Proclamation to us," Malachi asked Gabe on a chilly New Year's Day as a group of Gabe's men repaired collapsed breastworks. "How can a piece of paper make us free?"

"In many respects, it doesn't," Gabe said, dropping his eyes and messing with the dirt with a stick. "It only frees slaves in the states that seceded but doesn't apply to the border states, western Virginia, and parts of Louisiana. In other words, you're free, but Levi, who's from Kentucky but has been free in Canada for years, is still considered enslaved."

"Dat don't make sense," Billy said. You think the Rebs are goin' to treat me any differen' dan Levi when we done get captured? How dose people on plantations know dey be free? You think der massa's gonna tell 'em and just let 'em go?"

"You're right. Besides, it might not be Constitutional," Gabe opined, flexing his legal muscles. "Freeing the enslaved is taking property without compensation and violates the Fifth Amendment. Lincoln believes that certain presidential acts which would not be Constitutional in peacetime are valid and necessary as a military measure if public safety requires them."

"It also allows Negroes to be paid for their labor and inducted into the army, and to wear uniforms and be armed," said Luther, who appreciated having Blacks on the Union side.

"If'n Father Abraham's proclamation makes my Papa free, it's the best thing that has ever happened," Levi said.

"I think the Proclamation changes how we have to think," Gabe predicted. "Northerners will have to agree with Douglass that the war now has one real moral purpose: free the slaves."

"All we want to do is fight and prove our worth," Levi said with steel in his voice. "Remember Douglass also said: 'Once the Black man gets upon his person the brass belt-buckle stamped 'U.S.,' an eagle on his buttons, a musket on his shoulder, and bullets in his pocket, there is no power on earth that can deny he has earned the right to citizenship.'"

"Amen," Billy agreed.

"I still don't think most white soldiers want to stand on the lines with us," Levi said. "But it's about time we get a gun and a uniform, even if we don't get equal pay."

Buxton, Canada West, January 2, 1863

Dear Levi and Gabe,

Just a quick note so I can get this posted today. I've loved all of your letters. I hope you are getting mine. Today is an exciting day with Lincoln's Emancipation Proclamation. Papa is free—now, if only he can get away and find us! We miss him so much.

Mama and Glory say hello. Can you believe she is almost 9? Her singing has improved, and she's starting to write poetry. I'm enclosing a poem she wrote for Levi.

With Auntie Hattie being bedridden at times with her arthritis, I have to help out more at the bakery. I'm not teaching at night as much because there are fewer new adults to teach. We still have lots of kids at the school.

We all hope you are safe and healthy.

Fondly,
Jasmine

"Men," recently promoted Major Ritner announced in the early spring after the troops had moved to Milliken's Bend on the Mississippi River, "We'll be moving south. Vicksburg is the target."

"With Vicksburg," Gabe said, his voice rising, "we would control the entire Mississippi and could start pushing the Rebs back toward Atlanta."

"That's right," Major Ritner agreed. "But there's more. There is something in the works with your unit. Rumor has it that General Grant is under orders to transfer some wagons and men to the medical corps and turn the wagons into ambulances as they did at Antietam."

"If we're moving on Vicksburg," Gabe said, "there'll be many casualties. Grant and Sherman like to fight and won't stop until we succeed."

With that, Gabe went off to be by himself. He was having more and more flashbacks to Pottawatomie. The thought of more young men with bodies blown apart and blood and guts covering the field caused another episode of shaking, sweating, and nausea. *Why can't I shake it? Was what we did there the right thing to do? Were the killings at Harper's Ferry right? Are the killings during this war right?* Then, the battle in his brain came to a conclusion consistent with his beliefs. *Of course, they are, dammit. Jasmine deserves every effort to end the brutality of slavery. We've got to win this war.* He returned to camp with his body and resolve strengthened.

After a week of idleness, Major Ritner announced, "It looks like Grant gave up trying to blast a canal to bypass the horseshoe bend at Vicksburg that is protected by Confederate cannons. Our orders are to move south on the Louisiana side of the Mississippi River until we get below Vicksburg and join General McClernand's Thirteenth Corps at New Carthage."

The 23,000-man army moved south for several weeks through unforgiving swamps, stopping to ward off pestering Rebel pickets and conduct reconnaissance, as they searched for a spot where the men could be ferried to the Mississippi side of the river. An escaped slave led them to a dry staging area at the De Shroon plantation near Hard Times, Louisiana. Gabe's men helped load wagons, supplies, and troops onto barges that ferried the army across the river.

It took a second day to get all of the soldiers across the river, and Gabe's charges were the last to cross. Disembarking, Gabe could hear booming cannons and the faint, steady staccato of rifle fire in the distance. He told his men, "We need to move fast and catch up to the troops."

By the time Gabe's wagon train reached Port Gibson, the day had become very hot and humid, but the town was secure, and the Rebels had retreated to Grand Gulf, twelve miles north. The fighting had been fierce, and there were many casualties, which kept Gabe's men busy.

The next day, Gabe's eyes followed General Grant as he rode through Port Gibson, with John Rawlins and Michael riding behind him. Grant tipped his hat toward Gabe, and his brother smiled and waved.

"Men," Grant bellowed, "I know your standing orders are to burn buildings and supplies useful to the Rebels as we move forward. However, Port Gibson is too beautiful to burn. Do not touch it." The army headed north to Grand Gulf.

To the troops' great relief, Grand Gulf was a different story. The Rebs retreated to Vicksburg before the Union army arrived.

As the troops marched out of Grand Gulf, Major Ritner announced, "Our orders are to get between Pemberton's forces in Vicksburg and Johnston's forces near Jackson and keep them from joining. Let's move."

The army pushed northeast toward Jackson through intermittent hot, dry, dusty conditions and violent rainstorms that left the road nearly impassable. The Confederates put up little resistance except for a few bloody skirmishes.

Gabe couldn't believe his eyes when they entered Jackson. "Look, Levi! The Rebs left their capital city in ashes and shambles."

A messenger approached and told them, "Don't drink any water. The Secesh fouled the water supply with dead animals and poisons."

"I don't care. Look at that," Luther pointed, his finger shaking. "The Stars and Stripes are flying above the Capitol."

Gabe's troops caught up to the rear guard near Vicksburg. Surprising the Union army, the Rebs made a stand at Champion Hill and charged. Gabe and his men found themselves in the midst of the fighting.

"Flip the wagons and use them for protection!" Gabe yelled. "Fire as fast as you can!"

Within minutes, the raging battle turned into hand-to-hand combat around them.

"Fix bayonets!" came the order.

Luther rose to fire. A screaming Confederate soldier burst into the opening between two wagons and shot point blank at Luther's chest.

Gabe could see powder burns on Luther's shirt as Luther flew backward, blood beginning to spread.

Instinctively, Gabe stepped toward Luther's killer, buried the full length of his bayonet into the man's back, and drove him to the ground. He left the bayonet embedded for a few seconds, then stepped on the man's back for leverage so he could pull the long strip of metal free.

He jumped over the man to help Luther. There was nothing he could do.

Gabe turned back to the stabbed soldier and rolled him over. He couldn't have been older than sixteen. Gabe shuddered. The boy's eyes opened, and he pulled a knife from its sheath.

Gabe lunged forward and drove his bayonet into the boy's chest.

Dislodging his bayonet, Gabe realized the shouting and shooting was no longer close by. He looked up to see Union soldiers chasing fleeing Rebels. Levi and Billy were nowhere in sight.

Bodies from the North and the South lay in intermingled heaps, covering the hill of death. Flowering branches from magnolia trees littered the ground, and trees were cut to stumps of varying heights as if waiting to be carved into sculptures. The debris of an army—bodies, horses, mules, wagons, weapons— were strewn about in utter chaos.

Gabe looked at the boy he had stabbed and froze, realizing this was the first person he had killed since Kansas. He hyperventilated, and his pulse raced. Struggling to breathe, Gabe tried to gather himself, knowing he had a job to do, but couldn't. He crawled to Luther's body, put his head on Luther's stomach, and grieved.

TWENTY

"BATTLE CRY
OF FREEDOM"

May 16, 1863–December 22, 1864

Billy returned to find Gabe lying on Luther. "Oh, God," Billy moaned. "Not Luther." He knelt next to Gabe and pulled him to a sitting position by the shoulders. "Gabe, what happened to Luther is horrible, but we've got to go help others."

Gabe nodded his head and looked back at Luther. "I'm sorry, my friend." Billy helped Gabe to his feet and trudged to a wagon that still had horses harnessed to it. Gabe was numb to the sounds and people around him. Nothing seemed right. As they headed out to the field to help the wounded, his eyes regained focus, and he slowly became aware of his surroundings.

"Oooh, he'p me. I's hurt," came an anguished cry on Champion Hill.

"We've got you," Gabe said as Billy applied a tourniquet over the one the man had attempted to tie on his right leg, which was missing a foot. "Billy, get him into the wagon."

"There's not much room."

"Make room!" Gabe yelled, having regained his grit as he faced the task at hand. "Let's get these men back to the hospital." They squeezed the large man onto the wagon and began the bumpy ride. A soldier on foot, who had what appeared to be a slight flesh wound to his forehead, reached for the man who was missing his foot and cursed at him, "Dammit. Nigrahs walk, soldiers ride."

"Don't touch that man," Gabe threatened.

The soldier grabbed the wounded man to pull him out of the wagon.

"Stop! Step away, and that's an order." Gabe pointed his rifle directly at the private's chest.

"You're a damned bastard." The soldier slinked away, muttering about being treated so poorly.

The next day, Gabe walked through the field hospital, a long, strung-together series of tents held high in the center with long poles, their flaps open. Beds only a few feet apart lined both sides of the tent. He came to the section of the tent with the Black patients, separated from the white soldiers by a hanging white sheet. Gabe stopped to talk to several of them when he came across the man who had lost his foot. "How're you doing?"

"I's all right." Recognizing Gabe as the person who had helped him, he said, "I 'preciate wha' ya did for me. It's kinda funny. Massa cut off my toes on my lef' foot when I try to 'scape. Now, I lose my ri' foot to a Confed'ret cannonball. I jumps one ball bouncin' along, but 'nother one got me."

"How'd you get to our lines?" Gabe asked him.

"I 'scaped from da Loo-siana salt mines an' head north to freedom. I is gonna go lookin' for my fam'ly."

Something about this guy looks familiar, Gabe thought, his eyes squinting and his head tilting to the side, trying to figure out what it might be.

"What's your name?"

"Don't matter; a wounded nigga might as well be dead. I'll never find my wife or chillen."

Making conversation to comfort the man, Gabe asked. "What are your wife's and children's names?" he asked.

He told Gabe their names, his eyes downcast. "How's I gonna find them?"

"I'll be right back," Gabe said, running out of the hospital and sprinting toward his camp.

Gabe located Levi in his tent. "Come with me, quick," he demanded.

Levi was puzzled at Gabe's insistence and sense of urgency as Gabe practically pulled him to the wounded man's bedside.

"You know this man?" Gabe asked Levi with a racing pulse.

The men's eyes locked. The injured man shook his head to clear the disbelief raging between his ears. "My's eyes is lying to me," he cried.

Levi's eyes grew large and filled with tears. "Papa?"

"Oh, swee' Jesus. Levi? My Levi?"

Levi fell into his father's arms.

Gabe started dancing around the bed, using every nurse who came to check on the commotion as a dance partner. "It's

George! It's George!" He kept repeating, with everyone wondering what all the excitement was about.

Outside Vicksburg, Miss., May 20, 1863

Dear Mama, Hattie, Jas, and Glory,

Sit down. I said, sit down! Read the next part of this letter aloud so all can hear it at the same time. Someone wants me to write something for him.

My dearest Rose, my beloved sister, my precious little girl, and my beautiful granddaughter I haven't met:

Your Papa is coming home. The good Lord saved me and is bringing me back to you. I knew He would. After New Orleans fell, I escaped Avery's salt mine. My foot was shot off near Vicksburg, and glory be, Levi and me found each other! As soon as my leg heals and I can travel, I'm coming to you. I miss you all so much. Every day, I prayed to see you again. I never gave up. The Lord answered my prayers. I love you all. I'll see you soon.

Papa

Mama: I'll try to bring Papa home as soon as he can travel. He doesn't need to recuperate at the Camp Dennison hospital. He needs to be home.

Love, Levi

P.S. This is from Gabe:

Hello everyone. Isn't the news wonderful? You don't know how rejoiceful I am. My life is complete now that your family will be reunited. I can't wait to see all of you.

Gabe

Despite his other duties, Levi rarely left his father's side. He tended to the stump every day, keeping infections at bay. George didn't want to talk about his horrible life since his capture. He only wanted to talk about his family. "I let you all down by getting shot and caught," he would repeat in a whisper, almost talking to himself. Levi couldn't tell him about the last ten years fast enough. George broke down when Levi told him about Benjamin and was quiet for hours after hearing it. "My poor Rose. My poor little boy," he repeated over and over. "It wouldn't a happened if I'd been der. Dem men would be dead." His anger, however, was uncontrollable when he heard about Marcus, Jasmine, and Glory.

"Gabe," he snarled, "I 'preciate all you done for my family, but you better hope I *never* see dat cousin of yours. I'll take all dose years I spent in slavery thinkin' 'bout my chillen out on him. He'll wish he nebber been born."

"I don't care what you do to him," Gabe replied. "The good thing is that you have a beautiful granddaughter."

"Don't matter how Glory came into de world." George's nostrils flared, and his fists clenched. "I's come to love my gran'baby no matter who de father, like we all had to do all de time," George said, tearing up. "But he done defile my li'l girl. He'll pay."

"Papa," Levi said, looking into his father's eyes. His voice didn't have its normal upbeat sound. "He is a powerful man. There's nothing you can do other than get yourself in trouble. We need you home, not in some fleabag jail. Leave him be."

Buxton, Canada West, June 6, 1863

Dear Gabe,

The news about Papa filled our hearts to over-flowing—and then some. Do you think God has a purpose for you by finding Papa? Do you think His purpose includes me? I'm beginning to think so. Now that Levi has fulfilled his goal, will you allow him to come home with Papa? Maybe you can come with them. Glory misses you almost as much as I do. I hope to see you soon.

Affectionately,
Jasmine

Georgetown, Ohio, June 8, 1863

Dear Gabriel,

What a wonderful lift of spirits to hear about George amid all this suffering and turmoil.

We read the reports of the Negro troops hold-ing off the assault at Grant's supply depot at Milliken's Bend—how they did not back down, even after the white soldiers ran like whipped

*curs. The reports said many of the coloreds died
from hand-to-hand fighting and that no one
could show greater gallantry. They won't fight?—
Ha! I'm glad Gen'l Grant is arming the Negroes.
That gives us many more men and takes them
away from working for the Rebs.*

*Lee has moved into Pennsylvania. What if they
move farther north? The fear is that they will
make a dash for New York. Oh my, what happens if they split the North? We have no news
about Vicksburg.*

Accept our best wishes,
Pops

Gabe and his men were sent to support the troops holding
Jackson, Mississippi, and keep General Joe Johnston's force
from reinforcing Vicksburg. Those wounded at Champion Hill
and during the battles for Vicksburg were in hospitals set up in
Jackson, so Levi was able to spend time each day with his father.
They were not near Vicksburg when Grant ordered several
bloody and failed frontal assaults on the crescent-moon-shaped
defenses protecting the town.

Grant's troops tried digging a tunnel under the Rebel positions and filling it with tons of explosives. It created a huge cra-
ter when detonated, but the defensive position was not breached.
Grant's only recourse was a siege so tight that not a trace of food,
water, medicine, or ammunition could get through to resupply
the 30,000 troops defending the city or the more than 4,000

residents. The Union forces kept up a day-and-night bombardment. For forty-seven days, starving people in Vicksburg hid in caves and were reduced to eating cats, dogs, and vermin. Union trenches were dug to within feet of the Rebel line, but the line held.

On July third, Gabe was given new orders. "Men, get those horses hitched to the wagons. We've been ordered to get to Vicksburg."

"What's going on?" Levi asked.

"I'm not sure. I heard a rumor there may be another assault," Gabe answered. "It won't be much of a Fourth of July tomorrow."

They could hear cannons beginning a nighttime bombardment of the city.

The next morning, Gabe and his wagon came over a rise in the road approaching Vicksburg. "Oh my God, would you look at that," Gabe said, his jaw hanging slack. Along the escarpment protecting the city, men frantically waved torn pieces of white cloth attached to poles and rifles, making every effort to be seen, not shot.

"I could cry," Levi said. "Vicksburg surrenders with no more casualties."

The reality of the scene tempered the euphoria of the surrender. Gabe watched as thirty thousand men, not much more than skeletons, dirty and ragged, many too wounded or sick to walk without assistance, struggled down the steep hill from the Vicksburg defenses.

"Sergeant Adams," barked Major Ritner, "get your men and start collecting the enemy's arms and ammunition."

"Pile your weapons in this area and your ammunition over there," Gabe instructed the beaten troops. "Fall in at the field down yonder and wait for further orders."

"You heard him. Get moving!" yelled newly promoted Sergeant Wagner, whose bluster and braggadocio reminded Gabe of Marcus, shouting at the destitute mass of humanity as if they were animals. He shoved a man forward, snatching the company flag the soldier was using as a crutch, and threw it to the ground, grinding it with his heel into the mud. "I said, get moving!"

Georgetown, July 9, 1863

Dear Son,

Your letter of the 4th filled us with great pride. We celebrate the victories at Gettysburg and Vicksburg. Your friend, Zeb, was a hero at Gettysburg. We're told he rallied his men to hold off the Rebs on Little Round Top. He was shot but is expected to recover. God bless him. With your victory at Vicksburg and Port Hudson taken, the entire Mississippi is controlled by Union forces. Finally, the North has something to cheer about.

But we also have bad news—the elephant has come to us! Gen'l John Morgan led a Rebel force of 2,000 men and moved across Indiana and Ohio. They tried to attack Camp Dennison but got repulsed. They have hindered our mail for a week. Our Brown County militia, comprised of older men and some women, resisted as best they could. Part of his raiding band came into Georgetown several days ago, but other than scaring the daylights out of folks in town, all they did was loot Newkirk's, Shane's, and Theis's general stores, pour molasses over a pile of clothes at Colthar's, and knock down telegraph lines. The newspapers call the band's incursion "The Calico Raid." No one was hurt, but it sure terrified us all. It was distressing because the raiders were welcomed and supported by local Copperheads and Butternuts—how can Northerners be willing to assist the South against their neighbors? Henry Brunner repaired some of the Rebels' boots while Mary cooked them dinner! I never liked either one of them. The Rebs tried to steal money and gold from the bank but didn't get any. They crossed the river east of Ripley and, last we heard, are back in Kentucky.

Caroline moved to Charleston, South Carolina, along with Miss Barton and other nurses to tend to the soldiers. Pray for her safety. Her being in the deep South only increases our anxiety.

We are sick with apprehension. Neither of us ventures away from the farm unless we have to.

We don't even enjoy church or seeing people.
Please keep safe. Come home to us.
              Love,
              Mother and Father

George's stump healed, and Levi sought Major Ritner's permission to take George to Canada.

"You don't need my permission," Ritner said. "You're not in the army. You just work for us. I can't make you stay or come back. I hope, however, that you will return. We need you."

George had never been on a train or a ferry before and was like a child, taking it all in. The concept of freedom still had not sunk in, and he constantly looked over his shoulder, fearful it would end at any second. When he clumped through the door in Buxton on crutches, Levi by his side, Rose stood like a statue as if the scene was only a vision. No homecoming had ever been so anticipated or could ever match it. When George said, "Oh, Rose, my dear, beautiful, faithful wife," she collapsed in the strong arms of her long-missing husband.

"I shoulda never lef' you," George whispered in her ear. "I shoulda stayed hidden wid you."

"Shhh, shhh," Rose said, looking into his eyes and putting her finger to his lips. "I didn't wait for you just to dwell on the past. We've got a future to live."

He turned to Jasmine and motioned for her to join the hugging duo. "Oh, Papa. Oh, Papa. Welcome to your new home."

Glory hung back, unsure what to make of the hulking presence who looked like her uncle but was missing a foot.

"Papa, there's someone you need to meet," Jasmine said.

George released his grip on Rose and Jasmine and knelt, reaching out his arms. "Come see me, my beautiful little gran'baby. I'm your Gran'papa."

Glory looked at her mother, whose look and nod encouraged her to approach him, although she was still hesitant. She soon became lost in the giant cuddle, causing the rest to clap with joy.

By that time, Hattie had crawled out of bed and made her way to the small room. Like Rose, she stood rock-still, taking in the scene she never expected to witness. "Oh, gracious. The Lawd is good. Yes, the Lawd is good," as she took her turn in George's embrace.

George stepped back and stretched his arms as wide as they'd go. "My family! A real home!" In disbelief, he laughed the laugh they had missed for over ten years.

When Levi made the decision to return to his unit, George announced, "I'm goin' wid Levi. I wan' to find and finish off Massa Avery."

With steel in her eyes and voice, Rose said, "George, you won't take one step outside this house unless it's to pick me some flowers. You aren't leaving this family again."

"Dear Rose," he started.

"Don't you 'Dear Rose' me. You ain't going nowhere. You're here to stay, and I don't want to hear another foolish word out of your mouth. And I *never* want to hear the words 'massa' or 'Avery' ever again. He'll get what the Lord wants him to get."

On a sultry and stifling evening without a breeze, Gabe and his charges sat around a campfire, not to feel the heat but to keep the gnats and mosquitos away.

"Here's an article about riots in New York, Boston, and New Hampshire," Gabe said, holding a newspaper.

"What happened?" asked Levi, who had returned just a few days before.

"Apparently, low-class whites don't want to be drafted and fight to free slaves who will then compete with them for jobs," Gabe answered.

"Anybody hurt?

"No whites, but hundreds of Negroes were massacred before the army broke up the melee. Now, we have to fight our Southern *and* Northern brothers!"

"We have nowhere to go," Levi lamented.

Before anyone could comment further, Major Ritner ordered, "Sergeant Adams, I need you to come with me."

Major Ritner and Gabe joined Lieutenant Colonel John Rawlins, Major Michael Adams, and an assembled group of selected wagoneers. "Men," Rawlins began, "we've got a new assignment for you. General Grant ordered us to form an ambulance corps for the Army of the Tennessee. Each of you is being promoted to second lieutenant and assigned to a brigade. Major Adams will explain some details."

Michael began to address the men. Gabe thought he looked more gaunt and tired than ever, but he had a flash of excitement in his eyes. "As you know, up to now, recovering the wounded has been left to all of you after the battles without much organization. General Grant wants to copy what they did at Antietam. You will be part of the ambulance corps assigned to an infantry regiment. Each of you will have two sergeants under your command, one transport cart, two four-horse wagons, and two two-horse wagons converted to ambulances capable of carrying four to sixteen gurneys. Each artillery battery will have one two-horse ambulance. Each wagon will have a driver and two or four stretcher-bearers."

"Sir," Gabe said with a slight smile as he addressed his brother in such a formal way, "who will be the stretcher-bearers?"

"The infantry soldiers will no longer care for the wounded. That took too many guns off the field. The army is inducting the contrabands, and many will be assigned to each of you, just as they were before."

"Will we still have quartermaster duties?" one asked. "Because we have wagons, we keep being pulled from our work on the field to carry baggage for an officer or move supplies."

"No, that will not happen," Michael replied. "Now, your job will be to move the wounded and sick during battle, and you will still be responsible for overseeing the burial of the dead and gleaning the fields after a battle."

"Sir, I'm confused," another quartermaster said. "Are we to go onto the battlefield while the battle is going on?"

"Yes, that's correct," Michael replied.

"That will put our men in great danger," Gabe said.

"Yes," his brother replied with a lump in his throat, understanding Gabe, too, would be exposed. "But Washington has an agreement with Richmond to observe Henry Dunant's recommendations issued by the International Committee for the Relief of the Wounded that the army identify personnel and ambulances as such, and you will be treated as neutrals who are not to be fired upon. If captured, you are to be immediately released, unharmed."

"Sir, do you expect the Rebs to take a Negro captive, then let him go?" Gabe asked.

"That's the hope," Colonel Rawlins said, but it was clear from the dropped tone of his voice how doubtful he was.

"We are also putting into action Dr. Jonathan Letterman's Medical Corps protocol, which he developed after Antietam," Rawlins explained.

Michael started up again. "If we expect a battle, officers will find a safe place outside artillery range, hopefully near water, and you and your men will erect tents to make a field hospital. During the battle, your small ambulances will assemble near the rear lines, and your stretcher-bearers will comb the field for the wounded. They'll tie tourniquets when needed, pour powder morphine onto wounds, stop any bleeding they can, and carry the injured to the ambulances."

Rawlins further instructed, "The ambulances will take the wounded soldier to a triage center or dressing station not far from the action, where a surgeon and nurses will quickly examine him and do what they can to clean the wounds of dirt and debris, splint broken bones, stop bleeding, and make the patient comfortable. The four-horse ambulances will transport the wounded soldiers to the field hospital, where the doctors and nurses will treat them. We'll give you more information as we get the ambulance teams organized. Except for Lieutenant Adams, you're all dismissed."

The men filed out, chattering about their new duties. Some were excited with the assignment, others were apprehensive about the increased danger, while others were just happy for the promotion and the extra dollar a month it meant.

"Gabe," Colonel Rawlins said, "we also can dispense with military formality for now. We need you to pick your five best men to serve as sergeants in the Colored Regiments of the Tennessee forming out of the contraband camps."

"Sherman has inducted almost five thousand Negroes under his command, all uniformed and armed," Michael added, looking at Gabe and admiring his grown-up little brother.

"Major Ritner will be in command of the Colored Division and in charge of training them," Rawlins went on, "but we need reliable men of their race to help lead each regiment. Men who will follow orders without hesitation and instill that same response in the raw troops. We have to bring them in as sergeants rather than captains because Lincoln won't allow Negroes to be commissioned officers."

"I've got just the men for you," Gabe said, smiling, returning his brother's nod of approval.

"Tell them it won't be easy. Being sergeants will cause resentment."

Later that evening, while sitting around the campfire, Gabe said to Levi, Billy, Malachi, and two other men who had spent the last year with him, "I've got some interesting news for you. You'll be leaving the ambulance corps and becoming part of the infantry under Sherman," and then he outlined their new assignment.

The men were excited. "You mean," Levi said, his eyes growing big, "not only do I get a uniform and a gun, I'll be a sergeant?"

"And promised more pay, but not paid anything," Billy added sarcastically.

"White privates have to salute us?" Malachi chortled. "That'll be the day."

"You're going to take undertrained men into battle," Gabe said in a very serious tone.

"New white recruits aren't better trained than we'll be, but people above us will be overly critical of what we do," Levi warned warily. "White soldiers can retreat. If we retreat, it's 'cause we won't fight."

"Then I guess our men won't retreat," Billy said, his jaw clenched tight. "When do we start?"

"As soon as they can get it all organized," Gabe responded.

"Yee-haw!" Malachi said, slapping his old floppy hat on his leg, mimicking officers he had observed.

Chattanooga, October 24, 1863

Dearest Mother and Pops,

I'm sorry I haven't written lately. We have been on the move ever since Gen'l Rosecrans was defeated at Chickamauga and retreated to Chattanooga. We were deep in Alabama when we got orders to stop making Sherman's neckties— that's what we call the railroad rails after we heat and twist them into a bow. We were ordered to double-time it to Chattanooga to reinforce and resupply Rosecrans. In less than two weeks, we marched over 200 miles, often through almost impassable, bottomless mud bogs. Rosecrans's troops were starving due to Bragg's siege. Because we had a long string of wagons bringing thousands of boxes of hardtack and other sup- plies, Grant called it "The Cracker Line."

I'm assigned to one of Sherman's wing com- manders, Major General Oliver O. Howard. I won't see Michael as much, but to the extent we can ease your fearful heart, we are safe.

Taps sounds. I'm exhausted. It's time to turn in.

With much love,
Gabe

One month later, a battle raged around Gabe. *I used to only hear the boom and explosions of artillery and the crackle of rifle fire. Now, all I hear are the screams of the wounded.* "Get these men to the dressing station!" Gabe ordered as his stretcher-bearers ran, ducking to avoid the barrage around them.

This was the second major battle in as many days. The day before, Grant's army fought its way out of Chattanooga, scaling the cliffs of fog-shrouded Lookout Mountain and routing the Rebs in a surreal scene above low-lying clouds.

This day, the battle raged at the foot of Missionary Ridge. The soldiers would grovel into the slightest depression to avoid the rain of bullets, then leapfrog another soldier or a body to gain a few feet up the hill.

Gabe saw several of his stretcher-bearers slumped against their wagon.

"Keep moving," Gabe ordered.

"We're exhausted, Sir. We're doing all we can," one of his new men replied.

"These men don't have time for us to be tired," Gabe snapped.

The cacophony of battle stopped. "Look!" the man said to Gabe, pointing up the hill. "They've taken Missionary Ridge. There's our flag! The Secesh are on the run. I hope they run all the way to Atlanta."

"Celebrate later," Gabe commanded with ice in his voice. "We've got work to do."

Georgetown, December 6, 1863

Dearest Son,

Your news from Tennessee is glorious! Glorious!! Unfortunately, there is nothing new from Meade and Lee. They continue trying to outgeneral each other without a fight. I still cannot accept Raphael is gone, yet I am so thankful you are sound.

I'm sure you heard about Pres't Lincoln's short speech at Gettysburg. It received mixed reviews. Some papers criticized it as too brief and inadequate. Personally, I liked it. It was to the point, passionate, and poignant. Garrison thinks Lincoln's words about equality and a new nation seemed to offer hope for a better future.

Did you hear of yet another Indian massacre? This time, it was the Lakota at Whitestone Hill in Dakota Territory. About 300 Indians killed, many of them women and children. I don't know the answer, but it makes me very sad. Maybe if the settlers honored the treaties and stayed out of Indian lands, it would help.

Snow has fallen several times, but now the weather is beautiful, with no rain or snow for more than a week. We have our beef, hogs, etc., slaughtered and stowed away in salt. There are 10 acres of good corn to gather, which we will begin tomorrow if there is no providential hindrance.

Keep safe.

Love,
Mother

Chattanooga, January 5, 1864

Dear Mother and Pops,

Winter quarters in Chattanooga aren't too bad. Our hospitals have been emptied of the wounded but remain busy with the sick. Like many in our camp, I've got a bad case of the Tennessee Trots. Some of Chattanooga's finest whiskey appears to help—in moderation, dear Mother!

Levi is a sight to see training and drilling his regiment! Even though he's only a sergeant, he leads his colored regiment. They respond to him without question.

I doubt that you'll be surprised that I've reenlisted again. I'm called to see this struggle to the end. Because I re-upped, I'll get a furlough sometime soon. I want to eat your cooking, sleep in my bed, bathe in our bathhouse, and walk into the woods where I don't have to worry about being shot at by enemy pickets.

Your affectionate son,
Gabe

Gabe's furlough papers came through two weeks later, and he was off to Georgetown. Soon Gabe turned from the lane into his long-missed yard. Chester greeted him with the ever-present ball in his mouth and his tail wagging. "Mother! Pops! I'm home!" Gabe shouted, loud enough for the neighbors a half-mile away to hear.

"Gabriel Samuel Adams!" Ailene screeched as she rushed to her son, embracing him like never before. "Oh, Gabe," she wept in his ear.

Atticus joined in. "Son, we are so proud of you."

"Come in," his mother said, loosening her grip. "I need to get you something to eat."

The three practically never left the kitchen table for a week, which was always the family discussion area, because it meant a nonstop supply of Ailene's excellent cooking. Atticus and Ailene fatigued Gabe with all their questions and concerns. Gabe regaled them with stories about Mother Bickerdyke, Levi and his regiment, and his own promotion to lieutenant in charge of ambulances servicing an entire brigade. Jasmine was not an infrequent topic.

"Do you think she wants a relationship beyond being friends?" Ailene asked, raising an eyebrow.

"From her letters, I think so."

"Do you?" Atticus asked.

"I don't know. There are just so many obstacles. It's weird," Gabe said with a sigh. "Even if we win the war, whatever that looks like, she's still a slave and isn't a citizen in America. Ironically, George is the only free person in the family."

"And that's only if the Emancipation Proclamation withstands Supreme Court scrutiny once the war ends," Atticus said. "Besides, as my friend Wendell Phillips said, 'The Emancipation Proclamation freed the slaves but ignored the Negro.'"

"I sure don't like Lincoln's Amnesty and Reconstruction Proclamation," Gabe said. "I'm against giving full pardons and amnesty to those traitors, even if it also means states will have to abolish slavery in their constitutions to be allowed back in the Union."

They talked long into each night, and Gabe didn't want each day to end.

Before returning to his unit, Gabe made another trek to Buxton. The French family's emotional greeting rivaled the one Gabe had received from his parents. Only this time, George was among the welcoming party, and Levi was not.

Jasmine and Gabe resumed their long walks. The remaining snow changed their path from the woods to the road toward Lake Erie, which still was iced over in spots.

"When the war ends, would you consider moving to Canada?" Jasmine asked out of the blue.

Gabe was speechless. He held Jasmine's hand tighter. Not sure how not to commit without saying no, Gabe stammered, "I'm not sure I can stand the cold."

"I'll just have to keep you warm," Jasmine teased. "So?"

"What could I do up here? I don't know if I could be a lawyer. I don't know anything about Canadian laws."

"You could learn," she said softly, looking deep into Gabe's eyes. "I want to be near you, but I won't move back to a country where slavery exists anywhere."

The few days in Buxton went by in a flash. Glory and Gabe were great friends, and she followed him around like a shadow. "I've got to get back to my unit," Gabe told the group over dinner.

Each time Gabe left Buxton, it was harder than the last. George was moody about him leaving, still wanting to join the fight. Jasmine hated these goodbyes.

"Keep writing. I love your letters," she said.

"You, too. Your letters keep me going."

Gabe rejoined his division as Sherman was leading the way to Atlanta.

> *Outside Atlanta, Georgia, July 24, 1864*
>
> *Dear Mother and Pops,*
>
> *The march toward Atlanta is now in its second month. The battles I've already written about have taken their toll. Levi and his regiment continue to win accolades for their bravery. Many men are suffering mightily from heatstroke, but I am holding up well.*
>
> *We keep pushing the Rebs in front of us and destroying anything of aid to them behind us. Gen'l Sherman—we call him "Uncle Billy"—has Atlanta surrounded, preventing supplies from getting in. I doubt the Secesh will last very long before surrendering. When will all this suffering end? Why doesn't the South give up? Grant is tightening the grip on Lee, and there's no force stopping us. It's hard to believe that 3 years ago,*

we thought this would only take a few months, and it's not over yet.

It was a relief that the Republican National Union Party renominated Lincoln—but why did they choose Andrew Johnson—a slaveholder— to be vice president? At least they adopted a hard-line anti-slavery stance, declaring that slavery was the cause of the rebellion and that it needed to be utterly eliminated from the repub- lic's soil. Maybe there's hope for us.

Your affectionate son,
Gabe

As the troops advanced, Union forces took more and more prisoners. Black troops were often in charge of them, which angered the Rebels.

"Are you refusing to eat?" Sergeant Levi French asked a cap- tured Confederate officer, who, like his fellow captives, was worn out and hungry.

"I won't eat if I have to accept scraps from an armed escaped slave," the officer replied haughtily.

"Lieutenant Adams, you want to feed this officer?" Levi called out.

"Reb, aren't you hungry?" Gabe asked.

"Yes. I beg you to give me something to eat."

"Your pride must be more important than your empty stom- ach. You will take food from my men, or you can starve."

The man looked at Gabe, his head tilted to the side, his eyes opened wide. "I heard him call your name. You look familiar. Are you Gabriel Adams?" he asked.

Gabe looked at him with uncertainty, squinting to get a better focus. The officer was so dirty and emaciated that there was no way to recognize him.

"I'm Victor Packinfish."

Gabe gazed at Packinfish in disbelief. This was not the strapping young man he once had met. His lips were cracked and bleeding, and his eyes were sunken and sullen. "Quite a coincidence to see you."

"Mother and Father took you in and fed you. Please honor them."

"Leave your parents out of this. If you want to eat, Sergeant Levi's men will give you something."

"I'd rather starve."

"As you wish," Gabe said and turned to go.

"Wait," Victor rasped. "You ought to know that my parents would welcome a visit when this cursed war ends in a truce."

"What makes you think there will be a truce?" Gabe asked.

"Because we won't quit fighting until there is one."

"Well, unless you decide to eat, you won't live to find out how it ends."

Atlanta, September 3, 1864

Dear Jasmine,

I hope this letter finds you doing well. My health is good. Levi is healthy and impresses everyone with his leadership.

Atlanta held out longer than anyone thought they could. When they finally surrendered, the people were nothing but skin and bones. I don't see how or why these people hang on. Atlanta was reduced to ashes, and the stench from everything burning, including horses and mules, reminded me of the tannery.

We're on the move again. I'm still part of Gen'l Sherman's right wing, commanded by Major Gen'l Howard. Uncle Billy has severed all connections to any base and trimmed the force down to healthy soldiers capable of vigorous action and marches. As before, we're living off the land and burn anything we can't eat. We still have thousands of contraband trailing behind us who also forage for every morsel they can find. The Sesesh have nothing left but pride, which keeps them from giving up. Sherman vows to reach the Atlantic Ocean by the end of the year. We keep pushing the Rebs back, but they sometimes turn

and fight before being pushed back even more.
There is optimism that the end may be near.

Fondly,
Gabe

"Mother Bickerdyke," Gabe said as he helped unload a wagon containing numbered bricks so that the bread ovens could be reassembled daily, "this is ingenious."

"How else are we going to turn out 500 loaves a day, if we spend all our time trying to construct the ovens?" she answered, her eyes filled with merriment, the corners of her lips turned up.

"I can't tell you how much I respect and admire what you and your ladies do."

"We are glad to do all we can to make the wounded and sick comfortable," she said, placing another brick in the proper place.

"Don't you ever get tired?" Gabe asked.

"These men don't have time for me to be tired. I can be tired after this war is over," she laughed with her low, guttural chuckle.

Just then they heard a ruckus coming from the hospital tent. Gabe and Mother Bickerdyke dropped the bricks they held and ran to the tent.

"I won't have my bed next to a Nigra," a white soldier was yelling at a nurse. "Move me, now!"

"Sir, we separate men by the degree of care they need, not the color of their skin," Nurse Tally politely replied.

"Not for me, you don't. Miss Tally, tell those damn darkies I don't want them treating me."

"Then, I guess you don't want them scraping old cloth for lint and cutting wool into strips to make bandages for you, either," Mother Birkerdyke said.

The soldier softened. "I just want to go home."

"We all do," she said, placing her hand on the man's arm. "Get some rest."

Nearby, Gabe realized that a sobbing boy lying on a cot, his hands and head bandaged, was their drummer, Charlie. Gabe went to him, put his hand on the boy's forehead, and felt him burning with fever. He asked, "What can I do for you?"

"Please find my drum," Charlie said, barely audible.

"I'll see what I can do," Gabe said, placing a cool, wet cloth on Charlie's forehead.

Georgetown, November 14, 1864

Dearest Gabe,

Our greatest fear has been avoided—Lincoln has been reelected. The Northern "Rebels" who campaigned against him are beaten! Just 6 months ago, it didn't seem that Lincoln's winning was possible. I think he has Sherman's successes to thank. Certainly, Admiral Farragut's victory in Mobile Bay and Gen'l Sheridan's troops cleaning the Secesh out of the Shenandoah Valley helped turn the tide. The honorable conclusion of this horrible war hinged on Lincoln's reelection. Glory be to God.

We have had several touches of frost, and the ice on the pond is ½ inch thick. The wheat is in, and we're well along with the corn. I've cut and split nearly enough wood to get through the winter, although it's hard on my bent arm. The sun is shining today, brightening our prospects.

Accept the love and affection of the family tendered by,

Your father

On a cold, blustery day between rain showers three days before Christmas, Gabe watched Union troops sweep into Savannah, having slogged through swamps, marshes, and rice fields but with little Rebel resistance. The March to the Sea was over. He rejoiced at the sight of soldiers running the Stars and Stripes up the flagpole to once again flap in the Atlantic's breeze.

At that moment, the Black troops led by Levi began singing heartily the "Battle Cry of Freedom":

Oh, we'll rally round the flag, boys, we'll rally once again,
Shouting the battle cry of freedom,
And we'll rally from the hillside, we'll gather from the plain,
Shouting the battle cry of freedom!

The Union forever! Hurrah, boys, hurrah!
Down with the traitors, and up with the star;
While we rally round the flag, boys, we rally once again,
Shouting the battle cry of freedom!

"Is freedom even possible for them?" Gabe asked Mother Bickerdyke.

"Look at those faces on all the Negroes lining the street," she answered. "They seem to think so."

TWENTY-ONE

"There's no place like home!"

January 17, 1865–May 24, 1865

G abe and the troops had been in Savannah waiting for orders for three weeks. Gabe, Levi, and the other regimental sergeants who once worked with him sat around the fire. The rain had stopped, but the night was cold. The fire's heat felt good on Gabe's face.

"These oysters aren't bad," Gabe said as he cracked another one open using the blade from one of John Brown's pikes that Avis had given to him, which he kept in a sheath on his belt.

"I've never had 'em before," Levi replied, holding his rifle with an oyster impaled on its bayonette over the fire. "I have to cook mine first. The raw ones are too slimy for me."

"Me, too," Malachi added. "Ishmael," he addressed a newly freed man from Savannah who appeared to be in his fifties, "it shor is nice o' you to bring us dis here bushel of oysters."

"Ya'll came and tol' me I's free," Ishmael beamed. "I's bring ya'll all de oysters you kin eat."

"What are you going to do with your freedom?" Gabe asked.

"I don' rightly know. Massa's wife offer me a little patch o' land if'n I stay an' work for her. I's work for her, but if Massa show up, I ain't workin' for him no more."

"I hear some Negroes are heading out for the Sea Islands and setting up colonies," Levi said.

"I might just look into that," Ishmael said. "I need t' head back. I's bring more oysters an' clams t'morrow."

"Mighty nice of you," Billy replied, then turned to the others. "I wonder where we go next?"

"Halleck wants to transport us to Virginia, but Sherman wants to continue the march north through the Carolinas and destroy everything in our path, just as we did coming here from Atlanta."

"I've heard there's nothing but swamps north of here," Levi said, shaking his head. "I had all the swamps I care to see along the Mississippi and coming into Savannah."

"Either way, we put Johnston and Lee in a vice," Gabe smiled. "We've got to be near the end."

"I sure loved Sherman's message to Lincoln that he presented Savannah, heavy guns, ammunition, and tons of cotton to him for Christmas," Levi said.

Before anyone could respond, they heard drums in the distance. "There they go again. Must be seven o'clock," Gabe said, driving his blade into the ground. "Damned townspeople beating drums to warn the Negroes to get off the streets."

"We've taken their city and freed their slaves, yet their arrogance continues," Levi said. "Even if we win this war, they'll claim *they* did."

Sherman's plan won out. His troops spread out in a swath sixty miles wide and began the arduous march north, feinting toward Charleston but aiming inland toward the capital, Columbia.

"I wish dey'd turn an' fight so we coul' beat 'em an' end this war," one of Levi's men said. "Dey fire a few shots, den run."

"They don't seem to have much fight left in 'em," Levi said.

After two days of a relatively easy march, the troops came to the Salkehatchie swamp of waist-deep water and cypress roots, causing a slow and agonizing advance. Several days later, having moved only a few miles, the Union troops came to a bridge over the Salkehatchie River. Suddenly, an untold number of Confederate troops opened fire, and an artillery bombardment began from behind earthen berms on a high, dry spot of land on the opposite bank of the river. The cannonade kept the Union forces pinned down for a day.

That night, a battle plan for the next day was devised. Levi suggested that his troops lead the charge to take the bridge. "Reports are that thirty thousand Rebs are dug in to defend the bridge. A frontal assault could be a suicide mission," replied General Joseph Mower, whose division was the point of the anticipated attack.

"Somebody's got to lead the charge," said Levi. "We're that somebody."

At first light, Levi's men screamed like the Rebs and began the assault. "C'mon, men!" Levi yelled, up to the top of his thighs in swamp water. "Tighten up those ranks!"—not an easy task when each step took the effort of dislodging a foot from the muck then stepping over underwater roots and vegetation. "Drummer, signal *advance!*"

Drum roll. Pause. Two quick beats, called a flam. Pause. *Flam, flam, flam . . . Roll . . . flam . . . flam, flam, flam . . . Roll, flam, flam . . . Roll, flam, flam . . . Roll . . . Flam . . . Flam, flam, flam . . . Roll . . . Flam . . . Flam, flam, flam . . . Roll, flam, flam . . . Roll, flam, flam . . .*

Levi's regiment charged. The Rebs fired from the top of their protective mound and mowed them down. Smoke choked the battlefield. The whiz of bullets was like the sound of cicadas when they hatch every seventeen years. Artillery shells raged over their heads before exploding and raining terror on the troops. Despite heavy casualties, Levi again yelled to the drummer, "Advance!" *Roll . . . Flam . . . Flam, flam, flam . . .* Levi's men charged again. The Rebels held, and more men were lost. Levi ordered another charge. This time, aided by another Union regiment from Wisconsin that had crossed the river and flanked the Southern position, the charge was not repulsed.

"Keep going, men!" Levi yelled, watching the Rebs scrambling through the trees in retreat. "Huzzah! We got 'em on the run!"

Seeing only the backsides of the enemy, Gabe thought, *That reminds me of the Philippi Races*, remembering his first battle, which seemed a lifetime ago.

Salkehatchie Swamp, South Carolina,

February 5, 1865

Dear Mother and Pops,

We left Savannah three weeks ago and are chasing Gen'l Johnston north. I'm still with the Army of the Tennessee in the Ambulance Corps, under Gen'l Howard's command. He put me in for a promotion to captain.

We continue to teach South Carolina a lesson for leading the secession, burning just about every house or barn we pass. We spare the houses occupied by women with children at their feet. Just as during the march from Atlanta, we are not supplied, so we must forage for food and live off the land. There is little looting because the men don't want to carry additional weight. The Negroes still living on the plantations have been particularly helpful, showing us the location of hidden food and stores. Many fall in line at the back of our army and follow us north. Our clothing is practically gone, but our bellies are full of bacon, sweet potatoes, molasses, turkey, and chicken. The men have recovered plenty of tobacco and alcohol, too.

Although I remain in good health, dysentery and the ague are plaguing our men. We still have

many casualties from disease. Despite every-
thing, they are in high spirits.
> *As always, your obedient son,*
> *Gabe*

"Sergeant French," General Howard beamed while reading Levi's report after the Battle of River's Bridge, "you and your men are a credit to this army. Your troops leading the charge carried the day. I've put you and your regiment in for a special commendation."

"Thank you, Sir," Levi replied, "but all they want is equal pay, food, and treatment."

Gabe, whom the general had invited to his tent along with Levi, said, "A giant step toward that equality just occurred. Ohio became the thirteenth state to ratify the Thirteenth Amendment. Only fourteen states to go, and slavery will be abolished everywhere."

"The Lord be praised," Levi said. "That Amendment does what the Emancipation Proclamation didn't do. My family will be free!"

Two weeks later, Levi led his troops into a deserted Columbia and raised the Stars and Stripes above another Southern capitol building. Their stay in Columbia was brief, but like Atlanta, the troops left Columbia a smoldering wasteland. As the last wagon rolled out of town, a massive explosion shook the air and ground.

"I think they just blew up the armory, and probably took what's left of the town with it," Gabe said to Mother Bickerdyke as they rode at the rear of the advancing army.

"Look at that," she commented, pointing to the west, where great billows of black smoke rose, darkening the sky. "I heard they were going to set fire to the pine forests to destroy the pitch and tar used by the navy."

"Did you also hear that Sherman stuck another dagger into the Southern heart?' Gabe asked. "He issued a field order giving freed slaves forty acres of land along the South Carolina coast."

"My daddy worked that land, and my granddaddy before that," added Raymond Cress, a young freedman Gabe had befriended and invited to ride in the ambulance. "We earned every acre of that land with our sweat and blood. All we ever asked for was a chance. This gives it to us."

"Now," Gabe said, "all we have to do is finish off Lee and Johnston."

The army continued its relentless slog through South Carolina at the frustrating rate of about four miles per day.

"This swamp is the worst we've been through," Gabe said to Mother Bickerdyke several days later. "The unrelenting rain is miserable."

"How the army engineers get us through this quagmire is amazing. Every mule available is used to pull stuck wagons out of the mud. Even General Logan was in the muck, helping."

Eventually they approached yet another town already ablaze. "What town is this?" Gabe yelled to a Black man leaning on a hoe, watching the troops file by.

"Dis here used t' be Cheraw!" the man yelled back. Then he threw his hoe over his shoulder and joined the mass of Black humanity following the wagons heading north.

Georgetown, March 5, 1865

Dear Gabe,

I miss you but feel better when writing.
Mother's health has improved. My health is
normal, but we are having a disagreeable winter.

There are many peace rumors, but we can't
tell if they are true or false. I'm not sure I agree
with Lincoln's conciliatory tone in his Inaugural
Address. "With malice toward none and charity for all." I shouldn't feel this way as a pastor,
but those traitors don't deserve any charity.
They killed my son and are trying to kill you and
Michael! They are rebelling against the United
States. The Rebel leaders should be executed or
imprisoned for life. Lincoln invoking God's will
that the war continues, if necessary, "until all
the wealth piled by the bondsman's two hundred
and fifty years of unrequited toil shall be sunk,
and until every drop of blood drawn with the lash
shall be paid by another drawn by the sword" is a
sobering call for the Lord's righteous judgment.

Our new Vice President, Andy Johnson, was
in Cincinnati and was so inebriated he could not
speak with any sense and was a complete fool. It
is unfortunate. The Republicans made a mistake
in nominating him.

The popular opinion is that the rebellion
cannot stand another 90 days. We pray that is so.

> *Accept my best wishes. I remain,*
> *Affectionately, your father,*
> *Pops*

As the troops entered North Carolina, the swamps ended, the rain let up, and the roads dried out, uplifting their spirits. "It seems Sherman has changed his tune on the destruction of the South," Gabe said to Mother Bickerdyke. "It's as if he wanted to teach South Carolina a lesson for starting the war but is letting North Carolina off lightly. We're to order our bummers to stop plundering, and we're not to burn or destroy anything unless it has a military advantage to do so."

A week into their advance in North Carolina, Major Ritner alerted Gabe and his men to ready their ambulances. "We've got information that the Rebs are massing near Bentonville."

A battle began the next day. "This is as bad as we've seen!" Gabe shouted at Raymond, whom he had adopted as Luther's replacement. "The doctors and nurses at the dressing station can't keep up. We've got too many wounded to get to them all. Go to the field hospital, and see if you can get some surgeons to come to the dressing station to get the men stabilized."

"Yes, Sir," Raymond said, saluting like he had seen others do, and he ran off to the field hospital.

Gabe turned his attention to the field of battle. "Oh God, no!" Gabe cried as one of his stretcher-bearers fell, dropping an end of the canvas gurney and toppling a wounded soldier onto the dirt. Gabe rushed to his stretcher-bearer's side and saw the bloody hole in his temple. Gabe rolled the wounded soldier back onto the stretcher and lifted an end. "Let's get this man to the ambulance!" Gabe yelled at the dead man's partner, who stood in shock.

The hail of cannonballs splintered the stately oak trees, whose falling branches injured or killed men below. The forest and underbrush were set on fire from the constant artillery. Brambles, as thick as debris stacked after a flood, tore at their woolen garments. Gabe and the surviving stretcher-bearer fought through the fire and stabbing thorns to get injured soldiers to the ambulance.

Relief finally came when the sun went down. The burning trees gave off an eerie glow.

The next day, after the Rebs retreated and the Union troops emerged from the fields, Gabe said to Mother Bickerdyke, "Have you ever seen such a motley assembly of humanity?"

"And we were the victors!" she exclaimed, shaking her head in disbelief. "They are so covered with soot from the pinewood fires and gunpowder that, for once, there's no difference between Blacks or whites."

Gabe noticed that no one wore a complete set of clothes. Shirts and pants had more holes than cloth—shirts without sleeves and pants with little left below the knee. Most men did not have shoes, and those who did often did not have a matching pair. The stench from thousands of unwashed men matched the odor of Grant's tannery. Yet all stepped lively. Each man seemed to have one piece of food impaled on his bayonet and another in his hand.

"With Johnston slipping away to the north, Bentonville isn't the end of it," Gabe said, shaking his head.

"I pray he can't hold out much longer."

Bentonville, No. Car., March 23, 1865

Dear Jasmine,

I'm feeling excited and hopeful. I'm tired of all the fighting and taking care of wounded men. We've got to be close to victory. I want to go home. I want to come to Buxton.

I think of you so often and about what will happen if we win this war. Thousands of Negroes have escaped and followed us as we move north. Where are they going to go? Back into the South, where the only thing they know is slavery? No education, no money, no land, no live-stock—nothing! How will the freed slaves fight prejudice as strong in the North as in the South? I'm sure Lincoln and others are working on answering those questions.

I haven't seen Levi for several days, but I've heard he's fine. All of my questions make my head and heart hurt. I must get to bed. Good night.

Fondly,
Gabe

Three weeks later, Gabe said to Raymond in frustration, "Lee surrendered, but we're still chasing Johnston. We should be celebrating with our troops in Richmond."

"They'll give up. They just have to."

"I wish they'd hurry. Tomorrow is Good Friday, then Resurrection Sunday. I agree with President Lincoln. It's a time for rebirth for our God and country."

On Holy Saturday, Levi burst into Gabe's tent. "Gabe! We just received a dispatch that President Lincoln was assassinated."

"What? Nooo . . . " replied a stunned Gabe. "That can't be true." Exiting the tent into the bright sunlight, he paced aimlessly and absently, trying to collect his thoughts. Nothing made sense. *How could Lincoln survive the war, then be killed when the end is within grasp? It's not real. What will happen without him?*

The news spread like a prairie fire driven by a strong wind. The boisterous morning, filled with merriment due to Lee's surrender and the hope that the end of the war was near, gave way to mournful despair.

Gabe sat down on a stump next to Levi, staring blankly at the dying fire. "Who would do such a thing?" Gabe asked, not expecting an answer. "His goal was to crush the rebellion without harming his enemies any more than necessary, and to restore the Union. He sought no personal aggrandizement. He made no use of his vast opportunity to profit for himself."

"My people owe so much to him," Levi replied.

A stillness came over the camp. People sat in small groups and spoke in hushed tones. The somber beat of muffled drums sounded in unison. "Just a few days ago, we were festive and jovial," Gabe said to Levi and Raymond in a whisper. "Now, I've lost Captain Brown, Raph, and the president, all in the name of freeing the slaves. I didn't always agree with him and his views toward the Negro. But as the war progressed, his thoughts changed, and he began to see you as part of the future of America."

"He was a good man and taken from us when we needed him most," Levi added.

Learning more about the assassination and the assassin later in the day, Gabe shook his head and said, "I can't believe I met his murderer the day of John Brown's execution. I wish I would've killed him then and there."

"What happens now, with a slaveholder as president?" Raymond asked.

"It doesn't bode well," Levi said, putting his hand on Raymond's shoulder. "But we've come too far. We won't turn back."

That night things turned ugly. Some of the soldiers had spent the day easing their pain with whiskey, and the quiet became replaced with angry shouts: "Burn Raleigh to the ground!" "Avenge Lincoln's death!" Several thousand armed men began to head for Raleigh to inflict as much damage to the city and its people as possible.

General John "Black Jack" Logan stood between the mob and Raleigh. Twelve-pound cannons, primed and ready with canister shot, stood like sentinels on either side of him. "Turn back, or I'll light the fuse," he threatened. Only his reputation that he always did as he said stopped the advance and turned the men back to their camps.

Three days later, Sherman met Johnston at James and Mary Bennitt's farm outside Durham Station, North Carolina, and worked out the articles of surrender. However, Secretary of War Edwin Stanton went berserk over the terms offered by Sherman and rescinded the articles.

"Men," Gabe informed his unit, "we've been ordered to move on Johnston and clean him out." But the army had marched only about three miles before getting word that Johnston had surrendered a second time, this time with terms acceptable to both Stanton and Grant.

Later that week, Levi exulted to Gabe, "I've been given my orders to muster out and go home."

"I'm happy for you. I'm being sent to Greensboro to parole the Rebs; I'm supposed to go to Washington. Although it'll be good to see Michael and Caroline, I wish I were going home, too. At least we have a home to go to—what do you think is going to happen to all the Negroes in our camp?"

"Some are heading for a new life up north or west. Some will go back to their plantations to find family and work. They don't know anything else. But I'm worried. If the Emancipation Proclamation was just a wartime effort, are the slaves really free?" Levi wondered aloud.

"Let's hope the Thirteenth Amendment freeing all slaves gets ratified soon," Gabe responded. "At least Congress passed the Freedmen's Bureau Act to give the Proclamation some teeth. The army will provide protection while the Bureau provides food, clothing, and medical care, manage abandoned and confiscated land, and force Southerners to pay the freedmen for their work."

"You sound more optimistic than I am."

> *Alexandria, Virginia, May 21, 1865*
>
> *Dear Mother and Pops,*
>
> *I'll be coming home soon! After I finished the parole process in the lovely town of Greensboro, I caught up with Gen'l Howard and the 17th, and we marched through battle-scarred Virginia to Washington. A supply line was opened, and we had plenty of provisions and were outfitted with clothes and shoes. At Mother Bickerdyke's urging, most of the men even took a bath! Some brigades got into a challenge to see who could get to Washington first and were making bets on the outcome. Their officers pushed them to march harder than at any time during the campaign, and it's been very hot. Soldiers who made it through the war are dying of heat exhaustion. The officers of those units should be arrested and court-martialed.*
>
> *The Negroes cheer us loudly along the way, whooping, hollering, and dancing in exuberant jubilation. Many of the local citizens, though, have blistering resentment for us.*
>
> *We will arrive in Washington tomorrow. Even though Rebel forces are still fighting in Alabama,*

*Mississippi, and Texas, a Grand Victory Review is
planned. After that, I will go to Camp Dennison
to muster out and be home by the end of May.
Have some stew and bread ready! Oh, how I've
missed you.*

Eager to see you soon,
Gabe

"Michael!" Gabe yelled with glee as he entered Grant's Washington war offices.

"Gabe!" Michael cried, and the two embraced.

Releasing his brother, Gabe realized General Rawlins was in the room, and he must have interrupted a meeting between them. Embarrassed, he snapped to attention and saluted.

"At ease, Captain," Rawlins replied, returning the salute. "Your exuberance at seeing your brother is understandable."

"Thank you, Sir. I apologize for interrupting."

"Not a problem," said Rawlins. "Michael, I'm sure you two have some catching up to do. You are free to go."

"Thank you, Sir," Michael said with a salute. "Gabe, let's find Caroline. She's been back from South Carolina for a while and will be giddy with delight to see you."

Michael and Gabe strode from the War Department's headquarters to the Bureau of Records of Missing Men, where Caroline worked. "Ah, there it is," Michael said, looking at the drab building on Seventh Street. "Caroline's still working with Clara Barton, whom Lincoln appointed as the general correspondent for the Friends of Paroled Prisoners last March."

"What does Caroline do?" inquired Gabe.

"Why don't you ask her—there she is!"

Gabe barely recognized his sister, whom he had not seen since Raphael's funeral. Her hair was cut short, and even with a brother's bias, she had matured into a beautiful woman. *She looks so much like Mother.* "Perhaps you could show me the way to a Miss Caroline Adams's office?" Gabe inquired, trying to surprise his sister, who was absorbed in reading a report, but he had trouble keeping his emotions in check.

Startled, Caroline looked up. "Who needs to . . . " Upon seeing Gabe, she took two steps forward and leaped into his arms, papers flying. "Gabriel. Gabriel. Gabriel." Tears streamed as she kissed his cheeks. She backed away, still holding his arms, and admired him at arm's length. "Oh, Gabriel," she sighed.

The three spent the next hour chatting excitedly about everything that had happened in the past few years.

"Being with the two of you again is the best thing that could happen," Caroline gushed. "I just wish Raph could be here with us. I miss him so much." A somberness filled the air.

Michael cleared his throat. "Praise God we are all still here, and this war is finally over," Michael said. "It's getting late. I better get back to the Department."

"Let's meet for dinner at the Willard. Gabe needs to try one of their mint juleps!" Caroline exclaimed as Michael turned to leave.

After dinner, Gabe, Michael, and Caroline sat at the Willard's Round Robin Bar and talked until the bartender announced the bar was closing. Gabe was impressed by Caroline's warmth and compassion as she talked about her work identifying graves of the fallen in the south and helping with the wounded and orphaned. "My mission is to help us all come out of this terrible ordeal and begin new lives that have forever changed," she said.

"You and Michael are doing such important work," Gabe mused. "I wonder what I'll do."

"You'll figure it out," Caroline replied.

It was hard to end the evening. The night was healing and nourishing for everyone.

Early the next morning, Gabe sat beside Mother Bickerdyke in an ambulance, waiting to fall into place in the Grand Victory Review. Banners streamed everywhere—"Welcome to Our Western Boys" and "Hail to Sherman's Army." Flowers covered the street, and women threw bouquets to the men. Choirs sang "When Johnny Comes Marching Home," "John Brown's Body," and other favorites.

When the marshals organized the masses, they chose Levi's regiment to lead the review, with General Logan riding next to Levi. The men marched as smartly as ever a soldier did. Every regiment was led by color-bearers waving regimental flags with the battles they had fought embroidered on them.

"Oh, shit," Gabe said, and Mother Bickerdyke flinched a bit at his swearing. "There's my cousin leading his regiment. What's on his shoulders? He's a *major*?"

"What's wrong with that?" Mother Bickerdyke asked innocently.

"He was the captain of the regiment when my brother was killed," Gabe responded icily, watching Marcus sitting tall in the saddle and waving to the crowd, soaking in the adulation he craved. "We'll leave it at that."

As they approached Pennsylvania and I Street, Mother Bickerdyke ordered, "Let me out here. Those soldiers are suffering from the forced march and heat. I've got to tend to them."

"I'll get out and help you."

"No, somebody needs to drive this wagon. You've earned it."

"So have you," Gabe countered.

"Yes, but these men need me. You go on."

What an incredible woman. Reluctantly, Gabe continued alone down Pennsylvania Avenue. As he passed the reviewing stand, his heart burst with pride. Generals Grant and Sherman stood there along with President Johnson. Michael and John Rawlins were slightly behind Grant's side. Grant beamed as he looked over his troops. Sherman, with a haircut, beard trim, and clean uniform, was almost unrecognizable. Johnson stood stoically and motionless. *President Lincoln should be there, not that jackass.* Gabe rose to his feet in the ambulance and saluted.

Grant, Sherman, Rawlins, and Michael returned the salute. Then, with a well-chewed stump of a cigar clenched between his lips, Grant tipped his hat to Gabe.

The marching soldiers sang "Home, Sweet Home" with great gusto. They hadn't been allowed to sing it during the war because it made men homesick and caused desertions:

> Mid pleasures and palaces though we may roam,
> Be it ever so humble, there's no place like home.
> A charm from the skies seems to hallow us there,

Which seek thro' the world, is ne'er met elsewhere.

Home! Home!

Sweet, sweet home!

There's no place like home,

There's no place like home!

TWENTY-TWO

FREEDMEN'S BUREAU

June 3, 1865–February 15, 1866

After mustering out at Camp Dennison, Gabe arrived in Georgetown and strode up the tree-lined lane to the Adamses' whitewashed farmhouse. His home had always been a haven, and it seemed to him now as if even the cows and horses in the lush fields were perfectly at peace. But something was different. *Raph is never coming home.*

Chester bounded toward him, ball in mouth, as best as his arthritic hips allowed. Gabe gave him a big hug and a head scratch and threw the ball. Entering his familiar home, trying to be funny, he calmly and casually asked, "Mother, Pops. Mind if I stay for dinner?"

"I doubt there's enough for you," Atticus teased back as he dropped the book he was reading, sprang from his chair, and grabbed hold of his youngest son. "Ailene, dear, there's someone here to see you."

Ailene emerged from the kitchen, wiping her hands on her apron and brushing a few errant strands of hair from her face. She stood in stunned silence. Then the tears streamed, and her hugs and kisses smothered her baby boy.

Relishing his mother's love, Gabe told her, "Mother, I promised you I'd come home."

"And you're coming home a captain and a hero," Atticus beamed, his chest expanding.

"Come, tell us about your time in Washington," his mother held him at arm's length, examining him from head to toe. "How are you feeling? How are Michael and Caroline? Tell us everything!"

"Whoa, whoa. Take a breath, dear. Let the boy remove his hat and coat."

The questions continued nonstop as Gabe and his father sat at the kitchen table while his mother prepared dinner. Ailene placed pork chops, peas, and carrots on the table an hour later and sat with Atticus and Gabe. *Mother's not eating much. Knowing her, she's praising God and counting her blessings.* "Aw, Mother, quit staring at me," he teased.

"I can't. Having you here is a sight to behold."

Having told them all about the last few months, Gabe mused, "I wonder what's in store for me," staring at his bowl of freshly made strawberry ice cream as if it were tea leaves.

"It's probably best to leave the future in your dreams for a while," Atticus half-scolded. "There are two parents—and several young women, I hear—who have long awaited your return."

"But there is so much left to be done," Gabe countered. "I'm troubled by what will happen to the millions of Negroes who are suddenly free with no education, no citizenship, no basic rights, no money, and most without a skill other than picking cotton or hacking cane. I fear for their future, with Lincoln gone and Johnson in charge. Does God have a plan for me?"

"Of course He does," Atticus preached. "Sometimes you must be still. Listen and watch for signs that reveal His plan."

"He's been watching over you since you left for Kansas," Ailene said, pressing her palms together. "He will continue to do so."

"I wish I had the same faith you have," Gabe said.

"For now, just rest and recover," said Atticus. "Eat your mother's cooking—she's been waiting a long time to feed you. Besides, I need your help here."

Gabe couldn't help but notice Atticus's graying hair, the deepening creases in his neck and cheeks, and the constant rubbing of his crooked arm.

Gabe enjoyed every moment in his soft, warm bed, eating everything his mother put before him, helping his father with chores, and going to Georgetown to spend time with Zeb and his girlfriend, Martha. She always seemed to have one of her friends around whenever Gabe came to town. But, even though Gabe was polite to them, he didn't take the bait. He found that Jasmine filled his thoughts no matter which young woman he met.

"Son," Atticus said as they worked in the field on a hot, humid day. "It's sure nice to have you home. Maybe you can settle down here. You could practice law with my brother."

"Don't bet on it. Not as long as Marcus is in town."

"I understand he may run for Congress," Atticus said, knowing his presence caused his family grief. "Maybe he won't be around."

"Congressman? Marcus doesn't care a whit about people," Gabe said through gritted teeth. "He only cares about what is best for him and gaining power."

THE WAR DEPARTMENT

BUREAU OF REFUGEES, FREEDMEN, AND

ABANDONED LANDS

WASHINGTON, D.C.

June 10, 1865

Dear Captain Gabriel Adams,

I hope this letter finds you well and that you have fattened up on your mother's cooking, about which you so often bragged. I am sure you are glad to be home, but I know you understand that although the drumbeats of war may be over, beating the drum for justice and equality has just begun. Without question, the country still needs your able assistance.

As you know, the War Department created the Bureau of Refugees, Freedmen, and Abandoned Lands—the Freedmen's Bureau. My task is to assemble a staff of people, primarily ex-Army officers, to carry out my orders to protect the basic human rights of the newly freed slaves, to ensure equal justice for them, to supply, feed,

*and give shelter to the destitute, establish hos-
pitals and schools, negotiate and enforce labor
contracts, and to oversee and disperse abandoned
and confiscated land. In essence, the Freedmen's
Bureau has military powers to protect the freedmen, women, children, the elderly, and the
infirm and help bridge the chasm as many go
from enslavement to freedom.*

*I hope you will come to Washington immedi-
ately to discuss how you might fit in. Please wire
me that you are coming.*

Most respectfully and sincerely,
Major General Oliver O. Howard
Commissioner

Gabe sat on the edge of his bed, elbows on his knees, staring at the letter he had read over and over. *I can't leave Pops alone to do the farming. Mother needs my help, too. But so does General Howard. Will Michael and Caroline be disappointed in me if I stay? What about Jasmine? Why do my decisions always seem to let somebody down?*

Rising from the bed, Gabe slowly shuffled into the parlor, where his father was reading and his mother was knitting. He cleared his throat. "Mother. Pops. I'd like you to read this letter."

His parents leaned together, each holding one side of the letter. Ailene gasped and put her free hand to her lips, and Gabe knew she had just read, "I hope you will come . . . "

"Not again," she moaned.

"Mother, if a man like General Howard asks me to come talk with him, I don't know how to turn him down. I should at least find out what he is thinking."

"You know what he's thinking," Atticus said with an edge in his voice. "He wants you to be part of the Freedmen's Bureau."

"Yeah, I imagine so."

"Oh, Gabe," his mother lamented, her chin quivering. "You've done your service."

"But there's so much more to do," Gabe said, his confidence returning. "I have to at least hear him out."

A day later, Gabe was on the train to Washington. *This sure beats how I got to Washington the first time*, Gabe thought, reminiscing about the years and thousands of miles it took for him to zigzag to all points between Camp Jackson, Corinth, Savannah, and Washington. However, the more he thought, the tighter his stomach got. *It really all began in Kansas and Harper's Ferry.* His body shook and his heart raced.

Gabe stepped off the train into a sultry 90-degree day. Few people were out and about, most waiting for the cool of the evening before venturing forth. The bugs, which seemed to thrive in the heat, swarmed around him. He walked from the railroad station toward the former house of a senator-turned-Confederate near the White House, which Howard had appropriated and set up as his headquarters. Gabe stopped at a little cafe to purchase a newspaper and some lemonade. He was shocked to read about a small riot in Washington just a week prior, where two hundred soldiers had assaulted as many Blacks for no apparent reason, injuring a few and demolishing windows, doors, and furniture.

He shook his head and put the paper down in disgust. *I really am* needed.

Gabe arrived at the Freedmen's Bureau's headquarters. An aide directed him to General Howard's suite and announced the captain's arrival.

"Good afternoon, General Howard," Gabe said with a salute.

"Good afternoon, Captain Adams," Howard replied, returning the salute with his left hand, his right arm having been amputated after two minié balls shattered it. "But we can drop the salutes and rank. We're not in the army anymore. How've you been? You've put on some weight."

"I'm doing well, thanks. Yes, Mother's cooking is better than hardtack and dried sowbelly! You look healthy," Gabe said, noting Howard's face had filled out some, and he looked younger with his beard neatly trimmed and his eyes not so sleep deprived.

"Yes, I also am doing better."

"I'm eager to hear why you brought me to Washington."

"Have a seat," said Howard. "I appointed former Brigadier General Eliphalet Whittlesey as assistant commissioner of the Freedmen's Bureau in the Carolinas. I hope you will join him as the superintendent in Raleigh, North Carolina. Your work with the Negroes under your command gives me confidence that I could have no more exceptional person working with me on what may be a hopeless mission."

"That's very kind of you, Sir. Thank you. But why may it be hopeless?"

"Despite the grandiose expectations placed on the Bureau, President Johnson does all he can to make our job impossible. His proclamation of amnesty pardons all but the highest echelon of the Confederate soldiers and, despite promises to the Negro, restores confiscated property to the Rebels. He refuses to fund the Bureau or provide what we need; he's been stubborn, intolerant, combative, and unable to compromise. He is unfit for the office he holds."

"Sir, if things are so bleak, how can I help?"

"We've got to do all we can. We need to address those concerns I outlined in my letter." Howard rose, strode to the open window overlooking a park, and stared out. "The Southerners are bitter and physically and economically devastated. They will do all they can to restore life as it was before the war. Your country needs your skills, work ethic, and passion to construct a new social order. I need you to be my right arm, so to speak."

"I appreciate your faith in me. I need to talk with my parents, and I have some people to see before I decide whether to embark on another quest that takes me away from home. I need a week or so."

"Take the time you need, but there is some urgency in getting started. I suggest you go to Raleigh, meet General Whittlesey, and look around. You'll better understand the task. Thank you, my boy."

Gabe spent the rest of the day with his brother and sister. Most of the conversation was about whether he was needed more at home or with the Bureau.

"How can I do nothing?" Gabe wondered, searching for answers in their eyes. "You two are doing so much."

"It's a tough call," Michael said. "Don't compare yourself to us. Do what you think is the right thing to do for you."

"That doesn't help," Gabe groaned.

Gabe left early in the morning for Raleigh. General Whittlesey was waiting for him at the station.

"Good afternoon, General Whittlesey," Gabe greeted the dignified, straight-laced former minister from Maine. "I'm very pleased to meet you."

"It's nice to meet you, but call me Eli."

They talked as they walked, getting to know each other, and Eli said, "I'm glad you're here. I sure could use your help." He stroked his bushy white beard.

"I'm not sure what to do," Gabe said. "My father and mother need my help on the farm. One of my brothers was killed at Shiloh, and my sister and other brother work in Washington. Leaving my parents again after being gone for four years is not easy. But I realize the Bureau needs me, too."

"It certainly does, but I understand your dilemma." As they arrived at the just-built school, the hospital, and a camp of hundreds of tents housing Black refugees, Eli said, "Let me show you around," and the two talked about Gabe's duties.

"It looks and sounds overwhelming," Gabe said after listening to Eli.

"It might be. We'll never have the resources to do all that's expected of us, but anything we do will help. We especially need teachers. The American Missionary Association is sending teachers, including Black women, but we need more."

"Sir, I'll need about ten days to think this over."

"Before you leave, take another look at those freedpeople. They have nothing but righteous hope and desire. They deserve any assistance we can offer."

Upon Gabe's return to Georgetown, his mother pleaded, "You promised us you'd come home. Doesn't that include staying?"

"Mother, all I know is that I've got to do this. When I saw the condition of the Negro in that camp, I knew my work wasn't over. The South will never give the freedmen any rights or move toward equality, and neither will President Johnson. Remember what he said last year," spitting out Johnson's words as if each one was soaked in vinegar. "'The laws must distinguish between the races, or every thick-lipped, flat-nosed, woolly-headed Negro in the country will have equality with the white man. This is a white man's country, and as long as I'm president, it will stay that way.'"

"Johnson may be a bigoted slave owner," Atticus retorted, "but he hates the Southern aristocracy. He'll keep the landowners in line."

Shaking his head and frowning, his eyes focused, Gabe disagreed: "I doubt it. I need to be an agent of change. Seeing Jasmine learn to read and write, the reaction of George and Rose when they were reunited, Levi flexing his freedom muscles, hearing about Caroline working with Miss Barton identifying dead soldiers, and my working with the contraband all gave me meaning. This is my best chance to be a part of something bigger than myself that moves this country away from the pestilence of enslavement. I promised Jasmine the war didn't end my fight for Negro equality. I want to show her I'm a man of my word."

"I understand all that, but you're needed here," Ailene begged, her jaw set.

"Dear," Atticus said softly to his wife, "he's twenty-five. We've tried to talk him out of his quests before and failed. As Thoreau said in *Walden*, 'If a man does not keep pace with his companions, perhaps it is because he hears a different drummer. Let him step to the music he hears, however measured or far away.' Gabe needs to follow the beat of his own drum."

"Atticus Adams, don't be using my favorite book against me," Ailene admonished, knitting her brow and shaking her finger at Atticus, but she knew in her heart he was right.

"I think I'll go see Jasmine and Glory before I report to Raleigh."

Ailene's chin fell to her chest in resignation.

Gabe left the next day for Buxton. The reunion there was like before, except Glory had no hesitation in giving Gabe a hug and a kiss, beating Jasmine to the punch. Jasmine took her turn, and it was a long one. Gabe could feel some shoe-shuffling in the room as others waited for the infatuated pair to come out of their private world, but he couldn't stop looking into her dark eyes, which had focused on him as if she were looking into his soul. They both liked what they saw.

After dinner, George and Gabe sat in the room next to the bakery. George asked, "So, what's next for Gabriel Adams?"

"I'm moving to Raleigh, North Carolina, to work for the new Freedmen's Bureau," Gabe said as he described the Bureau and its responsibilities.

Jasmine interrupted. "You're going back to North Carolina? You just left there!"

"Yep. Wanna come? General Whittlesey says they are in dire need of teachers."

"You're not serious . . . are you?"

Later that evening, Gabe told Jasmine, "I am serious about you coming to Raleigh with me. The American Missionary Association—or the AMA, it's called—has opened two schools in Raleigh. You could work with them. You could bring Glory; she could teach singing, music, reading, and writing. I'll be living in an old army camp, and some teachers are in one of the buildings nearby. I'd *love* it if you were there with me." Gabe caught himself. "I hope that's not too forward or offensive."

"I'm not offended," Jasmine smiled as she took his hand in hers. "You've got me excited just thinking about being there with you, helping my people. I'd be afraid to take Glory, but I can't leave her."

"She'll be okay. Nobody will let anything happen to her."

Jasmine's parents thought differently. "No, you can't go," George scolded her. "You ain't goin' back to a country where people think dey are still better dan us whether dey los' the war or not."

"George is right," Rose said, her body tensing. "Remember, you are still a slave in that country."

"Mama, it's time to do my part," Jasmine said. "Papa, you lost your foot gaining your freedom, and Levi is a hero for helping free our people. I've done all I can in Buxton. New people aren't coming. Many are leaving to find their families. I can do more for our people working with Gabe than here. I have to go. The Bureau is only authorized to be in place for a year, so we'll be back then."

"Talkin' sense to you is like talkin' to a squirrel," Rose harrumphed. "You said 'we.' You planning on taking Glory?"

"Of course. I couldn't leave her."

"Over my dead and buried body!" George exploded. "You're an adult. I can't stop you from bein' foolish, but you ain't takin' my gran'baby to dat rat's nest of bigots who think *we* are the vermin."

Jasmine wrestled with what to do all night. In the morning, her eyes indicated she knew neither choice was good.

"This is my opportunity. I've got to go," she announced to her parents, "but I'll leave Glory."

Saying goodbye to Glory was the most challenging thing Jasmine had ever done.

"I wanna come with you, Mama," Glory whimpered, still in her red flannel nightgown, her hair flattened on one side from her pillow.

"It's not safe for a little girl to go, honey. Besides, I need you to stay and help Grannymama with the bakery and continue your studies and music."

"I'm eleven," said Glory, just over four feet tall and about 70 pounds, stomping her foot. "I'm old enough to go."

"I'm sorry. It's important that I go. But you cannot."

"Please don't go." Her eyes filled with tears and her chin quivered. "You either, Mr. Gabe. You stay here."

"No, you sweet girl, the work I have to do can't be done here," Gabe told her as he knelt before her. "Blacks and whites need to work together so little girls like you have a chance to live a better life. Understand?"

"I'll hate you if you leave!" Glory screamed at her mother, then ran to her bedroom.

Jasmine looked at Gabe, then her mama, who was wringing her hands. George glowered at Gabe for causing this trouble.

Jasmine went to Glory's bed, stroked her beautiful hair, wiped tears from her wet cheeks, and rubbed her tiny back. "I love you, honey. I don't want to hurt you. Please don't hate me. Sometimes in life, we have to make difficult decisions. When your grandpapa took us and escaped, he knew that if we got caught, we'd all be whipped, maybe sold or even killed. But he did what he had to do. I feel this is something I have to do."

Glory rolled over and put her head on Jasmine's lap. "I don't hate you. I love you, Mama. I'm afraid for you, and I don't know how I can live without you."

"Grannymama and Grandpapa will take care of you. I'll come back to be with you when I can. You'll always be with me in my heart."

No other parting was as difficult, ripping both of their hearts into shreds.

Gabe and Jasmine took the ferry to Cleveland and a coach to the train station. Gabe knew the train ride would be a strain because, even in the North, people frowned upon a Black woman traveling with a white man. In addition to being sad about leaving Glory and her family, Jasmine was apprehensive about taking her first trip back to the United States.

Gabe waved to Jasmine as she climbed aboard the ladies' car. "See you at the next stop," he said.

However, the conductor stopped Jasmine before she reached the top step. "Miss, for your travel through Ohio and Pennsylvania, you must sit in the back of the smoking car."

"Why?" asked Jasmine, who was well dressed, wearing a wide, flower-filled hat and her best shoes. "I'm a lady. Why can't I ride in the ladies' car? I believe my ticket allows me to ride there."

"Sorry, Miss. Rules is rules."

Gabe bristled but held his tongue. He could see the fury in her eyes. He nodded, wanting her to know he was also disgusted by the conductor's words.

Rather than cause a scene, Jasmine complied, her eyes downcast.

Angered at the irony of a prejudice that still existed after four years of killing to free the enslaved, Gabe found a seat in the smoking car near her. The two acted as if they did not know each other except for occasional glances and smiles.

Before entering Maryland, the only state through which they had to travel where the Emancipation Proclamation did not apply, Jasmine went to the back of the car, where a canvas sheet hung to give a person some privacy. She emerged, as planned, in her working clothes, a head scarf, an apron, and rough-leather brogans to blend in with other Black women on the train. She and Gabe held their breath until, without incident, they arrived in Washington, where they were to change trains.

Gabe said, "You can ride in the first-class car with me in Virginia and North Carolina. People here are used to seeing Negroes riding with their owner."

"This country doesn't make sense," Jasmine seethed. "I don't want anyone looking at me like I was your slave. I'm going to the free Black car."

"I'll come with you. You're not riding alone."

"I've been in Canada so long, I almost forgot how bad it is here. Maybe I made a mistake in coming."

"We're almost to Raleigh. Your work will be important. We'll settle in, and the situation will improve," Gabe said, trying to sound convincing.

Upon their arrival, Eli met them at the station. "It's nice to be here," Gabe said. "Please let me introduce Jasmine French. She'll be teaching at the school."

"Pleased to meet you, Miss French," Eli said, his head tilting and his eyes asking the questions he did not put into words—how Gabe knew her and why they were traveling together. "We need people like you to teach the freedpeople."

"It's a pleasure to meet you and to be here," she said. "I'm eager to start teaching. I've been teaching young and old alike in Buxton, Canada."

"It is impressive watching the freedpeople learn to read and write with such passion," Eli said.

"They are eager," Jasmine agreed. "I just never understood how white people could say we were stupid. Have they not read

David Walker's *Appeal in Four Articles*, William Wells Brown's *Clotel*, or anything by Harriet Tubman or Frederick Douglass?"

"Enslavers would undermine the very basis of slavery if they allowed Blacks to prove their capability to learn and achieve," Eli said as he guided Jasmine into his office, gently holding her elbow. "Please, have a seat." He held the back of a chair for her. "The opening of the Raleigh Institute should help overcome that stigma—the first college in the South open to Black men *and* women."

"Just like Oberlin," Gabe interjected as he sat beside Jasmine. Then he changed the subject: "I was wondering. As we got near Raleigh, it was different from just a few months ago. It's the middle of August, and the fields are bare."

"Yes. The war decimated the male population, and Negroes won't work for their old owners unless they get paid. People are starving and hurting," Eli said, shaking his head. "One of your first duties will be to procure unused army provisions—food, medicine, tools, wagons, horses, mules—and distribute them to the freedpeople."

"Doesn't that cause problems with the white folks who are in dire straits, too?" Gabe asked.

"Yes, they steal the supplies we distribute because they feel they deserve to get them first. We have to spend time each day recovering the stolen goods."

"Sounds like an endless cycle. What else do I need to plan for?"

"You'll be busy," Eli said, rolling his eyes at his understatement. "You'll have twenty things to do simultaneously with only one assistant. We've tried to distribute abandoned and unclaimed federal land, but antebellum owners lay claim every time we do, and the courts, which we don't control yet, uphold their land ownership rights. You must also find abandoned buildings to turn into schools or obtain the lumber and supplies to build them."

"How am I to know what is abandoned?"

"You'll use your best judgment, just as you will when you resolve disputes between whites and the freedmen, no matter how big or small. For instance, just yesterday, I had to intervene when a Southern 'gentleman'—I use the term loosely though he was a colonel, no less—pushed a Negro out of his way and sneered, 'Listen, Sambo, this *still* isn't your walkway.' The man pushed him back, and the colonel demanded his arrest. Having witnessed the altercation, I ordered the constable to let the Black man go and told the colonel I'd have *him* arrested if he pushed a man again."

"I doubt he took that well. I'll be leaning on you for guidance and support," Gabe said to Eli.

"I can help outfit the schools," Jasmine added with enthusiasm.

"Thanks. We need all the help we can get," Eli said. "We better get y'all to the school and the rooms where you'll stay. Tomorrow is another day in the quest to change hundreds of years of prejudice as a way of life. They may have lost the war, but they won't relinquish their misguided belief in their superiority; it's ingrained as the basis of their culture. I'm not sure it will ever change."

Gabe dove right into his duties. "This is frustrating," Gabe said to Eli a week after starting. "The traitors think they should be allowed the same privileges as the most loyal citizens of the U.S. government. They have no interest in our work or giving any equality to the Negroes."

"Your challenge is to get the landowners to honor their payment obligations. Landowners try to avoid their debts by driving the freedmen off for petty complaints after all the work is done, without paying them. I've been pressing the free-labor concept, for the landowners to pay honest wages in exchange for the freedmen's work. The Negroes don't like contracts or sharecropping, though. All they want is to own land and be independent."

"Actually," Gabe replied, "my next challenge is settling a dispute over a freedman's cow that wandered onto a white man's property, and the damn farmer won't give it back. I'm off to court."

The next week, Gabe stood in a field with Virgil Hazen. "I can't read dis here contract," Virgil said, wielding a hoe and using it to take out his anger on the dirt he and his ancestors had hacked for generations. Middle-aged, Virgil was a proud man, not afraid to stand up for himself, and was becoming a leader in the Black community. "How's I suppose to trus' what de man be saying?"

"I am here to help with that. You agree to work his field every day but Sunday, and he agrees to pay you at the end of the season after he sells the crop."

"How's I suppose to live an' take care of my family until I's gets paid?"

"The landowner agrees to provide you and your family with food, clothes, tools, and shelter. He'll deduct the cost of those things from your wages."

"He'll jist make up some story whys he can't pay me or whys he thinks de things he gave me cost more dan my pay. He'll make me his slave again."

"I'm here to keep him from doing that."

"I ain't entering into no contract wid no white man," Virgil stated as he vigorously muscled the hoe to take another bite of earth. "Dat's a fact."

Gabe needed to see a friendly face, so he went to visit Jasmine at the school. As he approached her schoolroom, he stopped to watch and listen.

A child, maybe eight, was standing before the class, reading from a copy of *McGuffey's Eclectic Reader*. "One . . . none . . . love . . . time . . . food," he read until he had finished about twenty words.

"Very good, Russell. That's the best I've ever heard you read. Who would like to go next?" Jasmine asked the class in a sweet, soft voice.

"I will!" an older girl squealed.

"Start here," Jasmine said, pointing to a poem, smiling down on the tall, pretty little girl with her hair braided tightly behind her head.

"The . . . gooey . . . gwei . . . Oh, I can't read," Bessie cried as the class giggled.

"Yes, you can. Try again. That's a hard word. It's 'guide.' Go ahead," Jasmine encouraged, glancing at the class out of the corner of her eye with a slight sideways nod. The giggling stopped.

"The Guide Post," Bessie started again, smiling. "The night was dark; the sun was hid beneath the mountain gray, and not a single star . . . app . . . apper . . . "

"Appeared."

"Appeared to shoot a silver ray," Bessie finished the stanza.

Gabe was transfixed, watching and admiring Jasmine's gentle demeanor, encouraging Bessie as she read the remainder of the poem.

"That's all for today, boys and girls. Remember to wash your faces before dinner and help your mama with the dishes," Jasmine said before noticing Gabe in the doorway. She blushed, wondering how long he had been watching her.

"That was wonderful to see," Gabe said, wishing he could greet her more intimately. "I want to be in your class!"

"Oh, Gabe, stop." But, as the last child left the room, she took Gabe's hand. "I wish you were, too."

It was Gabe's turn to blush. He shuffled his feet. *I could hug her if she were white, and no one would think anything about it. But just touching her like this could get us both into trouble. Someday, things will change.*

"I know what you are thinking. I feel the same way," Jasmine said, almost whispering, her sad eyes not matching her smile as she let go of his hand. "So, what did you come over here for— other than to see me?"

"I have some news. Eli asked me to go to the Raleigh Freedmen's Convention as a Bureau representative and quell any disruptions. Do you think you'd like to go? It would be nice to have you there."

"Here, sit down," Jasmine said, pulling up two small chairs facing each other. They sat with their knees touching. "What's that convention about?" Jasmine asked.

"Before a state that seceded can rejoin the Union," Gabe explained, "it must hold a state convention and ratify the Thirteenth Amendment, repeal the articles of secession, and repudiate the Civil War debt. The state convention will be all white men, so the freedmen are holding a meeting to pass resolutions and, hopefully, to influence the convention."

"Of course I'll go."

The end of September brought 106 Black men together for four days of meetings and debate.

"This makes me so proud," Jasmine exclaimed. "Negroes coming together to try to have a say in how we are governed."

"I hope the men at the state convention have open minds and will listen," Gabe said.

"All the freedmen want are basic rights like the right to testify in court, to serve as jurors, and to vote."

At the end of the four days, the freedmen passed a series of resolutions requesting that the state convention afford basic civil rights to the newly freed Blacks. The next week, the state convention convened. Eli went to present the petitions from the freedmen's meeting.

"No bones and banjo convention is gonna tell us what to do," proclaimed Tod Caswell, the convention's secretary. "We won't let white people be reduced to the level of the Black race in civil and political rights, which ends with miscegenation."

Eli pleaded. "Why can't you consider their requests along with your decisions on the three requirements for readmission?"

"I will not agree to take their petition up," Tod retorted. The state convention ended with no action on the freedmen's petitions.

On a cold and blustery January day, Gabe and his new assistant, Raymond, the former stretcher-bearer whom Gabe was able to locate through army records, walked past the shantytown camp next to the hospital where the homeless and helpless gathered to receive rations and medical care. "Conservative men will have to help with Reconstruction," Gabe said. "Radicals cannot do it alone. Even Northerners regard the Bureau as a 'Grand Humbug.'"

"We's got to make it work," Raymond replied, limping from an injury he received at Bentonville. He held his chin high and shoulders back, accentuating the limp like a medal of honor. "De glorious Thirteenth Amendment won't mean much 'less we makes progress toward equality."

"I don't think we'll ever get enough help. We can't even provide for the thousands of Negroes here, let alone the hundreds of starving whites also seeking handouts," Gabe replied. "No one ever considered what to do with Black or white orphans, older men and women, wounded soldiers still recovering from injuries, and those who will never be able to work due to amputations, head injuries, and the like."

"Hey, Bureau Boy!" a man missing a leg yelled at Gabe. "Quit givin' them darkies food. We need it and shouldn't have to stand in line with them to get it."

Gabe ignored him and said to Raymond, "These Southerners, stripped of their wealth and power, hate the Bureau almost as much as they hate seeing Blacks treated like humans."

As they entered the hospital, motioning with a sweep of his arm to the right, Gabe asked the first orderly he saw, "Why aren't these people being helped?"

"Some doctors are refusing to treat Black patients," the orderly replied.

Gabe and Raymond stormed into the hospital's chief doctor's office. "What's this I hear that some of your doctors won't treat the Negroes?" Gabe demanded.

Angered by the intrusion, Dr. Banschmidt waved Gabe off, ignoring Raymond. "As long as they're working, they can treat who they want."

"Not on my watch," Gabe said, his voice rising. "I order you to tell your team to treat everyone equally, starting with the most serious cases, or fire anybody who refuses. You may run the hospital, but I hold the money."

Dr. Bruce Banschmidt, a backwoods Indiana bigot better known for groping the nurses than caring for the patients, again waved Gabe off. "Get out of my hospital."

"Start treating the Negroes on an equal basis, or it may not be yours for long." Gabe turned to Raymond and said, "Let's go. We have to get to court to handle a couple of matters." They trudged dejectedly toward the courthouse.

Raymond called the first case on the docket.

"Is it true you whipped a young girl?" Gabe asked a planter he had had problems with before.

"She was insolent and lazy," the planter retorted. "If I have to pay them, I have the right to make them work."

"You better figure out a different way. I order you to give the girl and her family ten bushels of corn. You use that bullwhip on her or anyone else again, and I'll make it fifty."

The man stormed out of the courtroom.

The second case exposed the fundamental problem with sharecropping.

"Why haven't you given them their share of the harvest?"

"It was a bad harvest. I sold all the crops to pay my debts and feed my family. Besides, the way I figure, they owe me money for the food, clothing, shelter, and tools I provided all year."

"I don't care. You have to pay them. I'm sending one of my soldiers with you. Pay the hands their fair share, or he'll bring you in, and you'll sit in jail until they get paid. Sergeant, get this man out of here."

"I's afraid it'll take years before freedom mean the same thing to everyone," Raymond said, slumping into a chair.

"I don't know what will happen when the Bureau ends next year. These freedmen need the presence of authority to protect them."

A month later, Eli called Gabe into his office. "I'd like you to go to Greensboro and get things under control there. Take Miss Jasmine with you. You two seem to work quite well together," he said with a wink and a smile.

What was the wink for? I wonder if he knows there's more to my feelings about Jasmine than just being friends. Trying to ignore the innuendo, Gabe asked, "What's going on there?"

"The Night Riders of the White League burned down the school, and the teachers got scared and left. There's a carpetbagger there, Albion Tourgée, who leased an old nursery farm and set up a small community for the freedmen to work. He's going to rebuild the school, but he needs help. He says the Riders are scaring everyone to death. The military there needs direction to protect the Bureau. You're one of the few I can trust, and thanks to you, Raleigh is going smoothly."

"Greensboro? The two-week capital of the Confederacy," Gabe said. "I was there after Johnston surrendered while we collected weapons and sent the Rebel soldiers home. It doesn't sound like you're giving me much choice, but I can't speak for Jasmine."

"Jasmine," Gabe said as the two walked toward the school on a pleasant, sunny day. "I've been asked to go to Greensboro," telling her what Eli had told him.

"I won't stay here without you. I want to go with you," Jasmine replied, waving at two little kids playing on a makeshift swing. "But it sounds like a dangerous place for a Black woman to be."

"Probably not a safe place for a Bureauman, either."

"Then I better go to protect you," she smiled, but there was an uneasy feeling in the pit of her stomach.

TWENTY-THREE

"THERE IS A HAPPY LAND, FAR, FAR AWAY."

February 20, 1866–September 11, 1866

"Do you realize," Jasmine said to Gabe as their wagon bounced along the rutted road from Raleigh to Greensboro, "this is the first time we've ever been completely alone? Even on our walks in Canada, I felt like people were watching us."

"I was thinking the same thing, and I like it," as Gabe rearranged the blanket covering their laps. "I can't get used to the idea that you are free and we are here together."

"The Thirteenth Amendment is only the first step toward freedom and equality," Jasmine said. "I'm still nervous about this trip after what Eli told you about the Night Riders. But with you, I feel safe."

"We'll be all right. Um, I'm a little chilly. Can you slide over?"

"Ahh, that's nice," as she pressed against his side, laid her head on his shoulder, and closed her eyes. After a minute of silence, Jasmine said, "I'm glad I'm here with you, but I sure miss Glory."

Following Eli's directions, Gabe and Jasmine arrived at their destination. "Mr. Tourgée?" Gabe asked after the farmhouse's large oak door opened. The man nodded. "I'm Gabe Adams with the Freedmen's Bureau. General Whittlesey said you would expect me."

"Good to meet you. Call me Albion," said Albion Winegar Tourgée, a handsome man about Gabe's age and size, with a warm smile and caring eyes. By Albion's side was a plain woman a few inches shorter than Albion, with dark, sunken eyes. "This is my wife, Emma."

After exchanging introductions and greetings, smoothing her short brown hair pulled back in loose curls, Emma said, "Please come in. Have a seat in the parlor. Make yourself comfortable. Would you like some tea?"

"That would be nice," Jasmine said. Gabe nodded his head in agreement.

I'll bet this is the first time a white woman has served Jasmine, Gabe considered as Emma poured steaming tea into cups painted with colorful flowers and birds.

While the two women warmed themselves before the fire, Gabe asked Albion, "Where are you from?"

"I was born and raised in Ohio, near Cleveland on the Western Reserve, but I came here from New York," Albion replied.

"I'm from Ohio, too. Georgetown, near Cincinnati," Gabe said. "What brought you to North Carolina?"

"I injured my back in the war and had other maladies brought on by serving four months in foul Confederate prisons, and I thought a warmer climate would help. I felt I had to do something when I saw enslavement firsthand in Kentucky and came into close contact with the contrabands during the war. I answered North Carolina's recruiting call for Northerners to migrate, bringing capital and joining the state's Unionists in the noble work of Reconstruction."

"I worked with many contrabands when I was a captain of an ambulance division under General Howard's command. Many of my men enlisted in the colored troops."

"My brother served with Gabe and was a sergeant in a Black regiment," Jasmine added, already becoming comfortable with the easy-going Tourgées.

"He would have been the best officer in the army, if allowed," Gabe smiled at Jasmine.

"I applied to command a Black regiment but never heard from anyone about it, probably due to my injuries," Albion said. "I was outspoken, too. I made it plain I didn't care a rag that the politicians said the war was about the Union as it was. I wanted a Union *better* than it was."

"Well said," Gabe replied.

"Gabe, what brings you to North Carolina?" Albion asked.

"General Howard asked me to join the Freedmen's Bureau. I couldn't say no. He appointed me a superintendent in Raleigh but now has moved me to Greensboro."

Albion turned and spoke to Jasmine. "Miss Jasmine, where are you from, and what brings you to North Carolina?"

The question took Jasmine aback. No white person had ever shown interest in her history besides Gabe.

Sensing her hesitation, Emma said gently, "Yes, I'd like to hear it."

"I was born into enslavement near Lexington, Kentucky," Jasmine began slowly. She told them of her family's escape with Gabe's help, losing then finding George, and their settlement in Buxton.

"Oh my!" Emma exclaimed, her eyes wide. "That's quite a story. It seems God has his hand in your life."

"No question about that!" Jasmine nodded. "Anyway, I learned to read and write and taught school. Mama and Auntie Hattie have the best bakery in town. And, best of all, I have an eleven-year-old girl, Glory."

Gabe saw Emma's puzzled look. He glanced at Jasmine. *How is she going to explain that?*

Jasmine saw Emma's look, too, and said softly, "I was taken against my will by a white man before we escaped."

Emma leaned forward and touched Jasmine's arm, "That's just awful."

Gabe gave Jasmine a slight nod, indicating his appreciation for her nondisclosure of the actual perpetrator and to give her support.

"It's part of growing up as a slave girl," she said, her eyes dropping down. Quickly, she looked up with a smile. "But Glory is the light of my life. Here, I have a daguerreotype of her."

"My, she's beautiful," Emma said, almost in a whisper.

"I hated to leave her, but when Gabe asked me to come and teach, I knew I had to do it."

Noticing the sky was darkening, Gabe said, "We had better be going. Do you know of a place we can stay in Greensboro? Last night, it took a while to find an inn that allowed Jasmine to stay."

"I ended up sleeping in the *help's* quarters," Jasmine added, her jaw clenching.

"There will be none of that nonsense!" Emma exclaimed. "We've got lots of room. You'll stay here with us until you get settled."

"I don't want to impose," Jasmine said.

"Neither do I," Gabe added.

"Not an imposition at all. We enjoy the company," Albion added, putting another log on the fire. "We're pleased you are here." Lifting his cup, Albion said, "I'd like to propose a toast to our new friends and colleagues. Cheers!"

"Cheers!" said the others in unison. The four continued their discussion over dinner and into the evening.

The next day, they all loaded into Albion's two-horse phaeton for a tour of Greensboro. A bright sun warmed the day. The men sat on the coachman's bench while the ladies sat in the rear seat.

"Last night," Gabe said as they started toward Greensboro, "you mentioned you were a lawyer. I was studying to become a lawyer when I got General Howard's request. Do you think I can study under you in my spare time? I've kept up with current legal issues."

"Of course. Besides, much of what you do with the Bureau is legal work. Speaking of that, what do you think of the new Civil Rights Act and the *Milligan* case?"

"The Act goes a long way to help the Negroes by overriding *Dred Scott* and affording Negroes citizenship and equal protection of the laws, but the *Milligan* case will make it harder for the Bureau to enforce it."

Albion's brow wrinkled. "How so?"

"We were making progress settling disputes," Gabe explained. "But with *Milligan*, we can't try a civil or criminal complaint brought by a Black man against a white man if a state has a judicial system in place. Instead of the Bureau making the decision, an all-white jury will try the white man in the state court where no Black can testify."

"Has a Negro ever obtained justice in a state court?" Albion asked rhetorically. He pointed to the right. "There's the courthouse, and the small building beside it has the Bureau office where you'll be."

"The Supreme Court should protect us, not take rights away from us," Jasmine spoke up.

"Jasmine, don't you think ratification of the Thirteenth Amendment will help?" Emma asked.

Jasmine thought for a moment. "It's everything, yet it may not mean anything. We may be declared free by law, but my people have no property or money, and most still can't read or write. Black Laws block us from having any political or judicial status. The only areas of advancement seem to be educational opportunities, the ability to move around, and the right to have relationships without restrictions. Don't get me wrong—freedom is freedom, but what is freedom without basic rights?"

"I see your point," Emma said. "But you've come a long way."

Jasmine's eyes almost closed, and she let her guard down. "Folks seem to think so, but we haven't. How long will changing a person's opinion and hate-filled heart take? For every person like you, Gabe and Albion, trying to make things better, many others have no desire to give up an attitude of superiority, power, and entitlement."

"You can say Negroes are free, but convincing those who hate is a different story," Gabe added. "Where can the freedman go for justice when the police and the town leaders are part of the terror squads?"

"That's right," Albion agreed. "As Thaddeus Stevens said, 'A deep-seated prejudice against Negroes has disfigured the human mind for ages.' Without a sizeable military presence, I don't see how we can stop the lynchings, burnings, and fearmongering."

"We might not be able to," Gabe said. "Before we left Raleigh, I heard from Ben Runkle, a friend of mine and our Bureau superintendent in Memphis. He told me that Irish workers assaulted Negroes out of fear they would take jobs away from them. Things got out of hand, and whites, including police officers, mobbed the Black part of town, burning homes and all the churches and schools. Forty-five freedmen were murdered. It took three days for troops to arrive and stop the riot."

"That's terrible," Emma said, shaking her head. "We can't let that happen here."

"It would help if we had the right to vote," Jasmine said.

"Very true," Albion added. "Now that a former slave counts as a full person, instead of three-fifths of a person as originally designated in the Constitution, if a Black man can't vote, Southern whites will have increased representation in Congress and even more power."

Several weeks later, Wyatt Outlaw, one of Jasmine's adult students with a growing reputation as a carpenter, burst into Gabe's office. The Bureau had given Wyatt a small plot of land, part of which his young wife had turned into a productive vegetable garden. He had built a small house and shop with leftover materials from his carpentry work. "Mister Gabe, de overseer just walk into my workshop an' took all my tools. Said dey belong to de owner. I bought dem tools wid my money. You's got to help me get my tools back. How's do I work widout my tools?"

Despite being overwhelmed with work, Gabe said, "I know how important those tools are. Let's go. We'll get them back."

Soon after Gabe had retrieved Wyatt's tools, Gabe and Jasmine were repairing a chair in the back room of the schoolhouse that Gabe, Albion, and a cadre of men living on Albion's land had just finished building. Gabe reached for a jar of Upton's Liquid Fish Glue and accidentally tipped it over, spilling it on Jasmine's arm. He snatched a cloth and began wiping the smelly, sticky substance off her. The cleaning became caressing, and soon they were in each other's arms. Passions rose. Gabe held her cheeks and kissed her, and Jasmine didn't push him away.

A loud crash interrupted their intimacy as a rock came through the window, followed by a flaming torch.

"Get down," Gabe whispered as he moved toward an unbroken window and looked outside. As his eyes adjusted, he could see as many as ten Night Riders. Another crash showered him with glass. Another torch followed.

Flames rose above the windowsill.

"Let's get out of here!" one vigilante yelled as he and the others disappeared into the night.

Gabe and Jasmine rushed outside and grabbed buckets of water that had been set out along the front stoop just for this purpose.

Jasmine screamed, "Help! Fire! Help!" as she emptied two buckets onto the fire and Gabe rushed to the schoolyard's pump to fill more buckets. Albion, Emma, and members of the Tourgées' little community came running. They formed a bucket brigade and poured water on the growing inferno until they got the upper hand and extinguished the fire.

"That was close, Miss Jasmine!" exclaimed Raymond, who had just come from Raleigh to assist Gabe, holding the sides of his head. "Are you all right?"

"Yes, but very frightened," Jasmine said, only then noticing her singed dress and the burns on her hands. "Not only could the school have burned down, we could have been killed."

What would have happened if I hadn't been here? Gabe fretted.

Between the unexpected but much-desired passionate moment with Gabe and the frightening attack, Jasmine was utterly undone, shaking violently. "Why can't they leave us alone?" she said, and began sobbing uncontrollably.

Emma held her tightly while Albion and Gabe tried to calm their frayed nerves with a glass of whiskey. "Damn it!" Albion thundered. "They'll do anything to strike fear in us and ruin our attempts at improving the lot of the freedmen."

"Even if we knew who those men were, the courts wouldn't do anything to them," Gabe groaned. "We may have to station armed guards around the compound."

The next day, Gabe and Albion worked to repair the school's damaged floor and windowsill and replace the shattered windows. Gabe said, "After last night, I have trouble with Lincoln's belief of 'malice toward none and charity for all.' I wonder how his ideals would have played out with all the roadblocks the South puts up to prevent the formerly enslaved from moving forward?"

"I wish we could have found out," Albion said, wiping his brow on the hot and humid day. "Johnson gives all the charity to the Southerner and the malice to the Negro."

"Johnson expects the Negro to stay on the farms and work for their old masters while the landowner pays little or no wages and continues to whip and abuse them," Gabe said, holding the window so Albion could nail it into place. "Taking orphans or other children on as apprentices and indenturing them until they are twenty-five is appalling."

"Have you learned about convict leasing yet?" Albion said, hitching up his pants.

"No, what's that?"

"Towns pass harsh vagrancy laws and then arrest a Black man for not working or just passing through town. He gets convicted. A landowner pays the fine, then indentures the person until that debt is paid, including charges the landowner adds for food, tools, seed, and anything else the freedman needs."

"I'll bet the amount of charges is never earned," Gabe said, shaking his head.

"That's pretty much correct. The real problem is that the Negro no longer has a monetary value to the landowner," Albion added. "The owner can work the person literally to death, then go back to court, pick up another load of falsely convicted freedmen, and work *them* to death."

"That sounds like slavery by another name," Gabe replied.

"It's slavery all right, but the landowner doesn't have any responsibility for the welfare of the Negro, especially when they grow old or feeble. But that's where you and the Bureau come in. You can get the Negro released without a fine, try to find him work, and see to it the landowner pays a fair wage. Your work will eventually pay off."

"Most days, I don't feel like we're doing anything. The damned Confederates hate the Bureau and think we do nothing but cause trouble. One planter told me I'm an idealist and don't know the Black man and what he needs or what motivates him, whereas he does."

"The only thing an owner knows about a Negro is how much he paid for him and how to inflict the most pain."

Late August found Albion, Gabe, and Jasmine at the National Union Convention in Philadelphia. "I'm glad you invited us!" Gabe shouted over the raucous crowd. "Your speech on why Negroes should have the right to vote was powerful."

"You were wonderful," Jasmine gushed.

"I hope this convention accomplishes something," Albion intoned. "We have to counter President Johnson's opposition to giving Negroes the right to vote. After we're done here, I'm following Johnson's speaking tour around the country to counteract him. He gets sizable crowds of bigots and racists, and he just lies, makes stuff up, and misleads the public. He responds to hecklers by insulting or threatening them and puts the dignity of the office into the gutter. We will oppose his inflammatory rhetoric with the truth."

"That's what's needed!" Jasmine exclaimed. Then, looking over Albion's shoulder, her eyes grew wide, and she said, "Look! Frederick Douglass is coming this way."

Douglass approached the group and said with a slight bow, "Mr. Tourgée, it is a pleasure to see you again. Your words were stirring."

"Thank you, Frederick. Any oratory skills that I have I learned from you. Let me introduce you to . . . "

"No need to introduce me to Mr. Adams. We met several years ago," Douglass said with a warm smile.

"It is nice to see you again, Mr. Douglass," Gabe responded, vigorously shaking Douglass's hand and noting that Douglass's bushy hair and beard were much whiter, his vest fit tighter, and the creases on his cheeks were deeper than when he had seen him seven years before. "I wasn't sure you'd remember me."

"How could I forget John Brown's trusted aide? I miss the passionate old man and my friend, Shields."

"So do I," Gabe said, dropping his eyes and chin.

"And who is this lovely lady?"

"Mr. Douglass, this is Miss Jasmine French. She is a teacher at the school in Greensboro."

"Miss French," Douglass again bowed, kissing the back of her hand and grinning. "Someone as lovely as you shouldn't associate with these rascals."

Jasmine blushed. "Someone as renowned as you shouldn't either."

All broke into laughter. The four retired to a back room where they discussed life, family, and politics for some time.

Having heard Jasmine hold her own with the opinionated men, Frederick said to her, "I appreciate your strength, wisdom, and poise."

"No one admires you as much as I do. I learned how to read from your writings."

"You flatter me. Apparently, my writings taught you more than how to read."

"As a slave, I was ashamed to be Black and not allowed to have principles, ideas, or to speak my mind, to keep me in my place. You showed me dignity. I am proud to be Black because of you."

Frederick took her hand and looked her in the eyes. "I will always remember that compliment."

After their return to Greensboro and finishing a long day at the courthouse and his office, Gabe went to the schoolhouse. "Ah, I needed to see your smile," he told Jasmine as he helped her straighten the desks. "These planters use every ruse they can think of to cheat the freedmen. It makes me crazy."

"Just keep doing what you are doing. They'll come around."

"We've been here a year. I don't see a lot of progress."

"Speaking of that," Jasmine began, clearing her throat, "I need to talk with you about something."

Gabe braced himself.

"Although Congress extended the Freedmen's Bureau for two more years, I can't stay any longer. I need to get back to Glory. I've seen her only the one time I was able to get home for Christmas. I miss her so much. I also want to see *Captain* Levi before he goes west with the Buffalo Soldiers. With Auntie Hattie's health failing, they need me home."

"I knew this day would come," Gabe said with a lump in his throat. "I don't want you to leave. We are a great team, and . . . um," Gabe stammered.

"What?"

"Nothing."

"What?" she insisted, hands on her hips.

"I don't know what to do. I . . . I . . . I love you, but I can't act on it. Even if the states ratify the Fourteenth Amendment, I don't think it will change anything until people change."

"I love you, too," Jasmine said softly as she met his lips. "I've always loved you."

Gabe pressed against her, and his body heat rose like a fever.

"No, Gabe, we can't," Jasmine said sadly as she gently pushed him back. "It is too dangerous. If those Night Riders had known we were alone in that school, they would have lynched us. How I feel about you is why I need to leave."

On Jasmine's last day in Greensboro, Gabe watched the children cry their goodbyes.

"Wait," one child said, "we have something for you." The children gathered around Jasmine, the youngest sitting at her feet. They sang one of Jasmine's favorite songs:

> There is a happy land, far, far away,
> Where saints in glory stand, bright, bright as day;
> Oh, how they sweetly sing, worthy is our Savior King,
> Loud, let His praises ring, praise, praise for aye.
>
> Bright, in that happy land, beams every eye;
> Kept by a Father's hand, love cannot die;
> Oh, then to glory run; be a crown and kingdom won;
> And, bright, above the sun, we reign for aye.

As the children sang, Jasmine glanced at Gabe and smiled. But it was more than a smile. Gabe's face flushed. *This is how I'll remember her—standing in the sunlight, admiring the children she has brought so far.*

TWENTY-FOUR

"It's time to go home."

September 20, 1866–February 28, 1870

"I hate these goodbyes," Jasmine cried at the Greensboro train station.

"I do, too," Gabe replied with equal emotion. "Each goodbye is harder than the one before. I wish I could go with you. I don't like you to travel alone."

"I'll be all right, but there are many other reasons I'd like you to be coming with me," she said, taking his hands in hers.

"Send a telegram as soon as you get to Buxton," Gabe requested, wanting to take her in his arms. They had spent time alone that morning and exchanged the hugs and kisses he so greatly desired at this moment. Gabe handed her bags to the conductor and helped her up the three steep stairs into the railcar. He mouthed the words, *I love you.*

Jasmine found a seat next to a window. The train chugged and lurched northward. She gave a feeble wave and mouthed the same words back. And she was gone.

Lonely, Gabe immersed himself in his work. Several weeks after Jasmine's departure, Gabe met with local planters in the schoolhouse. To be heard, Gabe raised his voice above the murmurs and jeers. "They aren't slaves anymore. They'll work for you, but you have to pay them like you would any hand."

"I don't have money to pay them," objected Adin Badger, who was dressed in a slouch hat and greasy shirt, his britches stuffed into his boots. "This here free-labor idea ain't free."

"You had a bountiful harvest this year," Gabe retorted. "Pay them when you sell, or give them a portion of the crop so they can sell it."

"Why? The darkies come and go as they please, don't work as fast as I need them to, and they have an uppity attitude when they do work. After all we done for them, they repay us with ingratitude, insolence, and insubordination."

"You're lucky they don't repay you with revenge," Gabe retorted. "The freedmen will work with a contract, and I'll oversee that the contract is fair."

"Reck'n *I* don't need no contract to make the bucks work," spat Uriah "Baldy" Blount, a former enslaver and Confederate captain, "just a whip."

In a voice dripping with sarcasm, Badger said, "Using the bully ain't allowed, Baldy. Gotta be nice to the Neeegro and treat 'em like our equal." Returning to his normal voice, he added, "We ought to just exterminate the whole lot of them varmints like we're doing to the redskin savages, before they poison our blood more than they already have."

"It would help if you gave them a plot of land to call their own," Gabe said, although knowing his words fell on deaf ears. "They provided you with your lifestyle with their blood and sweat for hundreds of years. You exploited the slaves for your comfort and wealth. If you think about it, if they had some land, they'd stay and be available to work your land."

"Don' s'pose we have to pay those orphaned pickaninnies indentured to us until they are twenty-five, too?" Baldy sneered. "I don' give a damn about what you say. The Bureau is an unconstitutional force telling me what to do and how to do it. The war ain't over until we get rid of you and the federal invaders, and the South becomes a white man's land again. That son of a bitch Sherman ain't going to tell me to give a nigger forty acres, even if *you* throw in the mule."

"General Sherman's Field Order applied only to abandoned lands," Gabe corrected him.

"Well, Sonny, they are no longer abandoned. Your Pres'dent Johnson granted us amnesty, and he is givin' us our land back," Baldy shot back.

"Slavery might be dead," Badger shouted, "but what is most unfortunate, the Negro is not! Watch your back, Bureauman."

Two weeks later, a man rushed into the Bureau office. "Gabe, you need to get down to Baldy Blount's farm. There's trouble. I think you ought to take some protection."

Gabe yelled at Raymond and three soldiers playing whist, "Nick, Joe, Connor: Get your guns and get in the saddle. Raymond, let's go!"

They rode hard toward the Blount farm, about a mile outside Greensboro. When they got to the edge of the Blount acreage, they came upon a small group of white men confronting Wyatt Outlaw, who was standing next to the smoldering remains of his small cabin.

"Now get off my land!" Baldy yelled, holding a shotgun in the ready position. He looked at Gabe, Raymond, and the soldiers. "And you invaders ain't gonna stop me gettin' my land back."

"They just burned my house down!" Wyatt cried. "This is *my* land. I got this land from General Whittlesey himself. Gabe, you know that."

"I didn't burn your damn shack," Baldy snapped back. "You probably started the fire yourself to get rid of the lice. Your president gave us the land back. I got the papers right here."

Gabe dismounted but did not need to look at the papers Baldy was waving. He knew what they said.

"Dis ain't right," Wyatt pleaded, his arms stretched out to the side. "What's I gonna do widout my house? Dey can't take my land. Why do dem people who tried to overturn your gov'ment get all der land back, and we gets nothin'"?

"This here land has been in my family for generations," Baldy said, his hands on his hips. "It's mine. Now *git*."

"He'll stay put," Gabe said, inching closer to Baldy with the soldiers close to his back. "General Howard believes land declared abandoned and given to a freedman overrides you getting your land back, and what he says is as good as law. I'll see to it that you give him materials to rebuild his house."

"I don't care if that rogue Congress allows you to be here two more years," Baldy sneered. "We can wait. You'll be gone, and then we'll put them darkies right back where they belong." Baldy and his men turned to go back to his adjacent farm.

"We'll do all we can to protect you," Gabe said to Wyatt, exhaling slowly.

"You and your men gonna keep watch day and night? I 'preciate your help, but I'm not gonna be safe here no matter what you says to dem. 'Sides, he be right. You won't be here f'ever."

"I guess I was naive to believe that whites would see the benefit of the free-labor system that works so well in the North," sighed Gabe. "Forcing them to treat the Negro in a just and fair manner was too much to expect."

"We don't like de sharecropper system neither. Nothin's fair to us."

"Well, Wyatt, as Frederick Douglass said, 'The work did not end with the abolition of slavery, but only began.'"

Months went by. Gabe's work continued but with little progress. One day, as he was sitting in his office, Albion came to chat. "Gabe, this is wonderful," Albion declared as he read the Greensboro *Patriot*. "To get back in the Union, regain representation in Washington, and get the military out, a state has to give Negroes the right to vote, but if they let the freedmen vote, they'll be voted out of office. I take great delight when they sit on the sharp horns of a dilemma."

"They won't give up," Gabe said. "Too many people agree that the evil of Negro suffrage will not be tolerated, and they'll do all they can to prevent Blacks from voting."

Just a month later, Gabe exalted as he rushed into the Bureau office, waving a newspaper over his head. "Raymond. Mark this day in history. January 8, 1867—the day Negroes got the right to vote somewhere in the South. It may just be in Washington, D.C., but it's a start."

"So, Congress overrode Johnson's veto again," Raymond said with a big smile. "Hopefully, we only have one year left of that . . . that . . . what did you call him?"

"Megalomaniac!"

Greensboro, N. Car., January 12, 1867

Dear Jasmine,

Words cannot describe how empty I feel without you here. I miss seeing you at the school-house, and the days seem so much longer.

The Bureau is changing course for the better, but it will create more work for me. Congress overrode Johnson's veto and passed the new Reconstruction Act. The Act disbands the ten remaining Confederate states' governments and divides the states into five military districts, each commanded by a general backed by the army. The Freedmen's Bureau answers to General Howard, not the local government. We call it Military Reconstruction. We have a chance at making progress.

I'm pressing Eli to give me some time off so I can come to Buxton, but he says he can't afford to have me gone. I'll keep trying.

My very best wishes to you and Glory.

Fondly,
Gabe

Just a few weeks later, Albion came into Gabe's office, grinning broadly and waving his hands above his head. "I've been elected as a Superior Court judge!"

Pumping his fists into the air, Gabe cheered, "Hip, hip, hooray!" Then laughed, "It's hard to believe you could get elected for anything, with years of being outspoken about Southerners' attitudes."

"Not bad for a carpetbagger," Albion said, still beaming. "I wasn't even going to run until I was nominated at the convention."

"You had to overcome Governor Worth's comments," Gabe said, quoting him sarcastically. 'All respectable people would feel utter disgust putting Tourgée on the bench. He stinks in the nostrils of all men of honor.'"

"I don't care a whit what Governor Worth-less says. I just want to see that the means of light and knowledge are given to the freedmen. I will be evenhanded. Justice must be color-blind."

"In the meantime, seeing what happens at the presidential conventions will be interesting. With Johnson running as a Democrat, Grant should win the Republican nomination."

"I'm still upset the impeachment of Johnson failed by just one vote," Albion replied. "He was such a clown to challenge Congress the way he did. He was lucky there were enough gutless and spineless senators who didn't vote to convict him."

"No matter who the Democrats run, we need Grant to win. Reconstruction will be alive and well if he does."

Gabe's optimism disappeared a short time later.

"Outlaw, we're tired of your meddlin'," a hooded goon yelled, dragging Wyatt from his recently rebuilt home on a cool February morning. "You ain't never gonna vote or raise a ruckus again."

"Let's string him up at the courthouse," another man excitedly panted. "That'll teach 'em all a lesson."

Living apart from others on the outskirts of town, Wyatt couldn't hope for any help to arrive as the men dragged him through the dewy grass. His wife, Sabrina, and two young sons watched in horror.

"Y'all stay put!" one of the masked cowards yelled at Wyatt's wife. "You follow us, and we'll string you up, too."

A crowd gathered under a giant oak tree on the courthouse square. A disguised man yelled, "Throw that rope over the branch!"

"Wow, Mommy, this is exciting," said a little boy, taking a bite of an apple.

"This is what happens to uppity darkies," the mother said matter-of-factly to her son.

"C'mon, men, pull that rope!"

A guttural "Yea-ugh" exploded as the rope yanked Wyatt off his feet.

"Oh, look at him squirm!" the little boy's mother said, grinning. A young girl by her side clapped her hands, bouncing on her toes.

A breathless rider skidded to a stop at the Tourgées' house, interrupting Albion and Emma's peaceful day sitting on the porch. "Come quick! There's been another lynching at the courthouse."

Albion arrived at the courthouse. "Oh my dear God," Albion gasped upon seeing his friend and fellow vocal advocate for freedmen's rights hanging from the tree. "The damned Ku Klux Klan. We've got to stop them," he cried to Cato Crilbrow, a fellow judge.

The crowd had grown around Wyatt's body. "How disgusting," Judge Crilbrow said, his voice quivering. "Men, women, and children laughing, eating, and having a grand time. It's as if they're at the fair or having a picnic."

Gabe raced up and dismounted. Scanning the horrific scene, he told Albion and Cato, "To think this happened in broad daylight. They can't stand the fact that the Bureau and the Negroes are making progress. This is so atrocious."

"They killed him because he was a leader, trying to work with both sides," Albion said, his voice drifting off, unable to fathom what just happened. "C'mon. Let's get Wyatt's body down."

As the crowd jeered, Cato cut the rope and, along with several men who had arrived, carried the body to the courthouse.

"Look at this," Gabe exclaimed as he removed a note the murderers had attached to Wyatt's chest: "Which of you want to vote now?"

Six months later, standing on the Tourgées' front porch on a mild November day, Gabe mused, "What a great election for America.

With Grant winning, there is hope. He'll keep the army in place in the South."

"The army is not going to change the Southerners' prejudices, but with Grant and the ratification of the Fourteenth Amendment, we are going to provide them with a different paradigm," Albion said in his usual direct and firm way.

"Finally, Jefferson's promise that all men are created equal has constitutional status, and Negroes will get due process and equal protection under the laws. Black men can sit on juries and testify. There can be no more Black Codes."

"Times are changing. Can you believe North Carolina elected over twenty Negroes to the state Senate and House?" Albion asked rhetorically. "Despite the Kluxers stepping up their intimidation and violence, one hundred thousand freedmen voted, making all the difference."

"Enforcement is getting harder, though. Congress keeps slashing our budget and recalling our troops," Gabe said. "We had over ten thousand cavalrymen in North Carolina last year. Now it's down to about a thousand. Lynchings and assaults are directly proportional to the distance from the nearest army garrison."

Winter came, and with fewer planter disputes, Gabe pleaded with Eli to allow him a break to get home. He relented, and Gabe left for Ohio, where he spent two days with his mother and father before leaving for Buxton.

On his first night in Buxton, as everyone sat down for dinner, Gabe commented, "I sure enjoy coming up here. It is such a quiet and peaceful place. Glory, come sit by me," a request she obliged gleefully. He couldn't have been more content than sitting between Jasmine and Glory.

"You're not taking Mama with you again, are you?" Glory asked.

"No," Gabe laughed, breaking the sudden tension at the brazen question. "She belongs here with you."

"What about you, Gabe?" George asked.

"I don't know. Congress funded the Bureau until June. I'm not sure how much longer I'll be there. I have other things I want to do," giving Jasmine a glance that was not lost on George. "Maybe come back to Ohio and practice law."

While the women cleaned the dishes and kitchen, Gabe and George retired to the parlor, where George offered Gabe a glass of whiskey and he gladly accepted.

The two sat and chatted, Gabe first asking about how Levi was faring. George responded, "He's doing his duty, but he's not happy with the soldiers' treatment of the Indians or allowing the settlers to break the treaties. He's concerned that the army won't stop until all the Indians are on reservations—or dead."

"I'm not sure I fully understand how Black soldiers who just a few years ago fought for their freedom are now taking it away from the Indians," Gabe said.

"That irony is not lost on Levi. He has asked that his company guard some of the forts and escort mail and supply trains rather than fight the Indians." George began to hem and haw a bit, then said, "I love you like a son, Gabe, but I saw that look you gave Jasmine. What are your plans with her? Taking her away again?"

"Well, um, no, sir. I mean, not now. I don't know what might happen in the future."

"I like the present. I'm not ready for the future," George said emphatically.

Later that night, Gabe told Jasmine of his conversation with George. "He's just being protective. He is still not over being captured and leaving us alone."

"I love you, Jasmine, but our lives seem to go in different directions, and no matter what I do, I hurt or disappoint someone. After I finish in North Carolina, I'll probably go home, apply to be an attorney, and practice there."

"Why can't you be a lawyer in Canada?"

"I don't know anybody here, and the nearest courthouse is over fifty miles away."

"Well, I don't think I'm leaving, at least while Glory is here. I may not want to leave while Mama and Papa are alive, either."

"Why don't we let the future play out and see what happens."

"I don't see any other choice."

George's stern words and the uncertainties raised in Gabe's talk with Jasmine made the goodbyes a bit stilted. *Is this the beginning of the end of my time with Jasmine?*

Gabe hadn't been back in North Carolina for long when cloaked and hooded men bashed in his door one night. They were in his room before he could get out of bed.

"You tryin' to take our birthright away from us!" the Night Rider yelled. "I guess we need to make shore you git the message," and a club came down on Gabe's ribs, then another to the side of his head.

Gabe fell to the floor, curled up into a ball, and covered his head as the blows continued. A boot slammed into his side, knocking the air from his lungs. Gabe heard a *snap* as a blow hit his arm. Another smash to his lower back.

"Don' kill 'em—yet. I reckon that's about 'nuff for tonight," came a voice that sounded a lot like Baldy Blount's. "Now, Mr. Adams, leave town or else." One last blow caught the side of Gabe's head, opening up a large gash. Gabe lost consciousness as the men rode into the dark night.

The Klan was not done.

Albion's dogs were barking wildly. "Get up, Emma. Here's a pistol. Get under the bed. If anyone comes through the door, shoot 'em." Albion threw on a pair of pants, grabbed his shotgun, and ran to the front window just in time to see masked men dismounting from covered horses.

"Get the hell out of here!" Albion yelled as he let the hammer fly on the first barrel of his new Colt percussion shotgun.

A man went down. Illuminated by the light of the riders' torches, Albion could see the wounded man's white costume turning red. Men grabbed the motionless form and threw him across the saddle. Another man led the horse away at a rapid pace.

Crash! A bullet came through the window, just missing Albion.

With a flash of fire and an explosion in his ears, Albion discharged the second barrel. He snapped the breech open and jammed two brass shells into the chambers.

Another man seemingly was hit but was able to mount his horse and ride off.

Another flash and explosion. And again. Albion reloaded.

The mob of ten to fifteen disguised midnight marauders galloped off.

Shaken to the core, Albion embraced Emma.

"I can't take this anymore," Emma said, burying her face into Albion's chest.

The next day, they learned of the attack on Gabe and went to the room where he was being cared for by several teachers.

"How're you doing?" Albion asked.

"Been better, but I'll live."

Albion told him of what had occurred at the Tourgée farm. "At least, I believe, we have one less Kluxer," Albion said. "I heard that Deacon Tom Farley died last night. People claim a mule kicked him. I'm willing to bet that mule was my shotgun."

"Maybe we ought to go to his funeral and get a look at the rest of them."

Months later, Albion knocked on the door to Gabe's office at the Freedman's Bureau.

Opening the door, Gabe was delighted to see his friend. "Hi, Albion. Come on in. What brings you down here?"

"Well, now that the state adopted my civil code and our local courts have more autonomy, I thought we could discuss more efficient and effective ways to resolve cases."

"Anything to move things along. Have a seat. Let me get Raymond in here. He needs to be part of the discussion."

The two listened to Albion's ideas and asked many questions. Albion's thoughtfulness and depth of knowledge impressed Raymond. "I think there's a lot to work with," Raymond said. "I like your ideas."

After they finished with Albion's thoughts, Gabe leaned back in his chair and took a deep breath. "I'm glad you're here. There is something I need to tell both of you."

"After much consideration, I have submitted my resignation to Generals Howard and Whittlesey," Gabe sighed. "As you know, I stayed as superintendent of education and senior claims agent after the Bureau's virtual shutdown last year, but Raymond has proven he can continue our work."

"I can't do it without you, Gabe," Raymond pleaded. "If they treat you the way they do, how will they treat a Black man?"

"With the ratification of the Fifteenth Amendment, if Reconstruction is going to work, Black men will have to take the lead in many ways. You can do it."

Gabe and Albion went outside. Before mounting his horse, Albion turned to Gabe and said, "I didn't want to say this in front of Raymond, but I'm concerned that, despite Negroes gaining the right to vote, Southerners will still figure out ways to keep them from doing so. The South is falling back under the same supreme white control that sustained slavery and brought on the war."

Both men went silent, lost in their thoughts about the bigotry and hatred they had witnessed.

"Emma is talking more about leaving, too," Albion said, breaking the stillness. Looking defeated, he continued, "Ever since the Ku Klux raid on our house, she has wanted to leave. I don't think she can tolerate staying much longer."

"What do you think you will do if Emma leaves?"

"I don't know. I still have work to do here, but I don't see how I can stay if she leaves."

"I understand your dilemma," Gabe said. "I'm still struggling with my decision. I feel like I'm deserting you."

"No, my brother. We each must chart our course, and you must do what you feel is best."

TWENTY-FIVE

"Since I laid my burdens down"

March 15, 1870–May 15, 1870

Gabe arrived home, surprised to see Michael and Caroline there. His eyes darted from person to person, wrinkling his brow. "What's happening? Why are you both here? Where's Mother?"

Atticus said softly, "She's very sick, son. Breast cancer. I should have telegraphed you when I notified Michael and Caroline last week, but I knew you were coming home soon. We didn't expect her to slip so quickly."

The doctor came out of the bedroom. "Nice to see you again, Gabe. I'm sorry it's under these conditions."

"It's good to see you, too. What's going on with Mother? How is she?"

"She's not good. Her cancer is spreading fast."

"What can you do?"

"There isn't anything we can do except make her comfortable."

"Not even surgery?" Gabe asked.

"It's not an option. Surgery would be painful and disfiguring, with very little chance for success. Her lumps are large, and her lymph nodes are infected."

"Come see her, but be prepared," Atticus said, leading Gabe into her room. One curtain had been pulled back to allow light into the room. A candle flickered on the table next to the bed.

Gabe tried not to look shocked and choked back his tears. His mother's eyes were dull, and her cheeks were sunken into a colorless face. Ailene's torso barely made a mound beneath the quilt covering her. "Oh, Mother, I'm so sorry. I should have been here with you."

"There's nothing you could have done, Gabriel," Ailene said with a forced, raspy voice and a cough. "I'm glad you are here now. Come," she smiled, patting the edge of the bed. "Tell me all about your final days in North Carolina. We've worn out your letters, reading them over and over."

Gabe began telling her of the good things that had happened in the past couple of weeks, avoiding saying anything about the lynchings and other depraved acts against the freedpeople. Instead, he told her about the funny events, like making a white landowner plow the field of a Black man after he ruined the freedman's new plow. It pleased Gabe that he could make her laugh. After some time, Ailene appeared to fall asleep, and Gabe rose quietly to leave.

"Wait. How's Jasmine?" Ailene mumbled.

"She says in her letters that she is fine, but I haven't seen her in quite a while," Gabe replied, gently patting her tiny, frail hand.

"She's a fine woman," Ailene said.

Gabe telegraphed Jasmine when he saw his mother's condition to see if she and her parents might be able to come to Georgetown. Levi was with the Buffalo Soldiers in Wyoming, and Hattie's health prevented her from making the trip, but Jasmine, Rose, and George arrived the next afternoon. Jasmine said Glory remained in Canada to care for Hattie.

Michael roused from a nap to greet them. Caroline came out of her mother's room, and everyone exchanged abundant hugs, kisses, and tears. This wasn't the first meeting between some of them, as Michael, Caroline, Atticus, and Ailene had traveled to North Carolina for several visits while Jasmine was there. It was a surreal meeting for everyone else, occurring over sixteen years since Rose's escape, and no one except Gabe had ever seen George. Everyone expressed disbelief that the meeting was actually occurring.

Shortly, the talk turned to the matter that had brought them there. "How's your mother?" Jasmine asked.

"Not so good," Gabe said, peeking into her room. "Are you awake, Mother?"

"Yes, I'm awake," Ailene said, barely audible. "Come in. I understand I have visitors. Please open the other curtain."

"Hello, Mrs. Adams," Jasmine greeted her warmly as Gabe pulled the curtain back.

"Hello, Jasmine. Let me look at you." Her voice broke amid a coughing fit. She held out her hand, and Jasmine took it. Ailene gently pulled Jasmine toward the bed. "Thank you for coming. It means so much to see you. Rose, I can't believe my eyes that

I'm seeing you again. And who might that handsome man next to you be?" she teased.

"Ailene, it's time you met George."

"It does my soul much good," Ailene whispered. "It was a very sad day when we thought you were lost. God is good to have brought you home."

They all took turns talking with Ailene until she fell asleep, exhausted from all the emotional meetings and greetings.

That evening, Gabe asked George, "How about I show you around the property?"

"Of course," George said.

They hadn't walked far when Gabe stopped, turned to George, and stammered, "Um, I'm not sure, um, how to ask, but um, I was wondering if you and Rose, um, would give your blessing for me to marry your daughter?"

There was a long pause. "I've only got one daughter, so you must mean Jasmine."

"Well, yes, sir."

"Hmmm. Does that seem like a good thing to do?" he asked, squinting and looking off to one side.

"I think so, sir."

"Is this an emotional reaction to your mother's illness? Is this a good time for you to ask this?

"It has nothing to do with Mother. I've been thinking about this for a long time."

"I'm going to have to think about this and talk to Rose . . . ," George said with a far-off look, as if he wasn't prepared for the question or sure how to respond.

Gabe stood like a statue, fearing his request was going to be denied.

After a long pause, George emitted a deep, guttural laugh, grabbed Gabe, and cheered, "I was teasing. Yes, *of course*, you have our blessing!"

Gabe exhaled the breath he had been holding, raised his arms in joy, and embraced George.

Upon their return to the house, Gabe asked Jasmine to go for a walk. As they approached the barn, she deeply inhaled the air where she had first smelled the scent of freedom. "It seems like yesterday that we were hiding in the room under the stable," she shuddered.

"Let's go to my favorite part of the farm," Gabe said, leading her to an opening in the middle of a thick grove of towering oak trees. A swing hung from a massive branch. Jasmine sat, her toes barely moving the swing back and forth like a pendulum on a clock.

"Jasmine," Gabe held her hand, "I am going to stay here and get admitted to the bar, then open a law office. If Glory goes to New York to study music, maybe you could move down here so we can be closer."

"Why, Mr. Adams," a surprised Jasmine replied with a coy smile, "I'd still like you to come to Canada. But, there will have to be more to the offer than that to get *me* to move."

Gabe turned beet red and was speechless for what seemed like an eternity. He stepped in front of the swing, stopped it, and dropped to a knee. "Jasmine, will you marry me?"

"Oh, Gabe. I want to so badly," she uttered as she got down on her knees, enveloped his neck, and smothered his cheek with wet kisses. "It's against the law in Ohio for us to marry. What will people say? Would it be a mistake? What about your future?"

"I don't give a damn what people will say. I'm not afraid to marry the woman I love. You are my future. We can get married in Canada. Maybe Ohio will recognize the marriage someday."

Jasmine's face softened. "I've wanted to be with you for a very long time. But with all the hatred, prejudice, and brutality I grew up with, I didn't know how it would be possible."

"It *is* possible. Will you?" he pleaded, looking deep into her eyes.

"Yes. Of course. *Yes.* Being away from you has been agony. I don't want another day of it. I want to marry you no matter what difficulties lie ahead. I'd rather face a life of challenges with you than an easier life without you."

Gabe put his hands on her cheeks, pulled her face toward his, and pressed his lips firmly against hers. After a long while, he backed away, smiled, and said, "You should know that I got your father's blessing. I thought he was going to say 'no.'"

"I'm so happy. Of course he'd give his blessing. He already considers you a member of the family."

"Let's tell Mother," Gabe said with a lump in his throat.

They went back to the house. Gabe peeked into Ailene's room. Atticus was at her side, looking tired, holding her hand. "Is Mother awake?"

"Yes, come in," Atticus said.

Gabe took a deep breath, swallowed hard, and said, "Mother, Pops, I've asked Jasmine to marry me."

"What did you say?" Atticus said to Jasmine with a smile and a wink.

"I had to think about it," she winked right back. "But Gabe looked at me with his little boy eyes, and I had no choice. Of course, I said yes!"

A faint smile spread across Ailene's face. "That is wonderful. I'm so happy. Go tell the others, then Gabe and Jasmine, please come back in so that I might have a moment alone with you."

As they left, Atticus put his arm around Gabe's shoulder and gave it a squeeze. "Congratulations!"

"Oh, Gabe, we are so happy for you and Jasmine," cooed Rose, embracing Jasmine, before letting her go so that Caroline could join the celebration.

Michael clasped his brother behind his neck and pulled him close, their foreheads touching.

Jasmine and Gabe returned to Ailene's room, and each held one of her hands. Ailene began in a raspy, soft voice, punctuated with coughs, "I can't think of a finer person than you to care for my Gabriel."

"Thank you. I will love him and honor him."

"Marriage is difficult in the best circumstances. Yours will have additional challenges." Ailene continued before having another coughing spasm. "You will make each other stronger."

"I think we will," Gabe nodded.

"On my dresser is a small box. Please bring it to me."

Gabe went to the dresser and brought back the box.

"Jasmine, open it."

Jasmine opened the box to find a bejeweled brooch shaped like a butterfly.

"That was my mother's. She could afford only two pieces of jewelry, both pins, that she alternated wearing every day. I gave one to Caroline. I want you to have this one."

"Oh my. This means so much to me."

Some of the strength left Ailene's hand. Her eyes closed. "Please get Atticus and the children and ask them to come in," Ailene said. "Rose and George, too."

Atticus and the others entered the room and gathered around Ailene's bed. Atticus took her hand and whispered, "I love you. We all love you."

Ailene's eyes fluttered open. "I love you all," she said, her voice strained and scratchy. She exhaled her final breath.

Atticus's head fell to his wife's chest, his body heaving in anguish.

The next week was a blur, as neighbors and friends came to the farm bringing food and offering their sympathy and condolences.

The day of the funeral arrived. The church's wooden pews were full, but Marcus wasn't among the mourners, as Atticus asked Nathaniel to keep Marcus away from the house and funeral. Nathaniel was not happy with the request, but out of respect he complied. After the opening prayer and a reading of Psalm 23, everyone sang Ailene's favorite song, praising God for the life she had lived:

> Glory, glory, hallelujah!
> Since I laid my burdens down.
> Glory, glory, hallelujah!
> Since I laid my burdens down!
>
> I feel better, so much better
> Since I laid my burdens down.
> I feel better, so much better
> Since I laid my burdens down!
> Glory, glory, hallelujah!

Atticus leaned heavily on Gabe, choking back his grief. Michael eulogized his mother in a clear, strong voice, ending with, "When I was five, I got very sick with scarlet fever. I would have died, but for Mother being with me, cooling me and cleaning me, twenty-four hours a day for two weeks. Pops couldn't get her to leave my side. To the day she died, her tender caresses cared for me. Mother used to say she named her sons after angels, but *she* was the angel." Unable to go on, he stood silent. Gabe and Caroline hurried to the lectern and led him back to his seat.

After returning to the farm, Gabe told Jasmine, "I guess we need to figure out what we're going to do about our future."

"What do you mean?"

"Where are we going to live? We can't live here near Uncle Nat. I don't think I can make a living practicing law in Canada. What do you think?"

"Whither thou goest, I will go; whither thou lodgest, I will lodge," Jasmine said, quoting from the Book of Ruth.

"How about Cincinnati? Maybe I can finish reading the law with Mr. Dickson until I get admitted."

"Cincinnati is a fine idea. Let's go there."

One month later, Michael and Caroline, who were in Washington, met Atticus in Cleveland, and together, they went to Buxton for the wedding. The fine spring weather added to the enjoyment of the trip. As they arrived, Rose and George arranged for Arlis Robbins, the keeper of the Freedom Bell, to ring it in their honor.

Seeing Hattie again made Atticus glow. The thrill of meeting Glory was beyond description or imagination. "I'm sorry Ailene isn't here with us," Atticus told them.

"I can feel her spirit," Rose replied. "Come. We've borrowed the house next to ours for you to stay. Get refreshed. George has the meal of a lifetime planned."

Many of Buxton's and Chatham's townspeople attended the wedding dressed in their Sunday finest. Gabe and Levi, who was granted a furlough to travel to the wedding, stood outside the church. Levi introduced each guest to Gabe. The townspeople at the wedding were most gracious to the only white people in attendance.

The bride and groom repeated their vows, and the minister bound their hands with a strand of cowrie shells, an ancient African symbol of wealth and fertility. Glory sang:

I've found free grace and undying love,
I'm new-born again.
Been long time talkin' 'bout my trials here below,
I'm new-born again.

The ceremony ended with Rose waving a brightly decorated broom over Jasmine's and Gabe's heads "to ward off evil spirits." She put the broom on the ground, and the newlyweds jumped over it—"to jump into our life of marriage," Jasmine explained. The celebrants erupted into cheers and applause.

Jasmine remained in Buxton while Gabe went to his home and Uncle Nat's office to collect his personal items. His uncle enthusiastically greeted Gabe. "Congratulations on your marriage. I need to talk to you about finishing reading the law and getting certified. I really could use your help."

"I appreciate that, but, um, we're not going to stay in Georgetown," Gabe stammered, afraid to say anything more.

"Why not?"

"We just think we'd be more comfortable in Cincinnati."

"I assume this is . . . um . . . um . . . her idea."

"*Her* name is Jasmine," Gabe said, stifling his anger. "I would expect that kind of a remark from Marcus, not you."

"Mind your manners," Uncle Nat scolded. "I don't know what happened, but I'd like you to mend the fence. He's your cousin."

"The fence can never be fixed."

"Hogwash," Uncle Nat said, leaning back on the edge of his desk. "Whatever happened cannot be that big of an issue to hold a grudge so long."

"I'm tired of being told to get over it," Gabe said, turning red and clenching his teeth. "It's not a grudge."

"What is it?"

"You don't want to know."

"Yes, Gabriel, I do. I love you as a son, and it hurts my heart that you dislike Marcus."

"It's best to let it be."

"I've had just about enough of this. *Tell me.*"

Gabe erupted. "Jasmine was the little girl in the wagon that Marcus and I took north. On the way, Marcus raped her and got her pregnant. Jasmine's little girl, Glory, is Marcus's child."

Uncle Nat stood speechless. His arms dropped to his sides, his mouth agape.

Gabe immediately regretted his outburst. After collecting his things, he said, "He doesn't know, and I *never* want him to know. Thank you for all you've done for me." Gabe turned and walked out the door.

Gabe said farewell to his father and headed for Cincinnati. He met with William Dickson, who told Gabe, "I'd be happy to have you in my office. With your work at the Freedmen's Bureau and reading with your uncle, we should have you admitted in less than six months."

Jasmine joined Gabe, and they began their search for a home. "Where do you think we should look?" Gabe asked Mr. Dickson.

"Unfortunately, bigotry is alive and well in Ohio," Mr. Dickson said. "As soon as a house owner finds out Jasmine is one of the buyers, he'll refuse to sell it to you."

"So, where can we go?" Gabe asked.

"A few wealthy Blacks are starting to buy in Walnut Hills."

"We don't have much money."

"Then, the only area you might find a place is Bucktown, where the Negroes are forced to live."

"Where's that?"

"Near the waterfront, east of Broadway, between Fifth and Eighth."

"Well, we might as well see what's there," Jasmine said in such a way that Gabe wondered if she thought that leaving Buxton was a mistake.

Gabe sighed as he stood on Sixth Street, looking up and down the block. Small houses were tightly packed in a row. A few had fading and peeling paint. Most were bare wood, darkened over time, and in poor condition, some with broken steps, paneless windows, and crooked front doors.

The houses on Seventh Street were in slightly better condition. Gabe saw a sign in a window that said, "F. Burns. House Locator," and pointed to it. "Well, let's see what F. Burns has to say," Jasmine said, leading the way to the front door. *Knock, knock, knock.*

A portly, balding man opened the door. "Looking for a house?" he asked.

"Yes," replied Jasmine.

"For the two of you?" he asked, eyeing Gabe skeptically.

"Yes," Jasmine said. "We were married in Canada. Do you know of any houses available?"

"Matter of fact, there are a couple of houses on Seventh that are vacant, and one on Eighth where the people want to move and might sell to a Negro who's with a white man."

"Can we see them?" Gabe asked. "Will you help us?"

"S'pose so. Name's Frank. I charge $50, but only if you buy." He led them to the vacant houses, which were tiny and shabby.

"How about the house on Eighth?" Gabe asked.

"Well, it's not much bigger, but it's in better shape," Frank said as he walked a block north to the corner house on Eighth and Broadway. He walked to the front door and knocked.

Gabe was surprised to see a white woman open the door. "Miss Sclare," Frank said, tipping his hat, "these folks are interested in looking at your house."

A male's voice boomed from within. "Who's there, Marie?"

"Some people to see the house," she replied, then moved out of the doorway as a Black man walked onto the porch.

"I'm not sure you'll be interested," the man said, eyeing first Jasmine, then Gabe. "Most folks around here don't like the idea of a white person being with a Negro. That's why we're leaving Cincinnati."

"I'm not sure we have much of a choice," Gabe said.

After touring the house, Jasmine looked at Gabe with a slight nod. Gabe asked, "How much do you want for it?"

"Three thousand dollars."

"I'd only give them two thousand," Frank whispered to Gabe, but loud enough for the sellers to hear.

"We'll pay twenty-five hundred. That's all we've got," Gabe said, truthfully stating how much he had saved while working for the Bureau.

"Deal." Gabe and the man, Gordon, signed a contract that Gabe prepared with Frank's help, and the house was theirs.

"We can't take all the furniture. Can you use the furniture and give us a week to move?" Gordon asked.

"Yes, of course," Gabe answered, smiling at Jasmine.

A week later, Gabe and Jasmine sat on the sturdy front porch of their new home on rocking chairs the Dicksons had given them as a wedding/housewarming present. The houses across the street and next to them were not as close together as those on Sixth and Seventh and were in better condition. Neighbors walked past their house. Some gave a bit of a wave, some shook their heads, but none stopped to greet them.

"Will these folks ever accept us?" Gabe asked.

"As long as we have each other, we'll make it work despite the world around us," Jasmine said, rising from her chair. "I'm tired. Getting moved in has been exhausting. I'm going to bed."

As she walked away, she sang to herself, reminding Gabe of his mother:

Glory, glory, hallelujah!
Since I laid my burdens down.

Gabe slowly rocked back and forth, his hands clasped behind his head, his eyes closed. *Where do we go from here?*

Part III

Supreme Shame

TWENTY-SIX

"Old times there are not forgotten."

August 15, 1871–March 5, 1877

Over a year after purchasing the house, Gabe and Jasmine sat on their porch as the sun set, enjoying the cool evening air. Between Jasmine's contagious friendliness and Gabe's legal representation of clients from Bucktown, having been admitted to the Ohio bar, neighbors no longer just walked by but now would stop and chat.

In between visitors, Gabe commented, "Our little world here, and our country, seems to be making progress, with neighbors saying hello, the first and second KKK Enforcement Acts, and ratification of the Fifteenth Amendment."

"Despite all that Congress has done, though," Jasmine replied, her jaw tightening and her lip curling, "I still can't believe they didn't include women in the Fifteenth Amendment. Women are the only class of citizens wholly unrepresented in the government. Either the theory of our government is false, or women should have the right to vote."

"But Frederick Douglass and even the National Woman Suffrage Association didn't think the time was right to press for women's suffrage; they believed the states wouldn't ratify the Amendment if it included women."

"Someday," Jasmine dreamed, leaning back into her rocking chair and looking into the sky, "I'll cast a vote and be treated as an equal."

After saying goodnight to another couple, Jasmine took a deep breath and said, "Enough about politics. You know how we've discussed the difficulties we would face if we started a family?"

"Yes . . . ," answered Gabe, cocking his head to one side and raising his eyebrows.

"Well, we better start coming up with solutions—I'm pretty sure I'm pregnant."

His eyes grew wide, and he searched Jasmine's face. "You're not kidding! I'm going to be a father? Holy merciful God!" Gabe caught his breath. His heart pounded. "This is so exciting! But it's also scary."

Jasmine placed her hand on Gabe's. "I feel the same way. Life will be hard on our child. One foot in the white world, one foot in the Black world, and not belonging to either. Glory didn't have to worry about that problem, living in an all-Black community in Buxton."

"How can I help prepare our child for such a hostile world?" Gabe asked with trepidation as reality set in. "I'm not as equipped as you about bias and prejudice based on the color of skin. I haven't felt the sting of hatred like you have."

"You're equipped," Jasmine said reassuringly. "You have a good heart. You don't have to be Black to understand oppression and prejudice."

"I'll need your help," Gabe replied.

"Just as we've survived other challenges, we'll find a way to help our baby thrive."

Several months later, Gabe and Jasmine walked to Saenger Halle at 14th and Elm, where the Saengerbund Singing Society was hosting Fisk University's *a cappella* troupe, the Jubilee Singers, which Glory had joined after enrolling there. "I'm so excited to see Glory tonight," Jasmine said, beaming with delight.

"I am, too. And to think we get to see the group's premier."

Gabe couldn't believe his eyes or ears. Glory looked so grown up in her floor-length brown hoop skirt and long-sleeved bodice with its lace collar, standing tall and proud among her fellow singers. During her solo, "I'm Going to Sing 'til the Spirit Moves in My Heart," people clapped to the beat, and some danced in place.

After the performance, Jasmine hugged Glory. "Oh, it is so good to see you."

"It's such a lovely coincidence that we started our tour in Cincinnati, and you could be here. More importantly, how are you?" Glory asked, putting her hand on her mother's abdomen.

"I've been a little sick and somewhat tired in the morning. Otherwise, I'm doing well. That was a wonderful concert. Your

Jubilee Singers will change how white people think about Black performers—great entertainment without burnt cork and mockery!"

"It was interesting to watch the faces of the crowd," Glory said. "The people seemed genuinely pleased to hear our songs."

"I especially liked hearing the Negro spirituals," Jasmine said. "I've never heard them sung better."

"Your solo brought the house down," Gabe gloated.

"I was very nervous. I've never sung to such a large audience. But once I started, I let my heart do the singing." Then she added, "I'm especially proud that our director, Mr. White, donated the money we got tonight to the survivors of the Chicago fire. What a tragedy that was."

"Yes, that was very good of him," Jasmine agreed.

They spent a few minutes chatting about school, Glory's classes, and the friends she was making before Glory said, "I don't want this to end, but Mr. White is very strict and will not be happy if I'm not ready to leave for Columbus early tomorrow morning! I best get going. I love you."

"Goodbye, dear," Jasmine said, warmly embracing her.

"Good night," echoed Gabe.

Six months after the concert, Jasmine lay in her bed feeling miserable. Her labor had begun ten hours earlier. The curtains were open, allowing light to fill the room. It was a hot July day, and even though the window was open, she had thrown the covers off. Her nightgown was damp from sweat. "It's time. Glory . . . ," Jasmine moaned as she braced herself for another contraction.

Glory, who had arrived from Fisk several days earlier to assist as Jasmine's midwife, ran to her mother's side. "Bring in the water on the stove and the clean cloths," Glory demanded of Gabe.

Gabe ran in circles, trying to do as told, finally retrieving the water and pieces of cloth Glory had laid out.

Jasmine's contractions increased in their ferocity and frequency. "Hold my hand, Gabe. How much longer?" Jasmine groaned.

"I don't think much longer. Push, Mama."

"There's the head," Gabe squeaked as a tuft of black hair emerged.

"Push!"

Jasmine moaned and grunted, grimacing and biting her lower lip. She continued to push, with only brief respites in between the contractions.

Finally, "Here *he* is," Glory announced, cradling the bloody, wet baby and beginning to wipe him clean.

"Oh, Jasmine, he's beautiful," Gabe said as he cut the umbilical cord as instructed. He took the baby in his arms, swaddling him in a warm, soft cloth cocoon.

"Oh, thank you, Glory," Jasmine sighed. "How's the baby?"

"He's doing fine."

"This is the most amazing day of my life," Gabe said, although he couldn't help but be concerned at how tired and weak Jasmine appeared.

"Let me hold him," Jasmine said softly.

As Gabe gently laid the baby on Jasmine's breast, he gazed into her eyes and kissed her.

Something is wrong, Glory thought as she removed a bloody towel from under Jasmine. She led Gabe out of the bedroom. "Go fetch the doctor," she said, her voice quivering. "She's bleeding too much."

Gabe couldn't have run any faster.

"It's not looking good," Dr. Abraham said after arriving and caring for Jasmine in the tiny bedroom. His eyebrows knit together and his neck muscles tightened as he shook his head, puzzled. "She's lost a lot of blood, and I can't seem to stanch the flow."

"You've *got* to," Gabe pleaded. "What can I do? Can I be with her?"

"There's nothing you can do, but you can be with her. Glory, please get me more linens. And more hot water."

Gabe hurried into the bedroom. Jasmine's face was ashen, her eyes were closed, and her breathing was shallow. He reached for her hand. The baby lay sleeping in a crib next to the bed. "Oh, Jasmine. You'll be fine. I know you will," Gabe said, stroking his semi-conscious wife's arm and hand.

"Damn," Dr. Abraham said to himself as he crouched over Jasmine, pressing his fist into her stomach at her belly button. "I've got to get this bleeding stopped."

"She's going to be all right, isn't she?" Gabe choked out.

"I don't know." Dr. Abraham felt her weak pulse. "She's failing."

"What can we do?" Gabe cried.

"Pray," Dr. Abraham said, placing one hand inside her as he continued to press on her belly. Several minutes went by. Her skin was clammy, and her breathing became more irregular. Dr. Abraham leaned back and rubbed his eyes. "I've done all I can do. You need to say your goodbyes."

Glory held her mother's other hand and looked at her mother through tears. "Goodbye, Mama. I love you." Glory's chin sunk to her chest, and her whole body heaved with grieving sobs.

"Don't leave me," Gabe prayed, making every promise to God he could think of. "I love you," as if realizing for the first time the depth of his love for Jasmine and the devastation he felt at the thought of losing her. "I can't say goodbye."

Dr. Abraham continued to attend to Jasmine. After what seemed like an eternity, he said gravely, "I think the bleeding stopped."

"C'mon, Jasmine. C'mon!" Gabe cried. "I need you. Please, Jasmine. Please, God."

Jasmine opened her eyes slightly. Her faint smile might as well have been a beautiful sunrise. "Water," she whispered with a raspy voice. The doctor put a wet rag between her lips, and Jasmine slipped back into a semi-coma.

"Gabe, she's not out of the woods yet," Dr. Abraham warned, putting his hand on Gabe's shoulder. "Now let her rest. The next few hours are critical. There's nothing more we can do right now. I'll stay here in case there's a problem. Why don't you get some sleep?"

"I won't be able to," Gabe said, but his twenty-two hours without sleep won the battle, and soon he slumbered in a chair beside her bed.

Several hours later, Dr. Abraham accidentally kicked the side of Gabe's chair. Gabe jumped up, fearing the worst. "What's wrong?"

"Nothing. She's resting comfortably," Dr. Abraham reassured him. "I think she's going to be all right, and the baby is healthy."

Jasmine's recovery was slow but steady, and Benjamin Georatti Adams—whose middle name honored his two grandfathers—was healthy and thriving.

Gabe continued being mentored by Dickson, waiting for an opportunity to open his own office. One day, Dickson and Gabe walked the short distance to the courthouse, where each had cases set for hearing. "What are your thoughts on the new Supreme Court cases—the *Slaughter-House Cases* and *Bradwell v. Illinois*?" Gabe asked Dickson. "Am I crazy, or is the Fourteenth Amendment dead?"

"If not dead, it's seriously wounded," Dickson responded as they arrived at the courthouse and waited in the hall for the bailiff to call their cases. "How could the Court say that the Fourteenth Amendment wasn't meant for the federal government to be the overseer of the state's powers regarding civil rights? What else it is for?"

"The Amendment's intent was to protect people's, especially the freedpeople's, civil rights, not just those given as part of national citizenship. When each state makes its own rules, there can be no protections for Blacks," Gabe said, tapping the tip of his forefinger on the arm of the bench in time with his words. "We know what happens when a Southern state determines who can vote, get educated, or sit on a jury."

"Even with the Court saying that the Amendment was intended for the benefit of the freedpeople, as long as states can pass Black Codes, the Negro will never be given the rights guaranteed by the Fourteenth Amendment. Decisions like *Slaughter-House* allow those Black laws to exist," Dickson said, shaking his head. "Same with the *Bradwell* case. How can any woman practice law when the Court says that the Amendment does not include the right to practice a profession unless *the state* says it's allowed?"

"Jasmine was furious the Court agreed with Illinois, that 'the natural and proper timidity and delicacy which belongs to the female sex unfits them for many of the occupations of civil life' and it called that status 'the law of the Creator.'"

The men were interrupted by the court bailiff, Francis Lee. "Mr. Adams, your case will be called next."

"I'll talk to you later," Gabe said, gathering his books and papers.

As he did once a month, Gabe went to Georgetown to spend the day with his father. The train into Georgetown made the trip easy. "Hey, Pops!" Gabe exclaimed as he opened the door to his father's small, white-frame house next to where the Grants once lived. "Baby Benjamin is here to see you."

"Hello, you fine little fella." Atticus melted as he took Benjamin into his arms. "You are the happiest baby I've ever seen."

As they settled on the porch rockers, Gabe asked, "How are you after the move?"

"I miss the old place, but with everyone gone, I couldn't take care of it any longer. The arthritis in my thumbs and elbow just got too bad." While fawning over Benjamin, Atticus said shyly, "I've got some news . . . I've been seeing Myra Davidson for the past few months. I don't know if you heard that her husband died a couple of years ago. No one will ever replace your mother, but it's nice to know someone is out there who can bring joy to my life."

"Oh, Pops, I'm happy for you. I think Mother would have approved."

"I'm pleased you think so. Perhaps I should invite her for dinner."

Later that evening, after they had prepared dinner and Benjie had taken a nap, a knock sounded on the door. Atticus greeted Myra with a hug. "You remember Gabe?"

"Of course I do," said Myra, a petite, pretty, and perky woman with sparkling eyes. "How could I forget the class clown!"

Dimples appeared on either side of a warm smile. "It's nice to see you again, Gabe."

"Hello, Mrs. Davidson. It's a pleasure to see you. This is my son, Benjamin—Benjie."

"Oh, let me hold the little guy," she said, taking Benjamin from Gabe. "What a prize. He's so cute. He looks like his grandfather."

Gabe's law practice flourished, and he hired an associate, William H. Parham, to join him in his new office at Sycamore and Ninth, between Bucktown and the courthouse. William, a muscular, handsome man with an easy and frequent laugh, was the first Black graduate from the law school in Cincinnati and was also the superintendent of the Cincinnati Colored Public Schools. From the moment Gabe met William, he was impressed with his intellect and work ethic. William quickly picked up the nuances of a case, and the two of them enjoyed discussing cases and the problems of the times.

"Grant's in trouble," Gabe said to William, sitting in their office after reading the day's newspaper. "The Whiskey Ring scandal could bring him down. He does not want to believe his friends and aides can be so dishonest."

"You must admit, it looks suspicious. Regardless, we can't afford to lose Grant. He'll maintain the army in the South as long as he's in office. After *Slaughter-House*, it's the only thing keeping the Kluxers at bay. Hopefully, he'll run for a third term."

"Grant knows Northerners are tired of fighting the South over the fate of the Negro. But there is hope as long as the army is there."

"'As long as' are the operative words," William said, shaking a finger in the air. "If the army pulls out, the white supremacists win. Unless the Supreme Court steps up and gives the Fourteenth and Fifteenth Amendments some teeth, all gains made during Reconstruction will be lost."

"Don't you agree that the new Civil Rights Act gives Negroes a chance?" Gabe asked.

"No," William said, shaking his head vigorously. "Congress passed the Amnesty Act, allowing Confederates to return to positions of political power and ending the Freedmen's Bureau!" he said, becoming incensed, the veins on his neck standing out. "There aren't enough soldiers to stop the Kluxers from killing hundreds of Negroes all over the South as if it was a sport. Reconstruction is in full retreat. Besides, I don't think the Civil Rights Act goes far enough. It only dealt with equal public accommodations and transportation, not public education or voting rights."

Just as William finished his sentence, Jasmine stuck her head into Gabe's office on her way home from a suffrage meeting. "Hello. I hope I'm not interrupting."

"Never, my dear."

"You were talking about voting rights," she interjected. "We just discussed the *Happersett* case at the meeting. I am shocked and disgusted that the Supreme Court unanimously held that voting is *not* an inherent right of citizenship as part of the Fourteenth Amendment and that it's up to the states to decide who can or cannot vote." Jasmine's voice got louder as she became more riled. "I'm tired of being denied my rights by my state! The Supreme Court should uphold the Fourteenth Amendment and set national standards!"

"Allowing the states to determine a person's civil rights begets civil wrongs," William snapped.

"White men don't want to share their power with anyone," Gabe interjected. "Southerners are just making good on their threat they call 'The Mississippi Plan'—take back power peaceably if they can, forcibly if they must."

"We don't seek favors or patronage," Jasmine fumed. "We knock on justice's door, asking for nothing more than equality."

It wasn't long before two more Supreme Court cases caused Gabe distress. "Damn that Supreme Court," Gabe spat out his words, shaking the newspaper as he entered William's office. "Did you read the *Cruikshank* and *Reese* opinions? When will the Court adopt the spirit and morality of the Declaration of Independence and the Great Amendments?"

"Yes, I did," sighed William. "The South doesn't need the Kluxers as long as it has the Supreme Court. I could get murdered like Cruikshank and his cronies slaughtered over one hundred Blacks in New Orleans, and the killer would go free. It's absurd for the Supreme Court to say the Fourteenth Amendment and the Klan Enforcement Act don't protect me if the *state* doesn't take part in the killing."

"If the Amendment and the Enforcement Act can't be used by our courts to step in when a state refuses to protect a citizen, it's open season."

"With *Cruikshank*, I'm not sure I feel safe even here," William replied. "Without the federal court enforcing the Fourteenth Amendment, a white man standing trial for killing a Black man in a state court in Ohio stands no greater chance of conviction than in Louisiana."

"I agree," Gabe responded, scratching his head. "The *Reese* case is equally troubling. It's pure gibberish. What does it mean when the Court says the Fifteenth Amendment prevents the state from denying Blacks the *right* to vote but does nothing to keep the state from passing laws that *stop* them from voting? As long as the state doesn't pass a law stating outright, 'Negroes can't vote,' the Court will uphold it."

"States can create any sort of fraud—poll taxes, literacy tests, identification requirements, property ownership—any device to keep Negroes from voting."

"The bottom line is that the Court is relegating the burden and duty of protecting Blacks to the states," Gabe said. "Which some will never do."

His eyes downcast, William sighed, "Without the courts' support, we don't stand much of a chance.

In the spring, Gabe, Jasmine, and Glory traveled to Washington, D.C., for the unveiling of the Emancipation Memorial in Lincoln

Park on the eleventh anniversary of President Lincoln's assassination, which had been declared a federal holiday. They left Benjie with Atticus and Myra, who had recently married in a private ceremony in Georgetown. Frederick Douglass had invited Glory, now almost twenty-two, to sing the opening number at the memorial celebration.

The three joined Caroline, Michael—now President Grant's assistant chief of staff—and 25,000 others for the dedication. On a cloudy, 76-degree day with intermittent mist, they lined up along Pennsylvania Avenue to watch a glorious parade led by John Mercer Langston, the dean of Howard University's Law School and the master of ceremonies for the celebration. Gabe watched as brass bands, Black militia companies, fraternal orders, and other Negro organizations marched to honor the statue, which some were calling the Freedman's Memorial.

While the Marine Band played "Hail, Columbia!" Michael escorted Caroline, Jasmine, Glory, and Gabe to the speaker's dais as distinguished guests. Grant, Douglass, and justices of the Supreme Court climbed the steps behind them. Grant approached the Adamses, and they exchanged greetings. At first, Grant appeared stern and determined, but then he let his guard down. "Your presence relaxes me. Maybe I can enjoy the day surrounded by friends rather than demanding politicians."

Gabe took Jasmine's arm, pulled her to his side. "Forgive my manners. I'd like you to meet my wife, Jasmine."

"It's obvious you are a lucky man," President Grant replied, taking Jasmine's hand. "It is a pleasure to meet such a lovely woman."

Blushing, Jasmine said, "President Grant, it is my pleasure to meet you. You've done so much for my people and the country."

"You flatter me, and I find it less embarrassing to be the flatterer rather than the flatteree," Grant said with a chuckle.

Douglass interjected, "President Grant, this is Glory French, Jasmine's daughter and our featured singer today."

"Miss French, it is my honor to welcome you to Washington," Grant said, bowing slightly and kissing the back of her hand. "I look forward to your song."

"Folks, it's time to take your seats," declared Langston, as he ushered Glory to the podium.

Having trained in New York after her time at Fisk, Glory sang a beautiful rendition of "The Good Old Way":

> As I went down in the river to pray,
> Studying about that good old way,
> When you shall wear the starry crown,
> Good Lord, show me the way . . .

How comfortable she is in the presence of greatness, and in front of a large crowd, Gabe thought. *She has her mother's poise and inner confidence. I wish I had the same.*

Langston introduced the dignitaries and made introductory remarks about the Memorial, then a rapt silence enveloped the crowd as Grant stepped forward. Before the ceremonies began, Grant had told Langston, "I am not comfortable giving speeches, so I will make no remarks." Instead, Grant simply pulled the cord attached to the American flag and bunting to unveil the statue. As the fabric dropped, the band struck up "Hail to the Chief," cannons boomed, and the onlookers burst into cheers and thunderous applause. Gabe studied the statue, which depicted Lincoln holding the Emancipation Proclamation in one hand and stretching his other arm over a kneeling, muscular Black man dressed only in a loincloth and with broken chains at his feet.

Langston introduced the featured speaker, Frederick Douglass, whose dark eyebrows stood out from his now-all-white beard and white hair combed back into a thick mass above his collar. Gabe noted how dignified Douglass looked in his starched, bright white shirt and well-tailored black suit, vest, and tie, shoulders back and head erect. Speaking in his trademark loud, clear, and resonant voice, Douglass began with laudatory comments about the importance of the moment, then continued:

> With the long and dark history of our bondage behind us and with liberty, progress, and enlightenment before us, I congratulate you on this auspicious day and hour. We fully comprehend the relation of Abraham Lincoln, both to ourselves and to the white people of the United States. However, truth compels me to admit, even here in the presence of the monument we have erected to his memory, Abraham Lincoln was not, in the fullest sense of the word, either our man or our model. In his interests, in his associations, in his habits of thought, and in his

prejudices, he was a white man's man, entirely devoted to the welfare of white men.

Douglass's brusque and stinging rhetoric took Gabe aback. He looked over the crowd and could see the surprise, and even anger, in people's eyes as Douglass continued:

He came into the presidential chair ready to execute all the supposed guarantees of the United States Constitution in favor of the slave system anywhere inside the slave states. He strangely told us that we were to leave the land in which we were born. At first, he refused to employ our arms in defense of the Union. He was more zealous in his efforts to protect slavery than to suppress the rebellion.

Douglass's words were met with murmurs and polite applause. People looked at each other with astonishment. But then Douglass's message took a turn.

Viewed from the genuine abolition ground, Mr. Lincoln seemed tardy, cold, dull, and indifferent; but measuring him by the sentiment of his country, a sentiment he was bound as a statesman to consult, he was swift, zealous, radical, and determined. The judgment of the present hour is that, taking him for all in all, measuring the tremendous magnitude of the work before him, considering the necessary means to ends, and surveying the end from the beginning, infinite wisdom has seldom sent any man into the world better fitted for his mission than Abraham Lincoln.

Loud applause and cheers greeted the last part of his speech.

The marine band played a final song, and the festivities were at an end. The Adams group and Douglass retired to the Willard Hotel to enjoy mint juleps at the Round Robin.

"That was some speech," Glory said, still under the spell of the great orator. "Your mastery of language and oratory skills put others to shame."

"I'm not one to boast, but I am proud that it's self-taught. Much like you sing, I must speak on behalf of our people in a way that no one can question our abilities."

"I'm not sure people were prepared for such direct comments," Gabe added.

"I don't fear saying what needs to be said," Douglass responded, thrusting out his chest as he held the lapels of his jacket. "I know I ruffled some feathers."

"Well, I liked the speech," Jasmine said, "but I'm not so sure about the statue."

"I don't like it, either," Douglass said, pounding a fist into an open palm. "Negroes paid for it, but whites designed it. The Black man is still on his knees and nude. What I want to see before I die is a monument representing a Negro, not couchant on his knees like a four-footed animal, but *erect* and dressed like a *man*!"

In June, the Republicans gathered for their 1876 National Convention in Cincinnati. Grant declined to run for a third term, throwing the nomination wide open.

"I can't thank you enough for hosting me for the Convention," Frederick Douglass said to Jasmine and Gabe as he sank into an overstuffed chair in their small living room with a cup of tea. "I am glad to be away from the throngs of people who want either my ear or a piece of my backside!"

"Hopefully," Jasmine said, "a little peace and quiet will do you good after all your traveling and speaking engagements."

"There is no peace for the wicked," Douglass said with a grin.

Just then, William entered the room shyly, holding his hat in his hands. "Frederick," Gabe said, "I'd like to introduce my law partner, Mr. William Parham."

The two exchanged greetings and handshakes. William stood in awe. The group talked for some time before William asked, "What's your speech going to focus on tomorrow night?"

"Well, much like my speech at the Freedman's Memorial, I will offend some to make my point. How can there be emancipation without enfranchisement? What does it amount to if the Black man, after having been made free, is not able to exercise that freedom? Our infuriated old masters have replaced the lash with a rope. The Black man will not be free until he walks safely to the ballot box, even if we have to have someone with a bayonet escorting us."

Jasmine chimed in. "Are you going to argue for women's suffrage?"

"Not tomorrow," Douglass said. "My focus is on the Black man. I believe if we can enable Black men to vote, women won't be far behind. That will be my next mission."

"Although I see the logic in your strategy, I fear," Jasmine said, shaking her finger in warning, "if we miss this opportunity, it may be many years before we get another."

The next night, Douglass's speech brought the house down, but it was nothing compared to the fireworks of the nomination process. It wasn't until the seventh ballot that Rutherford B. Hayes was nominated. Gabe was thrilled that another Ohioan who, as governor, had done good things for civil rights, might be headed for the White House.

Several days after election day, William was helping Gabe fix a fence kicked over by a group of teens from Bucktown. "I'm sorry they took out their anger about whites' interfering with Black voters on you," William said.

"I get it from both sides," Gabe lamented. "First, it was the Klan. Now this."

"There's a lot of anger about the election," William said, shaking his head. "There may never be another one like it. Hayes lost the popular vote, but I believe he would have won it, if there hadn't been so much violence keeping Black men away from the polls."

"South Carolina topped the list. Do you know they advertised that every Southern white man should be honor-bound to control the vote of at least one Negro—by intimidation, paying him not to vote, or keeping him away from the polls, whichever way he may accomplish it?"

Although the voting was over, the election was not. Twenty electoral votes in three states remained contested, with both sides arguing there was voter fraud. Congress appointed a commission to determine to whom they should award the electoral votes. A few days before the inauguration date, after a series of back-room agreements, the commission awarded all twenty of the disputed electoral votes to Hayes, giving him the presidency by one electoral vote. Upon hearing the announcement, Gabe stormed into the office. William was already hard at work at his desk.

"The man I supported just made a deal with the devil," Gabe fumed. "Hayes won because he promised to pull the army out of the South and not interfere with the ex-slaveholders' return to power!"

"We might as well have elected Tilden."

"I feel awful. I was convinced Hayes was the right man. I was wrong about him."

"How were you to know he'd pull such a stunt?" William said. With a furrowed brow, he added, "With the Freedmen's Bureau already gone, when the army pulls out, the South will return to white supreme rule, and we'll lose any gains we made during Reconstruction."

"I agree. Reconstruction is over," Gabe lamented. "It's ironic that Hayes's betrayal of the Negro comes less than a year after the hundredth anniversary of the Declaration of Independence."

"The South has pulled the scab off of the wounds of oppression, and we will begin to bleed again," William said, stroking his throat and grimacing.

"I can't get over it," Gabe said, his voice rising and becoming agitated. "The South has kicked out the carpetbaggers, defanged the scalawags, and successfully intimidated the Negroes. The white supremacists have retaken the government, calling themselves 'Redeemers of the Lost Cause!' They are shooting fireworks celebrating Hayes's agreement and their victory right now! They are waving the Confederate Battle Flag as a symbol of the South. *We* won the war and passed the Great Amendments, but *they* celebrate."

"According to the newspaper," William sighed, keeping a concerned eye on Gabe, "they've been singing the unofficial Anthem of the Confederacy at the top of their lungs."

"Lincoln liked the song, but I hate it." Gabe couldn't help but think of the words, which he often heard the Rebels singing across the battle lines as he picked up the wounded:

> Oh, I wish I was in the land of cotton,
> Old times there are not forgotten,
> Look away, look away, look away, Dixie Land.

Gabe sank to his knees and became nauseated as the words brought back a flood of memories. Raphael. Cries of anguish. Piles of amputated limbs. The smell of gunpowder and smoke. Heat from the fires. He started to shake uncontrollably.

William kneeled next to Gabe and put his arm around Gabe's shoulders. "It's going to be all right. They aren't going to win."

TWENTY-SEVEN

"Jump Jim Crow"

May 6, 1877–December 15, 1887

Several months after Hayes's inauguration, Gabe received a letter from his Miami University friend, Harold Widepath, explaining that he was writing an article on Ottawa Jones and wanted to interview Gabe. In a return letter, Gabe invited Harold to come to Cincinnati.

When Harold arrived, the two did what they could to catch up on the past twenty-five years. Gabe was especially fascinated by Harold's description of his five years living with the Lakota. He was surprised when Harold said, "Now I'm living with my mother in Indian Territory."

"I thought your mother was in Indiana."

"My mother and others who had remained in Indiana by treaty were ordered to a reservation in Kansas Territory. And then, when Kansas became a state, they were forced to join the Western Miamis in the Indian Territory."

"I'm sorry," Gabe said, shaking his head, embarrassed by what his government did to people like Harold and his mother. "What are you doing there?"

"I work for a newspaper called the *Indian Journal.* The paper tries to give people a more accurate portrayal of Natives instead of the stereotypical picture and to give the Indians a better idea of the world." The discussion turned to the reason for Harold's visit. "As I told you, I'm doing a feature on Ottawa Jones. I remember you talking about him and figured you were a good source of information."

"His passing a few years ago was a sad day for me," Gabe said.

The two talked about Ottawa until Gabe had told Harold all he knew and felt about his friend. The discussion then morphed into a general discussion about the plight of the Plains Indians.

"I just finished an article about my time with the Lakota, the Great Sioux War, and the murder of Crazy Horse after he surrendered at Fort Robinson. I tried to paint a picture of what a future on the reservation would look like."

"I'll bet it's not pretty," Gabe said. "I've tried to keep up with their struggle. I see so many similarities between the treatment of Indians and Blacks."

"I agree. Like the Negroes, we are getting beaten down in every way," Harold said. "The army had us on the run the whole time I was with the Lakota, trying to move us to reservations. The government opened millions of acres to white settlers, and Grant offered to move the Lakota to Indian Territory, telling Spotted Tail the land was good."

"I doubt they wanted to go."

"Not at all. Spotted Tail told him, 'If it is such good country, why don't you send the white men invading our territory there and leave us alone?'"

"That comment would be funny if it weren't so tragic," said Gabe.

"We just want the land the government promised to us by treaty. We can't even live in peace on the land given to us! After Custer led prospectors into the Black Hills and discovered gold, it was only a matter of time before the government broke the Fort Laramie Treaty and allowed settlers to steal the sacred land from the Lakota. And when the government established the new national park, Yellowstone, it forced the removal of Indians who lived and hunted there for hundreds of years and then encouraged whites to cross Indian land to visit it and settle nearby."

"What's the answer?"

"For the life of me, I don't know. When settlers move into areas given to the Indians, the Indians fight for their land. When one side kills someone on the other side, the other side retaliates."

"Do you see any way to enforce the treaties and let the Indians keep the land given to them?" Gabe asked.

"I think it's too late for that. The buffalo are mostly gone. Tribes that are enemies of each other are forced to share the same small piece of land. The government forces us to adopt a way of life in a confined area that is foreign to our culture and heritage. It's complicated, and I don't think I'm making a difference."

"You can't give up. Your voice is needed," Gabe said.

"I feel like Chief Joseph of the Nimiipuu when he surrendered," Harold said, slowly exhaling through pursed lips. "'I am tired. My heart is sick and sad. From where the sun now stands, I will fight no more forever."'

"Some days, I feel the same way," Gabe said gloomily. "There are times I don't think any progress has been made for Negroes."

After a moment of silence, Harold said, "I probably ought to get going. I've got to start writing my article."

"I look forward to reading it," Gabe replied as the two said their goodbyes.

The years sped by. Gabe and William forged a strong partnership and friendship. Gabe's family moved from Bucktown to a house next door to the Parhams on Chapel Street in Walnut Hills. Gabe and William kept their office near the courthouse, traversing the two miles from their home to the office along Gilbert Avenue each day. Benjie grew into a bright, curious, energetic boy. Jasmine became even more active in the women's suffrage movement.

"We're not there yet," Jasmine told Mary Parham at the August meeting of the Cincinnati Central Suffrage Committee at Mary's home. "Black men are finally getting a place in line behind white men. In a few states, white women are allowed to join the queue, but Black women still haven't been invited."

"Revolution changed the circumstances surrounding Black men," Mary said. "Enlightened thought is what will change the progress of Black women."

"Well, there is some progress," Jasmine exclaimed. "Women have finally been given the right to practice before the Supreme Court."

"It's about time," Jasmine said.

Meanwhile, the United Colored American Association hired Gabe to appear before the Ohio legislature. Avondale, a town adjoining Walnut Hills to the north, was attempting to have the legislature pass a bill giving the Avondale Board of Health the power to declare the Colored American Cemetery a public nuisance and force it to move. Years before, the UCAA had purchased a plot of land in a rural area outside Cincinnati's city limit to create a Black cemetery. Over the years, the area became the town of Avondale, populated by wealthy whites moving up the hill, away from the stench and smoke trapped in low-lying Cincinnati. Now, the town hated having a Black cemetery in it and was seeking legislative help to have it moved. To Gabe's relief, Marcus was not on the committee handling the hearing.

"Your Honors," Gabe argued before a legislative committee, "the cemetery existed before Avondale was a town. These people moved in knowing that the cemetery was there. They have no right to desecrate the graves and force the removal of tombstones and coffins to another location. My law partner," pointing to William, "has family members buried there. Imagine if it were your family member."

"The cemetery has become a blight, overgrown with weeds and overrun with rats," the town's attorney asserted. "Time and weather have exposed some coffins, and vandals have stolen corpses. The fine people living in Avondale shouldn't have to put up with it."

"If that's the issue, give the Bucktown Home Improvement Association six months to clean the area and rebury any exposed coffins," said Gabe, mentioning an association he and Jasmine formed that solicited donations from area businesses for their projects.

Despite Gabe's offer, the all-white committee didn't take long to submit a bill to the full House giving Avondale the authority it sought, and the House passed it almost unanimously.

"That wouldn't have happened if it were a white cemetery," Gabe said to William when they got word of the bill's passage. "I am very sad for what this means to you and your relatives."

"I've come to expect nothing different from our government," was William's flat reply.

In March 1881, Gabe and Jasmine were excited to be on the train to Washington, D.C., for President James Garfield's inauguration, having been invited by Emma and Albion Tourgée, who had been a friend of Garfield's since they were ten. When their train arrived in Washington, Albion, who had recently moved back east after a short stint in Denver, met them at the station.

"I'm sorry your editor felt it would be best for you to move back to New York," Gabe said to Albion. "How are Emma and Lodie adjusting?"

"They liked Denver, but Emma is glad to return East. Coming back also gave me a chance to stump for Garfield."

"Well, we can use a decent Ohioan in the White House after the disappointment with Hayes. I hope Garfield will reinstate some of Grant's Military Reconstruction ideas. He needs to force the states to eliminate the Black Codes and quell the violence against Negroes."

"If he doesn't do something to reverse what Hayes allowed," Jasmine added, "we'll be right back in antebellum years."

"You'll enjoy his inaugural address," Albion replied. "I got an advance copy today. I don't mean to brag, but Garfield incorporated many ideas he and I discussed since his nomination, especially federal aid for education, intervention against violence, and access to the courts. He's going to tie illiteracy and disenfranchisement together and vow that educating the Negro is of utmost importance. He agrees there is no middle ground between slavery and equal citizenship."

"I look forward to meeting him," Gabe said. "With all you've told me about him, I think we could become good friends, too."

"He's a good, humble, honest, and decent man. I know you'll like him."

The inauguration was grand, but the party held at the new Smithsonian Institution was extraordinary. John Philip Sousa led the Marine Band in some of his famous marches. Jasmine had a wonderful time with Emma and with Garfield's wife, Lucretia.

Meeting President Garfield was a gratifying experience for Gabe. Although Gabe knew President Grant, Grant's superior rank and advanced age resulted in an undeniable, though unpretentious, inequality between them. With Garfield, who was Gabe's age and from a similar background, he felt an immediate kinship. Garfield had an intensity about him that was at once imposing and engaging. He was quick to smile, had a hearty laugh, and was known to give a slap on the back, just as Gabe's brothers had done. Gabe felt welcomed into the inner circle with Albion and Garfield and looked forward to bending Garfield's ear on civil rights issues.

Just four months later, however, William ran into Gabe's office. "Gabe! Oh my God, Gabe. Garfield's been shot!"

"What? That's horrific! Is he all right?"

"I think they expect him to live, but he's still in critical condition, according to reports."

"The country *needs* him to pull through. We *need* him in the White House."

Gabe's concern began to ebb as Garfield appeared to recover from the shooting. But, two and a half months after the attack, Garfield died. "This is a dark day for America," Gabe told Jasmine. "Alexander Bell's attempts to invent a machine to locate the bullet were futile, and Garfield's damn doctors wouldn't listen to Dr. Lister. Their fingers probing the bullet track looking for the bullet caused the infection that killed him."

"This is just one more gash on the Black man's back," Jasmine said. Vice President Arthur has neither concern for the Blacks nor the ability to lead. With Arthur, the hope I had with Garfield has turned into despair."

"This is a tragic setback," Gabe agreed.

"His loss isn't the only news setting us back."

"What do you mean?"

"The Tuskegee Institute named Booker Washington as its first principal," said Jasmine. "His belief that Negroes need to accept a subservient role to whites, instead of pressing for equal civil rights, will put us back to the day of emancipation. He says we Blacks must focus on handiwork trades and farming to slowly lift ourselves into equality. What a radical departure from the way Douglass and I look to make progress!"

"Whites will appreciate his calls for patience," Gabe remarked.

"Oh, Gabe. I'm so tired of people, including our own, telling us to be patient and come along slowly. I want equality NOW!"

"I don't see how that's going to happen," Gabe shook his head. "Tennessee followed up its laws requiring separate schools for Blacks and whites with laws controlling access to public accommodations, including a Separate Car Act. Railroads are now required to furnish separate cars with supposedly equal amenities for Black passengers. Other states are sure to follow."

"Separate can never be equal," Jasmine spit out the words.

Gabe rushed into the house, his speech high-pitched and rapid, "Jasmine, look what I've got for us!"

"Settle down. I can't understand you when you're so excited. What is it?"

"They've added another night for Adelina Patti at the Music Hall after canceling last night due to her laryngitis. I've got tickets!" Glory had met and sung with Miss Patti, the prima donna operatic soprano, and raved about her to Jasmine and Gabe.

Patti's admirers filled the music hall. Her rendition of Verdi's aria, "Aida," brought the 7,000 patrons to their feet with thunderous applause. However, she could only perform the show's first half because of her illness. The Opera Festival sponsors stacked the show after intermission with local singers and skits. Near the beginning of the second act, a white actor in blackface took the stage.

"I can't believe they have that act following Adelina," Jasmine whispered to Gabe. "How offensive."

Dressed in rags with thick, red lips painted on his blackened face, the minstrel began to sing. He danced and pranced around the stage:

> Come, listen all you gals and boys,
> I's just from Tuckyhoe;
> I'm goin' to sing a little song,
> My name's Jim Crow.
> Weel about and turn about and do jis so,
> Eb'ry time I weel about, I jump Jim Crow.

"We're leaving," Jasmine snarled through gritted teeth, not willing to join the laughter and sing-along of the well-known song that Thomas "Daddy" Rice, a Northern performer, had appropriated from a Black performer from Cincinnati for his variety show minstrel act. She got up, grabbed her coat, and began forcing her way out of the row with Gabe in tow.

As she pressed past a man, he uttered, "Sit down and enjoy the show. Don't you understand satire, you stupid Coon?"

Jasmine accidentally stepped on his toes with her heel.

"Black bitch," the man snarled.

When the couple got outside of the hall, Jasmine, her jaw clenched, said, "Why does a white person blacken his face, dance around like a buffoon mocking us, and think it's entertainment? The stuff they use, Stein's Burnt Cork, is actually advertised 'for Nigger Impersonation'!"

"It's so disappointing. I was looking forward to the show," Gabe lamented. "I find it ironic that the term 'Jim Crow' is now being used to describe segregation laws that keep Blacks under white thumbs."

"I'm willing to bet that, for years to come, people will cork their face thinking it's all in fun and forgetting what it really means."

"It will take generations to eradicate these ignorant things people do that are so prejudicial, hateful, and hurtful," Gabe predicted.

It was a long, quiet walk home.

Arriving home from the office one evening, Gabe told Jasmine, "I received a letter today from Frederick, and he invited us to come for a visit. It would also be a good opportunity to see Caroline, her family, and Michael."

"When do we go?" Jasmine responded gleefully.

A week later, they were on their way to Washington. First they went to Caroline's house. Jasmine and Caroline had become close friends during Caroline's visits to North Carolina and Ohio, and Caroline's husband of three years, Dr. Kendall Berk, had become close with Gabe. Their daughter, Gertrude, had just turned two.

Gabe, Jasmine, and Benjie spent a chilly but delightful February day in Washington, D.C., with Caroline's family and Michael. They talked about Caroline assisting the new American Red Cross after the Great Michigan fire. "They gave aid to over 14,000 people who lost their homes, including the families of over 200 who died," Kendall gloated. "Clara Barton calls her a hero."

"Oh, honey," Caroline replied, blushing. "I was just doing my job. My staff deserves all the credit."

"Helping others is who you are," Gabe said, proud of his little sister.

Gabe and Jasmine left Benjie with Caroline and Kendall and took a carriage to Frederick Douglass's house on Cedar Hill outside of Washington.

"Welcome, welcome, welcome," Douglass said, opening his arms and smiling broadly. "I'm so glad you accepted my invitation to come. Let me introduce my wife of one month, Helen." Helen's wavy hair was parted in the middle and pulled back into a bun. She wore a high, beaded collar with a cameo brooch tight against her neck, accentuating her alabaster skin.

"It is a true pleasure to meet you," Jasmine said to Helen, whom Jasmine already admired due to Helen's work on behalf of women's suffrage as the coeditor of *The Alpha*, a women's rights paper.

They began walking to a nearby restaurant Helen recommended for its Maryland oysters and veal cutlets. They discussed politics in Washington, Congress's passing of the Chinese Exclusion Act on the heels of anti-Chinese riots in Denver, and another blow to the Fourteenth Amendment in *Neal v. Delaware.*

"I can't believe the opinion," Gabe said. "As long as the state doesn't prevent Blacks from being *called* for jury duty, attorneys and the courts can kick every Black man *off* the jury."

"I agree. It's an extension of last year's *Strauder* case. I've about given up with the Supreme Court," Douglass replied.

Their discussion was suddenly interrupted by several Black men shouting at them. At first, Gabe thought they were just a couple of drunks, but then their epithets became clear.

"You goddamn Uncle Tom!" yelled one, jabbing a finger at Douglass. "Our women aren't good enough for you?" And, "Who are you with?" changing the finger's direction toward Jasmine. "Auntie Jemima?"

"Just keep walking," Douglass instructed his companions. "After Anna died and I married Helen, people harass us because she's white."

"You're nothing but a hypocrite!" screamed the other man. "Your turncoat voice ought to be silenced, and I'd be glad to do the silencing."

They arrived at the restaurant and were seated. "Although my parents were ardent abolitionists, they were against our marriage," Helen said, still shaken by the taunting men.

"My children think I am disrespecting their mother," Douglass added with sadness.

"I don't understand why," Helen said. "They should be glad that their father is happy."

"It's hard to explain," Jasmine said. "Even for Blacks who never felt the lash, the history of enslavement runs deep. Frederick, you know that. It takes a lot to overcome our bias and prejudice against whites. Give them space and time. They'll come around."

"I hope you're right," Douglass responded, his eyes momentarily losing their sharp focus.

Some people in the restaurant glared at the four. Others whispered and snickered.

"Maybe if we changed seats so it looks like I'm with Frederick and Gabe's with Helen, the abuse will stop," Jasmine offered.

"I'm not moving just because of unpleasant people," Frederick replied. "I've been trying to deflect some of the abuse by pointing out that Anna was my mother's color, and Helen is the color of my white father, but people don't care. I'm fed up with the animosity. I have the God-given and natural right to be with Helen. I get so angry! I've almost come to blows."

"We get the same abuse in Cincinnati," Jasmine tried to put Douglass's comments into perspective.

"How do you and Jasmine cope with it?" Douglass asked. "Besides growing an extra layer of skin, how do you live with the criticism?"

"Ignore them," Jasmine cautioned. "People who oppose you will say ugly things, no matter what. You can adjust in the same way you do with all the nasty criticism you receive fighting for our civil rights."

"The problem isn't the same for me," Gabe added. "A white man with a Black woman doesn't cause as much of a reaction toward the white man. People direct their scorn to the Black woman, just as they direct their scorn to you, a Black man."

"I certainly get my share of dirty looks, though," Helen added, jerking her head slightly to the side, toward a white couple sneering at her. "Why is who I marry any business of anyone else?"

"It's not, but people make it so," Jasmine said, her voice becoming softer but with a sharp edge. "I had to escape from slavery. I had my life threatened by the Ku Klux Klan. I've had to ride in separate railcars and bow down to every white person I see. Yet I have to put up with disrespect from my *own* people because I'm with a white man."

His anger rising, Douglass added, "Why can't I just be considered a *man* and be with the woman I love, not a Black man shamed by the very people I've tried to raise up? I'm not a different person just because I'm with Helen."

Jasmine took a deep breath and folded her hands in her lap. "We must go about our business. I consider the disapproval as part of my struggle for equality. If there is no struggle or pain, there is no progress."

"I appreciate your candor and wisdom," Helen said, her hands clasped in front of her bosom.

"As do I," Douglass added.

"Your Honor," Gabe began his argument before Superior Court Judge Judson Harmon as William watched from counsel table. "I submit you should not dismiss my client's claim for assault. Being thrown out of the St. Charles restaurant just because he was a Negro is a violation of his Fourteenth Amendment rights."

"Now, Mr. Adams," Judge Harmon said, stroking a thick mustache that stretched to the corners of his mouth and raising his bushy eyebrows, "you are aware the United States Supreme Court found the 1875 Civil Rights Act unconstitutional in the *Civil Rights Cases*. It decided the Fourteenth Amendment did not give Congress the power to prohibit discrimination by individuals. It only prevents state's laws or actions from being part of the discrimination."

"So he can throw my client out into the street without repercussions?"

"As long as the state doesn't have a law saying Negroes can't go into restaurants, private actions by the restaurant owner are not protected by the Amendment."

"But, Your Honor, they should be called the *Civil Wrongs Cases*. The intent behind the Amendment was to do exactly what the Civil Rights Act did," Gabe pled, his voice beginning to rise. "Not allow discrimination in public places."

"Mr. Adams: It's too late for that argument. Justice Bradley wrote that, when a man has emerged from slavery, and by the aid of beneficent legislation, there must be some stage when he ceases to be the special favorite of the laws."

"*Special favorite?* With all due respect, Your Honor, Justice Harlan's dissent gets it right. He said, and I quote, 'It is absurd to say the colored race has been the special favorite of the laws when the only purpose of the Civil Rights Act was to enable a Black man to take the rank of a mere citizen.' Harlan said that should be the law of the land."

"Well, it isn't, and I am duty-bound to follow the law as it is."

"Not if that law is wrong," Gabe said, slamming his fist on the lectern. "You ought to do what's morally correct and allow my client's case to proceed."

"Don't slam your fist on my lectern ever again," Judge Harmon raised his voice, almost losing his composure. "And don't you ever challenge my moral integrity. The state did not throw your client out, the proprietor did. Those aren't my rules, counselor. Case dismissed." Judge Harmon struck his gavel, spun his chair, and left the bench.

"I'm so mad I could spit," Gabe ranted as he walked to the office with William. When they arrived, he slumped into an over-sized, brown leather chair. "When will Blacks ever see justice?"

"Apparently, not in my lifetime."

"And *Bush v. Kentucky* upheld the *Neal* opinion," Gabe said, depressed.

"*Bush* and *Neal* make no sense," William replied. "Even if the state must call Negroes for jury service, they can get kicked off the jury for any reason."

"I understand your frustration. The Supreme Court has abandoned the Great Amendments by leaving it up to the states to decide who gets what rights, and it knows full well that whites will continue to find ways to keep those rights from the Negroes. I'm still furious about the *Pace* case and the prejudice it propagates. It strains logic to uphold the constitutionality of anti-miscegenation laws and the prohibition of sex between members of different races, just because the laws apply equally to whites and Blacks."

"It doesn't make sense to me, either," William said, standing up and beginning to pace the floor. "Look at the *Harris* case. Ku Kluxers drag four Negroes out of a jail cell and beat them all, one of them to death. Just like it did in *Cruikshank*, because individuals, not the state, killed them, the Court found that the Second Klan Enforcement Act doesn't apply."

"You're right, William. Freedom doesn't mean equality. Prejudice based on the color of one's skin is the root of the problem. There was a righteous hope for healing with Reconstruction, but with Reconstruction dead, inequality and the Negro problem will continue for a long time."

"It's not a Negro problem," William corrected. "It's a white problem. And it's not just a Southern white problem. Hate, oppression, and injustice come from Northerners as well."

A month after the November elections, Gabe went into the parlor, where Jasmine was reading Robert Louis Stevenson's new book, *Kidnapped.* He took the book from her hands and replaced it with a glass of champagne.

"Ooh, what's the occasion?"

"Ohio repealing the anti-miscegenation law."

"I agree that's a big step forward! But champagne?"

Gabe paused for a moment. "Being with you has been the best thing ever for me. You're a loving wife, a great mother, and a caring person. I'm a lucky man, but something is missing."

Jasmine looked at him quizzically.

Gabe dropped to one knee. "Jasmine, will you marry me—in Ohio?"

"Yes!" she exclaimed, her eyes lighting up. "*Of course*, I'll marry you—*again!*"

The wedding was a grand affair in the garden of Lyman Beecher's former house in Walnut Hills, now owned by the Reverend Joseph and Hannah Riggs Monfort, who had become Gabe and Jasmine's friends. Benjie, now fifteen, tall and lean with the hint of a mustache, was the best man. Frederick Douglass, Albion Tourgée, William, and Levi stood up with Gabe. Glory performed maid-of-honor duties while Emma Tourgée, Mary Parham, and Helen Douglass stood with Jasmine. The bride was beyond radiant, elegant in a cream-colored satin bodice and floor-length dress of brocaded satin and velvet, trimmed with ruffles of lace at the hem and around her waist.

George and Rose and Atticus and Myra beamed from the front row as Reverend Monfort presided over the first interracial wedding in Ohio.

Gabe's knees nearly buckled when Jasmine said, "I do," not only from her statement's historical significance but also from her beauty and poise. He cried unrestrained tears. He tried to compose himself to read his vows, but only Jasmine could discern the words through his squeaky voice and sniffles. No one needed to hear the words. All they had to do was watch Jasmine begin sobbing too, reaching out to touch his cheek. After being pronounced husband and wife again, they enveloped each other in a tight embrace and sealed it with a tender kiss.

The reception featured free-flowing champagne and macaroons from Rose's bakery that the guests could dip into a vat of heated chocolate. It was well past dark when the last of the revelers took their leave.

TWENTY-EIGHT

"WILL THIS BE THE FINAL BATTLE?"

December 31, 1888–December 31, 1890

"**D**o you know who just came in, and who that elegant woman on his arm is?" William innocently asked Gabe as they got a drink at the 108th Regiment Mutual Aid Association's annual New Year's Eve bash. Gabe was with William instead of Jasmine because she hated the event's drunken arguments between Civil War veterans, including Confederates, and their bravado-laced exchange of stories about battles and killing.

Gabe looked up. Bile rose in his throat. Marcus, epaulets on his shoulders, a purple sash adorned with military insignia across his chest, and an officer's hat with a major's gold oak leaves on the crown, had just strutted through the door. Holding his elbow was a woman, seemingly about Gabe's age, with a dazzling smile. She was dressed in a pink, floor-length dress with a Lillie Langtry bustle and a matching hat, which she wore slanted on her head over a loose chignon bun, the hat's single pheasant feather extending to the rear. "That's my cousin Marcus. I should have known he'd be here. He always likes to sing his own praises about his war heroics. I don't know the woman."

Gabe kept as far from Marcus as possible, generally avoided eye contact, and had a few more drinks than usual due to his discomfort with his cousin's presence. However, his evasive actions ended when Marcus approached, pointing at him and slurring loudly, "Hey, Cuz, where've you been?" Marcus weaved through the crowd, bumping into a few people along the way, his date trailing behind. "It's been so looong," Marcus crowed, nearly losing his balance. "Why haven't you come to Washington to meet with your new senator?" Without waiting for a response, he continued, "Oh, I'm being rude. Miss Chase, I'd like you to meet my cousin, Gabriel Adams. Gabriel, Miss Kate Chase. You may have heard of her father, former Ohio governor and senator, presidential candidate, and secretary of state, Chief Justice Salmon P. Chase," he said with braggadocio.

She is beautiful. I've heard she's intelligent and witty—what the hell is she doing with Marcus? "Nice to meet you, Miss Chase," Gabe said with a courteous bow. "Of course I knew your father. Although it has been some time since his passing, my condolences for your loss."

"Thank you," Kate said, accepting his sympathies with a gracious smile. "It's a pleasure to finally meet you. On multiple occasions, my father spoke about your work on behalf of equal civil rights for all."

Gabe glanced at his cousin, who looked shocked and stunned that his date knew who Gabe was and was complimenting him.

Smiling to himself, Gabe said, "Let me introduce my law partner, William Parham."

After an exchange of greetings, Marcus took a long drag off his cigarette, drained his whiskey, and laughed, "Well, Gabe, it's nice to see you aren't wearing my hand-me-downs anymore."

"You haven't changed," Gabe declared despisingly.

Marcus ignored the gibe and said, "Would you join me on the veranda to discuss some family business?"

Gabe tried to decline, but Marcus grabbed Gabe's elbow and tugged him toward the open door. Determining that resistance was futile, Gabe said, "Please excuse me, Miss Chase."

William and Kate continued to chat, as Marcus turned to address Gabe. "My father, may he rest in peace," Marcus began, taking another drag off the cigarette, "told me a story on his deathbed, which I'd like to confirm. Is it true that the famous nigger singer, Glory French, might be my daughter?"

Gabe tensed as never before. He stood like a post, trying to control every emotion coursing through his body. He finally spoke, lowering his tone and volume and spacing out the words: "Yes, but if you *ever* contact her or tell anyone else, I'll expose you to the world for what you did."

"You wouldn't dare," Marcus said, snarling. "So, how is my little girl?"

"Don't you ever say that again," Gabe said menacingly.

"Who's going to stop me," Marcus sneered, shoving Gabe's chest.

Gabe exploded. His right fist caught Marcus flush on the jaw with a sickening thud. Marcus went down and was out cold, blood pooling around his distorted face.

"*Gabe*," William gasped, horrified.

Kate screamed.

"Somebody get a doctor," Gabe said calmly. "Miss Chase, I'm sorry if my actions have upset you."

William grabbed a clump of Gabe's shirt and pulled him out the door.

"What the hell did you do that for?" William demanded, eyes wide and eyebrows raised.

"Doesn't matter. It's private," Gabe said, rubbing his throbbing hand. "It's been brewing a long time."

"I hope you don't get arrested for assault. He's a United States senator, for God's sake!"

"I don't care. He got what he deserved," Gabe said, straightening his shirt.

When Gabe got home, he told Jasmine what had happened. "I knew telling Uncle Nat was a huge mistake."

"Oh my God. I've always been concerned about him knowing. I doubt that's the end of it."

"I don't think Marcus will want the reason for my action to come out, although we can't control what he might say," Gabe said, looking down at the floor. "Do you think we must tell Glory who her father is?"

"I already told her."

Gabe's head shot up, his eyes opened wide. "When?"

"When your mother died and we came to Ohio. She needed to know. That's why she chose to stay in Canada with Auntie Hattie. She felt horrible, but she was afraid she'd see him."

"How did she react to being told?"

"Actually, quite stoically. I had already explained to her that a white man raped me. What's done is done. We'll wait and see if anything comes of it."

1889 was a busy year for the Adamses. Benjamin, as he now liked to be called, turned seventeen. He was serious and determined, the class president, and was fascinated by the emerging scientific work in astronomy and biology, especially Darwinism. He was a talented baseball player and the fastest runner in Cincinnati, having won the annual dash at the Hamilton County Fair. Benjamin wanted to go to Yale, but Yale didn't have integrated sports or activities, so he eagerly opted for Howard University and planned to follow his father into law.

Jasmine became even more involved in the suffragist movement, joining Mary Parham in a march in Painesville, Ohio, the home of the Ohio Women's Suffrage Association. "Look at all these women. Maybe now, with all of us working together, women's rights will get traction," Jasmine exclaimed, holding a sign proclaiming, "Ohio—Let Women Vote!"

"I think it's ironic . . . " Mary said, leaning toward Jasmine's ear to be heard over the chanting women, "Sojourner Truth and

Harriet Tubman began the women's rights movement, but they were denied a voice in the discussion because they were Black."

"That's why it's nice to belong to the OWSA," Jasmine said over the din, which was turning more boisterous. "Negroes are encouraged to join. We're not the only ones that look like us, for a change."

"I'm still angry the Fifteenth Amendment didn't include women," Mary said, raising her voice to be heard, "Susan Anthony and Elizabeth Stanton were justified in refusing to support the Amendment because it didn't include women."

"But Susan and Elizabeth spewed so much anti-Black rhetoric, I can't support them either," Jasmine declared, her chin set and lips tight.

"At least the two groups finally stopped arguing with *each other*," Mary said as a group of women began uncharacteristically yelling epithets against men in general and suggesting that violence might occur if the marchers' message was ignored.

"I hope I live long enough to vote," Mary exhaled slowly.

"You might have to live to be a hundred," Jasmine laughed but was fully aware of the reality of her statement.

Entering his fiftieth year, Gabe began working closely with Andrew DeHart, who had formed the Cincinnati Civil Rights League. DeHart took over the job of superintendent of William Parham's district when William became the principal of Gaines High School. Ironically, DeHart's wife, Jennie Jackson, had been a Fisk Jubilee Singer with Glory.

"Our next stop is city hall," said DeHart, a thin, balding man with a droopy mustache. "Our aim is to urge reform of the civil service patronage system. People with connections rather than qualifications do not make government run well."

Gabe explained their plan to the mayor and city council. "Candidates for city jobs will take a test to establish competence, and those doing the hiring will choose from the highest-rated applicants. The person hired becomes a permanent employee and not subject to termination just because a new person is elected."

DeHart added, "We also believe that Negro applicants be screened without prejudice and ensure that Negroes are selected when they are in the pool of qualified applicants."

"Are you suggesting that we should show a Negro favoritism and hire him over a similarly qualified white person just because he's a Negro?" the mayor asked.

"If he's similarly qualified, yes," Gabe answered.

The mayor and city councilmen had difficulty stifling their chuckles.

William and Gabe sat with several lawyers at Arnold's on Eighth Street after a long day in court. Gabe ordered a round of beer from the new Hudepohl brewery.

They engaged in banter about the Cincinnati Red Stockings baseball team, about the newest addition to the profession— female attorneys—and about funny things that had happened in court. On the third round of beer, the discussion turned more serious.

"Robert," William addressed an older district attorney who was in line for a judgeship, thinking he might enlighten the others on a topic about which William had a question. "There seems to be a mood shift among the Northerners, who no longer speak out against the Southern methods of dealing with race issues. Why do you think that is?"

"I think you're right," Robert said, taking a long drink. "Northerners are tired of being the country's conscience. They have rightly focused on industrial issues, Western expansion, and the economy. It's time your people stop looking for favoritism and rescue at every turn."

William leaned across the table as close as he could get to Robert's face and growled, "I shouldn't have asked. The echoes from Thaddeus Stevens and Charles Sumner's voices have been silenced. The South is reasserting itself as a white-dominated political system. And you say we are looking for favoritism? All we want is equality."

"William is right," Gabe said, edging closer to William in case he needed to intervene against physical violence. "The Supreme Court sanctioning prejudicial segregation laws and attitudes has made things worse."

"Give it time," Robert retorted, seemingly unperturbed by William's anger. "Negroes will learn to live with segregation. They can rise or fall on their own."

"Says the man with the wind at his back rather than in his face," William taunted, looking Robert in the eye. "Before the war, segregation was unnecessary because Negro status was a given. Southern customs resulted in a separation of the races without segregation, like a horse and its rider. Blacks freely mingled with whites in the North. Now, to keep the races apart, legislatures pass Jim Crow laws. With decisions like the *Texas Railroad* case, the courts are doing nothing to stop the immorality of it all."

"The courts are upholding the Constitution," Robert replied. "Don't blame them."

"I disagree," Gabe interjected. "The courts have effectively reversed or frustrated all legislative advances since Reconstruction, including the Great Amendments. The North is apathetic about the Southern way of dealing with Negroes."

"I'm sorry," Robert said, taking another swig of beer, "segregation is necessary to preserve peace and prosperity for everyone, including Negroes."

"I think we better go," Gabe said. "C'mon, William."

It took the entire walk to the office before William calmed down enough to talk coherently. "What chance does a Black man have when *he's* the prosecutor, or even worse, the judge?"

Jasmine came home from shopping at the new Kroger store in Walnut Hills to find Gabe with his elbows on his knees and his head in his hands. "What's wrong, dear?" she asked.

"Another somber day for America," Gabe replied softly, his words muffled. "The army slaughtered several hundred Indians in South Dakota at a place called Wounded Knee. It's worse than the Sand Creek Massacre. I wonder how Harold is doing? These were the people he lived with."

Sitting down next to him, she asked, "What happened?'

"After soldiers murdered Sitting Bull, Spotted Elk surrendered and began leading what remained of Sitting Bull's tribe to the Pine Ridge reservation. The Miniconjou and Hunkpapas in his care were mostly older men, women, and children, all starving and nearly frozen in the bitter cold. When they encamped, the soldiers tried to disarm the few warriors there. Someone fired a shot, and the army opened fire from hills overlooking the camp with rapid-fire Hotchkiss howitzers and Gatling guns, mowing down the defenseless Indians as they tried to run away."

"Oh, dear me. That makes my heart hurt. Why would they do a thing like that?"

"The army is on edge because of the Ghost Dancers, who believe if they dance a certain dance, the buffalo will return and the invaders will die. The army is making tribes cede the remaining land given to them by treaty and forcing them onto reservations as if they were prisoners, where they're given spoiled food, inadequate clothing, and flea-infested blankets."

Jasmine wiped a tear from Gabe's cheek. "You're such a decent and caring man. All you want is justice and equality for all. That's one of the things that made me fall in love with you." She kissed his cheeks dry and let silence envelop them.

Straightening up, Gabe said, "The Natives aren't considered citizens of their own country—they have fewer rights than the Negro. The United States government has tried eradicating the Indians since Andrew Jackson was president."

"Have they succeeded?"

"I hope not. Indians are proud, strong, and resilient."

TWENTY-NINE

"Glory, Glory, Hallelujah!"

September 30, 1891–April 13, 1896

As predicted, Louisiana followed Tennessee and other states in passing a Separate Car Act, requiring that railroads operating in Louisiana "shall provide equal but separate accommodations for the white and colored races" in a separate or divided car and that "No person shall be permitted to occupy seats in coaches other than the ones assigned to them on account of the race they belong to," subject to fine or imprisonment.

Thorheim, September 30, 1891

Dear Gabe,

A significant opportunity has arisen. A group in New Orleans formed the Citizens' Committee to Test the Constitutionality of the Separate Car Act. The law has many problems. Does one drop of Negro blood make a person colored? Or will it be up to the conductor to decide if a person is colored? How can cars separating the races ever be equal? I am joining them, and we plan to fight it to the Supreme Court. Would you be interested in joining us? We could use your fine legal mind and passion. William and Benjamin are welcome to come, too.

I'll be traveling to New Orleans on October 15 to plan strategy.

My best to you, and kind regards to Jasmine,
Albion

Cincinnati, Ohio, October 6, 1891

Dear Albion,

Your letter was music to my ears. It is time we come alongside Black leaders and fight these Jim Crow laws before they take hold like a boa constrictor. The Great Amendments gave the Negroes freedom, and now they must fight for liberty and justice! It is our fault if we do not exhaust every legal remedy which the law holds out against such evils as this audacious and insulting slap in the face anytime a Negro wants to travel across town.

Of course, we will join you. Thank you for inviting William and Benjamin. They are as excited as I am.

Will this be the final battle that convinces the Supreme Court to give

*meaning to the Constitution and the
Reconstruction Amendments?
Jasmine sends her love to you and Emma.*
Gabe

William looked out the window as the Louisville, New Orleans, and Texas train they boarded in Lexington sped south. "You know," he said to Benjamin and Gabe, "it gives me the nervous shakes traveling in Southern states."

"I can imagine. Jasmine feels the same way."

A conductor approached Gabe. "At the next stop, sir, the law requires you to move to the white car before we pass into Tennessee."

"I'll sit where I damn well please," Gabe said, rising to his feet and getting within inches of the conductor's face. "I'd be glad to move, but only if my *son* and *law partner* accompany me."

Shocked at Gabe's audacity and the stated relationships, the conductor backed up a step. Not wanting to create a scene, he merely said, "As you wish," and turned to leave.

"He'd really be shocked if he knew why we were going to New Orleans," Benjamin muttered.

Gabe sat down, breathing heavily and shaking his head. "We've got to win," slapping Benjamin's thigh.

The three arrived in New Orleans on a warm fall day and took a coach to Rodolphe Desdunes's office at the *Crusader* newspaper. "I am glad you are here," Albion greeted them. He began a series of introductions. "Rodolphe is head of the Citizens' Committee and has led the challenge to the Separate Car Act."

"Nice to meet everyone," said Rodolphe with a strong French-Creole accent and intense eyes. He was thin, light skinned, and his short, combed-back hair accented his high cheekbones.

"This is Louis Martinet," Albion continued, motioning toward a handsome Black man with short, graying hair, a receding hairline, and a neatly trimmed mustache that turned up at the corners of his lips. "Louis is a well-known lawyer and holds the influential position of civil law notary in New Orleans."

"Nice to meet you," the forty-one-year-old man said, shaking their hands.

"And this is James Walker, our Louisiana criminal law expert." Walker, a white man, had short, spiky hair, downturned lips, and a large forehead, made more prominent by his almost invisible light eyebrows. He was known to be a good, solid, and conscientious man.

"I am honored to meet all of you. I'm Gabriel Adams," Gabe replied, dipping his head in respect, then introduced his son and law partner.

The men sat around a large table piled high with law books and paper and quickly got to work.

"Albion shared your thoughts with me," Gabe said to Louis, whom Albion had called courageous and energetic. "Your attacks on the Act are solid."

"Respectfully, sir, when it comes to civil rights, nothing is solid with the Supreme Court," Louis replied. "It's an uphill fight to get this case to the Supreme Court and then even steeper to get the Court to overturn the ban on segregated railcars. If they do that, it will impact similar Jim Crow laws, possibly including segregated schools and other public facilities. Will they be willing to do what's morally right and protect minority interests, or will they succumb once again to the majority of Americans with their biased and prejudiced views?"

"If the Court follows the Fourteenth Amendment, they'll have to overturn the law," Walker said. "When the law depends on the color of a person's skin and not that person's actions, it is inherently unconstitutional."

"Yes, but I agree with Louis," said Albion. "The Supreme Court has been the foe of Negroes' civil rights until forced by public opinion to do otherwise. I'm unsure if the general public agrees with us to the extent that it will pressure the justices. If we lose, it may be many years before another Court will see it differently. The Court has never reversed itself on a constitutional question of this magnitude."

"I think we also ought to argue the effect of the law on the Thirteenth Amendment," Louis chimed in. "Segregation, like slavery, is a form of a caste system and maintains us in a degraded and inferior position. It perpetuates discrimination based only on the color of our skin."

"The issue of defining 'who is Black?' is important," Gabe said. "Is 'one drop' of Negro blood enough? One-sixteenth? One-eighth? Every state is different. Depending on where you live and draw the line, a person is deprived of rights because he is not white enough."

"I agree," Walker replied. "Louisiana doesn't even have a definition of 'colored.' How can any conductor be expected to make a lawful determination, especially in New Orleans where so many Negroes could pass as white?"

"I'd like to work with Gabe on that argument," William offered.

"That would be good. We should put as many arguments before the Court as possible, but I still think the Fourteenth Amendment may be our best chance," Albion said. "Segregation clearly denies equal protection of the laws and deprives citizens of liberty without due process."

"Who would be the ideal person to test the law?" Rodolphe inquired. "Should we have a woman or a man? Do we want someone who can pass as white or someone with a full measure of Negro blood?"

"I'm not sure," Louis pondered, "but I do know we need someone with tact who can resist just enough to get arrested but not cause a scene."

"Getting arrested is important," Albion stated with emphasis. "We need a criminal case under the Separate Car Act so that the Court cannot dodge the real issue—that Louisiana has made it a crime to resist a conductor's determination that a person is colored."

"If that's the case," Walker said, "then I think we should use a person who can pass for white to expose the law's absurdity."

"I agree, and I think a man would be best," Gabe added. "A male is more of an unspoken threat than a female."

"How about my son, Daniel?" Rodolphe asked. "He's large, soft-spoken, and can pass for white."

"Daniel would be perfect," Louis said to everyone, his eyes brightening.

"Your word is all I need. Does anyone disagree?" Albion asked. When no one objected, he said, "Let's get Daniel in here and plan the masquerade. We can work on the issues later."

"The railroad owners don't like the law either because of the added expense of the separate car," Walker added. "They will cooperate with us."

After working with Daniel and setting up the plan with the railroad, Daniel boarded a train, sat in the white section, and refused to leave when ordered. He was arrested, his father posted bond, and the case began its slow march through the Louisiana judicial system.

Shockingly, the judge on Daniel's case went missing while going for a walk along the levee abutting the Mississippi River; whether it was by accident or due to foul play was not known. The case was put on hold. In May, Gabe received a letter from Albion. "Alas," Gabe moaned to Jasmine, "the best-laid schemes of mice and men often go awry."

"What happened, dear?" she asked.

"Bad luck. In another railroad case, the Louisiana Supreme Court ruled that the Separate Car Act does not apply to interstate travel, just intrastate travel. Because Daniel had a ticket to Alabama, he can't be convicted. Albion thinks it's best to start over with another person traveling intrastate."

Post Office Department

TELEGRAM

New Orleans, June 1, 1892
To AW Tourgee-Mayville, New York; Gabriel
Adams-Cincinnati, Ohio
We got our man. Homer Plessy. He is a free,
light-skinned Creole, extremely polite, carries
himself well, and is committed to the cause.
He will board a local train heading north to
Covington. Conductor is in on the plan. See you
in New Orleans soon. James Walker

On June 7, 1892, a hot, muggy afternoon in New Orleans, Homer Plessy and Gabe walked separately into the Press Street Railway Depot.

"I'd like a one-way ticket to Covington, please," Gabe requested, even though he knew he wouldn't be riding the East Louisiana No. 8 train that far.

Homer, twenty-nine, a local shoemaker dressed in a suit and wearing a fedora, did the same.

Gabe's job was to observe, intervene if there was any trouble, and report on the arrest. Besides Albion and Walker, he was the only team member who could sit legally in the segregated white car. Walker was too well-known in New Orleans, and the team could not take a chance that Albion would get involved as a witness. Gabe found an open seat and waited.

Homer boarded the whites-only car, found an empty seat, and sat down. He turned to see where Gabe sat, and Gabe acknowledged him with a slight wink. Homer turned his head and looked straight ahead, unsure that the rehearsed next steps would succeed without violence. He hoped everything would happen quickly, as his stomach did not match his forced calm demeanor. Second thoughts crept into his throbbing head.

Soon, he was confronted.

Gabe moved to the edge of his seat, his hands white from clutching it.

"Are you a colored man?" the conductor, J. J. Dowling, demanded of Homer in the scripted set-up.

"Do you think I am?" Homer replied as calmly as his anxious voice would allow.

"Yes, and you'll have to retire to the colored car."

"I think I'll stay right where I am. I paid for a first-class ticket," Homer answered, fearing what his response might trigger despite the staged plan.

The conductor put his hand on Homer's shoulder, squeezing it, and he summoned the police.

The conductor is either a good actor or he's not playing along, Gabe thought. *Should I try to get Homer out of here?*

Gabe noticed people around Homer were uncomfortable with the situation. Some moved back a few rows to distance themselves from the ensuing confrontation. Others appeared willing to help the conductor and police forcibly remove Homer. Within minutes, two policemen arrived and boarded the train.

"What's your name?" Detective Chris Cain asked.

Uh-oh. He doesn't seem to be in on this. I thought we hired a private investigator to arrest him. Where'd we mess up? Gabe was puzzled, realizing there was nothing he could do to help Homer now that the police had arrived.

"Homer Plessy."

"You've got one last chance to get to the car where your kind belongs," Detective Cain commanded.

"No, thank you," responded Homer. Gabe could see Homer's eyes grow wide and his mouth tighten, fearful of what defying the policeman might bring.

Detective Cain grabbed Homer's arm in a vise-like grip, shoved him out of the car, and handcuffed him. Gabe was worried. There wasn't to be any force. Cain and the other policeman took Homer away in a horse-drawn patrol wagon. *There's nothing I can do. I've got to get to the station.*

Homer was jailed and charged with violating the 1890 Louisiana Separate Car Act.

Despite the intended purpose of Homer's arrest, Gabe shook his head in disbelief that they had to stage a disgusting event that, unfortunately, occurred every day. He went to the jail and asked to see his client and make arrangements to bond Homer out.

"How are you doing?" Gabe asked as Homer rubbed his wrists, raw from the cold metal cuffs, and his arm, bruised from Cain's grip. "I'm sorry. I don't know what went wrong."

"I'm okay. When we got in the wagon, Cain told me it was all an act, but he had to make it look real so that people wouldn't interfere or try to help him. I told him he was not much of an actor. He made it too real. Scared me almost to death."

"Well, let's get you out of here. The worst is over."

The case was assigned to a newly appointed judge, John Howard Ferguson, a carpetbagger from Massachusetts with a bushy white mustache extending almost to his ears and equally bushy white eyebrows like low-hanging clouds over his tired eyes.

"He might prove to be helpful," Walker told Gabe when the bailiff called Homer's case. "We think he'll be a fair judge."

However, nothing in Judge Ferguson's demeanor indicated he would be friendly to Homer or his case. Without fanfare, he set October 18, 1892, as the date for both sides to submit statements regarding the constitutionality of the Separate Car Act and other arguments supporting their respective positions. Counsel for Homer headed for their homes.

Albion worked on the brief from his new residence in Mayville, New York, overlooking beautiful Lake Chautauqua. He called it Thorheim, roughly translated as "Fool's Home," named after his first sensational book, *A Fool's Errand*. He sent excerpts of the brief to Gabe and William in Cincinnati and to Louis, Rodolphe, and Walker in New Orleans for comments and editing. When done, Walker filed Homer's position, detailing fifteen points about why the Act violated the Thirteenth, Fourteenth, and Fifteenth Amendments. "As you can see," he wrote to Gabe, "in essence, I've argued that Homer should be afforded and enjoy the full benefits of national citizenship, and forcing him to ride in a separate car robbed him of those benefits."

In October, Walker argued the case for Homer Plessy before Judge Ferguson, making the vital points that Louisiana did not define "colored" and that no conductor was equipped to make that decision. As an aside, he argued that Homer acted as a complete gentleman as opposed to the derelicts or intoxicated passengers whom the railroads also relegated to the Jim Crow car.

POST OFFICE DEPARTMENT

TELEGRAM

New Orleans, November 18, 1892

To AW Tourgee-Mayville, New York; Gabriel

Adams-Cincinnati, Ohio

Judge Ferguson ruled against all of our points.

He found Act constitutional. He did not set a

trial date. Next step? J Walker

POST OFFICE DEPARTMENT

TELEGRAM

Mayville, New York, November 19, 1892

To J Walker-New Orleans, Louisiana; G

Adams-Cincinnati, Ohio

Proceed with writ of prohibition to Louisiana

Supreme Court. We now have direct path to US

Sp Ct. AW Tourgee

Within a month, in a 5-0 ruling, the Louisiana Supreme Court held the Act constitutional.

Gabe arrived in Mayville to visit and plan strategy with Albion a day before a fierce snowstorm blanketed the area near Lake

Erie with three feet of snow, which drifted up to the eaves on the west side of the house. They sat before a roaring fire in cozy Thorheim, counting their blessings and discussing politics and current events before getting to business.

Gabe asked, "Did the Louisiana Supreme Court ruling surprise you?"

"Somewhat. It went farther than I thought it would. The court gratuitously predicted that overturning the law on Fourteenth Amendment grounds would overturn all the Jim Crow laws—as if that was bad."

"Many people think it is," Gabe replied sardonically. "What's next for the case?"

"We file in the U.S. Supreme Court."

"What are our chances?"

"I think Harlan goes our way, and four others are a maybe," Albion said.

"That's a bit optimistic, isn't it?"

"Perhaps. Let's hope President Cleveland doesn't get to nominate any new Supreme Court justices. An appointment by him will certainly be a vote against us."

The two put their heads together. Albion's typewriter clicked and clacked well into the night and for three days thereafter.

Thorheim, December 31, 1893

Dear Gabe,

I'm frustrated because Plessy keeps being pushed back on the docket. To make matters worse, my greatest fear has been realized.

Cleveland gets to make an appointment to name a new justice after the death of Justice Blatchford, who might have been a vote for us. This will tilt the scales further against us. It is of the utmost consequence that we should not have a decision against us. Separate but equal cannot become the law of the land.

Hopefully, 1894 will be a blessed year for you and Jasmine.

Albion

After the Court delayed the case for another year, Albion, Gabe, Benjamin, William, and the Plessy team met in the office of the *Crusader* to discuss the brief they would file with the United States Supreme Court. A pall hung over the group due to recent news of Frederick Douglass's sudden death due to a heart attack in his Cedar Hill home.

After a moment of silence in Douglass's honor, Louis announced, "Albion and I have invited a good friend, Samuel Phillips, here to help us. He is an experienced litigant before the Supreme Court as the solicitor general for over twelve years."

"It's a pleasure to meet you all," said Phillips, a clean-shaven older gentleman with short, white hair and deep-set, focused eyes, nodding to each team member. "I have read your work to date, and it is exemplary."

"Thank you. Each man has helped significantly," Albion responded, then started the discussion about the case. "All of the attention on Douglass's death might help us. I think, with the focus on the things Douglass was unable to change, and with all the court delays, we might have a chance to sway public opinion."

"Sometimes, that's the only way to get the Court to do the right thing," Phillips added.

"It might be," Gabe said, "but the Supreme Court upholding the Chinese Exclusion Act in the *Fong Yue Ting* case is another indication the Court isn't ready to grant non-whites any rights in this country. How can it be constitutional to arbitrarily select groups of American citizens and require them to carry special documentation and subject them to deportation or imprisonment if they don't?"

"That's not our problem right now," Albion said. "However, I agree it's a sign our uphill battle hasn't gotten any easier."

"Speaking of battles," Louis said, "Albion, are you still getting death threats because of this case, as I am?"

"Yes, it concerns Emma, but I'm not as frightened as I used to be. Twenty-five years of threats and being chastised dulls the nerves."

The discussion turned back to the case.

"The brief is the best chance to convince the Court we're right," Albion said. "Some of you think we should focus on the equality of accommodations. However, I think the gist of our case is the unconstitutionality of compelling a person to ride in a car set apart for a particular race, not whether it is as clean and comfortable as another."

"I think we're strong on the issue of how a railroad conductor can be expected to sort citizens by race," William said. "It's a violation of equal protection when the railroad forces the arrest of a person it believes is Black but suffers no consequence if they jail a white man."

"But the Fourteenth Amendment is broader than that," Louis argued. "It created a *new* type of citizenship embracing *new* rights controlled by a *new* authority having a *new* scope and extent. The Court must decide *Plessy* in a *new* world."

"I agree with Louis," Albion said, pacing the room with his hands behind his back.

"Along those lines, I think we ought to argue that being white is a property interest," Rodolphe said. "To require a man to ride in a Jim Crow car deprives a person of the reputation and financial benefit of being white."

"I think that goes too far," Albion argued.

"That's because you aren't Black," Rodolphe challenged. "Most white people, if given a choice, would prefer death to a life in the United States as a colored person."

"I agree," William said. "How much would it have been worth to Benjamin or me to enter the practice of law as a white man instead of a colored man? Being white is the master key that unlocks the golden door of opportunity."

Gabe looked at Benjamin and shrugged his shoulders. "Do you feel that way?"

Benjamin stared into his father's eyes. Uncomfortable confronting his father, his words were deliberate and steady. "Do you understand the biases I face when I enter the courtroom, not because of my inexperience but because I am Black?"

Taken aback, Gabe said quietly, "Maybe I don't. You're always so confident. I'm sorry I haven't appreciated that before."

"That's because it's not your reality."

After a brief silence, Louis broke in, "Benjamin, I'd like you to work with William on that issue. It's a good point and might mean something, especially to Justice Harlan, who seems to be moved by that type of argument."

"Of course," Benjamin said, holding his chin higher and pulling his shoulders back.

Samuel Phillips, the new member of the team, said, "I'd like to work on the Thirteenth Amendment argument, specifically the connection between the stated purpose of the Amendment, which is the abolition of slavery and involuntary servitude, and the moral intent of the Amendment, which is to rid the country of the caste system that supported slavery. The Separate Car Act, among others, continues to subjugate the Negro, which is slavery in different clothes."

"You're right," William added. "Slavery was the very definition of caste and the climax of unequal conditions. By distinguishing between citizens based on race, the law's effect legalizes caste and restores the inequality that was essential to slavery."

"The law implies inferiority in civil society, reducing further the condition of a subjugated race," Rodolphe said. "The weak suffer from all class discrimination and all caste legislation. It is the colored race which must always be the victim of such legislation."

"But doesn't that raise a problem?" Benjamin asked, again testing whether the group of older, more distinguished men would listen to his opinion. "Doesn't that ignore prejudicial legislation against Indians, Chinese, women, and anyone else who is not a white male?"

"You have a point," Louis said, impressed with Benjamin's logic. "But, if we broaden the argument beyond Blacks, we lose impact because that's who the Amendments targeted."

"I appreciate your intent, Benjamin," Gabe said, "but I also understand the need to focus. Let's keep an open mind. I'm working on the argument about Louisiana's failure to define what is colored. Will the Court hold that a single drop of African blood is sufficient to poison a whole ocean of Caucasian blood?"

"Until we decide whether to take the shotgun or focused approach, here's something else to consider," Rodolphe said. "What about an argument that laws such as this are really for the gratification and comfort of whites? It's all about white supremacy and superiority. They do not object to the colored person being in an inferior or menial capacity ministering to the comfort of the white race. Only when the Negro, as a man, seeks to claim equal rights, privileges, and standing as a citizen does the need to exercise power over Blacks occur."

"These are all valid ideas," Albion said as the team began to disperse. "I'll try to get a draft out soon. We've got to convince the Court that a law requiring the accommodations of the white and Black races to be separate but equal cannot be constitutional because, if separate, it defies equality. Lady Justice is pictured blindfolded. Her daughter, the Law, ought to be color-blind."

"I like that," Louis said. "Make sure that's in the brief."

Thorheim, September 30, 1895

Dear Gabe,

I have filed our brief with the Court. Now, I can begin preparing my oral argument.

Booker Washington's popularity is not helping our cause. His Atlanta Compromise speech will hurt us. He degrades the hopes and dreams of equality when he says, "No race can prosper until it learns that there is as much dignity in tilling a field as in writing a poem. It is at the bottom of life we must begin and not at the top." This accepts a lower-class status.

How can he claim to speak for all Negroes when he says that Blacks will accept segregation and disenfranchisement in exchange for economic and educational progress, or that the wisest among Negroes understand that the agitation of questions of social equality is extreme folly? How wrong can he be?

Whites hated the agitation of Douglass but will love the subservience of Washington. How can we expect justices to do what is morally right if the public cries out for castrating the Great Amendments?

I have been asked to go to Boston to present a eulogy for Douglass at Faneuil Hall. After his comments about the Emancipation Memorial, I will say something about the Statue of Liberty,

*given to us in commemoration of the Thirteenth
Amendment, with broken chains and shackles
at her feet, I think he would have liked it. But
the thrust of the eulogy will be that Frederick's
life should be a warning to those who would put
aside and cover up the wrongs that measure
human rights, not by manhood but by race and
color, by citing science and the shallow claim of
superiority.*

*The land, which gave a million lives to
destroy the demon of slavery, should beware
of enthroning in its place the fouler and more
dangerous Moloch — CASTE!*

*As always, most respectfully,
Albion*

Post Office Department

TELEGRAM

Mayville, New York, April 3, 1896
To Gabriel Adams-Cincinnati, Ohio
Oral arguments set for April 13. Meet in
Washington. I leave April 10. AW Tourgee

"If the Court please," Albion began his oral argument in the old
Senate Chamber in the Capitol Building, facing eight old white

men. They sat at a long table with a row of green columns behind them and green velvet curtains hanging between the columns. Justice Brewer's chair was empty, as he was away caring for a seriously ill child. Albion held a stack of some fifty half-sheets of typewritten notes. He first presented several jurisdictional points and referenced the briefs Walker and he had submitted before launching into the heart of his argument.

"What is the purpose of this Act? Evidently," he answered his rhetorical question, "to assort passengers on the railroads according to color. They are called 'races,' it is true, but the only racial distinctions recognized by the act are 'white' and 'colored.' The statute does not use the ordinary scientific terms Caucasian, Mongolian, Indian, Negro, etc. They reduce the whole human family into two grand divisions. It is a new ethnology, but prejudice based on the lessons of slavery does not stop at trifles.

"The statute is a skillful attempt to confuse and conceal its real purpose to keep Negroes out of one car for the gratification of the whites—not to keep whites out of another car for the comfort and satisfaction of the colored passenger. A class or race claiming superiority always insists on special privileges. It naturally desires to see its exclusiveness crystallized into law. In all history, not one instance can be found of the class stigmatized as inferior, asking or demanding that such disparagement be legalized or perpetuated. The claim that this Act is for the common advantage of both races is simply farcical."

Gabe studied the faces of the men who would decide the fate of over eight million people. Though stoic, they appeared disinterested. The few people in the gallery showed disgust at

Albion's argument with scowls and whispers. Gabe's curiosity was piqued when two men in the back kept looking at the door as if expecting someone to enter.

"It may be said that every man knows to which race he belongs," Albion continued. "How shall a man who may have one-eighth or one-sixteenth colored blood know to which race he belongs if the law of Louisiana has not decided the issue? Science may decide one way, and common repute may decide the other. The passenger must submit to the conductor's judgment or lose his right to ride upon the train. It gives the conductor authority to eject for mere disagreement with him upon one of the most abstruse questions of physics and law. This is an interference with his liberty.

"The most precious of all inheritances is the reputation of being white. This is true from every point of view: socially, politically, professionally, even religiously. No word can paint the injury that may accrue from the reputation of being 'colored' or the advantage that may result from the reputation of being 'white.' Its effect is to perpetuate the stigma of color—to make the curse immortal, incurable, inevitable.

"As it was intended to promote injustice, it should not be perpetuated to establish justice. As it has been the seed of strife, its elimination is the guarantee of peace. The law, with its constitutional defects, must fail. Separate can never be equal."

Albion attempted to shine a light on the purpose of the Fourteenth Amendment, arguing that the object was to secure equality of rights for all against the fear of states' interference or failure to enforce it or to protect the weak, poor, and despised.

However, Justices Stephen Field and Edward White interrupted his presentation and peppered him with questions about the state's inherent police powers over its citizens. Their questions implied agreement with Louisiana's argument. Opposing counsels smirked at each other, amused by the discomfort they were sure Albion felt.

As he neared the end of his thirty minutes, Albion asked each justice to consider a hypothetical situation: "Suppose you woke up in Richmond, Virginia, this morning with nothing changed about you except that your skin was darkened, you had a wider nose, and black, curly hair. On the train to Washington to come to this courtroom, the conductor instructed you to move to the colored car, neither realizing you were a justice of the United States Supreme Court nor caring that your outward appearance was not an accurate indication of the quality of your personhood. It is easy to imagine the result. Humiliation. Rage. Indignation. Protests. How would the resources of your judicial mind not be taxed in objurgation?" Albion paused. "I thank you for your time." He turned toward his seat, looked at Gabe, shrugged his shoulders, and slumped into his chair.

Gabe searched the eyes of each justice. *I don't have a good feeling about this.*

Albion, Gabe, Benjamin, and the *Plessy* team silently left the courtroom. As they reached the bottom of the Capitol steps, a small group of Black men and women waiting outside greeted those with whom they had entrusted their hopes and began to sing:

> Mine eyes have seen the glory
> Of the coming of the Lord;
> He is trampling out the vintage

Where the grapes of wrath . . .

The singing was interrupted as about twenty men wearing masks and hoods marched toward the Capitol.

A police officer confronted them and asked, "Where are you going dressed like that?"

"We're on our way to the Supreme Court to interrupt the arguments in the Separate Car case and make sure the justices understand the right thing to do," their apparent leader challenged, pressing his masked face and body against the officer. The man assumed a stance with his feet spread, one foot slightly ahead of the other, reminding Gabe of how the military trained men to intimidate another person and brace for a fight.

"You're too late," the officer tried to explain calmly. "The oral argument is over."

"Dammit, Earl," a man next to the leader said. "Can't you even tell time?"

His voice sounds familiar, Gabe thought. The two men he had seen in the back of the courtroom approached the leader, whispered in his ear, and pointed toward Albion.

The leader turned his attention from the officer to the team. "So, you're the great Al-bee-yon Tour-jay," he said menacingly as he and his posse moved closer.

Gabe stepped between the leader and Albion. "You masked cowards can just go on home. Your mission has failed."

"We haven't failed," the person next to the leader said. "We've made our point as long as the justices know we are watching."

"Then, why don't you show them who's watching," Gabe countered. His hand shot out like a cat's paw, and he snatched the handmade hood off the man's head.

Senator Marcus Adams tried to hide his shocked and frightened face as he turned and scurried away.

THIRTY

"The Supreme Court's wall of shame"

May 18, 1896–July 4, 1898

G abe was sitting in his office on a lovely spring day when a telegraph agent delivered a telegram to him:

Mayville, New York, May 18, 1896
To Gabe Adams-Cincinnati, Ohio
News from Supreme Court is devastating. 7 to
1 rejecting our argument. We moved no one.
Justice Harlan's dissent was beautiful and
should be the law of the land. Jim Crow may
never be stopped. Our life's work is for naught.
AW Tourgee

Three days after receiving the telegram from Albion, Benjamin walked into Gabe's office. "Read this, Benjamin," Gabe said, looking up with droopy, red eyes. He slid his attorney's copy of the *Plessy* opinion across the desk to Benjamin. "The Court completely ignored our arguments and eviscerated the Reconstruction Amendments."

The fragrance of blossoming flowers, including the jasmine Gabe had planted years ago, wafted through the open window. Birds chirping were the only sounds accompanying the tick-tock of the pendulum on the office's grandfather clock as Benjamin read the Court's opinion. Gabe stared out the window, feeling a depth of despair he could not express. The clock gonged the hour and then the half before Benjamin took a deep breath, rubbed his eyes, and broke the silence.

"Legalizing segregation and Jim Crow keeps us at the bottom rung of the social ladder. Outcasts in India have more legal rights than we do. Will I have to go to a separate courthouse than the one you go to—or at least go in through a separate entrance?" Benjamin asked through a tightened jaw, emitting a disgusted snort.

"I don't know, but I do know the opinion is immoral and just plain wrong."

"How can they say the Act doesn't conflict with the Thirteenth Amendment?" Benjamin queried, squinting his eyes. "We now live in a country where the highest court in the land deems that a legal distinction and separation of whites and Blacks does not destroy the legal equality of the two races. How can they say keeping us in a lower caste doesn't reestablish a form of involuntary servitude?"

"Look what they did to the Fourteenth Amendment," Gabe intoned, massaging his temples. "They give lip service to *political* equality before the law but say that it wasn't meant to enforce *social* equality or commingling of the races. They say a Negro hasn't been deprived of property by being assigned to a separate car because he is not entitled to the reputation of being a white man."

"Confound it," Benjamin's eyes widened, and he turned a deep roan color. "They disagree that the enforced separation of the two races stamps the colored race with a badge of inferiority. Instead, they claim that the Negroes *choose* to embrace that construction? We *choose* that construction?" He slammed his fist on the desk so hard it knocked the statuette of Lady Justice and her scales to the floor.

"The only saving grace was Justice Harlan's lone dissent. He even used Albion's best phrase, 'There is no caste here. Our Constitution is *color-blind* and neither knows nor tolerates classes among citizens. In respect of civil rights, all citizens are equal before the law.'"

"Can you believe the Court says legislation conceived in hostility to humiliate Negroes is deemed consistent with the Constitution?" Benjamin groaned as he reached down to pick up the fallen statue. "We might as well remove her blindfold."

"I like Harlan's final words," Gabe said, brushing a film of dust off the windowsill. 'The thin disguise of *equal* accommodations for passengers in railroad coaches will not mislead anyone, nor atone for the wrong this day done. Justice Brown's opinion will hang next to the *Dred Scott* opinion on the Supreme Court's wall of shame.'"

"May God save America," Benjamin prayed, bowing his head in resignation.

Turning back toward Benjamin, Gabe put his hands on his son's shoulders. "How can we live as a family if we can't go to concerts, sporting events, dinner, or anywhere in public together?"

"I don't have an answer to that. It makes me mad—and very sad."

Tears formed in Gabe's eyes with the thought of how the Supreme Court's decision would allow others to denigrate his family solely because of the African blood coursing through their veins.

A month later, Albion traveled to Cincinnati to see the Adamses before he was scheduled to go to Columbus to work on anti-lynching legislation, the first of its kind in America, with William Parham, who had just been elected as a representative in the Ohio legislature. Losing William as a partner was a huge blow to Gabe, but he was proud of William and what it meant for Ohio.

After exchanging greetings and catching up on the current affairs of their respective household members, Gabe and Albion retired to the parlor.

"How are you coping with the *Plessy* opinion?" Gabe asked as he poured whiskey into two glasses. "I'm still upset."

"I am, too," Albion said as he swirled the amber liquid in his tumbler. "I was too optimistic. I am shocked at how little reaction there has been in the press. Northerners do not care whether Negroes' rights are upheld. They are tired of the fight and no longer vested in the outcome. Southern editorials, of course, laud the decision, just as they did *Dred Scott*."

"Justice Harlan's dissent is morally correct and will, hopefully, someday become the law of the land," Gabe said, taking a long swig.

"Well, until that occurs, we are in for a woeful existence," Albion said. His voice rose as he went on. "How can anyone expect a Black person to escape from illiteracy and poverty when everyone knows that "separate but equal" is a farce? What's next? Separate bathrooms? Separate water pumps? Segregation now and segregation forever will become the new battle cry."

"Adding to our *Plessy* misery are the new cases, *Gibson v. Mississippi* and *Murray v. Louisiana*," Gabe said. "Twice more, the Supreme Court failed to acknowledge that the Fourteenth Amendment means what it says, holding that the laws at issue are Constitutional because they are not discriminatory on their face."

Later that night, after Jasmine had gone to bed, a slightly inebriated Albion said, "Gabe. I think I'm done. I'm exhausted, and my spirits are as low as ever. I don't think I have any fight left in me."

"Aw, c'mon. You've been through some pretty tough times. Things will get better."

"Dammit, Gabe. I'm tired of hearing that. I'm done, I tell you. My mind is empty." Albion scratched at the floor with the toe of his shoe.

"What can I do?"

"Nothing. Absolutely nothing," replied Albion, finishing his drink and closing his eyes. "I'll go help William, but that may be the last anyone will hear of me."

"William," Gabe greeted his former law partner at the office, "it's nice to have you here for a few days. What's going on in the legislature?"

"First, I wanted you to know that, with Albion's help, we drafted a good anti-lynching law that comes up for a vote next week. I thought he looked very tired and drained of energy. The issue of the day is trying to keep Francis Galton's eugenics from being required teaching in Ohio's schools."

"I hope you succeed. His theory that superior racial groups inherit superior traits, including mental traits, has no basis in science and is only intended to 'prove' the inferiority of the Negro."

"Did you know that Galton is Darwin's cousin?" William asked.

"Yes, which is the only reason he has any credibility."

"Well, people believe it. It makes them feel better about discriminating against me."

"How can anyone look at and listen to you and think you're inferior?" asked Gabe.

"That's the point," William answered. "When Galton saw our successes and advances, he turned to fake science to prove our inferiority. All my life I've had to deal with whites finding new ways to stay on top of me and treat me as a lesser man."

"You don't include me in that statement, do you?" Gabe asked, hurt by the insinuation.

"Of course not. You know that. I'm sorry. I'm just in an angry mood. I'm in Cincinnati to try to stop the Freemasons from naming a lodge after Robert E. Lee. I'm not sure they'll listen to me." William had risen through the ranks of the Freemasons and was the Grand Master, a title he disliked immensely.

"Why would a Northern lodge do that?"

"The United Daughters of the Confederacy started a movement to reinvent the Civil War they call 'The Lost Cause of the Confederacy.' They're erecting statues and monuments honoring Confederates like Lee, Forrest, Stuart, Davis, and others and naming things after them as if they were heroes, all to glorify the Southern way of life. Some of our members who grew up in Kentucky bought into the hogwash. They think it might help our relationship with lodges in the South."

"That's disgraceful," Gabe said. "Those Confederates are traitors, not heroes."

"I'm tired of seeing the South sanctified, even in the North."

"Mind if I go with you?"

"Not at all. Even though you aren't a Mason, they might listen to you."

Gabe and William went to the all-white Mason's Lodge. They were met with flying Confederate flags and large drawings of Robert E. Lee.

"Honoring Lee and flying that flag are insulting," William told the assembly. "William Thompson designed the flag as a rallying symbol to maintain the heaven-ordained supremacy of the white race. I take it personally."

"Those flags and the monuments being erected all over the South are a constant reminder of the war to save slavery," Gabe added. "The inscriptions on them glorify and exalt the men who led the fight against their nation to protect and continue their enslavement of human beings."

The meeting went on for an hour with less pushback than expected. A vote was taken. The lodge was not renamed, and the flags and pictures were taken down.

As they rode the electric trolley up Gilbert Avenue to Gabe's house, William said, "I'm hurting, Gabe. When I started working with you, I felt like a man for the first time. But, as a lawyer and a legislator, I am still viewed as Black first. When was the last time—or was there ever a time—someone said about you, 'Here comes that white lawyer?'"

In an awkward silence, Gabe stood with the weight of William's reality. Benjamin's words also came back to him. "You've given me much to think about," he said. "Maybe I'm still not doing enough, but I feel like I don't have much left in me."

"One person can't do it," William replied. "It's the people who say or do nothing who are the problem. They claim they're all for equal rights, but when a Black person is put down, they don't speak up."

"I've tried to speak up, but no one seems to be listening," Gabe said dejectedly.

Later, William and Mary joined Jasmine, Gabe, and Benjamin for dinner.

After catching up on everybody's lives since they were last together, Gabe inquired between bites, "What do you think about McKinley getting the Republican nomination?"

"I like him," Mary responded. "I'm glad the Republican platform advocates for women's rights, including the right to vote and equal pay for equal work."

"It's what's *not* in the platform that troubles me," Jasmine said, putting her knife and fork down. "We have gone backward with *Plessy*. There is nothing about Negro rights. I think the North has surrendered."

Benjamin interjected, trying to sound sophisticated, "The North and the Republicans are more interested in American imperialism and industrialization than they are about rights for the Negro."

"That's true, Benjamin," Gabe replied, giving Jasmine a squeeze of her hand, proud of their son. "The Negroes' stumbling block used to be the KKK, but now it's the white moderates who are more devoted to keeping order than ensuring justice."

Mary added, "It boils down to some whites being afraid they will sacrifice personal and political power if Blacks make headway. It's viewed as an 'either/or' proposition when, in reality, both sides gain when everyone improves their lives."

"Power includes wealth and opportunity," William intoned. "That's why I'm introducing a reparations bill in the legislature."

"What would that do?" Benjamin asked.

"Over the past several hundred years," William explained, "whites have amassed most of the wealth in America and have kept most Blacks from having any. As an example, the Homestead Acts gave whites millions of acres of free or cheap land, but Blacks received very little. As land values rose, whites accumulated that wealth, passed it down from generation to generation, and it continues to grow today. Whites have always had the upper hand for good paying jobs and advancement opportunities."

"That gives them power in government, industry, school boards, courts—every place," Gabe said.

"And look what happens with that accumulated wealth," William added angrily. "Whites can buy land and houses in better locations, which increases their wealth. Laws relegate Blacks to the poorest locations with crowded conditions, which leads to other problems. Schools in white sections of town have better educated teachers, better supplies, and better facilities than in the Black sections."

"And people wonder why Blacks lag in education," Jasmine added.

"It's a continuous, vicious cycle," Mary lamented.

"Today's economics are a straight and unbroken line from those people, including Northerners, who got rich off the backs of slaves," William said to Benjamin. "My reparations bill will be an attempt to make up for being disadvantaged for so long."

"How will it work?" Jasmine asked. "You're going to give us money? Who would decide how much is given?"

"Reparations doesn't necessarily mean giving money, which might help a few people for a few days, yet doesn't solve the long-term issues," William said. "Instead, Blacks will be given preference in government jobs and admission to state-funded universities. State-owned land will be sold at a reduced amount with favorable loan terms. Those benefits would help bridge today's wealth and opportunity gap."

"Won't that upset white people?" Jasmine asked.

"Maybe so, but whites aren't hurt by my plan. They still have plenty of opportunities. My plan helps give Blacks a chance without whites losing wealth or power."

"Do you think our Supreme Court would hold such a law constitutional?" Gabe asked.

"Maybe not with the current Supreme Court. However, the Court decided several recent civil rights cases with 6-3 votes, so perhaps attitudes are changing. There's only one way to find out," William said emphatically. "We'll keep challenging the status quo."

"I'm glad you'll be leading the charge," Gabe said. "I think of everything done by Brown, Lincoln, Douglass, and Tourgée, but none of it seems to have made much of a difference."

THIRTY-ONE

"Lift Ev'ry Voice and Sing"

August 4, 1898–March 15, 1903

Gabe, Jasmine, and Benjamin were on the train to Alexandria, Virginia, to join Benjamin's fiancé, Daphne, whom he met at Howard University Law School. Benjamin and Daphne were both going to work in the Washington, D.C., office of the Department of Justice. Daphne's father recently passed away, and they planned to live with and care for Daphne's ailing mother.

"Welcome to Alexandria," Daphne said as she opened the door. She was an impeccably groomed woman, wearing a frilly dress with a ribbon tied around her neck, her hair recently hot-combed straight and smooth. "Come in."

They spent a lovely evening discussing Benjamin's and Daphne's plans, their work with the Justice Department, and what they needed to accomplish to get settled. During that conversation, Benjamin announced, "Now that I'm going to be living here, I'm going to register to vote."

"I'm going with you," Gabe said, his voice hard and eyes narrowed. "With Virginia adopting the holdings in *Williams v.*

Mississippi, allowing all sorts of registration requirements, registering might be difficult."

"That was a horrible decision," Benjamin said, shaking his head.

"Mississippi even admitted the law had a discriminatory intent," Daphne interjected.

Upon their arrival at the registration office, Benjamin and Gabe were directed to Hank Johnson, the old, white registrar, his belly falling over the top of pants that were held up with a pair of well-worn suspenders. "Do you own any land?" he asked Benjamin.

"No, sir."

"Did your grandfather vote?" Hank asked with a sneer.

"Which one?" Benjamin said, an edge creeping into his voice. "Yes, my father's father voted."

"What about your mother's father?"

"No, he wasn't allowed to vote," Benjamen said, lowering his tone and slowing his tempo. "He was a slave and now lives in Canada."

"Was your mother born free or slave?"

"None of your business," Gabe stepped in. "This man is my son. I'll vouch for him."

"If'n he wants to vote in Virginny, it's my business."

"She was born a slave," Benjamin said defiantly. "But she's free now."

"If she was born a slave, I only care about *her* father. You don't qualify to be automatically registered."

Benjamin started to argue, but Gabe said, "Careful, Benjamin, you won't win that battle."

"Can you recite the Preamble to the North Carolina Constitution?" Hank asked.

Having prepared for the possibility of that question, Benjamin recited it perfectly but with hostility rising in his voice.

"I'll need five dollars for your poll tax."

"That's a lot of money."

"Here," Gabe said, "I'll pay the damn tax."

"Don't you be talking that way around here," Hank scolded. Turning back to Benjamin, he said, "Well, boy, I'll get you registered if you can tell me how many jelly beans are in that jar over there."

"Here's what you can do with your jar of jelly beans," Benjamin said as he swiftly moved toward the jar, grabbed it, and threw it against the wall, spraying glass and red, black, white, and yellow beans everywhere. Benjamin took two steps toward the registrar, grabbed him by his suspenders and shirt, and pulled his face within inches of his own. "I may not live to see the day when Blacks can vote without your fat white ass getting in the way, but we *will* vote." Spittle sprayed Hank's face.

Gabe overcame his shock and pulled Benjamin off Hank, who was holding his hands up in self-defense.

"Well, one thing is for sure," Hank said, wiping his face and recovering his bravado, "you're not getting anything but jail time for assaulting a state official," and he shouted for the policeman manning the door.

Gabe watched in agony as the constable hauled Benjamin away.

Rather than posting the high bail or sitting in jail, Benjamin chose to plead guilty to a minor charge. Gabe paid Benjamin's fine and escorted him back to his house. "I don't blame you for being upset," Gabe told his son, "but you have to control your emotions and direct your anger and passion more constructively. There will always be a comment or a case that will overcook your grits."

Daphne was angry when they arrived at her house and told her of the day's events. "Why'd you do that? Now that you have a conviction for disorderly conduct, you can't vote in Virginia."

"I can't be mad at you," Jasmine said. "But your father is right. Someone or some case is always going to get under your skin. For instance, Daphne was just telling me about the *Cumming* case. How can funding white, but not Black, schools be constitutional? You have to attack such atrocities in a productive way."

Benjamin seethed, still angry as a hornet from his treatment and incarceration. "White America can't abide the thought of sharing anything with the Negro."

The next day, Jasmine and Gabe left to return to Ohio. When they entered the train station, Jasmine suddenly stopped and, gritting her teeth and with steam almost coming out of her ears, she said, "Look at that advertisement. Why is it considered funny to have a Negro baby sitting in a bathtub with the caption, 'How ink is made'?"

"It's disgusting. But there's another one equally bad," Gabe said, pointing to a large wood panel painted with a Black baby with a black face and a white body to show how well Pear's Soap cleaned.

They sat on a bench and waited for the train. Gabe slumped, head down. "Those advertisements make me feel used up. Remember when Albion told me he was done? That's the way I feel now."

"I understand and am feeling the same way," Jasmine said, rubbing the back of Gabe's neck. "We're not getting traction on women's suffrage, Booker Washington's speeches are fitting into the white narrative of Black subservience and second-class status, and Dunning's so-called scientific theory of Negro inferiority keeps us down."

"I can't believe Booker said Reconstruction failed because Negroes were given the right to vote before they were intellectually and emotionally capable of governance. We worked so hard at the Bureau, and it was all for naught. William's anti-lynching law passed, but his reparations bill didn't get out of committee. All my work on *Plessy* was nothing but a fart in the wind."

"Neither the courts nor Christian sentiment is willing to grant protection of our rights as people, much less as citizens. They are willing to give us unlimited promises of heavenly delights but will not accord us equal opportunities on earth," Jasmine added.

"What does all this mean for Benjamin and Daphne's future?"

Gabe was in Atlanta for an American Bar Association meeting and made arrangements to meet with W. E. B. Du Bois, the leading civil rights activist after Douglass died. He approached Du Bois's house with trepidation. He had met famous people before, but through introduction, invitation, or chance meeting; he had never invited himself.

"Dr. Du Bois will see you now," an aide told Gabe and ushered him into a study lined with floor-to-ceiling bookcases, every inch filled, and with more books stacked on the floor. Du Bois sat behind a massive desk littered with several inches of paper. He got up from his chair and came out from behind the desk. Du Bois was shorter than Gabe, thin, and balding. He had a well-trimmed goatee and mustache, each end coming to a point and turning upward.

"Welcome, Mr. Adams," Du Bois said, extending his hand. "It's a pleasure to meet you. The letter of introduction from Albion means much to me. I knew him well. We lost a strong voice when he left to be the United States Consul in Bordeaux."

"Yes, we did. I miss him," Gabe replied, his nerves quieting. "I appreciate you taking the time to meet with me."

"Have a seat," Du Bois offered.

After spending about ten minutes discussing Du Bois's work, Gabe leaned forward in the chair, his hands clasped between his knees, and brought up the reason he wanted to meet with Du Bois. "I've heard you're planning a meeting to confront Booker Washington for giving in to white supremacy. From my perspective, times are bleak, with Jim Crow and the Supreme Court. With Douglass and Tourgée gone, someone needs to become the driving force behind the change that isn't happening."

"You hear correctly. I'm thinking of inviting people, white and Black, to explore ways to attack bigotry and prejudice and enhance Negro development. Several friends with whom I've shared my ideas think we should develop a national association to advance colored people's interests, to remove Jim Crow laws, and to ensure the ability to vote. Would you be interested in attending?"

"I feel a bit like Albion—I'm not sure I have the energy to begin a new quest—but it sounds like it may be the only hope. Will you be inviting women to your conference? I'm sure my wife would want to come."

"Of course," Du Bois said with a smile and opened his arms. "Diversity and different viewpoints are important. Here, I have something for you. Maybe this will help reenergize you." Turning his chair and reaching toward a small, long table behind him, he picked up a book. "This is an advance copy of my latest book, *The Souls of Black Folks*. I think you might enjoy it."

"Oh, thank you. I'm sure I will," Gabe enthused, thumbing through the first few pages.

"In it, I coin a phrase I call 'double-consciousness.'"

"What is that?"

"It's the sense of always looking at one's self through the eyes of others, of measuring one's soul by the tape of a world. One ever feels his two-ness—an American, a Negro; two souls, two thoughts, two unreconciled strivings; two warring ideals in one dark body. I think it's possible for a man to be both a Negro and an American without being cursed and spat upon by his fellow man and without having the doors of opportunity closed roughly in his face."

Gabe was quiet as he absorbed the powerful statement and the truth and passion it embodied.

"Mr. Adams, I'm sorry to end our meeting, but my papers will not write themselves," he said, grinning.

Rising, Gabe extended his hand and said, "I thank you for the book and appreciate your time. You're the voice and leader we need."

"I look forward to seeing you again when I arrange the meeting."

Upon his return to Cincinnati, Gabe excitedly told Jasmine about his conversation with Du Bois. "He's exactly what is needed," handing her the copy of the book Du Bois had given him. "I read this on the train. You will enjoy it. But, I'm depressed with the news out of the Supreme Court," shaking his head in disbelief. "They've taken another swipe at the Reconstruction Amendments. As if *Plessy* wasn't bad enough, this *Giles* decision makes the disenfranchisement of Blacks almost complete. A white registrar is allowed to exclude anyone from voting if he determines the person lacks *good character*! The Negro won't recover from these rulings for a hundred years."

"Don't be so pessimistic," Jasmine replied. "This is probably a temporary setback. Jim Crow won't last but a couple of years."

"I disagree. The conservative justices believe they know the minds of the original writers of the Constitution and the Amendments, yet they completely ignore the spirit and logic used to pass the Amendments."

"Don't you think President Roosevelt will appoint justices who share his desire to see Negroes improve their lot?" Jasmine asked. "He doesn't want to shut the doors of hope and opportunity to any man purely upon the grounds of race."

"I'm not so sure about that," Gabe predicted. With his voice rising, he explained, "Roosevelt wants each person to have an opportunity, but he still believes in the superiority of whites. He's more interested in the Industrial Revolution than civil rights. I'm not sure the Supreme Court justices, except for Justice Harlan, even considered what the rulings would do to the Negro. Since *Dred Scott*, they not only propagate the notion of Black inferiority, they give legal effect to it."

"Laws will change; the Court will change; people's attitudes will evolve," Jasmine said.

"Not with our Supreme Court," Gabe snarled.

"You like the new justice, Oliver Wendell Holmes, don't you?" Jasmine asked, trying to calm Gabe down.

"*He's* the ass who wrote the opinion," Gabe declared, turning red and getting even angrier. "With the KKK gaining strength in the North and in complete control in the South, and the courts making things worse, Blacks haven't got a chance! This is a sad time for America."

"Take it easy," Jasmine said, patting his hand. "You're getting too riled up and not looking well. You must be exhausted from the trip. Perhaps a good night's sleep will help."

"You're probably right," he sighed. "I love you, my dear one," he said, lightly stroking her cheek, and turned toward the bedroom.

"I love you, too," Jasmine cooed. "Good night."

Gabe's dry cough awakened Jasmine. "Are you okay?"

"I feel like I fell off a horse. I've got a headache, and every muscle hurts. I think I have a fever."

"I'll get a cold compress for you and some of that Bayer's Aspirin."

"Don't fuss. I'll be all right. This will pass in . . . Uh-oh, I'm going to be sick," he said, grabbing for the chamber pot.

"Should I summon the doctor?"

"We'll see in the morning, if I live that long."

"Oh, don't be so dramatic."

The next morning, Gabe's condition had worsened. Jasmine didn't want to leave his side but needed to get the doctor. Throwing on a shawl, she ran to a neighbor's house and asked if she would get the doctor. The neighbor rushed out the door without hesitating, and Jasmine hurried home.

Dr. Miller responded quickly. After listening to Gabe's breathing, taking his temperature, and checking his pulse, the doctor told Jasmine, "It's the flu. Keep him hydrated and warm. He'll be better in a couple of days."

Two days later, a very concerned Jasmine had the neighbor summon Dr. Miller again. The doctor listened to Gabe's labored breathing and incessant cough. Escorting Jasmine to the outer room, he informed her the flu had become pneumonia. "This is serious," he said with a look of concern on his face. "He's not getting enough oxygen, and his lungs are filling with fluid."

"What can be done?"

"We don't know much about what we can do to make it better. I've tried all the latest remedies and given him some opium. I'll come back tomorrow morning to check on him."

Gabe's cough continued through the night. He was almost delirious at times. Dr. Miller appeared the following day and was greatly concerned. "He's in acute distress. I don't know what else to do."

Scared and distraught, Jasmine went into the bedroom. Gabe's eyes were closed. His breathing was shallow. She stood still, praying, until Gabe woke himself up with a coughing fit. "Come. Sit by me," Gabe wheezed. "What will you do if I don't make it?" Gabe asked Jasmine.

"Don't say such a thing."

"I've been thinking about all the special people in my life—Mother, Pops, Raph, John Brown, Mother Bickerdyke, Albion—and I need to know you'll be all right."

"If something happens, I'll probably go to Buxton and live with Mama and Papa. Other than with you, that's the only home I know."

Gabe fell asleep. Deeply concerned and needing support, Jasmine hurried to the nearby telegraph office to summon their family.

The next day, Atticus and Myra appeared from Georgetown. Benjamin, Daphne, Caroline, Kendall, and Michael arrived from Washington. Glory came from New York, and Levi from Buxton. Jasmine said to them, "Prepare yourself. He's not doing well today."

"Jasmine," Caroline asked, "how are you holding up?"

"I'm all right, but I get pretty weepy and weak sometimes."

Michael put his arm around Jasmine's shoulder and pulled her to him. "We're here for you," he said. "Let us know what we can do to help."

"You being here is all I need. Let's go see Gabe," she said, and they huddled around Gabe's bed.

Gabe awakened and, his voice weak and gravelly, asked, "Why are you all here? I'm not going anywhere. I'm even starting to feel better. The mercury as a laxative and the opium seem to be working."

"We just wanted to make sure you're all right," Benjamin said.

"Actually, we came to see Jasmine," Caroline teased.

Jasmine sat in a chair next to the bed. Caroline went to the other side of the bed and knelt, grasping Gabe's hand, concerned that it was cold. The others stood around the bed. At times, Gabe seemed to improve, only to erupt into a coughing fit that discharged a worrisome amount of bloody phlegm.

Glory wouldn't leave his side. "You gave me everything," she whispered in his ear while wiping his forehead with a cold, wet rag. "You took me in. You've given me opportunities few get. You've given my mama every ounce of your love. You gave my family hope. I love you."

"You're a very special person," Gabe replied. "You've been a gift from God to all of us. Take care of your mother."

"Father," Benjamin cried, "I need your love and teaching. What can I do to carry on your mission? I want you to be proud of me."

Gabe opened his eyes, smiled, and said hoarsely, "I couldn't be prouder of you. I suggest you contact Dr. Du Bois and get involved with whatever he's planning."

Michael and Caroline held each other. "I love you, Gabe," they said in unison.

"I love you, too," Gabe choked out. "I love all of you so much."

Jasmine laid her head on Gabe's chest so she could hear his heartbeat through the horrible rattle in his lungs.

"Please get my Bible," Gabe rasped.

Caroline ran from the room. She returned clutching the Bible.

Barely audible, Gabe said, "Jasmine, read the Beatitudes. They were my guiding light."

Caroline handed her the Bible. As Jasmine opened it, a torn piece of paper, marking Matthew 5, fell out. It was the scrap of paper with her name scrawled in pencil, the one she had so proudly given Gabe almost fifty years before. Jasmine began to sob and clutched the jeweled butterfly she had worn daily since the day Ailene gave it to her. Unable to read, she handed the Bible back to Caroline.

Caroline read the verses. Gabe smiled. "Blessed is my life because Jasmine entered it. I remember the little girl with terrified eyes as I helped you into the wagon at the Rankins'. Look what you've become. So strong. So beautiful. So talented."

Jasmine grasped his hand, which went limp in a short while. She put her ear to his chest. She looked at her children. "He's gone." They surrounded Jasmine, their bodies slumped against hers.

At the funeral, William gave a stirring and emotional eulogy. A pregnant Daphne read one of Albion's poems, "With Drum-Beat and Heart-Beat." Glory rose to lead the singing of a final song. Before she began, she said, "The only father I knew told me this song touched his soul and reflected his life's work. He filled my heart with all he meant to me and my people."

She sang:

> Lift ev'ry voice and sing
> 'Til earth and heaven ring,
> Ring with the harmonies of Liberty;
> Let our rejoicing rise
> High as the listening skies,
> Let it resound loud as the rolling sea.
> Sing a song full of the faith that the dark past has taught us,
> Sing a song full of the hope that the present has brought us.
> Facing the rising sun of our new day begun,
> Let us march on 'til victory is won.

As they left the church, Benjamin held Daphne's hand, looked her in the eyes, and said, "My father's work must not be in vain. We must beat his drum until there is justice for all. For the sake of our child, we must not fail."

THE END

Afterword

The book ends in 1903. Why do we still have the lingering effects of slavery, overt racial discrimination, and systemic racism over one hundred and twenty years later? Is it possible we're repeating history?

At best, we are slow learners. Half a century passed before *Brown v. Board of Education* (1954) overturned the Supreme Court's imprimatur on segregation and Jim Crow in *Plessy*. Even then, school desegregation was to occur only with "all deliberate speed," and it is still not accomplished today. Kentucky did not ratify the Thirteenth Amendment until 1976, and Mississippi did not ratify it until 1995 and did not certify it until 2013. Colorado did not abolish slavery completely in its constitution until 2018.

Lynchings persisted into the 1960s, and there are many modern-day versions of hate-filled violence against Blacks: James Byrd Jr.'s dragging death behind a white supremacist's truck in 1998; George Floyd's death due to a policeman kneeling on his neck in 2020; Ahmaud Arbery being chased and shot to death by avowed racists while jogging in 2020. As of 2023, the Southern Poverty Law Center identified about 345 hate groups, including nine male supremacy groups, against people of color in the United States.

From the end of Reconstruction in 1877 until the 1964 Civil Rights Act and the 1965 Voting Rights Act and beyond, Black citizens and other people of color have been denied equal opportunities and access to jobs, education, and wealth accumulation (especially in housing and land ownership). The advances of the civil rights movement of the 1960s and '70s now seem to be eroding due to apathy among many whites. Some people seem to see racism as a Black or white, not an American, problem, and some believe it has been eradicated. Our current Supreme Court appears to be backing away from the advancement of civil rights with its abolition of affirmative action and consideration of race in college admissions, school quotas, and job opportunities. In *Shelby County v. Holder* (2013), the Court eliminated a key component of the 1965 Voting Rights Act that required states that historically deprived people of color the ability to vote to undergo scrutiny before changing a voting law. States are again passing laws restricting voting rights.

South Carolina did not remove the Confederate Battle Flag flying over its state capitol until 2015. Some Confederate names, statues, and symbols are being removed from public places, but many remain. Flags, banners, and other symbols, all dog-whistling white supremacy, fly at political rallies, in front yards, and on vehicles. Blasted into Stone Mountain, once owned by a Klansman and on top of which the Ku Klux Klan held cross burnings, is the largest bas-relief sculpture in the world, and the most visited tourist site in Georgia, depicting Jefferson Davis, Robert E. Lee, and Thomas "Stonewall" Jackson towering over the masses.

The first enslaved people were brought to American soil in 1619. Black Americans had twelve years of hope and advancement from 1865 to 1877 and maybe twenty years of renewed hope in a Second Reconstruction during the Civil Rights Era of the late 1950s into the 1970s—thirty years out of four hundred. And Blacks are not alone. Is it any wonder people of color live with significant gaps in wealth, education, and opportunity today? Many Americans are in denial that white privilege or racism exist or that they play a part in its history or current expressions.

Only by being knowledgeable about these issues and honestly and openly discussing them can we establish a Third Reconstruction. This book was written to provide knowledge. It is incumbent upon each of us to accept our role concerning racial injustice, confront it, and bring it to an end in America by exercising our right to vote and joining frank but painful conversations about race. We all have a drum to beat for justice.

ACKNOWLEDGMENTS

I could not have written this book without the assistance and encouragement of my wife, Nancy. She helped edit the book, gave great suggestions to improve it, compiled email lists (among a myriad of tasks), and was a wonderful travel companion who never complained about living out of a suitcase, missing lunches, spending the night in "dives," or wandering for hours around small towns, historical sites, museums, and libraries.

I would also like to acknowledge two groups of friends who helped shape concepts in the book, read and edited manuscripts, and gave suggestions for improvement: the Colorado Judicial Philosophical Society (a pretentious name I gave a group of fellow judges who have met biweekly for over fifteen years to read and discuss books on the philosophy and history of law); and the Author's Breakfast Club—a group of published authors and wannabes like me who meet to encourage each other through the arduous processes of writing and (more so) editing a book.

I especially thank Mary Sklar and Catherine Stevens for being my unwavering cheerleaders (and for the beautiful quilt Catherine made depicting scenes and people in the book); my research buddy, Don Ryan; and my beta readers, Addison "Spike" Adams, Robert Dill, Virginia Horton, Jen and Neil

Lewis, Kurt Lewis, Linda Danielle Murrell, Annie Ollada, and Jonathan White. Thanks also to Professor Kennard Bork; Peg McHugh; my sister, Christina Collier; and my sister-in-law, Margaret Cross, for their suggestions. Everyone's wonderful comments and edits were invaluable.

Special and sincere thanks to my first-class editor, Mark Chimsky, whose insight and talents were indispensable to making this story come alive. I also thank and deeply appreciate the amazing and outstanding abilities of my copy editor and proofreader, Amy Chamberlain, and book and cover designer, Veronica Yager. Finally, I thank my son, Joe, who helped me navigate through the intricacies of self-publishing, web page design, and teaching an old-timer about social media. All of them made the process more enjoyable and the book better. Thank you.

One of the highlights of writing this book was the encouragement I received from noted authors. After reading the late Otto Olsen's biography of Albion Tourgée, I contacted him, which led to a wonderful exchange of emails. I had finished writing the first half of the book when I read *March* by Geraldine Brooks. There were so many similarities between my book and *March* that I was concerned about plagiarism. I wrote to Ms. Brooks about my concerns, and she immediately replied, graciously encouraging me to "just write the book YOU want to write." Ironically, I happened to meet her late husband, Tony Horwitz, the author of several books on John Brown and the Civil War, and he also encouraged my writing. Ann Hagadorn, author of many books, including *Beyond the River* (the best book I've read on the Underground Railroad), met with me, gave me a personal tour of Ripley, Ohio, read part of the manuscript, and made excellent suggestions. Jeff Miller and Mark Shaiken selflessly provided insight into the writing and publishing process. The encouragement from "real" authors was a wonderful collateral experience for a tyro. I am saddened that Professor Olsen and Mr. Horwitz passed away before I completed the novel, and I cannot share it with them.

Similarly, when I was even further along with the book but still did not have a title, I read Bryan Stevenson's[1] *Just Mercy.* In it, he tells a story of meeting an elderly African American man who said, "I'll tell you what you're doing. You're beating the drum for justice! . . . You've got to beat the drum for justice" (pages 293 and 298). I got chills as I realized *that's the title of my book!* I wrote Mr. Stevenson to ask permission to use that phrase as my title. He wrote back and gave his blessing.

Other pleasurable experiences were made possible by people I met along the way, too many to count—tour guides, librarians, archivists, rangers, museum staff (see Appendix B)—everyone willing to help with research, ideas, and information. One such person was the most delightful Nona Mae Marshall of Maysville,

---

1 Bryan Stevenson is the founder of the Equal Justice Initiative and developer of the Legacy Museum, the National Memorial for Peace and Justice, and the Freedom Monument Sculpture Park in Montgomery, Alabama, all of which he established, as is the purpose of this book, to "educate people about racial history and the need for racial justice" and to "deepen the national conversation about the legacy of slavery and lynching and our nation's history of racial injustice."

Kentucky, the matriarch of the Jonathan Bierbower House and Underground Railroad Museum, who passed away at eighty-nine in 2023. After a tour of the beautiful museum, I sat down with Ms. Marshall and listened to her tell story after story. As we ended our conversation, I shared with her that this was my first attempt at writing a book and that I wasn't sure how well I was doing. She gave me the best advice I've ever heard, for *any* situation: "Don't tell me your sad story; just write the book."

So, in memory of Nona, it's written!

Appendix A:

ACTUAL HISTORICAL FIGURES DEPICTED

- People in the Civil War chapters (except Gabe, Levi, any of the named Black soldiers, and Lieutenant McIntosh)

- People in Kansas, Harper's Ferry, and the trial and execution of John Brown (except Gabe, the Packinfishes, and Iris)

- People involved with *Plessy v. Ferguson* (except Gabe and Benjamin; although William Parham was an actual person, I have no information that he was involved with the *Plessy* team)

- All U.S. presidents, vice presidents, candidates, federal, state, and local politicians, and judges

- All Supreme Court justices and parties and people involved with the named Supreme Court cases

- Individuals:
Bancroft, Ashley

Jones, John C.
Jones, John Tecumseh "Ottawa"
Jordan, Isaac M.
Langston, John Mercer
Linnell, Joseph and Samantha
Miller, Samuel
Mitchell, Richard
Monfort, Joseph and Hannah Riggs
Outlaw, Wyatt
Parham, William and Mary
Parker, John
Pate, Henry
Peck, Henry
Rankin, John, Jean, and family
Reid, John
Reid, Whitelaw
Robbins, Arlis
Runkle, Benjamin Piatt
Sackett, E. C.
Sherman, Henry "Dutch Henry" and William "Dutch Bill"
Stowe, Harriet Beecher
Sumner, Charles
Sumner, Edwin V.
Thompson, Henry
Tourgée, Albion, Emma, and family
Truth, Sojourner
Weld, Theodore

White, George
Whittlesey, Eliphalet
Wilkinson, Allen
Wood, Hannah Ingham

Appendix B:

Sources and Resources

Words cannot express my gratitude to the museum curators and personnel, National Park rangers, historical society members, gift-shop hosts, library and bookstore personnel, and others at the following locations for their selfless assistance and helpful answers to my unending telephone calls, emails, and questions. Thank you! If this book is interesting and historically accurate, it is because of you; if not, it is because of me.

16th Street Baptist Church, Birmingham, Alabama

Black History Museum of Corinth, Corinth, Mississippi

Black History Walking Tour, 40 Acres and a Mule Tour, Savannah, Georgia (Fritz Rumpel, guide)

American Civil War Museum, Richmond, Virginia

Amherstburg Freedom Museum, Amherstburg, Ontario, Canada

Atlanta History Center, Atlanta, Georgia

Battle of Rivers Bridge State Historic Site, Ehrhardt, South Carolina

Battles for Chattanooga Museum, Lookout Mountain, Tennessee

Bentonville Battlefield State Historical Site, Four Oaks,

North Carolina

Birmingham Civil Rights Institute, Birmingham, Alabama

Black Wall Street Walk of History, Tulsa,
Oklahoma (self-guided)

Brown Chapel AME (African Methodist Episcopal) Church,
Selma, Alabama

Buxton National Historic Site and Museum, North Buxton,
Ontario, Canada

Charles H. Wright Museum of African American History,
Detroit, Michigan

Charleston Black History, Gullah Geechee, and Porgy
and Bess Sea Island Tour, Sights and Insights Tours,
Charleston, South Carolina (Al Miller, guide)

Chatham-Kent Museum, Chatham, Ontario, Canada

Christian Waldschmidt Homestead and Camp Dennison
Civil War Museum, Camp Dennison, Ohio

Cincinnati and Hamilton County Public Library,
Cincinnati, Ohio

Cincinnati Railroad Club, Cincinnati, Ohio

Civil Rights Memorial Center by the Southern Poverty Law
Center, Montgomery, Alabama

Confederate Memorial Carving, Stone Mountain Park,
Stone Mountain, Georgia

Confederate Memorial Hall Museum, New Orleans,
Louisiana

Constitution Hall State Historic Site, Lecompton, Kansas

Denison University Library, Granville, Ohio

Fayette County Historical Society Museum, Washington

Court House, Ohio

Freedom Rides Museum, Montgomery, Alabama

Grand Gulf Military Monument, Port Gibson, Mississippi

Granville Historical Society, Granville, Ohio

Greene County Ohio Historical Society, Xenia, Ohio

Greensboro History Museum, Greensboro, North Carolina

Greenwood Rising Black Wall Street History Center,
Tulsa, Oklahoma

Harriet Beecher Stowe House, Cincinnati, Ohio

Highland County Historical Society, Hillsboro, Ohio

International Civil Rights Center and Museum, Greensboro,
North Carolina

Jefferson County Museum, Charles Town, West Virginia

Jessamine County Historical and Genealogical Society,
Nicholasville, Kentucky

John Brown House, Summit County Historical Society,
Akron, Ohio

John Brown Memorial Park and John Brown Museum State
Historic Site, Osawatomie, Kansas

John Parker House, Ripley, Ohio

John Rankin House, Ripley, Ohio

Josiah Henson Museum of African-Canadian History (formerly Uncle Tom's Cabin), Dresden, Ontario, Canada

Kentucky Gateway Museum Center, Maysville, Kentucky

Legacy Museum by the Equal Justice Initiative,
Montgomery, Alabama

Louisiana State University Library and Archives, Baton
Rouge, Louisiana

Mary Todd Lincoln House, Lexington, Kentucky
McClurg Museum, Chautauqua County Historical Society
    (home of the A. W. Tourgée papers), Westfield, New York
Miami University Library and Archives, Oxford, Ohio
Mississippi Civil Rights Museum, Jackson, Mississippi
Museum of African American History, Boston,
    Massachusetts
National Afro-American Museum and Cultural Center,
    Wilberforce, Ohio
National Center for Civil and Human Rights,
    Atlanta, Georgia
National Civil Rights Museum at the Lorraine Motel,
    Memphis, Tennessee
National Memorial for Peace and Justice (aka National
    Lynching Memorial) by the Equal Justice Initiative,
    Montgomery, Alabama
National Museum of Civil War Medicine, Frederick,
    Maryland

United States National Park Service:

National Underground Railroad Freedom Center,
    Cincinnati, Ohio
National Underground Railroad Museum/Jonathan
    Bierbower House, Maysville, Kentucky
National Voting Rights Museum and Institute,
    Selma, Alabama
Amherstburg Freedom Museum, including the Nazrey

AME Church National Historic Site, Amherstburg, Ontario, Canada

North Carolina Museum of History, Raleigh, North Carolina

Ohio History Connection, Columbus, Ohio

Old Exchange and Provost Dungeon Museum, Charleston, South Carolina

Old Main, Lincoln-Douglas Debate Exhibit, Knox College, Galesburg, Illinois

Old Slave Mart Museum, Charleston, South Carolina

Rosa Parks Museum, Troy University, Montgomery, Tulsa, Oklahoma (self-guided) Alabama

St. Catharines Museum and Welland Canals Centre, St. Catharines, Ontario, Canada

South Carolina State Museum, Columbia, South Carolina

Territorial Capital Museum, Lecompton, Kansas

U.S. Grant Boyhood Home and Schoolhouse, Georgetown, Ohio

Walnut Hills Historical Society, Cincinnati, Ohio

Walnut Hills Walking Tour, Harriet Beecher Stowe House, Cincinnati, Ohio (Geoff Sutton, guide)

Watkins Museum of History, Lawrence, Kansas

Whitney Plantation, Edgard Louisiana (formerly Habitation Haydel).

Antietam National Battlefield, Sharpsburg, Maryland

Brown v. Board of Education National Historic Park, Topeka, Kansas

Chickamauga and Chattanooga National Military Park, Fort

Oglethorpe, Georgia

Corinth Civil War Interpretive Center and Corinth
Contraband Camp, Shiloh National Military Park,
Corinth, Mississippi

Fort Donelson National Battlefield, including Fort Donelson
National Cemetery, Dover, Tennessee

Fort Pulaski National Monument, Savannah, Georgia

Fort Sumter and Fort Moultrie National Historical Park,
Charleston, South Carolina

Gettysburg National Military Park,
Gettysburg, Pennsylvania

Harpers Ferry National Historical Park, Harper's Ferry,
West Virginia

Kennedy Farm, Sharpsburg, West Virginia

Selma to Montgomery National Historic Trail, Alabama

Shiloh National Military Park, Shiloh, Tennessee

Vicksburg National Military Park, including the USS *Cairo*
Gunboat and Museum, Vicksburg, Mississippi

Please visit www.beatthedrumforjustice.com for this book's
bibliography and the Supreme Court citations. Many of the discussions among the characters in this book come from the actual
person's words as quoted in the extensively researched works by
the notable authors and historians listed in the bibliography.

About the Author

Christopher C. Cross served as a county and district court judge for almost nineteen years in the most populous judicial district in the State of Colorado. An avid history buff, his interest in civil rights and the shame of slavery, segregation, and the treatment of African and Native Americans led to years of reading and research. A graduate of Denison University in Granville, Ohio, and the University of Denver College of Law, Judge Cross is married, with three adult sons, each with a wife or significant other, and one beautiful granddaughter.